I0610582

Cowboy Code

Louella Bryant

Black Rose Writing | Texas

2019 by Louella Bryant
All rights reserved. No part of this book may be reproduced, stored in a
retrieval system or transmitted in any form or by any means without the
prior written permission of the publishers, except by a reviewer who may
quote brief passages in a review to be printed in a newspaper, magazine or
journal.

The author grants the final approval for this literary material.

Second printing

This is a work of fiction. Names, characters, businesses, places, events, and
incidents are either the products of the author's imagination or used in a
fictitious manner. Any resemblance to actual persons, living or dead, or
actual events is purely coincidental.

ISBN: 978-1-68433-300-4
PUBLISHED BY BLACK ROSE WRITING
www.blackrosewriting.com

Printed in the United States of America
Suggested Retail Price (SRP) $19.95

Cowboy Code is printed in Chaparral Pro

For my mother
Margaret Bryant
1917-2004

Cowboy Code

1

Daddy

Summer 1947

Outside the chapel, Covey Fortune leans against the stucco wall, the stiff collar of his shirt buttoned high around his neck, a brimmed hat shadowing his face.

When his gray eyes meet mine, I slow down and say, "Hey, Covey." He's eighteen, just four years ahead of me, and fine-looking.

"Sorry about your father." He dips his head toward the chapel door. I know he won't go inside. Since I can remember, I've known things. Not sure how— I just get a sense. Like, Covey isn't welcome at a white man's funeral. People from the African settlement can't take any chances.

"Come on, Bobbie." Momma pulls me inside.

The coffin sits on the chapel's folding table, a spray of lilies atop the pine drooping in Virginia's heat. It could be anyone lying cold and silent in front of the altar. I wish it were anyone—anyone but my father.

From baskets around the table legs, the aroma of gladiola and meadowsweet battles the stench belching from the paper mill's chimneys. I've learned the word irony, and what is more ironic than the fragrant smell of death overpowering the rancid smell of life in this mountain town?

We start down the aisle as if we're in a wedding, Momma and me. I try to be brave for her even though my loss is greater than hers. She knew Daddy for fifteen years, not even half her life. I knew him all of mine.

Momma's brother Buddy has been home from the front for a few weeks and is wearing a tight-fitting suit instead of his uniform. Buddy offered to bring my brother to the service, but Smiley would have fidgeted. My grandmother sits in a flowered dress, a hat with netting over her white hair.

Beside her, Nandaddy tugs at the collar of his shirt. He looks more comfortable with the collar open and sleeves rolled to his elbows as he is at home on Lordsview Court.

Before we sit down, Momma goes up and pats the casket. She's wearing the smile she used to get before Daddy came in from work and she rushed to set the table for supper. The last thing she'd do was cut some flowers from the yard and arrange them in a glass. She said Daddy appreciated beautiful things. I remember the gap to the left of his front teeth that he stuck his tongue into. When his ship came in, he used to say, he'd see about a false tooth to fill the gap. We're still waiting for that ship.

While Reverend Singer preaches about the Lamb of God taking away the sin of the world, I think about how two weeks earlier, Daddy got the fingers of his right hand jammed in a window sash trying to close it during a hard rain. That night Momma crushed ice into a bowl for him to soak his fingers. Later when the nails turned black, he said they didn't hurt anymore.

Reverend Singer is admonishing the congregation to dwell on the virtuous qualities of the deceased instead of his transgressions. I know Daddy was no saint. Once a car woke me late in the night. Out the window I saw a lady with bleached blonde hair behind the wheel. He got out, eyes grazing the house as if hoping Momma wasn't watching. I never heard them argue about the blonde lady. Either Momma was afraid he'd leave us penniless or she truly loved him. I know I did.

When I was eleven, Daddy gave me money for matinees at the Visulite. I watched *Back in the Saddle* three times before he told me, "I believe I'm wasting my money on you, Bobbie Marlene—you've memorized all of Gene Autry's lines." After that we started listening to "Melody Ranch," the radio show where Gene Autry recited his cowboy code of morals. Law number one says that a cowboy must never shoot first, hit a smaller man, or take unfair advantage. But the boiler that blew up in my father's face at the Blue Ridge Pulp and Paper Mill is no cowboy.

When the service ends, Reverend Singer rushes to the back of the chapel to shake hands with the mourners as they leave, but Momma posts herself beside the casket. Nandaddy comes up the aisle and stops next to me.

"You ready, girl?" he says. "We'll wait for your mother in the car. She needs a few minutes."

"I'm staying."

He frowns at me. "Then we'll be outside when you're ready."

The undertaker is about to roll the casket away, and I go up and stand beside Momma.

"I want to see my husband," she says.

"That's not a good idea, Mrs. Grey," he says. "It was a bad accident."

"Please open the casket, Mr. Underwood," I tell him. "If you don't, Momma will open it herself."

I prefer to remember my father as he was, Bogart-handsome, the way he could wink with his right eye but not his left, the laugh that rumbled up from his belly. But Momma needs me and I will look death in the face with her, even if what I see haunts me forever.

When Mr. Underwood lifts the lid, the silk inside rustles. Surrounded by puffs of satin lies a body that has a human form wearing a white shirt and a blue striped tie in a Windsor knot. Above the knot is an overripe watermelon, oddly shaped, as if it has not had sufficient space to grow. The rind is black and green and cracked over moist fruit. Where the mouth should be is a crooked seam, lips wrinkled inward like a toothless old man's and two rotten spots for eyes. Someone has made a mistake—this is not my father.

The hands are folded across the stomach like charcoaled chicken wings, the left over the right. On the ring finger is a plain band of gold, a ring that could belong to any man. It seems strange, though, that the fingernails are as pink as a baby's bottom, except for the right hand. The nails of three fingers are black, as if they were caught under the sash of a window.

I feel as if a rag has been stuffed down my throat. My heart thrashes and I want to be standing outside with Covey pretending it's someone else's father lying cold and mangled in the crude box.

When I'm able to choke out the lump in my throat, my breath comes with a torrent of spit and tears. Between sobs, I give voice to a single word—"Daddy."

* * *

Outside, I scan the churchyard for Covey, but he's gone. Nandaddy motions us to the car, and the engine growls as we sweep down to Lordsview Court. Friends have gathered at Nandaddy's house because our place is too small for a crowd. He built the house himself, even laid the brick and sanded the wood floors and stairs smooth, finishing them with coats of varnish. The dining table is crowded with dishes neighbors have brought—tuna noodle casserole, potato salad, a glazed ham, string beans cooked so long they melt on the tongue, plump biscuits, jars of pickled beets, pineapple upside down cake and cherry pie. Reverend Singer says the blessing before people load their plates, but Momma doesn't bow her head. Neither do I. How can I give gratitude to a power so pitiless that it would slaughter my father in such a sudden and merciless manner?

"You should eat something," Mamaw says.

"Why?" My stomach is full of bitterness.

"If nothing else than to acknowledge that life goes on." She is holding a glass of ginger ale. Momma nibbles on a ham biscuit when she's not shaking hands and receiving cheek kisses from fellow mourners.

Harlan Joiner comes over to us. He worked with Daddy. Had a drink after work with him, too, just to wash the slurry out of their throats, Daddy said. When he scratches his head with one finger, Harlan's pink scalp shows through his thin hair, making him look naked somehow. Green shadows hang beneath his eyes. He grips a tumbler of iced tea against his round belly, and I am drawn to his fingernails, the straight trim, the ridges in the clear nails, the white moons.

Harlan stares into his drink. "Gus was up on the main drum, checking the seams." He's talking about the digesters at the mill, the tall cylinders that boil wood chips into pulp. Daddy led me on a tour of the mill for a school report, holding my hand because everything was hot or sharp or in danger of flying apart.

"He said everything checked out, and I told him, 'Let's fire up these cookers, Gus.'" Harlan has to get the story off his chest and I'm hungry to hear details about my father.

"Harlan," Momma says, "it's all right."

"No, it's not all right," I say. "Go ahead, Mr. Joiner."

He clears his throat. "He asked me to bring him up the blowtorch, said he'd found a crack in a seam. I climbed the ladder and handed him the blowtorch. 'Careful there, hoss,' I told him. The chemicals in the digesters are combustible, and he knew it. But he said to go on back down, he'd have it fixed in no time."

I imagine Daddy at the top of the ladder, pulling his handkerchief out of his pocket and wiping the sweat from his forehead, then stuffing the handkerchief back in his pocket. He takes out the lighter, flicks the spark wheel, ignites the torch, adjusts the flame. Just as he points the fire at the seam, there is an explosion. Chunks of metal go flying, taking Daddy with them.

Harlan looks at Momma from under his bushy eyebrows. "I thought you should know."

"Thank you, Harlan," Momma tells him.

"If you need anything—" He sets his glass on the table.

"Thanks, Mr. Joiner," I say.

*   *   *

That night moonlight slices across me as I listen to the bedsprings squeak under Momma's weeping. I remember one night watching from our bedroom—Smiley's and mine—as Daddy took Momma's hand and pulled her down beside him on the couch. He picked a hair off her shoulder, held it out and dropped it. Her dress hiked up over her knee when she crossed her legs. Daddy swatted a mosquito on her thigh and then licked his finger and wiped the spot of blood away. Then he licked his finger again and ran it up her thigh so high she slapped at his hand. Guy Lombardo was playing a slow song on the radio. Daddy let out a sound like a growling laugh and rubbed his bristly chin on her shoulder. She ran her fingers through his hair and then her head fell back. For a long time I listened to their low, rumbling laughter. Once I heard glass break, a gay tinkling on the linoleum and "Oh," Momma said. "Nevermind," Daddy said and then the rustling of cloth. I fell asleep feeling that everything was just as it should be.

I wait until Momma has cried herself out and then I creep in and slip into bed with her. She is lying on her side, facing the vanity. I spoon myself to her back, and her elbow tightens on my arm. When Momma was upset, Daddy always told her everything would turn out all right, but when I try to tell Momma now, the words strangle in my throat.

2
Bloodsuckers

After the funeral Momma starts acting strange. One day she comes out of the house and hangs a Kotex on porch post with the bloody stain facing the road.

Our neighbor Elsie comes over and her mouth drops open. "What in creation?"

I'm sitting on the glider trying to keep from perspiring in the July heat.

"Her redheaded cousin's visiting," I advise Elsie. The cousin has been visiting me for a few months now, but I can't say I welcome her. Who would?

"Why's she got to exhibit it to the whole neighborhood?"

"Because," Momma says, coming out the screen door, "rumors are flying that poor Widow Grey's expecting, and isn't it a shame, her with two already and no husband to provide for them. I won't have the whole town spreading tales about me."

She's right about one thing—a squalling baby is not a problem we need.

"They'll be talking about you losing your sanity with that hanging there." Elsie sucks her teeth and the sound reverberates across the street.

Momma pries out the thumbtack and folds the Kotex. "It's done its work anyhow."

Our house sits on a steep slope, the porch held up by stilt-like posts. Beyond the town's dwellings, mountains roll like green billows on an ocean. Not that I've ever seen the ocean or much else for that matter besides what lies inside the borders of Pine Cliff. The Jackson River snakes between the mountains, foul smelling foam from the paper mill floating on its back. The mill manufactures cardboard boxes for everything from wringer washers to laundry soap, and people all over America pour their morning cereal from boxes made in Virginia's Blue Ridge Mountains. Black smoke spouts from the chimneys like grimy apparitions seven days a week, including Fourth of July and Christmas, and soot falls over the town and settles on the streets and the bed linens hanging on the clotheslines. By suppertime, my brother Smiley has dirt in his ears, between his toes, and in the creases of his neck and elbows. On the best days when the wind blows toward West Virginia, I escape the confines of our tiny house and venture outside. But when no breeze blows at all, the stink settles on the town like tarpaper, and every breath requires effort.

For the rest of July, I spend time swatting gnats, slapping mosquitoes, and waiting for something to happen. In the meantime, I reread old movie magazines until Momma shoos me outside and I sit on the steps and watch Smiley shoot imaginary villains with a stick gun and run toy trucks through the black mountain dirt. His real name is Archer Timbers—Archer to make sure he always hits his mark and Timbers so he'll grow up strong and straight as the hardwoods of the Appalachian hills around us. He arrived after I had settled into the consideration of an only child. I know it's not his fault for making a late appearance into the Grey family, so to appease my resentment I call him Smiley after Gene Autry's sidekick Smiley Burnett.

Momma is strict about the boundaries she set around our neighborhood—the back yard with mole tunnels weaving through the roots of her prickly rose garden, the top of the road we live on, and Trott's gas station at the bottom. We're not allowed into the woods where copperheads lie in wait with poisonous fangs. Neither are we to wander up the mountain to the African settlement. Those people don't want us up there, Momma says. They have their own ways. She's not more specific than that.

On the hottest days, I like to visit the creek that runs in back of the brick shed housing the water pumps. When my feet are gluey and dirt wedges like jelly between my toes, I stand mid-calf in the spring-fed stream, splashing crusted salt from my neck. Cupping my hands, I scoop guppies or tadpoles into my palms, but a crawdad is a bigger treasure, a lobster-like creature the length of my thumb, translucent with pincher hands. His shotgun pellet eyes twist about, antennae twirling.

"Lookit this," I once said to Smiley. He inched a finger close to it, pulling back when a claw snapped his way. When the crustacean got him, he ran crying to Momma. The spikey creature spidered to my wrist, and I nudged it around to crawl back toward my fingertips then offered my other hand to extend its course.

I've spent hours watching crawdads in the creek, fanning themselves ahead with spoonlike tails, spooning algae into tiny mouths with precision claws, and maneuvering rocks with spindly legs. In the water they're graceful and delicate, and I envy their intricate beauty. As much as Momma urges me into skirts and dresses, I prefer dungarees. I guess you'd call me tomboyish. I'm gangly and awkward, but alone at the creek I forget the judgment of others and imagine myself as lithe as Ginger Rogers.

I can feel things shifting, though. Just weeks ago, Daddy said I shouldn't sit on his lap anymore.

"Why not?" I liked to press my nose against his neck and smell his aftershave, feel the bristle of his whiskers when he hadn't shaved since morning.

He bit his bottom lip. Then he said, "You're fourteen now, Bobbie. You're turning into a woman." I didn't need him to tell me what was happening to me. My breasts have popped like dogwood blossoms, and the monthly bleeding amounts to one day of aching and five of messy inconvenience. I cry for no reason, and if I hold in the tears, my sadness turns to fury and I need to break something. It's as if a fog has moved into my brain. Who am I? What is it I'm supposed to be aiming for?

I have no one to talk to about these thoughts. Smiley is too young, and Momma's busy ridding the house of dirt which I think she largely invents. She calls to us now and again but has little to worry about. A passing automobile is cause to gawk, and what Momma calls meanness is absent from Pine Cliff's streets. The *Messenger*, our local newspaper, makes a point to feature robberies in nearby Clinton Forge, but attempted break-ins reported in town are most likely the fiction of the *Messenger*'s editor to sell a few extra copies of his daily.

It's the mill that presents real dangers. For many of its victims, including my father, the final ride is to Cedar Hill Cemetery between the railroad tracks and the Jackson River. One of my first life lessons was about the tentative nature of life.

Summer days, however, seem endless. When I'm not at the creek, I chase butterflies, hypnotized by their metamorphosis from disgusting multi-legged worms into the most elegant and colorful of God's creations. In the evenings, crickets black and big as two finger digits start their high-pitched songs signaling mosquitoes to feast. But the greatest of summer's annoyances are the eight-legged fiends with indestructible bodies that can go without eating for two years hanging onto the tips of grass blades, waiting for a whiff of warm blood. When they sense a meal, they grab onto a follicle of fur or hair and work their way down to the skin, digging in and sucking until they're blown up like blisters, fat as a grape. After they pull out their heads, they fall off and lie around, living off the lifeblood of the prey. Little hard-shelled vampires.

Nightly Momma does tick checks, running her fingers through our hair while Smiley and I scratch chigger bites. Chiggers are tiny red bugs whose venom swells to an itchy lump bigger than a mosquito bite.

Outside, Momma sits on the step above me and massages my scalp. I pull away from her.

"Daddy checks me for ticks." I know it's mean of me to bring up Daddy, but there's an emptiness in my soul without him.

"You want to do it yourself?" Momma's voice has a hard edge. When I don't answer, she presses my head to one side and then the other, her nails scratching my scalp. I reach for an itchy spot on my ankle, and she yanks me back.

"Be still," she says, stopping to puff on her cigarette. She perches the cigarette on the glass ashtray that has a picture of Natural Bridge painted on it. Daddy said the bridge was one of the Seven Natural Wonders of the World because Cedar Creek carved right through the rock. We went there for a picnic one Sunday in a car he borrowed from Nandaddy. We had to drive over the bridge, then turn and come down below before we saw how the river ate through the mountain, making a giant archway that looks like an ancient ruin. At a picnic table we ate fried chicken and potato salad. Afterward, Daddy bought us all soda pops from a machine and the ashtray from the souvenir shop for Momma. That was just two summers ago but it could well have been a century for all the changes we've been through.

"This one's already dug in." Momma grazes over a small lump behind my ear. When she digs the nails of her thumb and forefinger into my skin, the pain gives me odd pleasure. Then she pulls, firm and slow.

"Ow," I protest.

"Got to get the head, Sister—you know that."

I don't want the fever, so I sit motionless and bite my lips. Often I've found the vermin myself, but if I miss one or if it's buried in, there's danger of Rocky Mountain spotted fever, a disease so evil that victims go insane before death overcomes them—slow, painful, and sure.

"Got him." She holds up the tick, its stubby legs wiggling and trying to get a purchase on something. It has a piece of my skin in its jaws. I've seen stray dogs in town, ears lumpy with bloated ticks. Dogs can go mad in the summer, but I don't believe it's from Rocky Mountain Spotted Fever. More likely it's snakebite or rabies.

"We need to get rid of this one before I check A.T.," Momma says. She blows on her cigarette, making sure the tip shines red. Then she scrapes the tick from her finger onto the step and lowers the hot end of her cigarette to its body and holds it there. Smiley comes up close, his nose inches away from the drama.

In the distance a dog barks and the evening train blows a shrill whistle. Then a soft pop.

"He's gone," Smiley says.

Momma sucks her cigarette and smoke flows around her face. She's too pretty to be a widow.

"Your turn, Smiley," I say.

"I wish you wouldn't call him that," Momma says, pulling him between her knees.

"Can I get a bicycle?" Smiley's watching an ant crawl over his hand.

"We don't have the money for a bicycle, honey."

"Why not? Richie Marshall's got one."

"You're lucky we're not out on the street," I snarl, hoping that will shut him up. I picture us living on the street, cooking supper over a fire like in Gene Autry movies and sleeping on the packed dirt road so we won't get covered with ticks.

"Daddy'll buy me a bicycle," Smiley says. He's almost six and cried every night for a solid week when Daddy didn't come home. Who'll teach him to be a man now that our father is gone?

Momma doesn't answer him.

"Daddy's not buying you anything," I say. He did the best he could with us but when he died, he left as if we'd never existed at all, as if we didn't amount to a hill of beans. As it is, we don't amount to much.

"No bicycle," I say. "No nothing."

"Aw," he says. "You wait. One day I'll wake up, and there it'll be. You just wait."

Smiley's hair is nearly white, cut in a bowl shape. Pale colors attract ticks and Momma picks three out of him, two of which have started their evening buffet on his blood. Each time she pinches one of the freeloaders, Smiley wails and I feel a slow thrill. It isn't that I hate him, but some malevolent spirit has possessed me. My father's death has made us the pity of Pine Cliff. Church ladies bring cakes and cluck their tongues at what a shame it is that Mrs. Grey has fatherless children. I thank them for their concern, but underneath my courtesy I wish they'd leave us alone.

Momma presses the ticks into a tissue from her dress pocket. Then she drops the balled-up tissue on the cement step and lifts a box of matches from beside the ashtray. When she strikes the match, the tissue flares up. In a few seconds, I hear pops like tiny firecrackers.

I have no sympathy for ticks, but no creature deserves a fiery death.

When Momma sweeps the ashes off the step with her shoe, rage flares in me like a tree struck by lightning that burns from the inside. I grab the ashtray, draw back my arm and let it fly. The tinkling of shattered glass on the sidewalk cools the burning in my chest.

"Sister!" Momma gasps.

"What'd she do that for?" Smiley says.

"Hush." Momma grinds her cigarette on the step and pulls me to her chest. She smells of smoke and talcum. When I breathe her in, I pretend we're waiting for Daddy, his thin frame and easy step coming up the road from the day shift.

"Sister," Momma whispers into my hair, clean now of the blood suckers that would end my life. "Get the broom and clean up that glass. It's not right to leave your grief all over the sidewalk." She gets up and stands over me. "When you're finished, both of you come in for your bath." Then she goes inside and the screen door catches against her behind.

I take my time sweeping the glass into the dustpan. The town below us is turning dusky, like the moments between waking and sleep when color drains away and what's real becomes dreamlike. The first star, the wishing star, hangs bright over Oliver Mountain. I know not to wish for something big, like our own motor car or a horse. Once I wished my name would appear in the *Messenger*, and the following week I won the fifth-grade spelling bee and my picture appeared on page six along with the winners from the other grades. I'd spelled Paleozoic, which is a much harder word than the sixth graders had to spell. I thought I deserved special mention instead of being lost in the crowd. I had also wished that I'd win the spelling bee, so I know I can put stock in small things.

Just after Momma goes inside, a figure ambles up the street, a covered pail swinging in his left hand, a book under his right arm.

I know that hand, that dawdling step. Even when he's running late, he's not in a hurry.

"Hey Covey," Smiley says before I have a chance.

"Evening," he answers.

"Where you going this time of night?"

"Got a job at the mill." Covey's voice sounds like a song.

I'm tongue-tied, but Smiley asks, "Did you quit working with my Nandaddy?"

"Just making some extra money."

A black man working for a white man is an acceptable arrangement. But anyone who violates the unspoken code of behavior among light and dark-skinned folks pays serious consequences. Covey's father was one of those who paid the ultimate consequence.

"You run those big machines, Covey?" Why does conversation come so much more easily for Smiley than for me?

Covey's mouth twists to the side. "If I'm called to, I do." He switches hands with the lunch pail, taking the book in his left. "But when I get a nest egg, I'm going back to school." He wags the book in the air and swishes his gray eyes at me. "Anatomy."

Covey's too intelligent for mill work. But like everyone else, he has to scrape together a living. I try to think of a topic to talk about that will make him linger a little longer.

"Are you still boxing?" Daddy used to go to the Golden Gloves matches at Peters Auditorium. He said Covey fights like a rooster.

"When the prize money's good," he says.

"Maybe I could watch you sometime." I feel the blood rush to my face—too bold?

"That might be nice—if I win." He swings his pail. "Don't want to be late—see you later."

"See you later, Covey," Smiley echoes after him.

I want to continue our conversation, but I know it's dangerous to get too friendly.

When Momma calls Smiley into the house, I rock on the glider and watch crimson cinders escape the mill chimneys and rise into the night. Now that we no longer have my father's paycheck, Momma must be struggling to pay the rent. We haven't had a treat in weeks, except when we went to Nandaddy and Mamaw's on Sunday and had a popsicle from their freezer. Momma has been charging milk and butter at the store, and I expect we've run up a hefty debt. When cold weather comes, we'll have to buy coal for the stove and warm clothes for Smiley and me because none of our clothes will fit us by then. Money doesn't just float down from heaven even if Daddy's up there running a mint.

Momma comes out and sits beside me on the glider. She pushes back with her toe and the glider rocks forward and backward a few times.

"I thought after A.T. started school I'd take a job in a dress shop," she says. Besides Ruggel's Department Store and Thrifty Second Hand there's Monique's, run by a northern woman. Momma doesn't have clothes nice enough even to be a salesgirl there.

"Are we running low?" I ask.

"We can get by the rest of the month."

"Can't we ask Nandaddy to help?"

"I can handle this myself," she snaps. Obviously, I struck a nerve. Momma is independent, and I know to leave her alone to work things out.

I chew the inside of my jaw and shiver at the first cool breeze that marks summer's end. Now that I think of what to wish for, the sky is thick with stars.

3
Deep Dark Well

Pine Cliff and the Shenandoah Valley are all I know. The old-timers say the word Shenandoah is Sioux for beautiful daughter of the stars. At night the sky is so deep and inky and studded with a million twinkling lights that it strikes awe in me. Oftentimes I see a heavenly body moving faster than an airplane but not so fast as a shooting star. UFO, Daddy used to say. If aliens have landed near Pine Cliff, they must be hiding out in the hundreds of caves along the ridge. Now that he's gone, I'm almost an alien myself. Everything around me is familiar, but nothing fits. It's as if I've outgrown this old town.

To meet the rent, Momma and I take in ironing, first from Elsie next door. She gave up pressing her own sheets and pillowcases, but her husband likes the ironed crispness. We have a wringer washer out back, and a cup of bleach goes in with the whites. I hang the laundry on the line in the yard and just before it's dry, we fold the pieces, roll them into cylinders, and pack them in a basket. The ironing board has wooden legs that fold so we can store it in a closet, and on ironing day I set it up in the living room, the coolest place in the house. Momma taught me to iron the linens, being careful not to set a wrinkle. You'd think ironing a flat piece of linen would be easy, but the burn scar on my thumb is a warning to be careful.

We can count on Elsie to bring over her husband's work shirts, and she gets the members of the Ladies Auxiliary to take advantage of our services. I imagine half the women bring us their washing out of sympathy and the other half are happy to be rid of the toil. Momma's better at ironing shirts than I am. First, she pins up her hair to cool her neck. As soon as the iron is hot, she begins with the collar, then sleeves, front, and finally the back, keeping the iron moving so as not to leave a scorch mark. If a shirt scorches, the whole process has to begin over.

"There's a right way to do things," she once told me, "and that's the way they should be done." Momma is rigid about her ways. Furniture has to be dusted and polished, floors mopped, ashtrays emptied and wiped, and all items in their places.

When summer ends, so does my sweaty labor. The town turns ochre with ragweed, sunflowers, marigolds, seedy pods of tall grasses, and ears of ripe corn. In autumn Pine Cliff is the color of gourds and pumpkins and the strap the school crossing guard wears diagonally over his chest. I'm starting ninth grade at the high school, which isn't much different from eighth grade. Penny Rearden still acts like she's better than everyone else, and Kenny Schneider still makes googly eyes at me. I hate math but like English and history. Mrs. Davenport manages to make history interesting by explaining how twenty-eight thousand years before Christ, women wore bronze bracelets and necklaces and gold combs in their hair. In the Byzantine Empire, they wove gold threads into their clothes, and even their furniture was made of gold. I wish I lived back then. I don't have a single piece of gold jewelry to my name.

In the afternoon I find Momma at the ironing board. She's been standing there most of the day, tendrils of hair falling from the barrette in wet ringlets at her neck. At night her legs ache and varicose veins are starting to form. I fix supper so she can sit at the table and smoke a cigarette, but we never have much food in the house. From time to time Mamaw and Nandaddy bring over a ham from their smokehouse and okra or mustard greens from the garden. Other than those occasional windfalls, we make do. Momma hasn't taken Smiley and me to a Saturday matinee since Daddy died. Some days she never changes out of her housedress.

One Saturday Momma's not up yet by eight o'clock. Smiley whines that he wants some toast, but all I can find in the icebox are sad-looking carrots and a sticky jar of jam. I've got no choice but to wake up Momma.

"We're out of everything," I say. "If you give me some money, I'll go to the store."

Momma brushes back her hair and sits up. She looks over to Daddy's side of the bed and runs her hand over the flat blanket.

"There is no money," she says.

"I thought you had some saved up." I don't mean to sound like I'm accusing her, but that's how it comes out. Smiley's hungry and so am I.

"It's gone." Momma draws up her knees under the covers, coils her arms around them, and drops her forehead.

"Momma?" I whisper. "What are we going to do?"

I've seen that look before—when she wages war with Pine Cliff's filth on housecleaning day and on nights she used to wait for Daddy to come back from the Gypsy Tavern.

Raising her head, she says, "Give me a minute." She steps into a pair of pants that have been lying on a chair and pulls a sweater over her head. She brushes her hair back, stretches a rubber band around the ponytail, and passes the bureau mirror without glancing at her reflection.

At the grocery store, I carry the basket down the aisles behind Momma. She's all business, tossing in items without even checking the prices. What's the point anyway?

At the checkout, she drops the food on the counter: a loaf of bread, pinto beans, grits, a can of evaporated milk, coffee, and a pack of Kools.

"How are you doing, Maggie?" Mr. Isobel asks.

"Fine, Sam." Momma's voice is limp.

He rings up the groceries and bags them then winks at Smiley and tosses in two butterscotch drops.

"Can you add this to my bill?" she says.

Taking a binder from a drawer, he jots a note in the ledger. Then he pushes his horn-rimmed glasses up on his nose and presses both hands on the counter. When he leans forward, his eyelids sag behind the thick lenses.

"I don't mean to meddle, Maggie," he says, "but you should think about applying for the welfare program. You've got the children to consider."

Welfare is for poor people, people who have no other options, people like Linda Stadler, a girl in my class who wears patched hand-me-downs and eats her lunch from a crumpled brown bag. Her father works odd jobs and makes just sufficient to drink himself stupid. Linda has come to school more than once with bruises on her face, which makes me suspect he's a mean drunk. I'd rather die than be as bad off as Linda Stadler.

But Daddy's not coming back and from the way I saw him in the coffin, I wouldn't want him to. If we don't find a solution soon, we'll start looking like those concentration camp prisoners the allies liberated.

Momma picks up the bag of groceries. "Thanks, Sam," is all she says.

Rain is drizzling down outside the afternoon I empty pennies from

Smiley's piggy bank onto the coffee table. When a knock comes at the door, I hope it's not Reverend Singer checking why we haven't been to services since the funeral. It isn't prayer we need—it's a different kind of salvation.

"Hello, Mr. Trott," I say. Lowry is a big man and fills out his coveralls, "Allegheny Esso" stitched onto the pocket.

"Your Momma here?"

"Where else would she be?"

Momma comes from the kitchen. "Bobbie, don't be rude." Then she says, "Lowry, come on in."

There has never been call for Lowry Trott to come to our house. We don't have a car, but even if we did, Daddy would have met him on the porch instead of asking him in. He wipes his feet on the welcome mat and steps inside. There follows an awkward moment, all of us waiting to discover what it is he wants with us.

Lowry twists around as if checking whether anyone has seen him.

"You have a minute to talk, Maggie?" He fires a look to Smiley and me. Whatever he's come about does not involve us.

"Bobbie, heat up the coffee." Momma has on the same dress she wore yesterday and the day before, the cotton so wrinkled it looks as if she slept in it, and her hair hangs wilted on her shoulders. She'd never have let herself go like that if Daddy were alive.

She leads Lowry to the kitchen and points to a chair at the table. I remind myself to wipe off the seat after the oily lug leaves. When I give him the coffee, I don't offer milk.

"Bobbie, can you take A.T. outside for a bit?" Momma says.

"It's raining."

"You're not sugar," Lowry says. "Not gonna melt." He makes my skin crawl.

"Don't want us to catch our death, do you?" The word death presses a trigger, and Momma jumps at the impact.

"All right then," she says.

When I check on Smiley, he has lined up the pennies like a train, moving the last one to the front and curving the line around like a railroad track around a mountain.

Lowry rubs his arms. "You got the heat turned down?"

We are almost out of coal, but Momma put off asking Mr. Neddleton for a load on credit. I take the dishrag and wipe a sticky spot off the table, taking my time.

Lowry sips his coffee, rubbing his thigh with his free hand.

"I know times are tough for you," he says after he sets the mug down. Lowry can't know about how tough times are. His gas station is so busy he has two men working for him. "Why don't I cover your rent for a few months and give you some grocery money?"

Lowry is not one to dole out charity. I can smell a rat when it sits at our table.

"You've got a wife of your own, Mr. Trott," I say but I might as well be a ghost for all he notices.

"I need someone to straighten out my records. I could bring them by and have you make some sense of them." He holds up his mug. "Have a neighborly cup of coffee while we're at it."

Lowry is soft around the middle, grease under his nails. He smells of motor oil and the hair tonic he must have splashed on for Momma's benefit. He's pushing fifty if he's a day and as rusty as the junk cars around his station.

"I'll let you know, Lowry," Momma says. I hope "no" is the operative word.

After he leaves, Momma drops onto the sofa. "Well, I guess we've hit bottom."

"Bottom of what?" Smiley says.

"Nevermind," I say.

Momma looks at her fingertips. Her nails need filing. "I think I'll go down to the paper mill and see if they have any openings."

I've lost count of how many times ambulance sirens have squealed away from the mill carrying the injured to the hospital—bones to be set, gashes stitched, burns soothed. How can Momma think about taking that risk? She's all Smiley and I have left.

"What about the pin factory or the rayon plant?" I ask.

"I don't have money for a bus, but I can walk to the mill. Besides, don't you think the foreman owes me a favor?"

"Bottom of what?" Smiley says again.

"Of a deep, dark well," I tell him.

"I don't want to be in a dark well."

"Me neither." Momma brushes her palms together. "So I guess we'd better start climbing out."

4

The Jackson

When Momma peels back my sheet, for a minute I'm not sure if it's morning or the middle of the night.

"Come on—we've got a big day ahead."

"It can't be time to get ready for school." I rub my eyes. "It's not even light out." Ninth grade has been a big disappointment. Mrs. Davenport is determined to spend the first term on subject-verb agreement ("One of the cats IS screeching"), and I don't see the use in going to school at all until she moves on to the semicolon. She's reading *Great Expectations* to us, which I am perfectly capable of reading on my own. The story agitates me. Miss Havisham isn't so bad, and I wish Pip would stop whining. His prospects are more promising than mine.

I slide my feet from beneath the covers and dangle them over the side of the bed until weak light struggles through the window. Fog hangs in the valley so thick the tops of the mountains seem to float. Cold clutches at my throat and I catch a faint scent of lilac and rose in the darkness. But when I'm fully awake, I realize it isn't flowers at all, just the thick and acrid air that has filled me every day of my life, penetrating the pores of my skin and threatening to turn me to pitchy vapor.

Smiley perches on a kitchen stool with a glass tipped up, blowing bubbles so that the milk we borrowed from Elsie runs over onto the table in a white puddle.

"You're too big to be doing that," I reprimand. "Now get the dishrag and clean it up."

I go to Momma's room to see why she's gotten us up so early. The shade of one dim lamp on the vanity casts pink on the walls like new skin after the scab's been picked off. She's filling a pillowcase with my father's socks, BVDs, razor, bottle of Old Spice aftershave, a toothbrush, his tube of Brylcreem. Next she sorts through undershirts.

"These'll be cleaning rags." She lays aside three worn ones and stuffs the others into the case. There are four ties laid out on the bed, one with a naked lady painted inside the lining. I discovered the lady one evening when Daddy and Momma were fixing themselves up to attend a dance at the Grange Hall. While we waited for Elsie to come over and watch Smiley and me, I leaned into his chest. When I turned over the tie to see the inside, I found a hidden drawing of a naked woman.

"Who's this?"

"That's your Momma," he said. "Isn't she pretty?"

I'd never seen Momma naked, but the woman didn't look anything like her as far as I could see.

"Who painted it?"

"I did."

"You can't paint." I'd seen him draw pictures of horses and cows for Smiley—two circles and four straight lines.

"When it comes to your Momma," he said, "I'm a veritable artist." Then he winked at her in the mirror as she was patting her hair into place.

The pillowcase is bulging with shirts and trousers Momma folded and pushed in. She lifts Daddy's Bulova watch out of the top drawer and turns it around in her hand. It has a gold face and a genuine leather band curved to the shape of his thick wrist.

"I gave this to your father the day we were married."

"Can't we sell it?" It's Daddy's only possession that has much value, but this isn't a time to be sentimental.

"He'd want A.T. to have it someday." She sniffles and lays the watch back in the drawer.

On top of the pile Momma places the polished wingtips Daddy had shined with polish and chamois cloth. She takes two corners of the case and ties them together in a granny knot.

"Get A.T. to put a jacket on," she says. "It's cool out."

"Where are we going?"

She grabs the pillowcase at the top like she's strangling a goose. "Grieving's not going to feed us."

Outside a hook of moon has pulled aside night's curtain, and trees are taking shape. Downtown, the sidewalk is an eerie path leading into the unknown. The shops are closed up tight as we head toward the Jackson River. The Jackson is a liquid highway for transporting logs—clean wood goes in one chute and raw sewage comes out the other end. The mill is a big eating machine that devours trees and evacuates its putrid waste into the river.

Momma stops on the high wooden bridge. I've never seen fishermen dangle their lines into the Jackson. Any fish that survive the poison aren't fit to eat.

"Stand back," I warn Smiley.

Momma gets her footing, swings the pillowcase in a half arc and sends it flying out and down. It hits a soaked log, which rolls out of its way. Smiley cranes his head over the bridge railing, and we watch as the Jackson swallows up all that's left of our father in one greedy gulp.

5
Waves

While I boil grits for breakfast, Momma sweeps black dust from the porch. At seven o'clock she two-steps into her beige suit, the one she was wearing in the photograph of her and Daddy on their wedding day. I watch her try to fasten the waist on the skirt, but the buttonhole doesn't meet the button so she leaves it undone and wraps a belt around her middle. The jacket is tight, so she lets it hang open over the blouse.

She looks at her legs, pivoting on one toe to see the side of her calf.

"Wish I had some hose," she says. "But we can't afford that extravagance."

I hand her a bottle of makeup from her bureau.

"Maybe this'll help."

She dabs the make-up on her finger and then rubs it on her bare skin. Her legs are shapely and nice even without nylons.

In the kitchen, she stands over the boiling kettle and steams her hair, squeezing it with her fingers. Her hair has a natural curl to it, not pin straight like mine—I inherited Daddy's hair. When she has trained the waves into place, she pulls her compact out of her purse and uses the mirror to paint on a band of rose-colored lipstick.

"Do I look okay?" she asks.

"Beautiful, Momma." And I mean it.

Smiley and I walk her as far as where he and I fork off for school. From the rise, I survey the mill yard littered with logs like clipped fingernails. Men with cant hooks snag logs from the chutes and drag them onto neat piles. Stripping machines cut off the bark before feeding the wood into the chipper, a blade like a giant fan that cuts the logs into pieces smaller than stew meat. The mill is a universe of noisy machines, hacking, chopping, scalding, reducing trees to mush and mush to cardboard. Men's livelihoods depend on the dirty, stinking business. And as I watch Momma traipse into that odiferous universe, I shudder to think that once in a while it costs them their lives.

6
Phoenix

"Sixty-four cents an hour to start." Momma tosses her jacket on the couch. "I can work up from there."

"Doing what? Not working on the boilers." Climbing up the vertical ladders bolted to the cylinders is men's work, if there are any men left that haven't gone to soldiering or been blown up.

"Cutting paper," she says. "I stand by a stack higher than my waist and guide a huge blade through it. Phoenix showed me how to do it."

"Who's Phoenix?" Smiley asks.

"Assistant foreman. She's teaching me the ropes."

"Cutting paper sounds dangerous," I grumble. "How sharp are those blades?"

"Sharp as razors."

Momma wears a narrow gold band on her left ring finger. I imagine the blade cutting off the fingers at the second knuckle, the blood spurting out, the fingertips tumbling like pink Tootsie Rolls, Momma's lips pressing flat as she watches them bounce once and roll away.

"You sure you'll be all right? What if I quit school and work beside you? The little I'm learning in ninth grade I can pick up on my own." I don't really mean it. I like school and besides, except for a chance of running into Covey, the mill holds no promise for me.

"As long as I don't fall asleep on my feet I'll be fine." She pushes my bangs back from my forehead, the fingers of her hand still attached. "Don't worry, honey. Phoenix will make sure nothing bad happens to me."

I've never met Phoenix and have no reason to rely on her. In fact, I don't rely on anyone to look out for Momma but me.

*   *   *

The bustle of mornings is like music—spoons clinking against bowls, the shuffle of Momma's slippers across the linoleum, blub-blub of the percolator. I've started having a cup with Momma, more milk than coffee. She's almost sassy these days, swinging her hips the way she did when Daddy was around. When we leave the house together, I hate to see her disappear through the metal entry, but Cowboy Code number seven says that a cowboy must be a good worker, and Momma is sure to be.

After school I make Smiley a snack and wait for Momma to come in. She's usually so tired that supper has become my regular duty. Now that we have grocery money, I can get creative. After I dredge pork chops in flour and fry them in shortening, I make a paste of flour and water and simmer the scrapings into rich gravy. Other nights I make a meatloaf, adding thyme and a teaspoon of mustard to the pork and beef. I'll even hide a hardboiled egg inside as a surprise. When we run low on food, I scramble eggs with chopped ham. If all we have are grilled cheese sandwiches, I curl carrot strips with the potato peeler to perk up the meal. Momma says I have a flair for cooking.

We're almost like sisters, Momma and me. She gives me a summary of her day, how she moved up from cutting to working with huge spools. Phoenix tilts one up on an angle and dances it to the wrapping platform. She and Momma lay the spool down and pull the paper around it, pleating the ends so they lie flat. Then they glue it all into place.

"Seems like Phoenix is involved in everything you do at work." I can't help the tone of my voice. I haven't even met this Phoenix and already she's moving in on Momma.

"Just about everything, yes." Momma adds a little laugh as if she shares a private joke with Phoenix. I can just see them, heads together giggling like girls over their secrets.

Evenings are precious when I have Momma to myself for an hour or two before she falls into bed. But I start losing ground there, too.

I've got supper waiting on the table when Momma comes home late one night.

"Phoenix and I went for coffee," she says without apology.

"I could have made coffee."

"Girl talk—you know." She says it as if the topic of their conversation excludes me. I tell Momma what Penny Reardon and I talk about, which doesn't amount to much—movie stars, who we'd want to marry (I never mention Covey Fortune), and whether Mrs. Davenport has ever been in love. We make up stories about a heartbreak that sent her into the classroom to distract her from her lost love who was run over by the C&O engine when his foot got caught in a railroad tie. Somehow we thought that was funny—maybe because we knew it wasn't true. I don't see why Momma can't tell me about her conversations with Phoenix.

Momma shrugs out of her coat and eyes the chicken I've fried in Crisco. She picks a crispy flake from a thigh and drops it onto her tongue. What do she and Phoenix have to talk about? The fine points of wrapping spools of paper?

I fume over my dinner while Momma tells Smiley how Phoenix can whistle Yankee Doodle Dandy all the way through without missing a note. My grandmother says a whistling girl and a crowing hen come to a bad end, which is about all that gives me satisfaction that night.

* * *

After work the next day, Momma is radiant.

"I asked her to come to supper."

"Tonight?" I don't need to ask who.

She opens the bottom cupboard, chooses the clean cotton cloth that she reserves for those rare occasions that we have guests for supper, and spreads it over the oilcloth we keep on the table, smoothing out the creases with her palms. She sets the table for four, the extra plate at the head of the table.

I move the plate beside Smiley's. "That's my father's place."

"Don't be superstitious." She slides the plate back.

"Here she comes," Smiley calls. "And she's got Covey with her."

"Covey?" I trip over the rug as I dash to the window. Phoenix must know Covey, and my heart swells. I hope he's coming to supper, too. But then she flaps a hand at him and he continues up to the settlement alone.

Phoenix's cheeks are blushed from the cold and she dabs at a nostril with a gloved finger. She's mannish, baggy trousers cinched at the waist with a thick belt, a shirt tucked into the pants. The sleeves are rolled up to the elbows, and she wears it open at the neck, showing a tee shirt.

She greets me with "Hey, Sister—you don't mind if I call you that, do you?"

I do mind. But at least Momma has told her about me.

She shakes Smiley's hand. "Howdy, partner."

"What was you doing out there with Covey?" Smiley asks. Momma never mentioned Covey working with them at the mill. How does Phoenix know him?

"We ran into one another on the way over here."

"From Rosedale?" Momma says. Rosedale is a neighborhood across the river where businessmen live in grand houses and have their shirts laundered at May's cleaners.

"Naw," Phoenix says. "I didn't go home. After you left work, I hung out with the boys chewing the fat. Since I've been having lunch with you, we haven't had a chance to catch up. A few of us had a cup of joe at Marilyn's Café."

I wish she'd stayed hanging out with the boys.

"I hope you're hungry," Momma says. "Sister has cooked us a nice supper."

I made a stew with some hamburger, a can of beans and leftover vegetables I found in the icebox. Nothing special since I wasn't expecting company, but it's too late to fix a fancy meal.

"You mind if I use your bath first?" Phoenix says. "I need to wash some of this slurry off me before I'll be fit to eat with."

Since when does a dinner guest ask to take a bath?

"Let me find a fresh outfit for you to wear," Momma says.

While they're in Momma's room, I spoon the stew into bowls and slice the skillet of cornbread. I can hear a cackling laugh followed by Momma's soft chuckle. I won't deny Momma the enjoyment of having a new friend, but Phoenix rankles me. Although she isn't much bigger than Momma, smaller-hipped and flat-chested, she seems to fill our place up to the corners.

After the water starts running in the tub, Momma comes back to the kitchen.

"Isn't she something?"

"Why'd you invite her to supper?

"Is that cornbread all right? Smells burned." Momma is avoiding my question.

The walls of our house are thin so that the sound of splashing in the bathroom makes its way to the kitchen, and so does Phoenix's off-tune singing: *She'll be driving six white horses when she comes.* I click the radio on to drown her out, and Gene Autry croons out a chewing gum commercial advising me to double my fun. I wish I had a stick of Doublemint right then— I could use some fun.

I arrange the cornbread on a plate—the bottom is dark brown but not burned—and Momma pours iced tea into glasses.

When Phoenix presents herself, smelling of my mother's spring-scented soap, she is wearing a pair of pajamas I've never seen before. They're a silky scarlet material, embroidered with gold vines and amethyst birds. The top closes with coiled cords wound into knots that hook over each other, four sets down the front of the jacket that match the pants. The sleeves come to just below her elbows, and the pants stop above the ankles. She looks clownish, but there's also something refined about her, like the royal fool who entertained a king in a book I read in elementary school.

"Where'd you get those?" I ask Phoenix, but Momma answers.

"Your father gave me the outfit for our wedding night," she says. "They're too nice to wear except for a special occasion."

What makes Phoenix coming over a special occasion? I've got the same feeling as when I discover a tick in my hair, aiming for my scalp.

"Something smells appetizing," Phoenix says. Her hair is braided into a rope the color of cardboard. When the braid falls over her shoulder, she flicks it back.

When we sit down at the table, I won't look her way, won't look at Phoenix wearing my mother's special clothes and taking up my father's space.

"Glory, I'm hungry," she says, stretching for the cornbread.

"Why don't you explain to the children what we do all day, Phoenix?"

"You already told us what you do, Momma," I say.

"Did your mother tell you how we check the rolls of paper for moisture?" Phoenix says.

"How?" Smiley's legs are too far under the table for me to kick.

"You whack it," Phoenix says.

"You what?" Smiley likes that word—whack—which is what I'd like to do to him about now.

"You take a yardstick and whack the roll once or twice. If it sounds hollow, that means it's dry. If you hear a thud, the paper's wet. Wet means heavy paper, and heavy paper tears easy."

"What's heavy about something thin as paper?" I'm talking to my bowl of stew.

"You have a roll of it tall as your mother, and it's plenty heavy." Phoenix slathers margarine on her bread.

"She's right," Momma says, emphasizing their alliance.

"Give me your arm, Sister." Phoenix leans over, grabs my left arm, and pushes up my sleeve. "See this fuzz on your skin? You run your arm over the surface of a roll without touching it and watch what the fuzz does. If it stands up, the paper's too dry. Too dry means too brittle. It'll fall apart. You want the fuzz to stay put."

I pull my arm away.

"Where'd you learn all that stuff?" Smiley squints one eye at Phoenix.

"From the old-timers. They know all there is about paper." She helps herself to a second serving of the stew. There won't be leftovers tonight.

I'm surprised at how delicate her hands are. Hands that can tip a thousand-pound bolt of paper on its side and draw a blade through a stack of reams like paddling through water are smooth and graceful as swallows. Her nails are cut even with the tips of her fingers, and they move quick and sure for someone as boyish as Phoenix. She doesn't wear jewelry, no rings—not even a bracelet. Momma left her wedding ring on her bureau when she started at the mill. She said she was afraid it would get caught in the machinery.

After we finish supper, Momma says, "I'm sorry we don't have any dessert."

"Hold on." Phoenix snaps her fingers and slides her chair back. She disappears and comes back, holding her fists out to Smiley.

"Pick one," she says. He touches the back of her left hand, and she turns it over, a candy wrapped in silver foil perched on her palm. Smiley grabs for it, works the paper loose and pops it into his mouth.

"This one's for you, Sister." She uncurls her right fist to me.

"No thank you," I say, although I can almost taste the chocolate melting on my tongue.

"Suit yourself." She goes over to Momma, pushes a strand behind her ear, and looks in. "Hold still a minute, girl." She pretends to reach into Momma's ear and comes up with a third silver chocolate.

Momma giggles. "What about one for you?"

Phoenix looks at Smiley "Why, I believe A.T.'s got mine growing out of his nose." She pinches Smiley's nose, and another candy materializes in her hand.

"You going to eat that?" he says.

"Sure," says Phoenix. "Anybody else's nose and I might not, though."

From the look on his face she has won him over, but I am determined not to like her, even when she washes the supper dishes. Even when she crouches down on the floor, outlines roads with matchsticks, and plays cars with Smiley. Even when I find a foil-wrapped chocolate in my pocket, which I swear I will never eat.

"Hey," Phoenix says, "what say we make the table talk?"

How does Phoenix know about table talking? I thought my family were the only ones privy to the secret ceremony, a combination of religion and magic. Mamaw has hosted table talk sessions since I can remember. I haven't told anyone about it, not even Penny Reardon. No one would believe me anyway.

Mamaw never allowed me to participate when we got the table to levitate. I think she was afraid the devil would take a shine to me, but when I was little I sat underneath to make sure no one was moving the table with their knees.

"We need four people," Momma says, "and the children are too young."

"Sister's old enough." Phoenix winks at me, chipping at the layer of ice I've built up around myself.

"We need one more person, then," Momma says.

"How about I go ask Elsie while you get A.T. into bed?" Phoenix is already slipping her jacket over the pajamas.

While she's gone, I slide the card table out of the closet and set it up, locking the folding legs into place. One summer during a drought I saw Mamaw raise one side of the heavy picnic table off the ground and it tapped the days until the next rainstorm. And three days later, right on schedule, thunderclouds moved in and rescued Nandaddy's vegetable garden.

I wait, sticking my hands in my pockets and fingering the chocolate, rotating it and loosening the foil. At the risk of having the chocolate melt and make a mess in the cloth, I figure the best precaution is to dispose of it, and the least telltale place to dispose of it is in my mouth. When was the last time I ate chocolate? After so long, even such a small piece should quench my appetite for it. Instead, the sweetness starts a craving so deep in me that I can't see the bottom.

I place the four kitchen chairs around the table, one on the east and one on the west sides. Two sit on the south side. The north side, the one facing the mill, is to be left empty for the talking.

Phoenix comes in rubbing her hands together.

"Let's get this show on the road," she says.

Elsie follows her in. "Mercy," she says, "I've got a list of questions I need answered."

"Sister, pull those curtains," Momma says, having settled Smiley down. We don't want people thinking we're practicing witchcraft in here."

"Is that what we're doing?" Elsie says.

"If it is, I come from a long line of witches," Momma says. "My mother's great-grandmother was making tables rise before she came over from Europe. Solid wood tables two inches thick."

"How'd she do it?" Phoenix asks.

"Nobody knows. And neither she nor the table will talk about it." Momma sits in one of the chairs on the south side. "I'll take the driver's seat."

Phoenix plops next to my mother, and I slide onto the seat across from Elsie.

"Bobbie, are you up to this?" Elsie looks skeptical.

"I raised tables before I was her age," Momma says. Then why did she wait to let me be part of the raising, and why did it take Phoenix to advocate for me?

"Now, rest your fingertips on the table," Momma says. "No need to press down." She closes her eyes. "Let the table warm up a minute."

I raise my wrists so they aren't touching the table, the way Momma has hers. No part of me is in contact with the table except for the tips of my fingers. My fingers begin to sweat, and it's hard to keep them in one place. Every time I breathe, my hands slip back and forth. I hope I'm not sending the table a wrong message.

After a minute or two, Momma exhales and says in a low voice, "Rise, table, rise. Up, table, up." She looks like she's in a trance, directing all her energy into the table.

"Rise, table, rise," she says again.

A chill passes over my skin.

"Rise, table, rise."

The table shivers, and then the north end starts rising into the air. I crane my neck around the corner without moving my fingers and see that the legs are at least six inches from the floor and hanging steady. Momma has a calm expression, which keeps me from going into panic.

"Good table," Momma says. "Now, can we ask you a few questions? Tap the floor once for yes and twice for no."

The table is slow to drop down and rise again.

"You must be pulling it," Phoenix says.

"No—look at my hands." Momma's fingertips are slipping over the tabletop like mine and not at all straining.

"Somebody's using her knees," Elsie says.

I know I'm not using my knees, and I don't see how Momma can be either.

"Now, table," Momma says. "Is today Saturday? Tap once for yes and twice for no."

The table lowers and rises back up, lowers and rises.

"Is today Friday?" The table makes one affirmative tap.

"Now we know you'll tell us the truth." Momma looks at Elsie. "You have a question?"

"I sure do. Table, what is Earl going to give me for my birthday next week?"

The table hangs steady.

"You've got to ask a yes or no question," Momma explains.

"Oh," Elsie says. "Then, is Earl going to give me that little do-hickey I been wanting?"

The table taps twice.

"Aw," she says.

"What do-hickey are you talking about?" Phoenix raises her eyebrows at Elsie.

"It's supposed to be a surprise." Elsie ducks her head toward me. Do-hickeys are another adult secret to be revealed.

"Am I going to get that raise I asked for?" It's Phoenix's question.

The table bounces once on the floor and rises again.

"Hot dog!" she yells.

"Okay," Momma says, "My turn. Is Lowry Trott going to leave me alone?"

"Trott, that grease monkey?" The table cuts Phoenix off, tapping one definitive time.

"That's a relief," Momma says. "Okay, Sister, you ask."

My mother inherited the ability to conjure spirits, the same talent that threads back through her foremothers. Which means I've been given it, too, the knack of calling up souls. The power is a responsibility—and a weapon— and I have the sense to use it with caution.

I have questions about the upcoming history test and how I'll score on it, but the table's answer to Momma steers me in a different direction.

"Will somebody try to take my father's place?"

"Sister, I don't think—" Momma starts.

The table hits the floor with one definitive tap.

"I'm not surprised," Elsie says. "Who'll it be?"

The table starts to fall and then makes an effort to resume its position. Phoenix stares at Momma.

"There are some questions the table has no business answering," Momma says, "and we have no business asking."

"Well how about this," Elsie says. "Will Maggie live happy ever after?"

The table gives one strong tap and then lowers to the floor, touches down and is slow to rise, as if it can't make up its mind.

"What's that supposed to mean?" Elsie takes one hand off the table and scratches her scalp.

"It means the table's had just about enough for tonight." Momma rubs her palms on her thighs and the table flops to the floor.

"I'm about worn out myself," Phoenix says.

I had one more burning question that I thought better than to ask. Anyway, I already know the answer, even though with regard to Covey Fortune, it's not the answer I'm looking for.

*　　*　　*

After Elsie leaves, I fold the table.

"It's all a bunch of hooey," Phoenix scoffs.

"We'll see if it's hooey when you get that raise," Momma says.

"If the raise comes through, I'll take you all to the Chinese place downtown. My treat."

We went to the Chinese restaurant once with Daddy and I had my first taste of chop suey. I didn't get the hang of using chopsticks, so he asked the waitress to bring me a fork. If Phoenix uses chopsticks, I swear I will, too, even if it means leaving hungry.

"I'd best be on my way before the boogey man comes out." Phoenix starts for the bedroom. "I'll just fetch my clothes."

Momma stops her. "It's too dark out to be walking all that way."

"I'll get her the flashlight." I figure it's the least I can do since she spoke up for me about the table raising.

"Tomorrow's Saturday—she may as well stay over," Momma says as if she's asking my permission. A dinner guest is one thing, but an overnight is a commitment.

"Won't somebody be watching for her?"

"I live with my father," Phoenix says. "He's turns in early. Won't even notice I'm not there."

"What about your mother?"

"She's been dead since I was young." Her braid falls across her shoulder and she strokes it as if the woven hair is a pet. "If you'll give me a blanket, I can just curl up here on the divan." A flirty smile smears across her face.

"Don't be silly," Momma says. "I've got the double bed. It's plenty big for both of us."

No one has slept with Momma since Daddy died, except for the night after the funeral when I tried to comfort her. When she rolled over in the morning and found me next to her, she said that I had my own bed and I belong there, her words slapping my cheek. What gives Phoenix the right to sleep there now?

"What's wrong with the couch?" I say.

"I don't want to make an issue of it." Momma sweeps her arms out in a gesture of finality. "The bed's more comfortable, and that is the end of it."

Simple and direct, Momma has declared the way things will be.

7
Boxing Match

The smell of splattering sausage wakes me sometime after sunrise, the most delicious aroma there is. In the kitchen Phoenix scrapes a spatula across the skillet. She's still wearing Momma's pajamas but with an apron tied around her waist.

"She got up in the night and shoveled coal in the stove." Momma crosses her arms in a pleased manner. "Now she's fixing breakfast for us."

"What's she trying to do, take over?" Breakfast is my job. Grits and toast. A fried egg apiece if we want it.

"Chow's on," Phoenix yells. She does a cha-cha around the table, serving the plates over our shoulders. When she serves Momma's, her hand goes to Momma's back and rests there.

"You going to fix your own plate and sit down?" I sound friendlier than I mean to.

"I'm waiting to see if any of you keels over first." She squeezes Momma's shoulder before filling her own plate.

"It's delicious," Momma says, swallowing a mouthful. "And I don't taste any rat poison, Sister."

The scrambled eggs sit like a lump of yellow brains on my plate.

"I like my eggs over easy."

"Don't waste those eggs," Momma says. "They're ten cents a dozen."

"Leave them," Phoenix says. "We'll feed it to the hogs."

"What hogs?" Smiley has a spot of sausage grease on his chin.

"It's just an expression," I say.

"We ain't got any hogs."

"A.T., we don't have any hogs," Momma corrects.

"That's what I said."

"Eat your breakfast." I have no patience for his foolishness.

I push the eggs to the side but can't resist the sausage and toast. Phoenix scoops a forkful of eggs from my plate and feeds it to Momma, who hums approval. The rest she scrapes onto her own plate and consumes as if they're some rare delicacy. It's a performance, but if she expects me to be an appreciative audience, she's got another think coming.

*   *   *

After breakfast Phoenix changes into her own clothes to amble back to Rosedale, and we walk downtown with her. Smiley rides his tricycle although he's too big for it, his knees pointing out like an awkward bug. At the top of the Lexington Avenue hill, Phoenix says, "Wait here."

She jogs down ahead of us, stops at the bottom and tosses her hands over her head. Smiley pushes off with his feet and the tricycle bombs down the sidewalk and under the railroad bridge. His feet out to the sides, he hollers until Phoenix catches him, turns him around, and pushes him back up the hill.

"One more time," she says, then trots back down the hill.

Smiley wants to keep going but after three times, Phoenix says she's worn out.

"Tell you what, though," she says. "I'll come over tonight and teach you all how to play checkers."

I plant my hands on my hips. "I know how to play checkers."

"I don't," Smiley says.

"Can't but two people play at a time anyway," Phoenix says. "But how about this—after A.T. beats me twice, we all go out to Peters Auditorium, my treat."

"What's going on at Peters Auditorium?" Momma asks.

I know what's going on. The flyers are taped to light posts downtown—a boxing match, and I suspect Covey's going to be in the ring. We have to go— we just have to.

"Clinton Forge Mountaineers are fighting the Cougar Leather Pushers. Should be a good line-up. Ten matches. What do you say?"

"You mean a fight?" Momma says.

"Sure—left to the chin, right to the gut." She skips backwards, jabs the air, and knuckles me on the chin. For a chance to go to Peters Auditorium, I'll endure even that. Boys at school talk about Joe Louis and dance around the playground at recess, stabbing fists and ducking imaginary punches. Even Mrs. Davenport goes to matches every now and then. She says boxing is one of the oldest sports known to man. Art in motion, Daddy used to call it.

"The children are too young," Momma insists, "but Sister can watch A.T."

"You can have Elsie watch him." I'm going to the boxing match or die trying.

"Oh, come on, Mags. Let's bring her." Phoenix must sense how hard I'm trying to resist her, and she's trying just as hard to win me over.

"Please, Momma?" I never beg, but it would kill me not to go.

"I guess Elsie could come over," Momma says, "but what do I know about boxing?"

"I'll tell both of you everything you need to know." Phoenix leans in and kisses Momma's cheek before she trots off to Rosedale and we turn up Allegheny Avenue.

*   *   *

Momma applies fresh makeup and a flowered shirtwaist that hits just below the knee. Phoenix has on loose trousers and a clean shirt with a blazer over it and has combed her hair into a ponytail. She doesn't use makeup. Doesn't need it. She has a fresh scrubbed look just shy of pretty. As for me, dungarees don't seem right to wear to a fight. A Sunday dress is overdoing it, so I settle on my plaid skirt. It was Momma's that she altered to fit me. I add a cardigan, ankle socks, and my oxfords. It's a plain outfit, but Covey isn't one for putting on airs. Besides, he may not even notice me.

Momma kisses Smiley goodbye and she, Phoenix and I walk across town to the auditorium. Inside, smoke hovers like smog, and I cough at the smell of burning tobacco. Cigarettes. Cigars. Pipes. Voices drone in low tones, broken by a shrill laugh or a high squeal. We're looking at a wall of backs and buttocks wrapped in linen and rayon. Women are outnumbered by at least four to one, but that ratio seems not to bother Phoenix. She runs interference, and we squeeze by soft bellies and corseted hips. A hand brushes my ear, an elbow pokes my back, and I choke on cologne marbled with sweat.

We side-step into seats four rows from the ring, a soft-floored square raised a yard from the ground with three layers of rope strung around its edge.

Two low stools squat in opposite corners and overhead bulbs hanging from wires glare so bright they make my eyes burn. Two men dressed in bathrobes hop around the ring, throwing punches at the audience.

"We missed the first two matches." Phoenix produces a program from somewhere. "I don't mind skipping the flyweights—they're not over a hundred twelve pounds. I could take one of those twerps myself." I imagine her in the ring, satin shorts bagging around her thighs, fists up, on the attack.

"I wish we'd seen the bantams, though," she says. "The welterweights are coming on now."

When a man in dark pants, button-down shirt and bowtie climbs through the ropes, voices gush like a swollen river.

"Be right back," Phoenix says.

"Where you going?" I ask.

"Got to place a bet. Keep your eye on Aubrey Hicks. The one with the cauliflower ear? He's a mean turd."

I try to fathom what a cauliflower ear looks like.

"Who's the other one?" Momma asks. I know who it is. I hold my breath waiting for Momma's reaction.

"Don't you recognize him?" Phoenix says.

"Is that Covey Fortune?"

Phoenix flaps two dollar bills over her head. "I'm laying money on him."

"I've known Covey since he was a boy." Momma slips a dollar bill out of her purse and hands it to Phoenix. "Here—put this on him, too."

I had no idea that Momma knew Covey so well. I guess nothing escapes Pine Cliff's grapevine, not even news from the African settlement. Now I have another reason to cheer for him.

In the ring, the two men shrug out of their robes and prance around, pulling on the ropes and stretching their torsos. Aubrey has straight russet hair and glowering eyes. Covey's hair rests in soft coils. His muscles are like twisted leather, and a triangle of sparse curls is growing on his chest. His skin is beautiful, like the velvet of a deer's horn. What is it about dark skin that generates an aversion—even hatred—in white men? Those men would be giddy to see Aubrey punch Covey senseless, but I will that not to happen.

The bowtie man grabs a microphone that hangs from a rafter and introduces Aubrey, who slams his padded gloves together. He looks at Covey, bares his teeth and snarls. When Covey's name is called, he bounces on his feet, holding his gloves over his head. The announcer runs down the rules and introduces the referee, a short fellow in a white tee shirt, all business.

Phoenix gets back as the fight is about to start. When they spring out of their corners, Aubrey pistons his left at Covey's stomach. Covey grabs him around the neck, and they hug like brothers, pale skin against bronze. The referee breaks it up, and they come at each other again. Covey takes Aubrey's punches standing. When he staggers, my breath catches. I'm relieved when the bell rings.

"Did we win?" Momma says.

"First round, silly goose," Phoenix says. "They'll fight ten rounds, if they make it that long."

Covey is holding his own so far, but there's still a lot of fighting ahead.

The announcer pries the ropes apart for a girl in a short skirt and high heels to enter the ring. She holds up a placard that says "Round 2."

Phoenix is studying the program. "A well-placed punch is like being hit with a ten-thousand-pound bag of sand," she says.

"Lord," Momma says. "That could kill you."

I've seen Covey help Nandaddy wrestle hogs into the pen. If he gets the whack of a snout, Covey always ends up on his feet. No swine—not even a pig like Aubrey—is going to drag him into the slop.

In Covey's corner, the trainer gives him a drink from a bottle, but he spits it into a bucket that appears at his feet. The crowd seems to settle back. Flasks come out of jackets, and the air is sticky-sweet.

When the match begins again, Covey and Aubrey swagger around each other, dodging flying gloves and tying themselves into another clinch, as Phoenix calls it. Aubrey hooks one into Covey's stomach and he doubles over, but he lashes back in time to block the next wallop.

By the third round, the crowd is yelling. Aubrey dances Covey to the ropes, throwing full-speed punches to his belly, every blow of leather on flesh making a dull thud that causes my heart to jump. When Aubrey hits Covey's jaw, sweat sprays off his head like rice thrown at a wedding. The folding chair is hard and cold under me, but I can't tear my eyes from Covey taking Aubrey's cuffs. Bright lights blur, the ring blurs, and just as I think I might pass out, the bell clangs, giving both Covey and me a chance to recover.

The man sitting on my right rips a match into a flame that casts an orange light around his hands. The fire seems reckless and alive as he brings the match to the cigarette he holds with his lips.

As the next round starts, Covey's nose is bleeding and he has a cut over his left eye. The gloves guard his face like hands engorged with pus, dark as clotted blood—black balloons that with a needle prick would rupture and leave leather skin hanging in shreds from skeleton fingers. I bite hard on my thumb cuticle, pull off a strip and chew on it. Covey's bloody lip stains the rubber mouth guard like scarlet lipstick smeared on with a drunken hand. My thumb is bleeding, and when I suck it to stop the flow, it tastes of liquid iron sweetened with molasses.

Covey's right eye squints shut now, the brow swollen up. His whole face is enlarged, a bigger target for the force of Aubrey's fists, and I think of my father, his face unrecognizable as rotten fruit lying discarded among the folds of satin. He didn't have a chance to fight back. The explosion killed him faster than Aubrey's quick cross to Covey's eye socket.

When the round ends, Covey stumbles to his corner. I don't know what keeps him going.

Momma squeezes my knee and wheezes in her breath. "I think we'd better go."

"I'm not leaving." I shake my head. "He's got to win—I'm staying until Covey wins."

She takes her hand from my knee and crosses her arms over her breasts.

The trainer pours water over Covey's head, sways a bottle under his nose, rubs his shoulders, croons into his ear. When the ninth round starts, Covey lurches onto the mat. He finds his legs, begins a rain dance, and moves his lips over the mouth guard, talking to himself. Aubrey's glove shoots out, but Covey jerks his head aside, throwing his opponent off balance. They change positions and Covey lunges. As if in slow motion, he throws a right hook at Aubrey's head—the ten-thousand-pound bag of sand. When the glove pulls back, it's covered with blood and Aubrey's nose is lying flat against his left cheek.

Someone roars, "Kill him! Kill him!" It's Phoenix.

Momma's on her feet with the rest of the crowd. Men and women with blood-hungry looks scream in one loud commotion. I step onto my seat to see over heads. Aubrey's gloves cover what's left of his nose, but he doesn't fall, which seems to make Covey mad. He hits Aubrey's forehead, his ears, any part of his head that is unprotected. Aubrey's neck is like rubber, his head snapping back with each punch. Covey waits for an opening and when Aubrey drops his fists for a split second, Covey's glove is there. He hits, steps back, and watches Aubrey crumble to the floor like a sleepy man falling into bed.

"Hot damn!" Phoenix yells, throwing her fist into the air. "Be right back."

"Where are you going now?" Momma needs Phoenix's self-assurance close to her. The boxing ring is not her security zone.

"To collect. I'll get us a drink, too." And she's gone.

When the referee raises Covey's hand, I swear his eyes meet mine just at the moment he's being declared the winner, and I have a feeling beyond pride at knowing him although I can't attach a word to it.

Momma draws a cigarette out of her purse. She doesn't like to smoke in public, but everyone is too busy watching Aubrey's coach scrape him off the floor to notice. She stirs inside the purse, looking for a light.

A hand appears and a match shoots into flame. When I follow the arm up to the face, I see the man who had been sitting on my right. He's thin and handsome with soft lips and watery eyes. He lights Momma's cigarette and she inhales a deep drag.

"Thanks." She pulls the hem of her skirt over her knee and taps an ash onto the floor.

"Did you enjoy the match?" His voice is polished and out of place in the coarse noise of the auditorium.

"I don't think enjoy is the right word," Momma says.

"Covey had me worried for a minute," he says.

"You know Covey?" I ask.

"Know of him. It's a small town."

"You're from here?" Momma asks.

"Name's Lesley Burrows. Burr, most folks know me as. I can't figure how we managed to avoid each other, unless you moved in while I was at sea. I've been back a couple weeks. Surprised I haven't seen you."

Momma's eyebrows arch. "I've lived here all my life, sad to say."

I picture a life at sea, stopping on islands with palm trees and flaming sunsets, buttery sand and clean air. No soot to sweep off the porch. No whistles blowing shift changes or squealing sirens signaling a limb lopped off at the mill.

"Hey there." Phoenix holds a half-empty Dr Pepper bottle in one hand, two full ones by the neck in the other. She hands one to Momma and inspects Burr up and down.

"This is Mr. Burrows," Momma says.

Phoenix ignores him and sits down, handing the other bottle to me.

"Middleweights come on next." She's looking at the ring, empty now except for men setting bottles of water in two corners.

"I don't think Sister can take more boxing." Momma hasn't consulted me, so she must be thinking of herself. Anyway, I've seen the only match I'm interested in tonight.

"This here's the biggest fight on the program," Phoenix protests.

"You can tell us about it tomorrow," Momma says.

"You all can't walk home alone."

"I'll walk with you," Burr says. "I was just leaving."

"Well." Phoenix shoves a wad of money into Momma's hand. "Here's your winnings, then." I haven't heard the bitter tone in Phoenix's voice before, but I don't have the energy to decipher what it means.

8
Bobo

Momma says after watching the thrashing of the boxing match we should start going to church again to cleanse our souls.

Reverend Singer's right hand clamps the pulpit, and he raises his left hand, fingers pointing skyward, holding his congregation with a force that sprays out shotgun-like from his palm.

"Lord God, give us the fortitude to banish Satan from our lives and to walk in the path of righteousness," he prays. "Grant us strength to withstand temptation and light our path with thy eternal wisdom. Touch those without faith and fill their hearts with the glory of thy name."

I squint open one eye and scan the faces bowed in prayer, all of them Caucasian. The African settlement has its own church, but I doubt Covey is in any condition to praise the Lord this morning.

It is the habit of my grandparents to sit at the front of the sanctuary during the service, Nandaddy's brimmed hat on his knee and Mamaw fanning herself with the cardboard-on-a-stick that has a drawing of the church on one side. In the summertime one of the fans is stuck in every hymnal rack. After the service, we pile into Nandaddy's Ford and head to Lordsview Court for one o'clock dinner, but this morning someone else is sitting in their pew. A worry begins to form in my mind. My grandparents must be fifty, at least, and Mamaw's stomach is prone to upset. I worry about her.

I wish Reverend Singer would get on with the benediction. He's already running overtime. I was saved two years ago when I stood before the congregation in a robe borrowed from the church storeroom. Daddy said I was already saved in his opinion, but Momma insisted I go through the ceremony just to be sure. Reverend Singer dipped his fingers into the blessed water and dribbled a few drops onto my head. Sprinkling is better than what the Baptists have to go through for salvation. I've seen them gathered at the bank of the Jackson, upriver from the mill. A candidate for glory waded into the river where the preacher waited chest deep, his robe floating around him like flower petals. He said a prayer over the malefactor and leaned her backward, spread his hand over her face and dunked her, holding her under the water long enough for the Lord to wash away her sins. Evidently she forgot to take a breath before the baptism and came up kicking and fighting. I thought for a minute a black snake had wrapped itself around her ankle.

It will take more than the Holy Spirit to save me. If He's watching out for us, why did He blow my father to the mill's roof and break his back against the rafters, smash his skull and burn out his eyes? Daddy was not a heathen. He believed the Lord was watching over us from the summit of Spruce Knob, the highest point in the county. A church roof just got in God's way, he said.

Reverend Singer must have turned up the heat in the sanctuary to give us the idea of how uncomfortable hell can be, and I'm willing with all my might for the service to be over. The preacher pauses in his entreaties unto heaven, gearing up for the grand finish. He swings his words upward like the Lord's chariot itself, coming to carry the believers to eternity.

"For those who hear thee calling today, oh Lord, make them riiiiiise up from their seats and come down the aisle to kneeeeel before thee, as the cup of salvation is presented to their lips." He ends with an exclamation point. "We ask it in THY name! Amen."

"Amen is right," I sigh. Momma elbows me in the rib. When we stand up to sing the final hymn, she shrugs out of her jacket. Her brassiere shows through her thin blouse, and she has the clean smell of starch ironed into cotton. She's the best-looking woman in the sanctuary, and I'm proud to stand next to her.

As we filter out into the blessedly cool air, Reverend Singer shakes Momma's hand.

"It's good to have you back, Maggie," he says. "I'm sorry Gus never came to Sunday service. We might have coaxed him into the fold."

"My father had nothing against the Holy Spirit," I break in. "It was the tithing that bothered him." Daddy said if the Lord had the whole kingdom of heaven, what did He need with the little we had?

"Sister!" Momma acts as if I've insulted the entire Methodist creed.

Reverend Singer shakes my hand and presses his lips into a grudging smile.

The steeple bell is gonging when Momma and I walk around the building and in through the back door to retrieve Smiley from Sunday school class. I don't go to Sunday school and haven't absorbed the lessons about baby Moses's trip down the river in a basket and Jesus walking on water, but Smiley can fill me in on the details when he gets to them. We have to wait while he finishes his stained-glass window made out of colored cellophane. He's fashioned it to look like a rooster, and when he holds it up, its head shines blue and its yellow wings blaze.

"What's a rooster got to do with Sunday school?" I ask him.

"It's a chicken," he says. "I hope Mamaw's cooking one up. I'm hungry."

"We've got to go." Momma tugs his sleeve. "Your grandmother will be waiting dinner on us."

Out front, I'm surprised to see Phoenix sitting on the bottom step, parishioners brushing around her as they exit the sanctuary. She has on a coat that comes almost to the wide cuffs of her trousers. Her hair is twisted up as if she's tried to do something with it.

"Going my way?" She sticks out her thumb.

"I've never seen you at the service before," Momma says.

"I figured I'd better thank somebody for the bundle I hauled in at the fights last night." She stands up and swipes a hand at her coat, brushing off the grit from the step.

"Did you bet on fights after Covey won?" I ask.

"Cleaned house. How about we grab a bite to eat downtown?"

"We going Mamaw's house for dinner," Smiley says.

Phoenix looks out at Oliver Mountain and buries her hands in her coat pockets.

"Why don't you come with us?" Momma offers.

I bite my cheek. I could tell Phoenix that Mamaw doesn't like surprises, although I know she enjoys sliding another chair up to the table. And she always has enough food with some left over.

"What do you think, Sister?" She wants approval from me, but it's not up to me to proffer an invitation.

"Suit yourself."

"You reckon she's fixed some beans?" Phoenix lifts her eyebrows.

Mamaw's way of making green beans is snapping them in two-inch pieces and simmering them all morning with a slab of salt pork.

"Always beans on Sunday," I say.

"Then let's go." She hooks an arm through mine, but I shake it loose. I'm warming to Phoenix, but I'm not ready to be cozy with her.

It will take us half an hour to walk to Lordsview Court—longer if we dawdle down Main Street or have to wait for Smiley. The stale smell of the mill is faint, as if a heavy blanket has been rolled back to allow the town air. On Sundays business operates at half power, but tomorrow the plant will heave its mantle of tarry smoke back over the town.

"I'm going to escape this smelly place one day," Phoenix says.

Momma glances at her sideways.

"Do you have a plan we don't know about?" Much as I hate to admit it, Phoenix has settled herself into our lives and now just as I'm getting used to her she's talking leaving. I almost wish she'd take me with her.

"I'm thinking of applying to Tech. The engineering program."

"Engineer on a train?" Smiley says. "Can I ride along?"

"Not that kind of engineer." I shove Smiley's shoulder. "I think she means making complex things."

"Sure," Phoenix says. "Like bridges—designing them, I mean."

"Building bridges." Momma laughs. "That's right up your alley."

I wouldn't blame Phoenix if she burned her bridge when she leaves Pine Cliff. She didn't grow up here. Mrs. Davenport says the Blue Ridge is older than the Rockies and at one time was just as high. They've worn down over the years and now look fur-covered with evergreens, rolling one after the other like thick rugs blowing on a clothesline. They have funny names—Mud Run, Lick, Oliver, Pignut, Hawksbill, Peaks of Otter. I've never hiked up their slopes for fear of rattlers, but they're part of me, these friendly hills with hidden hazards. People are like that, too, I guess. Underneath every benevolent quality, some evil lurks.

"Sister ought to start thinking about college." Phoenix kicks at a stone.

"College?" Momma says. "It's all we can do to pay the rent much less scrape together college tuition."

In fact, the thought of what comes after high school hasn't entered my mind. But Phoenix has me thinking. If Covey can make plans to study beyond high school, why not me?

"When are you going off to Tech?" I want to know about Virginia Tech or any college for that matter. College could be my ticket out of Pine Cliff if I can figure how to make it happen.

"Oh, it's down the road a spell," she says. "Let's not talk about that now. All I can think about is sitting down at Mamaw's dinner table."

When we pass the train station, I search for anyone famous or notable who may have come down from the Homestead Resort in Hot Springs to catch the train. Today the platform is empty, but on Fridays it's not unusual to see a shiny black car waiting outside and a *Messenger* reporter standing by the curb, notepad in one hand, camera in the other. I used to imagine easing myself into one of those cars, pretending I'm the daughter of somebody rich and riding up to the Homestead to see the fancy ladies swinging their racquets on the tennis courts or having facials in the spa. It's a silly dream, of course. I'll never see the inside of the Homestead unless I get hired to hand towels to ladies coming from a soak in the springs.

When we reach the town hall, Smiley comes to a dead stop.

"How come we got to walk?"

"We could take the nickel wonder," Phoenix says. "Put in a nickel and wonder if you'll get there."

"Put a nickel in where?"

"She means the bus, Smiley. She's making a joke. Now hurry it up." My Sunday shoes are rubbing blisters on my heels, and I walk on my toes to keep them from bleeding.

"You all seem to be dragging this morning," Phoenix says. "Did that fella keep you up late last night?"

Momma is as calm as film over heated milk. She takes her time studying the granite statue standing sentinel by the courthouse, a begrimed memorial to the confederate soldiers from Allegheny County. There never were slaves in the Shenandoah Valley. Families worked their own farms, and farmers went to soldiering to protect their fields from the ravages of union armies, not to preserve slavery.

"What fellow might that be?" Momma says.

She knows as well as I do that Phoenix is talking about the guy who walked us home from the fight. He was coat hanger thin and talked to me instead of to Momma, even though I sensed it was Momma he was addressing. He asked me if I like pie and did I think we might have a slice at a restaurant with him sometime? I told him we were busy and didn't have time for pie. Momma butted in and said she was watching her waistline. When we got to the house, he shook my hand and then he shook Momma's, and I thought he held it a minute longer than was necessary, us just having met him. Then he said maybe he'd stop by sometime, but Momma didn't tell Phoenix what went on. It isn't any of her concern.

"You're acting kind of coy," Phoenix says. "I hope you're going to be civil to me at your mother's house."

Momma lifts her hair from her collar, acting coquettish the way she did with Daddy.

"Lady, you're trying my patience," Phoenix says. Momma laughs.

Up Main Street we pass the post office and an Italian restaurant owned by the Maruyama family, the only Japanese people in Pine Cliff. Down Maple Avenue is Ruggel's Department Store and the Visulite Cinema, where the last movie I saw was Gene Autry's *Mexicali Rose*. Cigarette smoke billows out of the Gypsy Tavern and Pool Hall, the only establishment whose doors are open after nine.

Houses on Locust Street are clad with crushed stone and bits of mica that sparkle in the sun. Every one of them has a wide front porch where people sit and watch the goings and comings of their neighbors. The smells of bacon frying waft from one house and Sunday's brisket from another.

My grandparents live just outside town. A few enterprising people like my grandfather bought land there and built houses. Theirs is a two-story brick that, except for pouring the foundation and doing the plumbing, Nandaddy constructed with his own hands. It's so solid and substantial that even fierce winds blowing off Lick Mountain won't shake it.

Mamaw is sitting outside on the rocker, studying the pine grove across the road as if she's deep in thought. Smiley races up the concrete steps to the porch that runs across the front of the house. Mamaw struggles to her feet and kisses him and then hugs me.

"Mother," Momma says, "this is Phoenix. Maybe you know her father, Doctor Goode."

Phoenix offers her hand, and Mamaw hesitates. Pine Cliff women don't shake hands. It's a head nod if they're meeting for the first time, cheeks pressed together at the second meeting if the first went well, hugs if they've become fast friends.

"I've got some lemonade made." Mamaw gives Phoenix's hand a quick squeeze. "You all come in—I just need to finish up the biscuits."

"Thanks, Mamaw," Phoenix says. "We've worked up a thirst." I wish she'd call her Mrs. Persinger like the ladies at church do and show some respect.

No dust balls lurk in the corners of my grandmother's house. The oak floors shine and cut-glass knobs glisten on closet doors. We follow her through the parlor, which smells of Pine-Sol and linseed oil. In the kitchen, the chicken lies dredged in flour and ready for frying, and a pot of beans simmers in the kettle, giving off the thick aroma of the meat Mamaw throws in for flavor.

Phoenix looks for glasses in the cupboard and Mamaw takes the pitcher from the icebox. Momma helps Smiley tie his shoelaces, which came undone on the walk, and I wander to the kitchen door and push it a crack to check on a commotion coming from the yard. Nandaddy has a victory garden behind the house, now in late autumn rusting except for some hearty kale and an hourglass or two of winter squash. Hens peck hopefully among the drooping weeds. Beside the garage is the pig sty where Doc Campbell, the town veterinarian, is searching through his black bag. He's called on to tend creatures of all sorts, from the ailing bear at the Allegheny County fair to Mrs. Bromer's French poodle.

"What's going on?" Momma comes up behind me.

"Mug! Get on out here," Nandaddy yells. I hate his pet name for Momma. A mug is an ugly face and Momma is far from ugly.

Inside the pen, Uncle Buddy holds his arms out to the side, herding Bobo into a corner.

"Is there trouble with the boar?" Momma calls.

"Bobo's been rutting on everything," Nandaddy says. "Broke the fence down twice this week and nearly ruined the sow." He wipes his forehead with his sleeve. "Wish we had Covey Fortune over here to help. Should have gotten this done months ago."

Just the mention of Covey's name sets my pulse rushing. I wish we had him here, too.

Phoenix sets a lemonade on the table for Smiley, and Mamaw starts kneading flour and shortening for the biscuits. How many times have I seen her flatten out the dough with the rolling pin and cut circles with an upside-down tumbler? Whatever is left over she gives Smiley to roll between his palms, making snake shapes she bakes in with the biscuits.

"Hurry it up, Mug."

Momma looks at Phoenix. "Dad needs my help."

"I'll go," I say. "You stay with Smiley." I unsnag a rumpled jacket from the wall hook and wrestle my way into it, slip off my Sunday shoes—a relief to my blistered heels—and slide my feet into a pair of rubber boots standing in the corner. The tops of the boots come to my knees, and I tuck the hem of my dress into them and wade out to the sty, buttoning the bulky jacket as I go. A mud dauber staggers toward a pitted nest near an eave. A crow caws a way off and another answers. I suck in and hold the smells of my grandfather's yard—pungent pong of pig, acrid hen droppings, rich earth, autumn harvest, and the ubiquitous odor of paper mill, aromas of hard work, without apology.

Inside the pen, Bobo has planted his hooves in the muck. His snout holes snort low grunts.

In a rumbly voice, Uncle Buddy works Bobo to one side, droning "Come, Bobo—Come, Bobo." When he has the pig pinned to the fence, he lunges and clamps his arms around the neck, wrestling Bobo to the ground. Nandaddy takes hold of Bobo's back end. Doc Campbell jabs a hypodermic at the giant rump, but the needle breaks off like a toothpick. The pig's scream echoes off the barn wall.

"It's no good," Doc Campbell says. "We'll have to cut him awake."

Buddy braces Bobo against the sty, and I think of Cowboy Code number four—be gentle with children, the elderly, and animals. But what's happening to Bobo can in no way be defined as gentle.

"Get the rope, Bobbie," Nandaddy yells. I waddle through the mud, snag the rope off the fencepost, and toss it to him. Quick as a clap, he wraps the rope around a foreleg and slips a loop around a back leg. Then he jerks the back and forelegs together and ties them off. Even trussed with two men leaning their full weight on him, Bobo threatens to cause an earthquake.

"Have that pan ready and lay those tools on the tarp," Doc Campbell orders. I spread the canvas on the driest plot of ground and open the surgical bag, take out curved needles and several small sharp knives. Doc Campbell extracts a bottle of clear liquid and pours a dose onto a cloth, then holds the cloth to Bobo's snout.

"Don't breathe this in," he warns Buddy. "Don't want you falling asleep on me."

Within seconds, Bobo starts to relax and then his rump goes down, but his eyes shoot out warnings.

"Okay," Doc Campbell says. "Give me that pan."

I pass it to him and he slides the pan under Bobo as Nandaddy holds up his top leg. Then he washes the testes, which are as big as an acorn squash. I've never noticed Bobo's privates before, but I've seen them on some of the stray dogs around our house when they lift a leg to do their business.

"Scalpel—quick, now," Doc Campbell says. When I hesitate, he says, "That sharp knife."

I take the largest of the silver instruments from the tarp and give it to the vet, who holds Bobo's privates and starts to carve. Bobo tries to rouse himself and screeches, but Buddy is clamped on him. I can almost feel the blade graze my skin, blood from the incision trailing down my leg. Thick hatred arcs out from the wound, dancing and twisting, threading through pig stink.

I tremble in the cold and snuggle my arms around myself.

"Hand me the sutures," Doc Campbell says. "And hurry it up." He has to yell over Bobo's bellowing. Is the pig is dying?

He must mean thread for sewing up the wound and that's what I give him. When he tightens the final stitch and ties it off, Nandaddy loosens his grip on Bobo's hind end and Buddy releases the neck. Bobo is tranquil now, lying in the mess of his sty, but I swear tears are streaming down the sides of his snout. My face is wet, too. I suck in a bitter breath and wipe my cheeks with my fingers. These are my people and this is what they do, even if it means mud and muck and blood. They gather pluck to meet the demands of living in this old mill town. When I start back to the house, I realize it's up to me to summon those qualities, too.

*   *   *

After Doc Campbell leaves, Nandaddy invites Smiley to his basement workshop saying he needs help hammering something while he cleans up. There are no thanks for my assistance and I don't expect any.

Momma gives me one of Mamaw's housedresses to wear so she can scrub the mud from my dress and hang it on the line to dry. Uncle Buddy is outside peeling out of his coveralls and cleaning up at the spigot by the garage. Mamaw sits on a kitchen chair, a fist wedged at her stomach, while Phoenix fries the chicken. She looks pallid, and her eyes are sunk in and ringed with dark circles.

"You feeling okay, Mamaw?" I ask. She nods, but her soft lips are pressed in a hard line. She's dwindling away in front of me.

"Sister, slice that cantaloupe that's in the icebox." Momma is mashing the potatoes. In the colder months, Mamaw serves fruit with dinner after the tomatoes and cucumbers have gone by.

I set the table, folding a napkin beside each of seven plates. When there are the six of us, Smiley and Momma sit on the kitchen side, Buddy and I on the other, and Nandaddy and Mamaw at opposite ends. Now I set Phoenix's place beside Smiley, as far from me as possible, forgetting that when we say grace at Mamaw's house, we hold hands. When Mamaw reaches for Phoenix's and their hands rest on the clean tablecloth, a barb of jealousy pierces through me.

I expect Nandaddy to deliver his shortest prayer, "Bless this food to thy use and us to thy service," the one he uses when he's been working outside and is too hungry for a long speech of gratitude. But today he improvises his own prayer, thanking the Lord for the clear day, for Doc Campbell's help with Bobo, for the rooster who gave his life for our nourishment, and for Phoenix, who had the good sense to befriend us and who is gracious in accepting our humble dinner offering. While he rambles on with God, I squint over the platters to see Mamaw's pale hand held captive in Phoenix's paw and wonder what their palms are communicating to each other. Mamaw, her neck bent at an angle like some tall, delicate bird, seems as though she'd float upward on pink wings had Phoenix not fettered her to the table.

When Nandaddy finishes his blessing, we pass around the food. Mamaw pokes at a thigh, stabs at a green bean, rearranges the potatoes on her plate. She hasn't even bothered to butter her biscuit.

"Have you taken a quinine for your stomach, Mother?" Momma asks.

"No, dear," she says. "It'll pass."

"Something's been at her all week," my grandfather says.

"Why didn't you let me know, Dad? I would have come over."

"I tried to get her to see Doctor Cummings," Buddy says. "She'd have nothing to do with it." I remember Buddy's jovial nature before he joined the military. He gave bear hugs and piggyback rides then, but since he's been back, he's solemn most of the time. He rarely offers as much as a comment on the weather and, except for an almost desperate clutch of my hand during grace, he hasn't given me the time of day.

"Couldn't the doctor come here?" I offer. Doctors make house calls, for which they charge the same as office visits. Doctor Cummings came to our house when I had the mumps in first grade, saying he didn't want the disease spreading to the pregnant and elderly in his waiting room.

"The patient has to be willing to let him in the door." Nandaddy winks at me. I hope his gesture means Mamaw isn't as bad off as she looks.

Phoenix chimes in. "Mamaw, you go lie down and I'll mix up a potion that'll settle your stomach, soon as we get these men folks to help us clear the table." Nandaddy frowns. I've never seen him lift more than a cigar after dinner. She leans over and whispers into Smiley's ear, then says out loud, "Isn't that right, Archer Timbers?"

Smiley wiggles off his chair, babysteps up to Mamaw, and tiptoes a kiss on her cheek. "You go rest, Mamaw," he says. When he slides her plate off the table, the fork clatters to the floor. Phoenix snatches it up and follows him to the kitchen.

Not wanting to be part of Phoenix's command, I offer to turn down Mamaw's bed, and I take her elbow to lead her to the stairs.

Upstairs, Momma helps her out of her dress.

"Sister, wet a washrag for her head."

I take a clean washcloth from the bathroom rack and run it under the cold-water faucet and then under the hot. Which temperature is better to purge the evil spirit that has hold of my grandmother? The hot water steams, so I decide on cold.

Momma lays the cloth on Mamaw's forehead, and we sit with her as she fusses about how this is no way to treat company and what will Phoenix think. Had she felt better, I'd have told her that Phoenix isn't company and to be careful she doesn't elbow her way into Mamaw's life the way she has ours.

Momma must sense what I'm thinking when she says, "Go on down and see if they need help with the dishes. I'll stay with Mamaw."

In the kitchen Uncle Buddy has an apron tied around his waist and is shaking suds from his hands into the dishwater. It's an absurd picture, and I smother a giggle that bubbles up.

"How do you women stand it this hot?" he says.

"You have to get used to it." Phoenix is standing at the counter scraping bark from a root no thicker than her finger. It smells like the root beer pop Daddy bought me one Saturday at Kresge's soda fountain.

"Archer Timbers, take this up and have Mamaw chew on it." He's been kneeling on a kitchen chair, watching her.

"What is it?" I take a sniff before she hands the root to Smiley.

"Haven't you ever had sassafras before?"

I haven't, but I won't admit it.

"When I was a little girl, we used to chew on it all the time. It's growing all over the field out there." She hands me a section of root. "Try it."

When I bite down on the bare root, the sharp, sweet taste brings the wet under my tongue.

Phoenix lays out a dishtowel with some tree bark on it, then inspects the cupboard.

"Saucer?" she says.

"Over your head." Buddy nods toward an upper cupboard, his hands now occupied with the frying pan.

Using the saucer, she pounds the chunks of wood.

"See if you can find some thyme," she says. "Ginger, too, if she's got it." She rubs the bark with her fingers. "Wish you had some chamomile or peppermint, but this slippery elm bark will do." I've fallen into her brigade, as Buddy and Smiley seem to have.

I take out jars labeled thyme and ginger. When Phoenix has crushed the bark so some sap is oozing out, she moves to the stove and drops the bark and herbs into a pot of roiling water.

Nandaddy comes in and sniffs. "What's cooking?"

"Take this a minute, will you?" Phoenix holds the spoon handle up and folds Nandaddy's hand around it. "Just move it around in the pot, like this." She raises his elbow, wraps her skinny hand over his plump fingers, and pushes the spoon in a slow circle around the pan. I've never seen Nandaddy at the stove before. The cellar is his domain. Phoenix pushed her way into our house and now she's taking over Nandaddy's. The worst part is, they all seem to enjoy it.

"You have some sweetening that'll help her get this down?" Phoenix scans the kitchen.

"There's a syrup jar on the table." I've seen Mamaw make the corn syrup with sugar, water, a smidge of cream of tartar, and a pinch of salt. Sometimes she adds molasses to make it darker so it looks like the maple syrup they have up north.

"Take a cup and scoop a heaping teaspoon in."

I do it for Mamaw, not because Phoenix gave the order.

Buddy sets the last dish in the drain rack and wipes his hands on his apron.

"That about does it," he says.

Phoenix takes the spoon from Nandaddy and uses it to hold back the herbs as she pours the liquid into the cup. Then she hands the cup to me.

"It should cool off a minute before she drinks it," she says.

Nandaddy taught Smiley that if he just presses the black keys on the piano, he'll always make nice music. From upstairs, I can hear him at it now, improvising some staccato melody. With the notes, voices hum as they talk, Uncle Buddy's bass anchoring Nandaddy's baritone, and Phoenix adding alto harmony. The cigar jar clinks and chair legs protest over the wood floor, and then the dizzy aroma of burning tobacco drifts up the stairs. Momma inches open the window in Mamaw's room.

"You'd better go back down and check on A.T.," she tells me. "And close the door after you to keep that smoke out."

In the dining room, Phoenix is cracking a deck of cards on the table, and Buddy presents a jar of pennies.

"Are you all going to play cards? Mamaw would have a fit if she knew. Sunday's the Lord's Day, she says, and the Lord wouldn't approve." I try not to sound accusing, but Sunday is for visits with neighbors, for relaxing, and for contemplating mortality.

"What's wrong with a few games of penny-ante poker?" Phoenix shuffles, arching the cards and fanning them in her palms.

"It's not fitting." I can hear myself say the words, but I don't believe them. Sunday has stopped having a sacred meaning for me. I wish we could go back to the tradition of Sunday afternoons at my grandparents' house, struggling to stay awake after a big meal, Daddy smoking on the porch with Nandaddy, even when it rained, dripped off the roof, and splattered lazy and happy in the gutter. Or, in colder weather, they sat inside in easy chairs and talked about politics, the impending election or the high school football season, balancing a dish of ice cream on one knee.

"Fitting?" says Phoenix.

"We can fix that," Buddy says. He leans for the radio on the buffet, switches it on and twists the dial until an organ quavers out the hymn, "I've Come to the Garden Alone."

I watch Phoenix deal the cards, organ whining, piano banging, and the lingering taste of sassafras sharp on my tongue. It seems to me that Reverend Singer's garden of blessedness is overrun with thorns and grass blades sharp as scalpels.

9
Hot Iron

The mill foreman assigned Phoenix to the night shift, which is fine with me. She says they reckoned that she had no family, other than her father, and men returning from the war want to be home with their wives and children in the evenings. Even though they gave her a raise, she says she'll stage a protest if they don't move her back to days by the first of the year.

One day Mrs. Davenport is explaining about the First Amendment and how America doesn't care if you're Jewish, unlike Hitler, who sent millions of Jews to the camps. You can believe whatever you want in America, dress the way you want, have any color skin, she says. She's wrong, though. Freed slaves moved to Pine Cliff because it felt safe, but with Jim Crow laws, nothing is safe for a brown-skinned person. Certain residents wish the people living in the African settlement would up and move to another town, another state. I've even heard talk of sending them back to Africa. Unfortunately, that would include Covey Fortune.

I'm thinking about Covey—the freckles on his nose and how odd it is that his eyes are gray, not brown—when I start to feel dizzy. I prop my elbows on the desk to hold my head up, but it doesn't help. The mucous on my tongue is getting thicker, and I swallow hard. I like Mrs. Davenport and don't want her to think I'm not paying attention to her explanation of my personal freedoms, but I'm shaking as if my bones are rubber bands. I fold my arms on my desk, rest my forehead on them, and stare at an A-shaped gouge in the wood. The desktop is the same color as my skin, a pinkish beige, and someone traced the gouge with pencil so that it has a shine to it. If you are an ant and start at the top of the A with another ant and each crawls down a different leg, you'll have one chance to meet at the crossover before you end up separated at the bottom. It seems so far to go.

I'm longing for sleep when a hand touches my head. I try to raise it, but my neck is not cooperating. It's as if my forehead is stuck to my skin.

"Barbara, honey?"

If I stop swallowing to answer, I'm not sure what will happen. I roll my head over so I can see her out of the corner of one eye. She's squatting beside me, short blonde curls around her soft face. She would be pretty if she didn't have to wear glasses. She's never called me honey before, and I like the way it sounds. Then I sense her cool hand on my forehead.

"Oh, my," she says. "You're burning up." She takes my hand. "You come on with me now," she whispers, and then she says in her teacher voice, "Penelope, you're in charge until I get back."

I'm aware of my feet carrying me and Mrs. Davenport's hand on my elbow. As she guides me down the hall, the dark wood of classroom doors blurs and light flashes through their windows. Teachers' voices mutter, and chalk scratches on blackboards. The stinging smell of cleaning fluid stabs me in the stomach like a wide blade slicing me open. Bending over a round metal trash can by the wall, I stare at the crumpled paper on the bottom, pencil shavings dusted in the wrinkles like sand settled in quartz crystals. Then the pain flows out through my mouth, a sour taste and a burning in my throat.

"She doesn't have a phone," Mrs. Davenport is saying to someone. Then I hear, "Do you think you can make it home?" No, I'm thinking, but I nod my head. It's all I can do to get air in and out of my lungs and I can't manage to form a word.

Outside my coat flaps in the wind, but the cold revives me. I wish Momma were home to take care of me, but every time I picture her, Phoenix's face pushes her aside. Phoenix with the wide green eyes and the nose that flares out sideways, Phoenix's thick hair pulled back from her cheekbones and winding over a shoulder. In that moment I cannot for the life of me remember what Momma looks like. All I can recall is the way over the bridge that crosses the railroad tracks, past the mill yard, down the hill to our house where my bed is waiting for me.

*　　*　　*

My fevered dreams make no sense. A dog lying in the street, cars whizzing by on either side. A train speeding past the Pine Cliff station and whirling people around on the platform like tornadoes. A dank cellar with giant pieces of furniture, all covered with flowered sheets, spider webs strung from sheet to sheet and draping themselves from the joists above.

When I wake, Momma is there. She looks as if her skin is too heavy for her face. I try not to worry her because she has enough on her mind with Mamaw not well.

"I'm fine, Momma," I say but I don't mean it. If only I could rest my head in the crook of her elbow, but when I raise my arms to summon her, she's gone. I drift back into a dream of corridors, of light coming through solid walls and strangers passing by without looking at me, as if I don't have a body, as if I'm just imagining myself. Then I'm at a boxing match, and Daddy is fighting a man twice his size. He is getting pounded, his nose flattened against his cheek, his skull bruised and blue, veins popping out and splitting and blood running down his cheeks like tears.

* * *

Daylight struggles through my window when the pain starts in my neck, creeps up and lodges deep in the side of my head. The ear is so painful I don't want to touch it. I can't sit up, much less go to school. The ache crashes over me, recedes, crashes over me again. Pounding, pounding, pounding. In order to swallow past the egg in my neck, I grit my teeth but that hurts, too.

Vaguely I hear a ringing. Do I imagine Momma telling me Mrs. Davenport called to see how I was? And did Penny Reardon call to say she would stop by if she wasn't afraid she'd catch what I had? But we don't have a telephone. So what is that ringing?

Momma wants to get Doctor Cummings, but I ask her not to. My whole body feels as if I've been rubbed raw with sandpaper, and he's likely to give me a shot or poke something into my ear.

Momma says I need to go back to my classes or I'll be too far behind to catch up. And if I'm too pigheaded to have the doctor look at me, she'll have to try one of her own remedies. She's already taken off two days from work and I'm afraid if she loses her job we'll be back depending on charity. So I agree to take sulfur pills and let her drop sweet oil into my ear. When I complain that my ear still hurts, she brings the iron, hot enough to bounce spit, and wraps it in a towel. At first when she props it between my ear and the pillow, it's pleasantly warm, and I can sense it drawing out the infection.

"When it cools down, I'll heat it up again," she says and goes out.

The towel gets hotter as the iron's fire seeps through the cloth.

"Too hot." I try to yell, more like a croak.

"Leave it there," she says from the living room. "It's supposed to be hot."

Not this hot, I'm thinking. Not so hot dragons are breathing on my skin. Not so hot my ear is melting and running to a steaming puddle on the floor.

In the intervals when I catch my breath amid moans, I'm aware of Momma saying, "Oh, Lord." She presses a bag of ice to my cheek to cool the fresh blisters and bring their boiling to a simmer.

At least the heat took care of the earache and it did break the fever, but the burn on my face means another night of sleepless torment. I'm ready to go back to school, even to see Penny and her know-it-all attitude. I miss Kenny, too, and think about the time he passed me a note asking me if I would be his partner for a history project, even though he had the worst case of chapped lips I'd ever seen. He kept licking the rash, which made it spread. But no school for me today. Momma caused the burn on my cheek. She doesn't care about me at all.

*　*　*

It's been a solid week with the flu.

"I'm expected back at work," Momma says. "But since Phoenix is on the night shift, she'll check on you."

"I'll be fine, just sleep most of the day," I say. "Don't bother Phoenix." But she turns and shuts the door behind her.

Sometime in afternoon Phoenix comes in. She heats up some nettle soup and I stagger to the table.

"I'm not hungry." I'm too weak to eat, but the Dr Pepper she sets by my bowl makes my mouth water.

"You need your nourishment." She sits and watches until I've finished the bowl and drunk half the pop. I swear it's the Dr Pepper that helps me on the road to recovery.

"You can leave now if you want," I say. "I'm feeling better and Momma and Smiley will be back soon."

Phoenix doesn't answer. She does the dishes and stacks them in the rack to dry. "How about I read to you for a bit?" she says, folding the dishtowel.

"I'm not a child. Besides, I'm going back to school tomorrow."

"Humor me, then." She pulls a book out of her bag and points to the couch. I am, in fact, woozy and lie down with my head on the arm. She starts reading from a Dashiell Hammett mystery and it isn't kid stuff at all: *My glass was empty. I asked her what she would have to drink, she said scotch and soda. I ordered two of them.* Phoenix makes the story come alive, and I remind myself to order a scotch and soda when I'm an adult so I'll appear sophisticated. Having her read aloud reminds me of nights Daddy read to me what seems like eternities ago when I felt safe and peaceful. In that hour with her sitting close, voice droning, I find myself thinking Phoenix isn't so bad.

10
The Bullet

Christmas is just ten days away, but my grandparents' house looks barren compared to past Christmas seasons. Mamaw hasn't arranged her holly centerpiece on the table, red candles on the piano, nor a garland up the staircase. It seems like sitting at the supper table with us is about all she can do, and even then she hardly touches a bite. There's no tree, no popcorn trim and none of Mamaw's shining glass baubles.

Weekdays Uncle Buddy works as shift manager at the rayon plant outside town, but on Saturday he says to me, "What say we go out and cut us a tree?" I like walking in the woods in the winter. There are no ticks or snakes, and the pine trees block the wind. Mamaw is particular about the tree. It has to be tall and just full enough to fit in the space between the kitchen and the stairs.

Smiley is in the basement with Nandaddy, so I go out with Buddy alone. The woods are across the cornfield, the narrow trail mottled with brittle leaves. I lead and Buddy follows me with the axe. The air is cold but not bitter and as we wind up the hill, I warm up. He's following, whistling and his shoes crushing the crisp pine needles.

"What do you think?" he says. "Blue spruce or balsam?"

"What's the difference?"

"Spruce smells better, but balsam has longer needles."

"I like a Christmas tree to smell piney." The aroma of rich earth mixes with moss and sweet pine and makes me feel clean inside.

"Spruce it is, then," he says.

We come to a clearing as big as a baseball diamond. Across the field, a fallen log has rusty paint cans set up on it.

"I used to come here for target practice." He dips into the pocket of his heavy jacket and presents a pistol, square at the grip with a dull green barrel.

"Eight rounds in the clip," he says, "and one in the chamber." He snaps the clip out of the handle, pries one bullet out and holds it upright with his thumb and forefinger.

"This baby blows through a man's skull at close range and takes a chunk of brain with it." He tosses the bullet up, catches it, then presses it into my palm.

"Keep this in your pocket. When you need power, you'll have it."

I curl my cold fingers around the colder metal and feel a shiver that vibrates from my fingertips down through my calves. When I slip the slug into my coat pocket, the bullet's weight pulls at my side, reminding me of its authority.

"This is the breach," he says. When he plucks back the top of the gun, a bullet flies into the air and he catches it and drops it into his own pocket. Then he hands the gun to me, butt first. He's squinting even though we're in the shade of evergreens. He isn't joking.

I figure there's no harm in holding the pistol.

"Where'd you get this?" In my bare hand the steel is icy and I taste the metal as if my fingers have tongues. The gun is much lighter than it looks. It isn't a hunting pistol, I know that. Hunting is done with shotguns if you're looking for birds, or rifles for bigger game.

"Off a dead German." He says this as if he'd said he bought his jacket downtown at Ruggel's.

"How did he die?" All I know about the war is what Momma read us from the newspapers, vague accounts of ships and airplanes and troops moving here or there. Nothing up close. Nothing about what it's like to be in a war.

Buddy takes the pistol back from me, pulls a single bullet out of his pocket and slides it into the breech.

"The A Troop went in before us." He blinks, talking to the pistol as if I'm not there. "We followed them in to clean up." His lips work against each other for a minute, and his jaw jerks up and down.

"We found one of our boys hanging from a tree by his wrists. They'd stripped him naked. His legs were kicking like they were having spasms."

He fits the clip back into the handle, jamming it up into place. I know he shouldn't be telling me these things, but who's here to stop him?

"Must have used a blow torch on him. Don't know what else would have burned his privates like that."

Steam comes out through his mouth like an old chimera whose fire has gone out. Creases shoot from the corners of his eyes, and his chin is starting to sag. He's become an old man in the two years he's been gone.

"His name was Stevens. Infantryman. He was from Kansas." He yanks back the breech, cocking the gun, his movements mechanical, as if he has prepared guns to fire thousands of times. In fact, he may have.

"After dark we sneaked up on their camp."

In the distance, the C&O train screams. Low clouds float like smoke around the treetops. I picture Momma getting the decorations down from the attic and Smiley threading popcorn on a string—anything familiar and safe to protect me from Uncle Buddy's story.

"At night," he says, "you come up behind a man fast, hanging your weight on the air so your feet don't make a sound. You grab him and cut across the throat clean and deep." As he utters the last words, he aims the pistol at the buckets across the meadow, steadies it with his big paw, and squeezes the trigger. A can leaps backwards and lands ten feet beyond the log, spraying paint like yellow blood. His lips broaden and he bares his teeth in a smile so grim it makes me shudder.

My uncle slashed a man's throat and watched him die. It was war that made soldiers commit such cruelty, I want to believe. Brutalities like he's describing happen in wartime, not here in Pine Cliff.

Buddy hands me the pistol. "You try it."

I'm not afraid of guns. Daddy had a twenty-two he hunted rabbits with. I've seen him take the rifle apart and clean it, but I never shot it.

Buddy wedges the pistol into my hand. Then he's behind me, gripping my elbow.

"Hold your arm out straight." He slips his other hand between my knees and pushes them apart.

"Spread your feet to get a broader base." He braces his body against mine, one arm around my waist, hand pressed at my stomach.

His voice is hoarse. "Pull the trigger gently."

I squeeze, the pistol answers with a sudden blast, and my body jerks backward into Buddy's. When I check, I see a wound in the log below the cans.

"This time, watch where you're shooting," he says, not letting me go.

I think of the bullet, its craving to destroy, and I tremble. Buddy hugs me tighter and holds most of the weight of the gun. Heat comes through his coat.

His aftershave smells spicy, and my hair clings to the stubble on his face.

"Slow and steady," he says.

When I focus on a paint can, the gun seems to go off by itself and the can disappears from the log. Buddy keeps hold of me as if I might fall over if he lets go. I like the cool feel of his breath, the heaviness of his hands on me. After a minute, he takes the gun from me and holsters it back into his pocket.

"We've got a secret now," he says, winking at me.

Gene Autry's Cowboy Code number two: Never betray a trust. I take the secret carefully—as if it might go off.

"Now—" He looks around the woods as if we've been out for an innocent hike. "Did we decide balsam or spruce?

Marilyn's Café

Linda Stadler is the fattest girl in my class. She lives on a dirt road, her house slumped in a thick growth of brush. It's no more than a shack covered with black shingles nailed in snaggletooth fashion. In winter, someone nails plastic over the windows to keep out the wind. The yard is bare dirt and a board leads to the step, which helps her family navigate the mud in rainy weather. Her family is comprised of an absent father who appears specter-like when the relief check comes around, a mother so stout she can hardly walk, and a mess of children. Linda's clothes look homemade, and she alternates between two shifts, one purple and one green, sewn in straight seams with rickrack around the armholes. When it's cold, she wears one of three blouses under the shift, provided through the generosity of the Trinity Baptist Church Charity Society who also brings the Stadlers food baskets. From the looks of Linda and her mother, they're getting plenty to eat.

In spite of Linda's corpulence, she has a delicate nose and deep eyes. She never smiles—maybe her teeth are bad—but her high cheekbones give her a pleasant expression. She comes to school with her hair combed, her face is clean, and her fingernails are scrubbed clean. She never raises her hand when Mrs. Davenport poses a question, but her compositions come back marked with red-inked As. In math class, she finishes worksheets before everyone else, and when I ask her to help me with equations, she shows me what I'm doing wrong. Most of the other students, including Kenny, keep their distance from her, but I like Linda.

A week before Christmas, Linda comes into history class with a web of mucous dangling from her nose to her upper lip. She must not have a hankie.

Nevertheless, she keeps her shoulders back and her head high and looks straight ahead when she walks to her desk. She slides into her seat as if balancing a plate on her head, careful not to move too much, but the snot jiggles nevertheless and glistens in the light coming through the window. When Kenny sniggers, Mrs. Davenport looks up and stares at Linda, horror coloring her face. I reach into my pocket for a tissue and hold it out to Linda. She takes it with two plump fingers and deposits the mucous into it. Even though she doesn't thank me, we have made a pact, Linda and I. She will not deride me for my poor math skills, and I will not pity her for her poverty.

Mrs. Davenport requests us each to bring a present on Friday of that week, the day before Christmas vacation. When Linda looks worried, Mrs. Davenport says, "Don't spend more than twenty-five cents." She must think that the Stadlers can afford a quarter, but I have my doubts.

"Aren't we too old for Secret Santa?" I say, thinking about Linda's quandary.

Mrs. Davenport bites her lip.

"Oh, it'll be fun," Kenny offers. His father works at the bank and they have plenty of money.

"On Friday we'll select names to see who receives which gift," Mrs. Davenport says. I realize that for some of the students of Pine Cliff, the gift exchange is all the Christmas they'll have.

I won't be surprised if Linda stays home that day and I think about playing sick myself. But Momma gave me the money and said I'll have to stop downtown after school to buy my gift. I invite Penny Reardon to go with me. She reads movie magazines and will know what to pick out.

On Wednesday we walk down Main Street. Penny is a C student—B if she applies herself—but what she lacks in ability, she makes up for in looks with chestnut ringlets and a grin like a switch that lights up her face.

"Kresge's has the best presents," she says. "My mother got me this bracelet there." It's a string of tiny glass beads on an elastic band. I have watched her pull it out and snap it against her wrist while we worked on a geography lesson.

"Are you planning to buy a bracelet?" I ask. "We're supposed to get a gift suitable for a boy or a girl."

"Of course not," she says. "It costs too much. I'm thinking of a kaleidoscope, if they've got one. Of course, if I draw Linda Stadler's name, it'll be a waste of money."

"She'd like a kaleidoscope." I'm thinking it would bring some delight into her life.

"A bar of soap would suit her better."

"You're just being cruel. Linda Stadler has some quirks, but they're not her fault. Her mother didn't teach her better." Someone should stand up for Linda, and I take on the duty myself.

Kresge's is at the end of Main Street, and we walk down the sidewalk goggling at store windows decorated for Christmas—holly garlands, miniature trees made out of pine cones, plaster Santas, cloth elves wearing stocking caps and bells on the toes of their pointed shoes. I haven't asked for anything for Christmas. The spirit hasn't gotten to me this year.

Main Street forms a wind tunnel, and the cold whips around us. I pull my collar close around my neck and lean into the wind. When we pass the Gypsy Tavern, I think about ducking in to get out of the weather for a minute. Through the big window, I see a fellow sitting at a small square table, a glass of what looks like beer in one hand. He holds a cigarette over the ashtray with the other and stares out through the glass. A familiarity dawns on me—I've seen him before.

Penny yanks my sleeve. "Come on—you're dawdling."

Half a dozen sidewalk squares ahead, I hear someone call my name.

"Keep going," Penny whispers. "My mother said not to stop to talk to people downtown unless you know them."

"I said hey there, Bobbie!"

I dislodge my sleeve from Penny's grip and stop. A nice-looking man is following us, about Momma's age, but fair-haired. He's the one I saw in the tavern.

When he catches up, he says, "Burr Burrows. Remember me?" When I don't answer, he adds, "The boxing match. I walked with you afterward."

"Oh." I thought after that night we were done with him. What does he want from me?

His face melts into a smile. "And your mother. How is she?"

Although I had shoved Burr Burrows out of my mind, I've relived every painful blow to Covey's body.

"She's fine," I say.

"Fine is just the word for her." He winks at Penny.

"We've got to be going," she says.

"Sure." He sticks a hand in his jacket pocket. "Say, Bobbie, can I get your telephone number? I'd like to talk to your mother sometime."

I believe except for Linda Stadler I am the sole person in my class without a telephone. Penny says Kenny calls her to find out what arithmetic problems he's supposed to do for homework and Mrs. Davenport called Penny's mother once to say how much progress Penny was making in her reading, but Penny likes to exaggerate.

"Go ahead," Penny says. "Give him your number." Her words are like pinpricks, sharp and irritating.

"That's all right," Burr says as if he can tell I've been assaulted. "You think she'd mind if I stopped by sometime?"

"I guess not." What I mean is I'd rather you didn't.

He fumbles in his pocket and unearths two quarters.

"Buy yourselves a pop—on me." He hands one quarter to Penny and the other to me and then goes back into the tavern.

Penny watches him walk away. "Is he sweet on your mother or something?"

"Maybe." What I mean is I hope not. From what I've seen of Burr, he'd be a poor substitute for my father, but I squeeze his quarter in my palm and follow Penny down the sidewalk.

*　*　*

At Kresge's I choose a box of colored pencils for fifteen cents and a drawing pad for ten. Kenny doodles in the margins of his math worksheets and if he draws my name, I imagine he'd enjoy doodling in color. I know he likes me. Last spring he brought a lilac sprig to class and kept it on his desk, fingering the petals and twirling the stem with his thumb. By lunchtime the blossom was limp with his handling and when he offered it to me, I accepted it without thanking him. He must have spent all day building up his nerve. Try as I might, I can't work up an attraction to Kenny. He's just a boy—not like Covey Fortune.

Penny buys a Dr Pepper and I pick out an orange crush. I like the orangy flavor and the way it fizzes going down my throat. We each buy a Mars bar to eat on the walk home and have a dime left over.

It's later than usual when Momma gets in, and I have supper almost ready. She's quiet, as if she has a lot on her mind.

"Anything wrong?" I ask.

"Tomorrow after school, meet me at the mill gate," she says.

"Why?" Smiley asks, as if it involves him.

"Someone has invited me for coffee, and I'd like Sister to come."

"I don't see what you need me for," I tell her.

"Because." She smooths my hair. "You're my guardian angel."

I'm grateful to be needed, and I touch my head where her hand was.

*   *   *

Elsie agrees to watch Smiley after school, and I clean Mrs. Davenport's blackboard to waste time before I'm to meet Momma at four o'clock. At quarter to four, I stroll over the railroad bridge. Momma's waiting for me outside the gate when I arrive. She has on fresh lipstick and has fixed her hair. We don't say much walking up Allegheny Avenue toward Marilyn's. She doesn't question me about school or my history project on Scotland. She just walks, our elbows linked like we're girlfriends.

Inside the café, daylight edges its way through thick curtains, and a layer of smoke hovers at the ceiling. Green and red streamers hang across the roof beams, and cardboard poinsettias are taped to the walls. Momma pushes a sigh through her mouth, as if she's exasperated.

Three women are at one table wearing gray and navy, hair pinned back, finger-roll bangs. At another table an elderly couple is eating an early dinner of what looks like chicken-fried steak and mashed potatoes. My stomach starts to rumble, and I hope this meeting won't take long.

"He's not here. I shouldn't even have come." Momma seems to be talking to herself.

As she starts for the door, Burr Burrows stands, tipping his chair and nearly knocking it over.

"Momma, he's here." I jerk my head toward him because pointing is impolite. He has on a pair of khaki pants and a sport shirt, a jacket slung over a chair. He wobbles as he stands there—he must have had a few at the tavern this afternoon.

"Maggie—" He snubs out a cigarette, third butt in the ashtray. He's been here for a while.

"Hello again, Bobbie." He manages what looks to be a fake smile at seeing me. I suspect he wanted to get Momma alone.

He's at a table for four and slides a seat out for me then one for Momma, leaving the coat on the fourth. We sit down and Momma plants her elbows on the table and laces her fingers as if she's about to pray.

"It's good to see you both." He rubs his nose and runs the backs of his fingers across his cheek. He's freshly shaven, and I can smell a coconut scent of aftershave.

"What can I get you?" the waitress says, a hefty woman who looks at Momma and me as if we're taking up too much of her time unless we order food. Just coffee means a barebones tip.

"Coffee for me," Momma says.

"How about a Coca-Cola, Bobbie?" Burr says.

"I'll have a coffee, too." I've been invited to an adult meeting, so I should act like an adult.

Burr widens his eyelids and dips his head. "Coffee it is."

When the waitress disappears, he evaluates the napkin he's holding in both hands, arms circled around his cup, and gambles a look at Momma. "You look better than I remember."

"It was dark." Negating his compliment is Momma's way of accepting it.

"Around you there is always light."

Momma looks into her cup and I clear my throat to remind them I'm still here. I try to picture what it would be like to have coffee with Covey and imagine what we would talk about. Not anatomy—what do I know about bones? History, then? Or boxing?

Me: I understand that boxing is one of the oldest sports known to man. In fact, some people believe that the gods boxed on Mount Olympus.

Covey: I've heard that, yes, but I'm no god.

Me: Oh, but we make men of gods and gods of men. Don't you think so?

Covey: I believe women are more god-like than men. After all, your gender has the ultimate power to create.

That's the way I would like the conversation to go. But it will never happen—a black fellow and a white girl sitting in a café having coffee and talking. Just talking. Not in this town and probably not even in my lifetime.

The waitress brings a fresh pot of coffee and a milk pitcher as tiny as a shot glass, not enough for me, let alone Momma.

"You go ahead, honey," she says, looking at the pitcher and then at my cup. "I'll drink mine black."

"But you like milk in yours, too."

"Sometimes I have it black."

I've never known her to drink black coffee. She sweetens it and drinks it blonde, as she calls it, with a heaping teaspoon of sugar. I pour in milk until the coffee comes to the rim of the cup, but it's barely the color of dark chocolate. When I take a sip to bring down the level, a cough chokes me.

"Too strong for you?" Burr has a smirk on his face. I suppose he thinks that's what I get for being where I'm not wanted.

"She likes a lot of milk in it," Momma says.

"Here." Burr leans over and clasps my cup, brings it to his lips and slurps it down, leaving room to add the rest of the milk. I drain the pitcher and pour in sugar from the jar on the table before I stir, making sure to drink from the opposite side of the cup where Burr had touched his lips. The coffee tastes better, but not like Momma's.

"Tell us about the Navy," Momma says. "Were you at Pearl Harbor when the Japanese bombed?"

"I left a week before. They shipped me to the Philippines." He tears the napkin at the corners. "I left some friends there, though."

"I'm sorry," Momma says.

His hair is combed to the side, and a wisp escapes and droops onto his forehead. Momma's hand goes out and stops just above her cup. I know she wants to push the strand back the way she does with Smiley's hair, but she catches herself, straightens her back and sends both hands to her lap. Burr seems to sense the change, pats the napkin down beside his cup, pulls a pack of Luckies from his shirt pocket, and offers Momma one. Smoking is a private activity for Momma. She smokes with friends inside the house and lights up on our porch, but I've never seen her light a cigarette when we're in town, except at the boxing match that night. But now she draws one from his pack and holds it to her lips. Burr strikes a match and she puffs in and blows the smoke straight up. He lights his own, turns his head and blows the smoke over his shoulder. They look as if they're performing a ritual, as if the lighting and smoking seals some agreement between them.

"We just do surveillance now that the war's over. Making sure there are no flare-ups in the Pacific." He winks at me, as if I shouldn't worry about him. I don't.

"What's the Pacific Ocean like?" I haven't even seen the Atlantic, just across the state.

"On calm days the sun glints off the water like silver dollars skipping across the surface." He holds the cigarette with two knuckles and works on the napkin again, tearing in a circular pattern, like a snowflake. His voice is boyish, sounding as if it will crack any minute. He clears his throat, takes a puff, and begins again.

"The Philippines are so lush you can see the bushes growing. Rain every day, and the land is black and rich."

He talks about the turquoise seas weaving with the golden sunsets like the silvery cloth worn by dark-haired women of the Orient. He describes Leyte, Samar, Palau and Saipan, names of places that spill off his lips like molasses. Pine Cliff, grimy as a coalmine, disappears and its gluey air thins into zephyrs carrying strange perfumes.

Coffee has spilled into my saucer, and I lift my cup and pour the milky liquid back in. Burr gurgles a laugh.

"Waste not, want not," he says. "I like that thriftiness." A smile tickles Momma's mouth. I suspect she likes that he's frugal. He folds what's left of the napkin and licks his bottom lip. His tongue is thick and pink and leaves a slick glaze.

"Will there be anything else?" the waitress says.

Momma checks her watch. "I have to go."

When I stick my arms into my coat sleeves, the waitress slides the bill beside Burr's saucer. Momma doesn't offer to pay, which is fitting since we came at his invitation.

"Have dinner with me," he says.

"We have to be getting home," I say, plunging my hands into my pockets. The bullet is hard and cold, and I run my thumb over the pointed tip.

"We don't have to eat here. We can go somewhere else."

"Elsie will be waiting, Momma. And Smiley—I mean A.T.'s sure to be hungry." I realize my purpose in coming is to be Momma's conscience.

"Will you meet me tomorrow?"

I unearth the bullet from my coat and hold it up to my eye the way I saw Uncle Buddy do. It stops Momma from answering. It stops Burr from pressing her to see him again. When I stand the tiny bronze missile head up on the table, Burr straightens up.

"Where did you find that thing?" Momma says as if accusing me of some crime.

With one delicate nudge, I push it over and the bullet falls with a soft click, pointing at Burr.

"Found it," I say. It's not a lie. I found it in Buddy's hand in the clearing.

Cowboy Code number three: Always tell the truth.

"You'd better get rid of it," she says.

Burr pushes his chair back. Momma is pulling on her jacket, and I sweep up the bullet and drop it back in my pocket.

*   *   *

At dinner that night, Momma doesn't ask Smiley what he did all day. She doesn't tell us what went on at work. She doesn't say much at all. She seems to be wrestling with herself, pushing Burr off her dinner plate with the fork, rubbing him off the dishes with the dishrag, sweeping him off the kitchen floor, letting him whirl down the drain with Smiley's bath water. When I peep in on her that night, she has the covers tucked up to her chin, as if to keep him from crawling in with her, but I imagine him seeping through the weave of the blanket and invading her dreams.

12
Brown Mouse

In the morning Smiley and I walk Momma down to the bridge. The air is damp, and someone is burning leaves. The sun has not yet come over the mountains, and it looks like twilight rather than dawn. Ahead, a slim figure is leaning on the bridge railing. A hand goes to the mouth and smoke floats out and up, blending with the fog. Burr turns his head. When he sees us, he drops his cigarette and it burns on the concrete.

"Mind if I walk a ways with you?" he says.

"Who are you?" Smiley looks up at him.

"Chief Storekeeper Burrows." Burr stands straight, clicks his heels, and salutes, a silly grin on his face.

"A little early to be up, isn't it, sailor?" Momma sounds happy to see him.

"If it means seeing a phantom of delight, I don't mind."

I'm about to ask where he dredged up that corny line, but Momma beats me to it.

"Did you make that up?"

"Would you like it if I did?"

"I wouldn't mind."

"Borrowed it from a chap named Wordsworth. I've never used it before. It never fit until I met you." If he's lying, he's doing it looking straight at Momma. He's smooth, but I don't trust his attempt at charm.

"These two have to skedaddle to school." Momma kisses Smiley then leans for my cheek and misses. "You all have a good day."

Burr slips his arm around Momma's waist and walks her to the gate. At least she has a day's work to do and no time to fool around with a seadog on leave.

I wrap the drawing set in tissue paper, tie it with green Christmas ribbon, and put it in my bookbag, setting it on top so the bow won't get crushed. At the beginning of class, Mrs. Davenport has us deposit all the gifts into a cardboard box where they stay most of the day despite our whining to give them out before class ends.

I start to feel the old tingle when the holiday season rolled around, raising my eyebrows every time Momma or Daddy brought a package into the house. "Tools," Daddy would say. Or "some of Elsie's old clothes I might make into a quilt someday," from Momma. I have a weight around my hopes, though, that keeps them from rising this year.

When the time comes to pass the box around, Brenda Miller draws my gift. She's a shy girl who talks with a lisp and hides during lunchtime so she won't have to sit with anyone. When she unwraps the pencil set, her eyes meet mine and she smiles with her lips together. Then she slides out a blue pencil and starts to draw.

People all around me are opening presents, but I haven't drawn one yet. Mrs. Davenport lifts the remaining gift from the box, a small bundle wrapped with plain paper and tied with twine, knotted with a sprig of evergreen for decoration.

"Barbara," Mrs. Davenport says, "I guess this one's yours." She has a tender smile as if she and I share some furtive understanding. I know Mrs. Davenport likes me, so I assume that she has saved the best gift for me. Maybe it's from her and worth a lot more than the twenty-five cents.

I hold the package in my fingers and check out my classmates. Jenny Marshall is flipping through a magazine. Tyler Worley has a bag of lemon drops and pops one into his mouth. Edward Paxton is tracing his pencil through a book of mazes.

Linda Stadler bites her lip. I tear the paper, hoping she's scraped up money to buy a gift at the store, something new like the others have, but I know the Stadlers can barely afford to clothe themselves, much less buy presents for other people. Inside the wrapping is not metal or plastic or even rubber. It's toffee colored and made of thread—a crocheted change purse fastened with a button at the top.

Penny Reardon leans across the aisle. "You got a—what is it? A pet mouse?"

With my peripheral vision I catch the smirk on her face.

"It's—" I'm trying to come up with a stylish name for the crudely crocheted object. "A coin purse. Haven't you seen them in your magazines? They're all the rage."

"For carrying all your money, I suppose." The sarcastic tone of her voice does not escape me.

I turn the purse in my hands. "I've been wanting one of these."

"Truthfully?" Penny says.

"Yes, truthfully." I swipe a look at her desk. "And what did you get?"

Penny's mouth worms to the side. "A fairytale book. Some story about animals—stupid."

"Let's see that book." I reach across the aisle and whip it off her desk. "*Animal Farm*?" I read the book last year, but I suspect the language is beyond Penny's ability. "Oh well," I say, sliding it back to her.

I respect Linda's gift because she thought about the change purse and spent time making it, and there isn't a false stitch in workmanship.

I take the dime out of my pocket, drop it into the purse, and button the flap.

13
Planter's Punch

When Momma comes in that night, Burr trails behind her.

She's grinning. "Look what followed me home."

Burr makes an awkward move toward me, recoils, and shakes Smiley's hand.

"Sit down." Momma motions for the couch. "I'll make some coffee."

Smiley stands and studies him.

"You want to see my broken thumb?" Burr shows Smiley the disconnected thumb I've seen a thousand times, and then the church and the steeple with the finger people inside. Nandaddy taught us how to do those tricks years ago, but Smiley seems captivated nonetheless.

In the kitchen, the coffee pot starts to perk. I almost wish Phoenix hadn't been relegated to the night shift. I'd ask her to whisk Burr off somewhere so he'd leave us alone.

Momma brings Burr coffee and Smiley goes back to playing with a piece of kindling, pretending it's a gun. He shoots Burr, who presses his hand to his shoulder, his stomach, his heart, feigning that he's wounded every time Smiley says "Pow." He's soaking up Burr's playfulness and I'm glad to have my brother occupied.

It's getting on to mealtime and while I set out plates, I hear Momma say, "You're welcome to stay for dinner, if you don't mind leftovers."

"I'm crazy for leftovers," he says to my utter disappointment. Smiley never eats much, and Momma and I are both watching our weight. But somehow I'll have to stretch the little we have to satisfy a grown man.

I take what remains of the pork roast we had the night before and cut it into cubes. Then I sauté onions in a pot and toss in the pork, keeping an ear toward the living room. Momma's alto voice tangoes with Burr's bass and Smiley adds his gun noises for percussion. I peel three potatoes and sniff some green beans we brought back from Mamaw's. They don't smell as if they've gone bad, and I pick out the fatback and add the beans and potatoes to the pot. I'm whipping in cornstarch to thicken the sauce when Momma comes in.

"Is this all we've got?" She sounds irritated.

"You told him we were having leftovers."

She peers into the pot. "Add a can of peas and see if there's any rosemary for seasoning." She gets the cornmeal from the shelf and measures some into a bowl, adds sugar and baking powder and cracks in two eggs. "He might forgive our meager offerings if we have fresh cornbread on the table."

"If he's going to complain about our dinner, he ought to find another place to eat."

"Sister," Momma says, "we'll talk about this later. Now do as I say."

In the other room, Burr is lying on the rug, his legs straight up, feet supporting Smiley's stomach, balancing him like an airplane, rotating him in the air and humming like an engine. Smiley screeches, wiggles off balance, crashes to Burr's chest, and they both laugh. I wish Smiley would be more careful with his affection. I should have a say about who invades our family circle, but Momma has become way too familiar with a person we hardly know. I didn't assert myself with Phoenix and look what happened—she horned in before I knew it. We ought to have a meeting about whether Burr should be invited back or not, one vote apiece. Majority rules. Just like the democratic process we're studying in history class.

With the cornbread in the oven, Momma goes back to the living room and I set the table. I resent the idea of seating Burr at Daddy's place, but he'll never sit there again. Besides, Phoenix has claimed the spot. It isn't Daddy's anymore.

After I take the cornbread from the oven and cut it into wedges, I call everyone to the table. Smiley watches Burr eat, copying his every move, asking for seconds on the stew, reaching for cornbread when he does. I've never seen him eat so much.

"Delicious," Burr says, laying his knife and fork on his empty plate.

"Momma," Smiley says, "can Burr spend the night?"

Momma rolls her eyes at Burr.

"Not a bad idea, A.T.," he says.

"Don't you have a place to stay?" I am the guardian angel, after all, and I have an impulse to swoop to the rescue.

"Sister, mind your manners," Momma scolds.

"We're up early," I add.

"Reveille is before daybreak on the ship," Burr says. "I need two cups of joe by sunrise or I'm good for nothing."

"Momma, it's not right." I don't want Penny Reardon talking about my mother when word gets around. And word always gets around.

"Help me clear the table," she says.

Burr rolls up his shirtsleeves, sprinkles soap powder into the sink, and begins filling it with water.

"I didn't mean you." Momma turns off the faucet. "Leave them. We'll do them later."

He takes a plate from Momma's hands, covering hers with his. "How do you keep them so soft when you wash dishes every night? Let me do them for you this time." He slides the glasses and plates one by one into the suds and rinses them under the faucet. Smiley dips his hands into the sink, and Burr lets him splash in the soapy water. Momma picks up a dishtowel and begins to dry.

"I've got homework," I announce, not wanting to be party to this household seduction. Sitting on my bed, I balance the science book on my folded legs. I know the yearnings of nature. I've seen a dog mount a bitch, I've seen Bobo rut on the sow, and I've seen Jane Wyman breathing heavy with Ray Milland in *The Lost Weekend*. I've had twinges myself, but they made me confused and frustrated. At the moment, I'm concerned with Burr working up a twinge in my mother.

I hear dishes clink as Momma stacks them in the cupboard.

Burr says, "It hasn't been easy keeping the house by yourself, I'll bet."

"Nobody has it easy these days."

"You'd get along better with a man in the house."

"There aren't any men around."

"I'll be coming home for good now that the war's over."

"I've got to get A.T. ready for bed."

"Can I help?"

I crane my neck to see him take the towel from Momma, fold it, and hang it over the top of the cupboard door beneath the sink. For a split second I visualize him tucking me in, kissing me on the forehead the way Daddy used to do. But he'll never measure up to my father.

"A.T.'s a handful," Momma says. "It may take a while."

"I can wait. I'll just make myself a drink. What have you got?"

"Just some milk and tea."

"Tell you what—you take care of the boy, and I'll just dash down to the corner. Unless you'd like to get rid of me?"

I hope Momma will come to her senses, but when he runs his fingertips down her arm, I know she's lost them. Momma probably just wants the same thing I do—someone to love her.

Burr squats down to Smiley. "Do what your mother says, okay sailor?"

"Okay," he says, but not convincing.

"Mind your mom, and there might be a treat for you in the morning." He ruffles Smiley's hair.

Momma puts Smiley to bed then says to me, "You'd best get some sleep, too."

"I'm not done with these problems."

"You've got all weekend to finish them." Her voice has an edge to it. "Anyway, it's almost Christmas vacation."

"Why is he coming back?"

"Just to talk for a bit." She sits next to me on the bed.

"About what?"

"Well—" She smooths the spread between us. "—whatever comes up."

"Do you like him?"

"I haven't decided yet."

"What about Daddy?"

"What about him?"

"Do you still love him?"

"Of course I do." Her voice is hard, as if she's angry that I've asked her about Daddy. Maybe she thinks I'm trying to make her feel guilty about Burr. Maybe I am.

The door opens and I see Burr pass into the kitchen, hear liquid tinkle into a glass. Momma leans toward me, the signal for girl talk, and whispers, "A woman has a need, and when her husband has passed away—" She circles my knee with her fingernail. "—she's got to settle for the next best thing."

"Isn't Phoenix the next best thing?"

Momma looks at the limp rug on the linoleum. I've upset her. I shouldn't have brought up Phoenix when she's about to settle for Burr.

"This doesn't involve Phoenix."

When I switch off the light and crawl between the sheets, I make out Burr on the couch, two pink drinks on the coffee table. He pats the cushion beside to him.

"What's this?" Momma asks, her voice low.

"Planter's punch. Ever had one?"

"I'm not much of a drinker."

"Oh, I think you'll like this. Try it." He plants his elbows on his knees and watches her.

"Tastes like cherries." She licks her lips.

"Old family recipe."

"I'll bet." She takes two short sips. Burr swallows long, sets down the glass, and stirs the ice around with his finger. He isn't Gene Autry handsome—more like Valentino. And soft. Softer even than Phoenix.

"You ever get lonely?"

I could have told him Momma doesn't have time to get lonely with the constant flow of people coming through the door.

"I have friends. And the children." She leans back on the sofa. Her hand is on his back. She must think I'm asleep.

"I'll bet you see lots of women in those ports, don't you?" Now she's asking the question.

"They're just girls. Not like you." He cups her face and gives her a slow kiss. His hand leaves her face and finds her leg, rests there, his thumb inside her thigh.

His touching her that way causes sadness to weigh on me and squeezes out joy, as if I'm being pulled down into a tight chamber with walls as high as Oliver Mountain, as sticky with pine needles, as musky as the rich dirt around the roots of the foliage.

The last things I remember are Smiley's heavy breathing of sleep and the gentle rustle of cloth.

14
Christmas

It's two days before Christmas when Momma takes leave from work. The house on Lordsview Court has three bedrooms. Smiley and I stay in the small room. Buddy gives Momma his and says he'll bunk on a cot in the basement. I consider Nandaddy's house a respite from the traffic through our house. If it isn't Burr, it's Phoenix, and how they've managed to avoid one another the past couple weeks is short of a miracle.

Smiley helps Buddy and Nandaddy tend the animals, and I sweep and polish the house floor to ceiling while Momma cares for Mamaw, who now has trouble getting out of bed. Christmas has meant bags filled with candies and nuts for Smiley and me. Four Christmases earlier, I got a Bilo doll with a porcelain head painted to look like a real baby, but on New Year's Day Smiley dropped it on the floor, smashing it to pieces. Daddy said he'd buy me another one, but he never did. Since then I've gotten practical gifts, a school skirt or a pair of trousers. They're always plain and tailored so I'll outgrow them before they go out of fashion. Smiley has gotten toys, and I build block houses for him to plow over with his cars or buildings flaming with imaginary fires for his toy firemen to extinguish. This year he requested a popgun.

Once we have the house in order, Momma offers to take us out to buy Christmas presents. Downtown the sidewalks are snarled with last-minute shoppers. We buy a new coffee mug for Nandaddy—Momma says it's because he calls her Mug—a pair of calfskin gloves for Buddy, and a lambswool scarf for Phoenix. Momma spends a long time looking at purses. Real leather ones with prong closings.

"Do you need a handbag?" I have two dollars she gave me to spend, but

that's not close to enough for the bags she's looking at.

On the sale table she finds a white leather model with a sign that says, "No returns."

"You know Mamaw's white spring coat?" she says. "Won't this be pretty with it next Easter?"

The truth is, Mamaw's not going to make it to Easter. Just as I'm about to remind Momma that the store has a no-refund policy on sale items, she tells the saleslady, "Wrap it, please."

Momma has me take Smiley to look around Kresge's so she can get his presents. I hope she's getting a surprise for me, too. She hasn't mentioned Burr, so maybe she's decided to let things cool off for a while. At least we won't have to include him in our holiday.

*   *   *

"I've got some work to do down in the shop," Nandaddy says that evening. Meanwhile, Buddy gets the box of decorations out of an upstairs closet. The tree has been sitting outside in a bucket of water, and when Buddy brings it in, the house fills with scents of pine forest, of wind, of secrets and promises. In the woods, I picked out a smaller tree but Buddy said he hadn't had a real Christmas in two years, and he wanted a tree we'd remember. This one lacks an inch of brushing the ceiling.

Nandaddy has let the coals die down in the furnace to cool the house so the tree can get used to being inside. Working on the trimmings takes my mind off the cold. Smiley hangs baubles on the bottom boughs, I work on the midsection, and Momma and Buddy hook them around the top. Colored birds, glass Santas, lacy angels, clothespin reindeer, decorations Mamaw bought or made or inherited. Her hands have held each treasured adornment, and she has kept them safe over the years. I believe some of them belonged to her mother and her grandmother, and someday I hope they will pass down to me.

Phoenix appears carrying a box of lead icicles which she begins draping over the needles, giving the tree a silvery glisten.

"Something's not quite right," she says.

"With the icicles?" Momma asks.

"No, with the mood. Sister, see what you can find on the radio."

I twirl the dial of the big wood box through voices and music until I come to a station playing Bing Crosby. Phoenix hums along with Bing crooning "Oh

Little Town of Bethlehem," and it's like old Christmases when Daddy's laughter rang up from the cellar with Nandaddy's as they sanded their handmade presents. I almost expect to see Daddy come up the stairs with crudely wrapped packages made happy with knotted ribbon, warbling Christmas carols out of tune, and pretending to hear Santa's reindeer as he tucks us in. Sorrow grabs at my throat when I think about him, and so I make believe he's at the Gypsy Tavern having a drink with his friends. I try to imagine this Christmas just like any other, except that Uncle Buddy is home and we have the addition of Phoenix. Thinking of everything as normal will get me through Christmas.

Buddy unrolls a parcel of tissue paper and finds a gauzy angel with pink wings and a golden gown shaped like a funnel. He hands the angel to Smiley and hoists him up to slip the finishing touch over the topmost branch. The tree is too tall for the angel to stand up straight, so Buddy bends the top of the tree so that she's looking down at us.

"Perfect," Phoenix says.

Momma plugs in the lights, and the tree comes alive with blue, yellow, red, shining on the glass balls and shimmering in the silver icicles.

Phoenix props one elbow on Buddy's shoulder and points to a thin space in the lower branches.

"Know how to pick 'em, don't you?"

Buddy chuckles. "You didn't see that when the lights were off, did you?"

"You planning to leave the lights off?"

"Is it safe in the dark with you?" He grins.

Phoenix coughs a laugh at the tree, specks of spit flying toward the meager spot. Buddy's laughing, too, his shoulders shaking up and down like quick hiccups, first time I've seen him laugh since he's been home.

Phoenix slugs him hard on the arm. "That's for the wise crack," she says. He grabs her in a neck hold and bends her over, but she twists around, gets a leg over him and pushes him backwards. He loses his balance and falls, pulling Phoenix with him and hitting the floor with a yell. Before he can move, Smiley is astride his chest. Momma stands with her arms folded, shaking her head. Thinking she's mad, I try to pull Smiley off Buddy, but he yanks me down, too. Smiley is sandwiched between Buddy and me, and Phoenix is on top of us. Hands press and tickle and for a minute it feels as if we're wrestling with Daddy, arms and legs twined like knots of string, giggling and squealing. I can almost believe we're in our own house, tussling on our braided rug, Daddy's rough cheek against mine, his hands around my back, and I fill up with delight.

When Buddy squirms around to get a better hold on Smiley, his shoe hits the floor lamp and knocks it over. Momma grabs for it, but she doesn't get across the pile of wiggling bodies in time. The bulb pops when it hits, and glass skitters across the wood floor.

Phoenix jumps up and rights the lamp, and Buddy pulls Smiley away from the shattered bits of glass. Then I hear footsteps coming up the cellar stairs.

"What's all the racket?" Nandaddy is rubbing his hands on a towel.

"We was fighting," Smiley says.

"So I see." My grandfather is drum chested, which makes him look taller than he is. He has never been good with words, but his skill with his hands makes up for his shortcoming with language.

"We were just having some fun," Momma says.

"Fun, my butt. Broken lamp don't look like fun to me." He switches off the radio in the middle of "Adeste Fideles" causing a screeching silence.

"It's just the bulb," Momma says.

"That poor woman's upstairs suffering, and you're acting like fools."

For once Phoenix has nothing to say. She looks back and forth at Momma and Nandaddy. Time seems frozen in place, except for the slow ticking of the mantel clock. It has a mahogany case, and Mamaw said her mother gave it to her and Nandaddy as a wedding present. It has been in her family for a hundred years. Mamaw winds it—or used to—the last task she performed each night, turning over what had been done, getting ready for what would come. I can't imagine my grandfather in this act of reflection and hope, but he must have wound it because the slow ticking fills the air now.

He throws the towel down onto the broken glass.

"Clean up this mess." Then he disappears through the kitchen, slamming the back door shut behind him. Momma and Buddy are a lot like Smiley and me. She and I are older and assigned to keep our brothers from swinging baseball bats in the house, from breaking garage windows with pebbles they use for pitching practice. From knocking over lamps.

After a minute, Phoenix says, "Well, I guess we better get busy." The tone of her voice has changed. She's finally met a man she can't stand up to.

*   *   *

On Christmas Eve, Buddy goes with us to church while Nandaddy stays with Mamaw. I've heard Reverend Singer's story of the birth of Jesus umpteen times, but I enjoy the carols. My favorite is "Angels We Have Heard on High," and I try to get through the Gloria without taking a breath. The choir is in high spirits and renders a song in Latin we are not expected to sing along with.

When we return to Lordsview Court, Momma serves eggnog with slices of a neighbor's gift of fruitcake laced with so much brandy that I can't get it down. Phoenix has gone with her father to a fancy party at the house of one of his wealthy patients. She might wear a dress, black velvet for the holiday, but I find it impossible to imagine her in high heels. Silk pants and a beaded sweater seem more her style.

With Mamaw in bed and just the five of us downstairs, Nandaddy's house seems cheerless. I sip my eggnog through nutmeg sprinkles and find myself wishing for the noise Phoenix brings with her. Smiley is on his hands and knees by the tree, as if his presents will magically appear. I keep expecting Mamaw to come from the kitchen, clean apron tied around her waist and carrying a plate of cookies decorated with colored icing. She'll set the plate on the end table, sit at the piano and play "Oh Come All Ye Faithful," and we'll sing our throats dry until we're ready to call it a night. The trouble is, some things are beyond my control. I can't make Mamaw well any more than I can determine which person my mother loves most. I think about Uncle Buddy's bullet in my coat pocket and will its power to work for me.

That night I lie awake and listen to the wind whine through the cracks in the window casing. Outside, bony fingers of bare trees tap the glass, bark pale as frozen flesh. The cold shoots pains under my skin and makes my throat ache. I wait for the sun to pour in and melt me into the bedclothes, but when the clock strikes three times, it's dark as hades.

*   *   *

"Wake up," Smiley says, poking me. "Nandaddy's already downstairs." He takes my robe from the footboard and lays it on the bed like Daddy used to do. He was the one to wake me on Christmas morning. Standing by the bed, he pulled back the covers and got me to fumble out.

I can hear Nandaddy whistling, can smell the coffee brewing. When I come downstairs, I see someone has plugged in the tree lights and piled gifts beneath the boughs. I stopped believing in Santa Claus at Smiley's age, but I hold a mystical belief in Christmas and the possibility of miracles, like Mamaw getting well or my father walking through the door.

"Good morning, Sunshine," Nandaddy says.

Smiley and I wait while Momma and Buddy help Mamaw down the stairs and sit her in an easy chair, blanket over her lap. Ill as she is, my grandmother has an aristocratic air—pride and modesty in balance, love pouring from her shrunken frame.

When Momma gives the okay, we tear into our presents. She gives us clothes, and Buddy has made Smiley and me wooden stepstools with our names carved on them. I'll use mine to reach the closet shelf above my clothes. Smiley unwraps his popgun, and before breakfast he has almost worn out the cork string playing soldier. Momma gets a blue checkered dress from Buddy with big red buttons down the bodice. It looks a little tight, but he says she can exchange it for a larger size. Nandaddy likes his mug so much he has his second cup of coffee in it, and Buddy works his hands into his new gloves and slaps them together.

When Mamaw opens the Easter purse, she blushes. She knows it's too lavish a gift even for Christmas, knows also the futility of a spring purse for a dying woman. But she thanks us even as she lays the purse back into its box and closes the lid. In a year or less, we'll find the box in her closet, the purse unused. It will go to charity, and one day a lady will walk down the sidewalk carrying the very purse proudly over her arm and neither Momma nor I will say a word.

"Something else there for you, Mug," says Nandaddy.

"Something else? From who?"

"Open the darn thing and find out."

The box must be heavy because Momma needs two hands to lift it. It's wrapped in freezer paper, the kind the butcher uses, and tied with string looped into a tidy knot. Nandaddy is reared back in his favorite chair, holding his new mug on one knee. Smiley drops his gun and helps Momma with the package. Inside is a cleaver with a shiny steel blade. The handle has Nandaddy's mark, sanded not quite smooth, but sturdy and dependable.

"Thanks, Dad," Momma says.

"Aw, it's nothing. I just thought you needed one." He flaps a hand. "It's for meat."

"I'm sorry I couldn't get out to buy you a nice gift this year," Mamaw says.

"Don't be silly. I'm just glad you're better." When Momma turns the cleaver over, it looks more like a weapon than a kitchen tool, and I derive satisfaction from imagining severing a chicken thigh with a heavy thwack.

Smiley crawls through the wrappings under the tree. "Who's this for?" He comes up from a sea of crumpled wrapping bringing with him a small square wrapped in shiny red paper with a curly green ribbon as a fancy store does it. I take it from him and look on all sides for a tag but don't find one.

"Is that from you, Buddy?" Momma asks.

"No," he says. "I don't remember seeing it last night."

Nandaddy points from his chair. "You better give Mamaw that one."

Smiley brings the gift to my grandmother and she runs her fingers over the bow, fanned out like a peony.

"It's too pretty to open," she says.

"Aw," Nandaddy protests.

Mamaw holds the box while Smiley twiddles with the ribbon. Her face is relaxed, not pinched in pain as it has been in the past weeks. Except for the streaks of mercury in her hair, she might have been a young girl, someone whose pale skin has not been toughened by hours in the sun. I'm pricked by the hope that I'll flower into a woman with her poise and beauty someday.

Inside the white box is nestled another box, black velvet and hinged like an oyster. Mamaw removes her fist from the space between her breasts and pries the box open. I squat in front of her and inspect what lies on the pearly satin. It's a locket, heart-shaped, a disk of smooth ebony laid on brushed gold with a delicate gold chain.

"Oh, my," Mamaw says. I've never known my grandfather to give her a Christmas gift, except one year a new teakettle. She stares at the necklace as if it will disappear if she looks away.

I lift the locket from the box and fasten the chain around her thin neck. She eases the lid shut and rubs her thumbs over the velvet without looking at Nandaddy.

"I've got some things need tending." He goes to the kitchen and lifts his coat from the hook before disappearing out the door.

* * *

Nandaddy has gotten a jar of raw oysters from somewhere and Momma presses the rolling pin over saltines to make cracker meal, dips the oysters in egg and then in the cracker crumbs and presses them into fat patties. I heat shortening in the skillet and get them ready to fry. The oysters, fried eggs, sausage patties and fresh biscuits are our Christmas breakfast tradition. Mamaw sits at the table with us and nibbles a biscuit with apple butter but turns up her nose at the eggs. On past Christmases I've relished the crispy oysters dolloped with ketchup, but Daddy never touched them and so this year neither do I.

It's almost noon when Phoenix pulls up to the house in her father's Hudson and parks behind Nandaddy's Ford, shabby by comparison. She's brought candy canes and an armload of presents, and we begin the second round of gifts.

For Nandaddy, a brass cigar trimmer.

"Now you don't have to bite the ends off," she says. "You can cut them like the rich boys." Nandaddy lights up, as much thanks as Phoenix will get.

To Buddy she gives a wool sweater, which looks hand knitted, although she says she bought it in Lexington. He pulls on the sweater, turtling his head through the neck hole. Phoenix nods approval.

"I don't have a present for you," he complains.

"Don't be a dunce. Didn't expect anything." She scratches her ear. "Of course, if you don't like it, I'll take it back."

"It will do just fine," he says and adds, "Thanks, Phoenix."

Momma gets a jacket, the one she marked in a catalogue from a Boston company, camel colored and too expensive. For Smiley a football and a toy telephone. He lifts the telephone out of the box and yells into the receiver. "Hello? Hello?"

I'm not expecting much from Phoenix, but I'm surprised when I open a box containing a pink plastic telephone like Smiley's. I'd think she'd know better than to give me a childish gift. Getting nothing at all would be easier than trying to escape thanking her.

She jerks her nose at my lap. "You ought to check that box one more time."

I shudder to think what more she has buried in the box, but I paw through the rumpled paper and pull out a square card. In Phoenix's scrawl is written: "This one's just for practice. The real one's waiting for you at home. Love, Phoenix."

I stare at the card. A real telephone? I dare not believe lest it prove to be a cruel joke. The card is signed "love." Does she mean she loves me, or is that just a common way for anyone to sign a note?

"Well?" Phoenix says.

"We can't afford a telephone, Phoenix," Momma says.

"The bills go to my father, at least for the first half of the year. Long as you don't call Paris too often."

"I can't accept—" Momma starts.

"It's not for you," Phoenix interrupts. "It's for Bobbie."

"Marguerite—" Mamaw speaks up in a voice that wields authority. When she uses that voice, I know it's useless to argue with her. "It is impolite to refuse a gift. Let Barbara have her telephone and thank Phoenix for it."

It's true, then—I'll have a real telephone. I lift the plastic receiver of the toy and hold it to my ear.

"Hello, Smiley? Merry Christmas, Smiley."

15
Crystal

Even though there's not much wealth in my mother's lineage, they have a noble character about them. My father's side is a different story. Daddy said he came from a hereditary line of scoundrels, including a horse thief. He said he didn't believe about the horse thief, though. The Greys were skillful with animals, and if the horse had sense, it would have come along of its own free will. The Grey thief was reputedly hanged, and his execution cast a shadow over the descendants. I shudder to think which side I take after.

I've never pushed Phoenix to talk about her people, and she hasn't volunteered. I don't see how she can link up with us unless she marries Uncle Buddy, but the fire isn't there. In my opinion, it's Momma Phoenix is sweet on. Everyone is sweet on Momma. Lowry Trott ogles her every time we walk by the gas station, and the men at church shift their eyes from their hymnals in our direction.

And then we have Burr Burrows.

* * *

On our porch we find three packages in graduated sizes—papa bear, mama bear and baby bear. Baby bear has Smiley's name on it. It's a silver-colored airplane with Navy insignias on the tail and a tiny pilot inside the cockpit window. The card stuck in with it says: "To a future pilot of the United States Navy. Merry Christmas, Burr."

"That weasel," Phoenix says.

Smiley holds the airplane up as if it's flying and gallops from kitchen to bedroom and back.

The middle-size package is for me, a blue sweater with embroidered pink flowers and green vines twining in graceful curls. I've never seen one like it. I put it on and twirl around. Won't Penny Reardon turn green with envy?

"I believe that cost a pretty nickel," Momma says, smiling.

"You got a note, too." Smiley hands me the card and I read it out loud. "Over your shoulder and down your arm, this summer garden will keep you warm." I'll admit I'm impressed that he thought enough about me to pick out a pretty sweater and then to write a rhyme about it.

"Beware of snakes bearing gifts," Phoenix says. I figure she's jealous because he hasn't left a gift for her.

"What's in the big box?" Smiley asks.

"Well, we won't know until we unwrap it, will we?" says Momma.

Smiley starts pulling at the bow and tearing at the wrapping. The box is square, a perfect cube. It's a minute before Momma can shake it open.

"What is it?" Smiley tries to see through the tissue paper.

Momma scoops out the paper, crumpled into blossoms like chrysanthemums, then lifts out a round bundle rolled in more paper. Smiley grabs for it, but Momma says, "It might be breakable. I'd better do it." By the flush of her cheek, I can tell that Burr is in pursuit. It's six months since Daddy died—half a year and I can still smell his cigarette smoke in the upholstery, see his imprint on the left end of the sofa where he sat, hear his laughter in the walls. And although he never wrote me a poem or gave me a gift as nice as the blue sweater, I'm not ready to erase his marks on my life.

Momma rolls out the bundle. The paper falls away and she's holding a vase of cut crystal, large enough to hold a fistful of spring tulips.

"Look!" Smiley says. "It's got colors all through it."

When Momma lifts the vase up to the light, the cuts reflect reds and yellows like a prism.

"Did you get a poem, too?" Smiley peeks into the box.

"Why, I believe I did." She hands the card to me. "Will you read it to us, Sister?"

"I'm not in the mood." It's an expression I picked up from Penny. Momma narrows her eyes at me.

"Well," she says, "I'll read it, then." She clears her throat as if she's about to stage a performance.

"'Roses are red, violets are blue. This vase is so beautiful, it reminds me of

you.'"

Phoenix shakes her head and makes a hissing sound like a tire losing air.

I bite a piece of skin beside my thumbnail. I've been picking at my thumb, rubbing around the nail for a rough place I can pull with my teeth, trying to smooth it out.

"Why is he being so generous to us?"

"That's a good question, Sister." For once, Phoenix and I agree.

"He's a nice man." Momma is smiling at the vase.

"Oh, and did he give everyone in Pine Cliff a Christmas present?" I have never before practiced the sarcasm that makes Penny sound smart. It makes me feel gritty.

"I think this would look perfect as a centerpiece for the table." She sets the vase on the dining table.

"We can watch the colors while we eat," Smiley says.

I think about Nandaddy's present, about how the cleaver could shatter Burr's crystal vase into shards. Then I pick the paper from the floor and begin wrapping it around the vase.

"What are you doing?" Momma is frowning.

Laying the vase back in the box, I stuff a cocoon of the thin tissue around it. "We should keep it for company." I taste the grit in my teeth when I add, "I'd hate to see something happen to it."

*   *   *

The day after Christmas someone comes to hook up our telephone. The first person I call is Penny, just to let her know she can call me for arithmetic assignments—or whatever else she has on her mind. I'm sure Linda Stadler doesn't have one, or I would have called to thank her for the change purse, even if I don't honestly think much of it. I'm desperate to use the new mode of communication.

Should I call Covey's house? What would I say if he picked up? *Hello, Covey? This is Barbara Grey. Yes, Bobbie. I was just wondering....*

What would I be wondering? If you ever give me a passing thought? Whether the color of my skin classifies me outside the realm of possibility for being your friend? To say girlfriend at this point is out of the question.

But, anyway, there's probably no telephone at Covey's place.

When the phone rings that afternoon, I race Smiley to the receiver, but he's a step ahead, which annoys me. It's my phone, after all.

"Hello," he says. I must educate him about answering the proper way: "Grey residence," the way Penny says "Reardon residence." I hear him say something about airplane and colors and then, "Momma, someone wants to talk to you." She stops at the mirror and runs her fingers through her hair, pushes the waves into place as if the caller will be able to see her. Then she takes the receiver from Smiley.

"Yes," she says. "It's lovely." I've never heard her use that word before—lovely. At least she doesn't say beautiful. He used that word for her.

"How did you know we had a telephone?" she says. "The operator? Already?" Then she laughs and says, "well, maybe" and curls her fingers to look at the nails. "I guess." And then, "All right," and "All right" again.

"That was him, wasn't it?" Phoenix sneers. Since Christmas came on a Thursday, the foreman gave her Friday off even though she'll have to work the weekend. And when Phoenix has time off, she spends it with us.

"Is it any of your business?" Momma answers. I resent her being rude to Phoenix after she gave us all those gifts.

Phoenix plants her fists on her hips. "I think I'm getting the picture." Her voice is hard. She picks up her coat and walks out without putting it on. Between Phoenix and Burr, she's the adversary I understand. I know the need for friendship, for someone to confide in.

At the door I call her name, but Phoenix is rounding the corner and Momma declares, "Sister, help me get some food on the table for supper."

16
New Year's Eve

When Momma calls Phoenix's house, her father answers and says she's not home. If Phoenix happens to answer, she hangs up the receiver as soon as she hears Momma's voice. She wants nothing to do with us, it seems.

"New Year's Eve is tomorrow," I tell Momma at breakfast one morning.

She presses her fingertips to her cheek. "Maybe we should have a few people over to celebrate."

"Can I invite Penny?"

"It'll just be for grown-ups."

Phoenix treats me like an adult but when it's not convenient for Momma, I'm a child again.

"You can stay up past midnight" is a concession I'll have to accept.

"Will you invite Phoenix to come?"

"We can't very well have a party without her, can we?" Momma winks as if she knows how to smooth the rough seas with Phoenix.

"I can try calling her," I suggest. "She doesn't have a feud against me." We both know that the feud with Momma involves Burr.

"I think it's better if we talk to her in person." Clearly, Momma already has a plan in mind.

*　*　*

Momma arranges for Buddy to pick up Smiley and take him back to Nandaddy's house. He says Smiley has to finish that birdhouse he started with Nandaddy, and Buddy needs someone to chuck the ball with.

Across the Jackson River bridge, the sidewalks end in Rosedale. No one there walks—they drive their nice cars. The exception is lean women in tailored trousers who lead small dogs on leashes, unlike our neighborhood where mongrels are let out the back doors to roam at will.

Phoenix lives in a brick house with stucco gables, larger than Nandaddy's. The steps rise straight to the oak door without the hospitality of a veranda. The absence of this architectural tradition must be due to the fact that Mr. Goode hails from up north where, according to Phoenix, most of the year it's too cold to sit outside.

The doorbell does not buzz as Nandaddy's does but chimes three notes like a steeple clock. Doctor Goode answers the door in suit pants and a vest of rich herringbone over a starched shirt. He fingers a chain that disappears into a pocket then adjusts his rimless glasses, squeezing top and bottom of one lens and lifting them higher onto his nose.

"Hello, Doctor Goode," Momma says, "I'm Maggie Grey. And this is my daughter Bobbie. We're friends of Phoenix."

"Of course," he says. "Come in. Cold as blazes out there."

In my grandparents' house, once inside the door a visitor is standing in the living room. But here the entrance is a short hall with doorways on either side. A wide staircase is carpeted with a bright runner, and beyond is the dining area with a polished table reflecting light from the crystal chandelier that hangs above it. Mamaw's dining table has hardwood chairs, but these are upholstered in a shiny violet fabric. The great room is cheered with a rug woven in designs of russet and gold. Over a tall mantel of wood hangs a painting of a seated woman in a white dress, young and frail, her pale skin contrasting with the dark background. She doesn't resemble Phoenix, who is at least twenty pounds heavier with suntanned skin.

Doctor Goode directs us to the parlor on the left. It's a smaller space with a grand piano, not a spinet like at Nandaddy's house, and a divan, the uncomfortable type with one thin cushion for the seat.

"Can I get you anything?" He seems embarrassed, as if he would have no idea what to do if we said yes.

"No, thank you," I say. Then he disappears without asking us to take off our coats or to sit down. Momma perches on the piano bench, and I wander to the bookcase. I breathe in the scents of old books, a damp odor mixed with aging leather and dust. Books cram the shelves, except for a gap here and there with a painted vase or a silver frame holding a picture of a young Phoenix. In one photo she's dressed in a cowgirl costume astride a pony. In another she stands on a beach, a rubber ball pressed to her hip. A third picture draws me and I study it. A young woman, hair tied from her face, sits on a straight back chair, a handsome dark-skinned boy standing beside her. He looks familiar.

"Who do you reckon this is?"

Momma comes over and studies the picture. "I can't say." She places the frame back on the shelf just as I hear Phoenix's heavy tromp on the stairs, mumbling to herself with every step. She appears and rests one hand high up on the jamb, cutting the doorway on a diagonal.

"Well, it's about time," she says.

"Bobbie wants to thank you for the telephone." Momma has that stubborn voice that makes me grind my teeth. Why won't she apologize?

"Bobbie does, does she?"

"And Momma wants to invite you over for New Year's Eve." I lock eyes with my mother. "Isn't that right, Momma?"

She yields. "Yes—that's right. Can you come, Phoenix?"

Phoenix leaves the doorjamb and hugs Momma, holding her bosom to bosom, Momma's chin hooked over Phoenix's shoulder. Then she leans back and bores into Momma as if our coming has more significance than just inviting her to a party. When she finishes with Momma, she pulls me close.

"Are you getting taller, girl?" It's the old Phoenix with her clean smell and her sassy way of talking. Her thick braid falls over her shoulder and tickles my neck.

"You waited almost long enough to spoil my New Year's Eve," she says.

*　　*　　*

Momma is checking off the guest list and writing down items she needs to pick up.

"Can I invite Covey to the party? He's a friend of Phoenix." I don't make it obvious that I hope to make him a friend of mine.

"Sister, Covey might not be comfortable as the only Negro."

"He's the only Negro every time he goes to help Nandaddy. Besides—his skin isn't black. More like sienna." Burnt sienna is my favorite color of all the crayons.

"It's different in social situations. They have their own school and their own church, and they prefer the company of their own kind."

"Seems to me he isn't any kind different from us."

Momma doesn't like it when I argue with her, and she shuts me down.

"You should go pick out something special to wear tonight."

My dark blue skirt goes with Burr's sweater. Might as well show it off for him.

I set the crystal vase on the dining table. We have no fresh flowers, but I rummage in Momma's closet and find some artificial ones. With some rinsing under running water, they look fine. Momma sets out dishes of candy in colorful wrappers and assorted flavors. Foil twisted on top, the candies lure me with their sweetness. Peppermints, butterscotch drops, horehound bits, squirrel nut zippers.

When I pick up a peppermint, Momma says, "Put that back—those are for the guests."

Around eight o'clock Buddy brings in a paper bag and sets it on the kitchen counter. I don't have to ask what the bag contains. He mixes himself a drink with some ginger ale and chips off a hunk of ice for his glass. Elsie leads in her husband, a lanky, balding fellow, followed by some people Momma works with at the mill, and everyone is given a glass of amber liquid to sip on.

I keep an eye out for Phoenix. It wouldn't surprise me if she brings in a ukulele to plunk on or wears an Indian headdress and does a war dance, and I'm almost right. When I open the door, she scissors me into a hug. She smells pungent, like a tropical flower.

"Phoenix!" Buddy spies her. "It's about time. Want a drink?"

"Just a short one." I take her coat and pile it on Momma's bed, and Buddy hands her a glass tinkling with ice. I suspect she started drinking before she got here to rouse her courage.

I check on Smiley, who's out like a light, and wonder how he can sleep through all the chatter. I'm getting sleepy myself, but I'm determined to make it to midnight. It will be 1948 in a couple of hours. Millions of people died in the war—some soldiers, some victims. But now that the war has been over for a while, maybe conditions on the home front will get better, too.

Burr arrives and in short order has Momma squeezed into a corner. She's not looking like she minds. Phoenix is still in the kitchen with Buddy, finishing up one drink and pouring another. Someone comes up to them and joins the conversation.

Groups form around the house, talking, laughing, getting louder as liquid runs from glasses. Buddy and then Burr offers to make refills. The two seem to hit it off, Burr saying how lucky Buddy is to be out and how he hopes to finish up his service and settle down soon. Maybe he'll even ask out his good-looking sister. The clock on the kitchen wall says half past nine and my ginger ale has gone flat.

"Where's your mother?" Phoenix is looking at me. I point to the dim corner by the bookcase. She goes over and nudges herself close to Momma.

"Hello, Phoenix," Burr says.

Phoenix looks at Momma, ignoring him.

"You ready to celebrate?" Burr sounds jovial.

"I don't see much to make merry about," Phoenix says.

"Come on—a new year's starting." He salutes her with his glass.

"When do you ship out?" She's hoping soon, if I know Phoenix.

"What's it to you?"

"This town's rank enough without you fouling it."

Burr balances his cigarette on an ashtray.

"Look, why can't we be pals?"

"She has no desire to be pals with you," I interrupt.

Burr swims his boggy eyes my way. "What's she got against me?"

"I don't like your looks." Phoenix spews the words as if ridding herself of a nasty taste.

I worry that any minute fists will fly. If that happens, my money is on Phoenix.

Momma breaks in. "What's gotten into both of you?"

Phoenix slips her arm around Momma's shoulders. "Let's get out of here," she says. "I've got a car outside."

"That would be rude, Phoenix." Momma pivots from her grasp.

"We can take Sister and A.T. and all of us can stay over in Rosedale." Her words are slurring together. "Nobody here is worth taking up our time." She pans around the room and locks on Burr, baring her teeth in a malignant smile.

"You two know each other?" Buddy ends the showdown.

"Sure." Burr is fixed on Phoenix. "We worked together at the mill for a short time before I went into the Navy. Phoenix isn't too crazy about me, I'm afraid."

"She's not too crazy about anybody, unless it's Stan Musial," Buddy says.

"Mags, I'm heading out." Phoenix bores into Momma's eyes. "Come with me."

Momma looks from Phoenix to Burr. Then she says, "I'm not leaving my own party."

Phoenix spins around, knocking the table. The vase teeters, indecisive. I clutch and grab a handful of the silk flowers before the crystal leaps, shattering on the green linoleum.

"Oh!" Momma breathes but nobody moves except Phoenix, who bulls past me.

"Get your coat," she says, wrestling with the sleeves of her own camelhair.

"Me?"

"Yes, you. If your momma doesn't want to come, I'd just as soon you did."

Phoenix is in a frenzy, and I'm not crazy about riding around with her agitated and drunk to boot. But Momma's told the truth about the party being for grown-ups. I'm not having much fun. Burr doesn't care about me the way Phoenix does. I'm afraid if she walks out alone, she'll never come back.

"Well?" she says.

"I'm coming."

*   *   *

"Roll down your window." Phoenix's window is already rolled down, winter slapping me like a slab of ice. I'm teeth-chattering cold, wondering why frost isn't forming on the windshield in sharp gemstone shapes, why birds aren't falling out of trees in frozen hunks, how the gaggle of teenagers we pass can be so rosy-cheeked and good-spirited in such cold.

"Slide over here by me." Phoenix must be trying to shiver the alcohol out of her system.

"What time is it?" I slip closer and she nestles me into her armpit.

"Eleven. Pull the gearshift straight down when I tell you."

I curve my hand over the knob and get ready to shift the way I've seen Nandaddy do.

"Now."

The engine revs and I pull down as she tells me, hoping that she's sober enough to know what she's doing.

"You ready for an adventure?" Her breath smells syrupy.

"I guess." I've been ready for the past six months. Crossing the bridge, I have imagined going past my school and walking all the way to Lexington, walking until I can't take another step. Someone would offer me a place to rest and something to eat, even invite me to spend the night. Maybe there would be a girl my age, and she'd be like a sister to me. She'd have a big house and a father who isn't dead. I allow myself this daydream for the time it takes to cross the railroad tracks, and then I realize how much I'd miss Momma and Smiley if I left without a word. I'd even miss Phoenix, if I'm big enough to admit it.

"This isn't the way to Rosedale," I manage through shaky lips.

"Be patient."

Papers rustle in the back. A copy of *The Messenger*, a shopping bag, sheets of typed letters fluttering up and down at the corners, all threaten to take wing.

"Something's going to fly out the window."

"Let it. We start over again January first, don't we?"

"I hope so." I couldn't bear another year like the last one with Daddy dying and Momma busy keeping coal in the stove and ice in the icebox, dust off the furniture and food on the table. Then it's Smiley, getting him fed, making him mind, teaching him to behave. It's Mamaw being sick, then Phoenix taking up her time, and now Burr. Why doesn't Momma make time to talk to me, to listen to me? But she never seems to have a spare minute.

Phoenix takes her arm away to maneuver a sharp corner. When the car leaves the hard pavement, I hear the crunch of pebbles in the dirt, and the road begins a gentle rise.

"Are we heading up to the African settlement? Daddy said I should never go up there."

"Why in heaven's name not?"

"Those people don't want us elbowing into their lives, he said."

"Those people? For your information, Covey is my people."

What does Phoenix mean by Covey being her people? Must be the booze talking, I figure. All my life I've burned with curiosity about the settlement. How do they live? What do they do? Daddy said they're descendants of freed slaves, but I've never heard of any of them visiting their families in Africa. Anyway, there isn't much to see in the settlement. No streetlamps, and the yards are dusky. Looks like nobody here celebrates New Year.

The headlights illuminate trees along the way, green pine and naked limbs stretching toward us, making soft scratching noises against the car fenders. A dog bays ahead, and when we slow down in a driveway, a hound is caught in our spotlight, standing on hind legs, digging at the trunk of an oak with his forepaws. He has an animal treed, coon or possum, I suspect. He dances around the tree, hopping on two legs as if he believes he can climb it if he tries hard enough and barking his frustration at not being able to.

"Franklin, quiet down!" Covey has come out, shielding his eyes from the lights.

The dog sits, ears perked, and then lopes to the car as if he's just discovered he has company. Phoenix gets out and the dog bounds to her side, tail swishing in time with a happy whine. He's seen Phoenix before.

"What are you two doing out at this time of night?" he asks.

"Hey, Covey." I'm hoping he'll recognize me—or at least notice me.

"Covington Fortune, tell those folks to come in out of the cold." A woman's voice. "And shut that door."

We stumble in the darkness toward the yellow shaft of light coming through the open door. Phoenix makes straight for the parlor stove and holds her hands over steam rising in lazy curls above a simmering kettle.

When I shrug out of my coat, Covey takes it and our hands brush each other for a second. He seems not to notice.

"We need to warm you up," he says.

I feel my face flush. Will I always blush around Covey?

"I heard there's a party at the Grey house," Covey says. "Why'd you two leave?"

"I don't think Phoenix liked the company," I answer.

"That's putting it mildly," she says. "Sorry you couldn't make it."

"Don't recall being invited."

"I'd have invited you but Momma said you wouldn't come."

I regret the words as I say them. Why do I blurt out things I wish I hadn't said? But Covey looks amused, which pleases me.

"You would, would you?" he says.

The woman standing by the cook stove gets two bowls down from a shelf. "I'll heat up some chili. Just made it today."

Covey must see me staring at her. "You know my Aunt Regina, Bobbie?"

Did I answer him? I'm too taken with the way she looks, tall and long-fingered, with hair that plays around her shoulders in coils. She's slender and gives dignity to the housedress she's wearing so late in the day. I don't want any chili, but I can't see myself saying no to Aunt Regina.

"And this here's my cousin Winona."

A girl younger than I am—eleven or twelve—leans on Covey.

"Hello," she says, sleepy-eyed.

"You still up, girl?" Phoenix asks.

"Uh-huh." She knuckles an eye.

Phoenix tilts her head. "Winona's a prodigy."

"What's a prodigy?"

"A virtuoso. She has a gift."

I consider Winona. "What kind of a gift?"

"Why don't you show her, Winona?" Phoenix says.

"Do I have to?"

Covey steps toward his aunt. "What time is it, Regina?"

She checks the small clock on the counter.

"Twenty past."

Covey lays his hand on Winona's shoulder. "You want to stay up 'til midnight, you'll have to earn the privilege."

She snatches a look at me with a sly smile and goes into another room. Through the doorway I can see a bed and a bureau with a lamp that casts a soft light. There isn't a speck of dust and the wood floor shines. See-through curtains on the windows, and the walls are free of the fingerprints Smiley leaves on ours. The savory smells mix together simmering supper, wood crackling in the stove, and sweet spruce from the Christmas tree in the corner, strung with red ribbon and hung with angels made of net and lace and eyelet. A handmade quilt, folded so the corners meet, hangs on the back of the sofa, and I want to curl up, pull the quilt over me, and fall asleep.

Winona comes back with a violin case, lays it on the rug, and raises the top of the case. As if she's handling a brown swan, she lifts the instrument with delicate care and fits the end under her chin. When she draws the bow across the strings, the violin produces a wail that sounds like a cat in pain. She stops, adjusts the pins that hold the strings and tries again. This time the notes sound right.

Winona's fingers are long like her mother's, and they drift up and down the neck as the bow glides back and forth. The air vibrates with music, tickling the hair on my neck. It has a pure quality, as if I'm in a forest of pine trees. I've heard music like this on the radio, but Momma always changes the dial, looking for a peppy song.

Lips pressed together, Winona stares straight ahead as if she sees the music in the air. She has her mother's doe color skin, the wavy hair.

When she finishes, she settles the instrument back into the case and sits next to Covey on the couch.

"I never heard anyone play a fiddle like that."

"It's a violin," Winona corrects me.

"What was the song?" I ask.

"It's called 'Greensleeves,' one of the first pieces I learned."

"Do you know 'Turkey in the Straw'?" Phoenix butts in.

Winona bites her lip. "I don't think we've learned that one. Which composer is it by?"

"Ha," Phoenix says. "You got me."

I'd like her to play "Mexicali Rose," my favorite Gene Autry song, but it calls for a guitar.

"Chili's ready," Aunt Regina says. "Covey, Winona—either of you want a bowl?"

"Naw, thanks," Covey says. He checks the clock. "You all better eat fast, though. It'll be midnight pretty soon."

Winona perches opposite me at the table and watches me eat.

"What are you staring at?" I ask.

"Are you white?"

"She looks white, doesn't she?" Phoenix says.

Winona cradles her chin in her hands. "I wish we could peel our faces off and trade them so I could look out through your green eyes and talk through your little mouth."

"You'd get sunburned in the summer." I blow on the chili and take a bite— shreds of pork, soft beans, pungent, foreign flavor.

Winona frowns. "There's got to be more to it than that."

"I guess I don't know any different. Besides, you don't look African to me."

"We've got Indian blood," Aunt Regina says. "Choktaw. Winona's name is Indian. It means 'daughter of the river.'"

"But Choktaw's not white, either," Winona says.

I can tell them what it's like to be white. It's about waiting. Waiting for my turn. Waiting for someone to notice I'm around. Waiting to grow up.

"Less than five minutes now," Regina says.

"Winona, get those noisemakers," Covey tells her. She goes to her room and brings back three cylindrical horns colored with confetti and stars.

"We got these knocking over bottles with a beanbag at the carnival that came through town last summer." Covey hands one to me, one to Phoenix, and the other to Winona. "Hold on one more minute—" He gets a jug out of a cabinet in the kitchen and brings some tumblers to the table.

"What's that stuff?" Phoenix asks.

"I've been saving this for a rainy day." He fills the glasses halfway with a liquid that smells like apples left in Nandaddy's root cellar too long.

"This is hard cider," Phoenix says. "I had a rough enough time driving out here as it is. A glass of this, and I won't be going anywhere tonight."

"We've got plenty of blankets," Regina says.

"Momma will be worried."

"Your momma knows you're with me." Phoenix lays a hand on my shoulder. "She knows I wouldn't allow anything happen to you."

Yes, let her worry. If she goes into a panic, she might come looking for me.

"Okay, here goes," Covey says. "Those hands on the clock look straight up to me. Let's drink a toast to the New Year." He clicks his glass to each of ours, and we all take a swig. The cider sends bubbles up my nose. I hiccup and Winona blows her horn at me. I blow mine back at her, and Phoenix toots quick quacks on hers. We click our glasses again, and from down the hill I hear firecrackers go off. Covey fills our tumblers again, and what with the tooting and the drinking and the late hour, I start to get lightheaded. I've forgotten how I got to Covey's house, forgotten about Momma's party, forgotten even that it's New Year's Eve. All I'm aware of is Winona's hand in mine, pulling my dress off and wrapping soft cloth around me, Winona's arm over me, her slow breath on my neck, and strands of violin music flowing like velvet over my skin.

17
The Burrows Sisters

New Year's Day 1948

Sticky glasses clutter the kitchen counter, and pools of liquid need wiping up. Momma is busy picking up candy wrappers crinkled on the floor.

"Well," she says, "I thought you might be holding my daughter for ransom."

"I don't need your money." Phoenix sounds like she's still angry.

"I'm not thinking about money."

"What have you got that I want?"

"Obviously something, or you wouldn't have been so unmannerly at the party."

What Phoenix wants from Momma is clear to me—the same thing I do. Didn't she worry about me at all last night? Did she stay awake, pace and check the window fifty times for Phoenix's car? Or did she laugh and smoke and sip so many highballs that it didn't matter to her whether Phoenix brought me back? Mothers are supposed to be wellsprings of love, saving their children from ugliness and unkind deeds of man or nature. But Momma's wellspring is pointed in one direction—Burr. And Phoenix, Smiley and I are left hanging out to dry. If we want saving, we'll have to save ourselves.

I check around the house. "Where's Smiley?"

"Burr took him for a walk," Momma says.

"Burr came by already this morning?"

Momma places a clean ashtray on the table, ignoring my question. "Are you two hungry?"

"Regina made cheese grits," Phoenix says.

"You've been up to Covey's?"

"Does that surprise you?

"Phoenix, nothing you do surprises me. But I'd have appreciated knowing my daughter's whereabouts."

"Well, here she is, none the worse for wear."

Momma runs water in the sink for the dirty glasses. I don't offer to wash them.

"I'm about to boil up some black-eyed peas," she says.

I wrinkle my nose. "I hate black-eyed peas."

"You're supposed to eat them on New Year's Day or you'll have bad luck all year."

"Covey's family doesn't believe in that superstition." I emphasize Covey to remind Momma I've been up in the African settlement. I don't care if it makes her mad.

She shakes the beans into a metal colander, a musical tinkling. "Well, I'm going to put some on to cook. Better safe than sorry."

Even though she has slept on it, Momma's hair is curly from setting it with bobby pins for the party. I catch her scent—pasty with a sprinkle of nutmeg. She washes the beans and picks through them for stones.

When I get the broom and start sweeping crumbs into a pile, Momma says, "Aren't you afraid of what people will think?" She speaks to the beans, but Phoenix and I both have overheard.

"I don't give a squat about what people think," Phoenix says. "You should know that by now."

"I'd rather you not take my daughter up there."

"You afraid I'll catch something?" That sour taste of sarcasm is back on my tongue.

Momma lifts her apron and rubs the fabric between her hands. "You remember what happened to Lorna Murphy. Now she's raising a little milk chocolate boy."

Phoenix scowls. "Look who's giving out free advice."

"What does that mean?" Momma plants her fists on her hips.

"I mean you're the one heading for the potholes."

Momma bends over the beans, raking her fingers through them.

"You should go, Phoenix," she says.

"I'm on my way out."

"Phoenix—" I bark out her name, and she stops. "I had a nice time last night."

"Happy New Year," she says, her voice scraping like chair legs across the floor.

* * *

Smiley holds out a piece of Bazooka bubble gum.

"Look what Burr gave you." He mumbles around the pink wad in his jaw. "And we going to a party."

Burr grins.

"What kind of party?" I take the gum and look it over, the rectangle of colored paper wrapped tight and folded at the ends. The candy smell makes my cheeks ache.

"It don't matter, long's they got ice cream," Smiley says.

Momma is stirring the black-eyed peas, a hunk of bacon floating on top. The sharp aroma robs my appetite. "What's this about a party?"

"My mother's a magician in the kitchen," Burr says. "You're all invited for dinner."

"Do you want to go, Sister?" Momma asks. Does she want me along, or does she mean that she'll decline his offer if I refuse?

"Do I have a choice?" If I admit it, I'm curious about Burr's family. They can probably tell me what kind of fellow is weaseling his way in among us.

"Stay here and eat black-eyed peas by yourself if you prefer," Burr says.

"In that case," I grumble, "I suppose I'll come."

* * *

Burr's arm is around Momma's waist as we walk toward Riverside Avenue, Smiley and I following a few steps behind. Thunder rumbles over the mountains. The sky is bullet silver and it's cold enough to snow. A page of *The Messenger* somersaults across our path and dry leaves flutter down like drunken butterflies.

"My sisters will love you," Burr says to Momma.

"How many sisters do you have?" I toss the question at Burr's back.

"Four." He starts to list them. Esther is so shy he doesn't think she'll ever get married, but Grace is on her third husband, an Italian aristocrat. Rhoda's husband Freddy stays drunk all the time because the army wouldn't take him, but he's good for a laugh. Pansy is living with her parents while her husband is stationed overseas, and her baby is due any day, thanks to a furlough he enjoyed in the spring.

"You must be spoiled without brothers," Momma says.

"Oh, I have two brothers. Eddy is in the Merchant Marines, stationed at Sheepshead Bay. I see him now and then, but I don't go in for getting pie-eyed and brawling like Eddy. And Pete's in the Navy, too, but he's at sea. I'm going to try to catch up with him when I ship out. You'd like him, but don't get ideas—he's married." He squeezes her shoulder. You'd think with all those brothers and sisters, there'd be a mess of little ones around, but he doesn't mention children.

The Burrows's house is nothing out of the ordinary—two-stories, bushes trimmed to look like round boulders. As soon as Burr walks in, happy chatter tumbles out. We follow him and find three men sitting in overstuffed chairs smoking cigarettes. Two stand when they see us. Burr's father, thin as wire, stays seated and bobs his head at us. One of the men standing is younger than Nandaddy but rougher around the edges—Freddy. He salutes with a glass of what looks like iced tea, almost slopping it out. The Italian aristocrat, I guess he is, narrow as Mr. Burrows, leans on a silver-tipped cane. He takes Momma's hand, bows, and brings it to his lips.

Women are smoothing the tablecloth, setting the table, carrying pots and plates around the kitchen. The rich smells of roasting meat and baking sweets are tantalizing. When she sees us, the pregnant one looks up first—Pansy, is it? Her big belly sits like a basketball on her lap.

The other women part, allowing Mrs. Burrows to walk between them. She's broad but no taller than her daughters and wears her hair about her face in short snowy wisps. Skin smooth as a young woman's, it's her eyes that tell her age, lids drooping over blue irises and deep lines in the brow. She stops in the midst of the younger women and surveys Momma.

"My son has told us so much about you." She brings Momma to her chest. "And these must be your young ones. Come here and give me a hug." She squeezes me with solid arms, kitchen aromas hanging around her. When she goes for Smiley, he backs away.

"He's bashful." I like her so far and don't want Smiley to start out hurting her feelings. Cowboy Code number nine: Respect women and parents.

When we gather at the long table, Burr's father sits at the head, Mrs.

Burrows at the opposite end. Burr is flanked by his sisters except for Esther, who sits by Momma. I'm next to Smiley, Freddy and the Italian on my other side.

Around mouthfuls of brisket, candied yams, turnip greens, and hot biscuits, Rhoda says, "Don't you all think Burr resembles Bing Crosby?"

"Don't sing like him, though." Freddy pokes me with his elbow. I hold back from correcting his grammar.

"He's much better looking than Bing," says Pansy. "Burr, I swear you ought to go to Hollywood and get into the pictures. You're Laurence Olivier's double."

"Pshshsh," says Freddy. "Lon Chaney's more like it." He pokes me again, as if the joke is just for me. I wish he'd stop.

"Now don't go talking about my brother that way, Freddy," says Rhoda. "He's protecting our country, which is more than I'll say about you."

Freddy bites off a piece of biscuit as if it's her head.

Mrs. Burrows says, "I'd like peace at the dinner table, if you all don't mind." She points to Esther. "Pass some greens down to Pop. He's all skin and bone."

Mr. Burrows meditates on each bite. I suspect he's missing teeth and that his gums are doing most of the work. He throws a look around the table now and then, seems to disapprove of it all, and focuses on his plate.

"Burr," says Grace, "Louise said she wants a picture of you in your uniform. You have an extra one? She wants to tape it to her mirror so she can look at it every day."

"Who's Louise?" Momma asks.

"One of his girlfriends." Grace lifts her chin as if to challenge Momma—big mistake. "And, Burr, if you don't stop in and see Suzie Barker while you're home, she'll chew her nails to stubs."

"I've got no hold on him," Momma says, her own chin lifted. I'm glad she's willing to let Burr go.

"Grace, you are ornery," Rhoda says. "Get up and help me clear these dishes."

"She's just teasing, honey." Burr gives Momma a weak smile across the table.

"Suzie that one with the pair of cantaloupes?" Freddy holds his palms out from chest.

"Don't you listen to him, Maggie," says Rhoda. "He's just an old lush."

Burr rears back in his seat, an arm on Pansy's chair, and winks at Smiley as if to say, "This is the life, boy." He pats Pansy's belly and raises an eyebrow at Momma. If he's looking to procreate, I wish he'd think about Louise or Suzie.

Strangely enough, I never met my father's people. They're all in Rocky Mount and deep into the bootleg liquor business. Daddy said he didn't want his children to get tangled up in that mess. At the Burrows house, the strongest drink they offer is lemonade.

Grace starts to clear the table and Esther and Rhoda bring out banana pudding and a pineapple upside-down cake. Burr gets up and stands behind his mother, pressing her shoulders. She folds one arm across her chest and clasps her son's hand.

"Burr, you cut the cake," she says. "And give Bobbie and A.T. an extra big piece."

A maraschino cherry perches in the center of each pineapple ring. I like a sad cake, and this one is so moist it almost makes me dizzy. When I finish my piece, I'm too full for the banana pudding, even though the creamy vanilla smell is tempting.

Some of the sisters start in on the dishes.

"Can I help?" I ask, but Pansy says she needs me to help get the men to push the furniture back against the walls. She calls directions with one hand on her swollen belly then threads a roll into the player piano, and "Sentimental Journey" purrs out. Burr waltzes his mother around the living room and then presents her to his father.

"Pop, you take over."

Mr. Burrows shakes his head, but his foot is tapping. Freddy steps in, twirls his mother-in-law too fast for the music and screws up the rug.

Mrs. Burrows stops and presses a hand to her chest. "Freddy, you need to take a lesson from Burr. You're stepping on my feet."

Rhoda whirls Esther, but Pansy sits close to the Italian and watches. Grace holds the Italian's hand, dancing and bending over to show him some cleavage. It's definitely a party, everyone talking and laughing. I admit that I'm enjoying the show—that is until Freddy holds out his hand to me.

Not me, not me, not me, I'm thinking.

But he has my wrist and is pulling me up.

Then I'm dancing, my cheek pressed to his shoulder. I can hear gurgling from his protruding belly. His breath, saturated with brisket and what must have been a secret flask of whiskey, falls heavy on me and I hold my own breath until I almost pass out.

Burr pulls Momma against him and spreads his fingers at the small of her back, holding her close. His chin is at her temple and he folds her hand between them and kisses it. He's a good dancer.

"Will you go to the movies with me tonight?" Over the music, I'm half hearing his low voice, half reading his lips.

"What about the children?"

"Can't Bobbie watch A.T.?"

"I suppose she could." He's luring her in—or is she luring him? Even if my father was burned to a cinder and buried under six feet of Virginia's rich dirt, even if she cleaned his clothes out of the closets, hid his watch and stored him in a box of time, even if she dies of longing, I expect my father to be the only love in her entire life. He's the only one in mine.

*   *   *

While Momma gets Smiley ready for bed that night, I ask her what movie she and Burr are going to.

"*Spellbound*," she says.

"That Ingrid Bergman movie?" I've been wanting to see it.

"It's probably scary," she says.

"I don't get scared."

"Me either," Smiley pipes up.

Momma is humming "Rum and Coca-Cola" and shooting looks into the living room where Burr is waiting.

"I'll stay up until you get back," I offer.

"No, Sugar—it's the nine o'clock show. You know it won't be over 'til eleven." She touches her lips to my cheek, cool and quick. "I'll tell you all about it tomorrow."

That familiar note of finality. I could use Phoenix here to advocate for me.

*   *   *

Sometime in the night a crack of lightning wakes me, sounding like metal ripping and followed by thunder's low rumble. Outside, wind is pushing hail down the street, splashing like banshees flying just above the ground. Rivers

are forming in the gutters and pooling in potholes. After the hail, water runs in a solid sheet down the window.

Did Momma make it home before the storm? In the darkness I can make out a figure on the couch, too big to be one person but moving as if the two parts are laced together.

"Momma?"

The form stops, and after a minute I hear her say, "Go back to sleep."

When I get back into bed, I press my palm to the window, so cold it hurts to hold it there. I bite my lip to keep from pulling my hand away. The cold moves through my wrist and up my arm as if I'm being plunged to the shoulder in ice crystals. Then it flows into my chest and sucks my breath. Still I hold my hand on the glass, winter searing my skin and ice forming around my heart with a film of frozen blue.

18
Prowler

The week school starts again seems endless.

"I hear you went up to that African settlement on New Year's," Penny Reardon says at lunchtime. She's holding her mouth in a sneer as if I've done something distasteful.

I refuse to deny it. "Is there a law says I can't go up to the settlement?"

"You know what people will call you if word gets around. I'm not saying I'd call you that because you're my friend." Penny's hair is not strawberry as I once thought but more like the color of dog turd and I'm just noticing that her teeth have come in crooked. If rumors are flying about me, it's most likely that Penny has launched them.

"What business is it of yours?"

She raises her eyebrows. "I'm looking out for you is all."

"I can look out for myself, thank you."

*　　*　　*

In class Mrs. Davenport is edifying us about the Niña, the Pinta, and the Santa Maria. Although I like the poetry of their names, I couldn't care less about the scurvy-wracked voyage to the New World. I'm looking for my own land to discover, providing one exists beyond these Allegheny Mountains. Mrs. Davenport says there's a universe outside Pine Cliff's limits, but all I have are Burr's naval reports to testify to it.

Burr is stationed in Washington, DC, while he waits for his ship to sail again. He promises to return on the weekend, a promise I don't care if he keeps. Momma seems restless, though, and one night she scrapes together enough money for dinner downtown. Smiley takes two bites of his hamburger and squirms in his seat. He unfolds his napkin and lets it float to the floor. Momma picks it up, and he lets it fall again. He pushes the salt shaker around his plate, making car noises. He shakes a pyramid of pepper onto the table and blows it at me, which makes my nose tickle. Momma doesn't notice. She's staring out the window as if waiting for someone to walk by. When I complain about the pepper, she says, "A.T., if you don't eat your hamburger, you can't have an ice cream." He tears at his hair and clenches his teeth.

"Stop it, now," Momma says. Then he slides off the seat onto the floor and tears at his shirt until a button pops off. I've seen him throw fits before, but never in public.

"Smiley, why are you acting this way?" I'm offering him concern rather than scolding, but he shrugs his shoulders. "Are you having a growth spurt?"

A couple at the next table are staring at us.

The waitress comes over and in a low voice says, "If you don't get the boy under control, I'll have to ask you to leave."

Momma doesn't offer apology but grabs Smiley by the shirt collar and yanks him out onto the sidewalk. I scoop up his coat and follow them outside. He's never acted like this when Phoenix is around, and when he's with Burr, he's mesmerized by a spell of goodness.

Back in familiar territory, Smiley calms down. Momma has never hit him, not even when he threw rocks at cars or said "hell" on purpose. She has tried to reason with him, even when he was too young to understand.

He's pouting, so I try my hand with him.

"Smiley, you're getting too big to make a scene like you did tonight. Don't you want to grow up to be a gentleman?"

"Like Burr?" His sweaty hair is glued to his forehead. His eyes are too big for his face, lashes so thick they cause a breeze, and his sharp chin juts out when he grins, like Daddy's. Maybe he doesn't remember our father, the soft fur of his arms, hands strong enough to chop wood to kindling, delicate enough to pick a chigger off my knee. It's Burr's angular frame that's familiar to him, the smells of aftershave and liquor swimming about him.

"If Burr was my daddy, I'd be a gentleman." Smiley leans on Momma, looking into her face. She tries to give us whatever we want although we know not to ask for the unreasonable. Momma is resourceful, and even when money is scarce she improvises, bartering with neighbors or making do with a needle and thread, scissors and paper, flour and sugar. I'm afraid if she sets her mind to it, she'll improvise Burr into becoming head of the household.

"Burr is not going to move into this house and be your daddy," I say, "so just put that idea out of your mind. We're stumbling over one another as it is."

"He can sleep in your bed," Smiley says, "and you can sleep with Momma."

Momma laughs. "That's not the way it usually works."

I continue to plead my case. "I don't find anything at all funny about the situation."

She sighs. "Our house is small—it's true. But we've got lots of space in our hearts."

I vow to protest any alliance concerning Momma and Burr until I have no more breath to speak. "Not my heart—my heart is full of Daddy."

* * *

Friday evening, Burr appears. Momma greets him at the door, and he kisses her. She looks up the street before pulling him inside as if she's cheating on Daddy, which in my opinion she is.

"I came right from the train station," he says. "And look what I brought for A.T." He holds out a bag, crumpled at the top from being folded down. Smiley tears open the bag, the surprise of a gift delighting him as much as whatever is inside.

"Candy wafers!"

He breaks the roll of quarter-sized discs in different colors and shakes out two flat wafers that tumble and crack into wedges on the linoleum.

"Pick those up," I tell him.

"Mind your own business," he answers.

Burr interrupts. "This is for you, Bobbie. Maybe you'll let your mother look at it when you're finished." He hands me a *Photoplay*, a latest edition even Penny Reardon hasn't gotten yet. I fan through the pages. Clark Gable, Ava Gardner, Mickey Rooney, Shirley Temple—stories and pictures about the most popular stars in Hollywood. No Gene Autry, though. For the past two years he's been flying Army cargo planes in China and India, and I've had to settle for reruns of *South of the Border* and *Be Honest With Me* at the Visulite until he gets back and makes some new movies. I sit down and study the pictures, planning which ones I'll cut out to hide in the back pages of my math book so I can look at them when I get bored with decimals. I suppose I should thank Burr, but he's moved Momma to the kitchen to talk while he makes himself a drink. I can hear them over Smiley bouncing a ball against the wall, catching it as it ricochets off the floor.

"I missed you," Burr says.

"Did you?" Momma answers.

"You know you missed me, too." Momma must have made a face because Burr says, "You little goat," and mashes himself against her.

He sips the drink while she rummages through the cupboards for what to fix for supper.

"Maggie, I need some advice," he says.

"I'm not sure I'm the one to give it to you."

"I think you are." He swirls his drink around in the glass. "I don't have anyone to worry about me while I'm at sea."

"What about your mother and that houseful of sisters?"

He sets his drink down on the counter and holds her by the shoulders. "I've got a two-week leave." He kisses her once on each eye.

No louder than a sigh, he adds, "Say yes."

I've forgotten about Smiley and his candy, forgotten about the magazine on my lap, about movie stars and math books. I'm focused on my mother's answer, like a pen poised above paper ready to draw a picture of the rest of my life.

"We'll see," she says.

*　*　*

On Friday night I wake when the door slams closed. I figure Burr is leaving and check the clock on my nightstand. Did I remember to wind it last night? Otherwise what were Burr and Momma doing until four in the morning—as if I didn't know. Seems to me Burr overstayed his welcome.

On Saturday afternoon Momma welcomes him back. At least he offers to take all three of us to a matinee at the Strand, a Fred Astaire dance movie. Afterwards we walk down Main Street like a real family. Every block or so we stop for Burr to shake hands with neighbors and talk about how he's about to ship out for another tour of duty, cruising around the Pacific and firing guns over the water to show the Japanese we still mean business. I watch Momma looking at him, the mill's smoke sailing up behind him, and wonder if she's drifting up like smoke and floating over the carpet of mountains. Can she smell the spices of Indonesia, feel the salty spray of the ocean? Is she sailing away from us the way my father left, heading out from home port without a goodbye, without a backward glance?

*   *   *

Late that night I listen to Momma's voice, louder than usual, sounds propelling from her like ammunition, although I can't make out specific words. Burr is trying to argue, more like pleading. Then the door closes hard, as if pushed from the inside rather than pulled from without. The springs of Momma's bed creak their welcome when she crawls in, and I drift into dreams of attics filled with cut glass figurines and painted patterns on the walls, furniture carved in scrollwork and covered with sheets to keep the dust off. I've never seen these objects except in books and wonder what they're doing in my attic, wonder why I even have an attic when all we have is a crawlspace above the main room.

Sometime during the night the moon shines in the window like torchlight. I run my hand across the sill. One of Momma's straight pins pokes my fingertip. I lift it with my fingernail and use it to etch tiny scratches into the glass. On the sidewalk, pebbles crackle under shoe soles. I swear I hear the shuffle of leather on the steps, the soft sound of palm gripping doorknob. The door rattles. It's too early for the milkman, and we don't have milk delivered anyway. Daylight is still hours off. I think of an animal coming down from Fore Mountain, looking for something to eat, a hungry tiger escaped from the Richmond circus and finding his way to my bedside for a tender bite, or a furry bear arising hungry from a winter nap. Will it look toward the window and see me huddled behind the thin glass? The wind is howling beneath the window, throbbing against the pane. "It's just the wind," Daddy used to say, pacifying me from the fearsome faces my imagination conjured. "Don't be afraid of nothing." But nothing is what I fear—the loneliness of nothingness, and I scratch at the window to keep from falling into the pit of nothingness.

If I squash my cheek to the window, I might be able to see who's at the door, but he might be able to see me, too. What if he's big and hairy, if he has drool dripping from sharp teeth and the look of crazy hunger about him? Then

the shadow moves slow as quicksand, too big for an animal. I scrunch my eyes shut and see red inside my lids, and I lie still as death, pulling the satin border of the blanket up to my nose. When I slip my thumb between my teeth, I taste sweet under the nail, count the ridges of my thumb with my tongue, and let the comfort of sucking take me to a safe place.

19
The Proposal

By morning, I've forgotten about burglars and fears that invaded the night. I have bigger worries on this Sunday. Burr is coming with us to Lordsview Court for dinner.

Momma stops in the doorway of my room. "I'd like you to wear your best Sunday dress, Sister. The one you wore to the funeral."

"But we're skipping church, aren't we?"

"We've got to have time to fix the dinner. You know your grandmother's not up to it."

She wants me to impress Burr by dressing up. If she's committing a sin with him, I hope God will forgive her, but I have the awful feeling that the Almighty will send a bolt of lightning down.

By noon, Burr has not yet arrived. Momma is sitting on the glider wrapped in her coat and smoking a cigarette. Smiley and I play catch to pass the time, but my stomach is growling. If Nandaddy's rooster is still pecking warm-blooded around the yard, it will be three o'clock before he's cleaned and plucked, baked and basted, and I'll have withered from hunger. Virginians are always on time for church and meals, no exceptions. They may drag their feet showing up for work, but they'll be at the dinner table with clean hands before the serving ladle dips into the gravy.

"There he is," Smiley says.

Burr is shuffling down Allegheny Avenue, head down.

"Am I late?" he says.

"A little bit," Momma answers.

"Hour and a half," I correct. "We're starving."

"I'll handle this," Momma says to me. She glares at Burr. "What's going on?"

He plunges his hands into his pockets. His breath is gray fog in the cold. "Didn't get much sleep."

"Was it something you ate?" Momma asks.

Something he drank, I think. He smells of stale whiskey, and his eyes are bloodshot.

"Met up with a few old friends after I left you. I had to make sure they don't forget me."

"I didn't appreciate your coming back," Momma says.

"When?"

"Last night. Trying to get into the house."

"I didn't come back last night."

I remember the sound of someone on the porch. "I heard you try the doorknob."

"It wasn't me," he says. "You can ask Percy Jamison. I was with him until sunrise."

"Then who tried to get into the house?"

"Maybe it was just the wind." He snugs up the waist of his pants.

"It wasn't the wind." I'm not letting him off that easy. "Someone came up the steps and tried the door."

"Did you get a look at him through the window?" he asks.

"Who'd want to take what little we've got?" Momma says.

Yes, who would? Maybe Phoenix felt lonely and wandered over from Rosedale, but she would have thrown stones at my window until I got up to let her in. Or one of the tavern clients was so oiled up he got the wrong house coming home.

"Could be that it wasn't your things they were after," Burr says.

"You reckon they were going to eat us?" A breeze lifts Smiley's hair on end.

"We shouldn't be scaring A.T." Momma tries to get his hair to lie flat, but he jerks his head.

"We ought to have a gun." My fist is in my pocket, the bullet comfortable in my fingers.

"What do we know about using a gun?" Momma's hand rises to her top coat button.

"It's not brain surgery. Full clip, one shot in the breech, steady, aim, pull."

"When have you ever shot a gun?" Smiley sounds skeptical.

Burr flips up his collar and buries his hands in his armpits. "You wouldn't have to keep it loaded. It would scare a prowler, loaded or not."

"If we have a gun, we'll keep it loaded," I tell him.

Momma buries her hand into her pocket, the pocket of the coat Phoenix gave her for Christmas. "I'll ask Dad if he's got one he can give us."

"We should get us a shotgun," Smiley says.

"I think I know where we can get a pistol." A German pistol. A war weapon.

Burr laughs. "We're talking about a real gun. One that shoots bullets, not corks."

I doubt Burr has ever killed a man or even glimpsed the enemy. When he came to supper that first night, he said his job was Chief Storekeeper, which means he makes sure the ship is stocked with towels, writing paper, pens, envelopes and copies of *Reader's Digest* to fill sailors' lonely hours. When the war was on, he stayed below deck. The Navy couldn't lose the officer who oversees the ship's supplies, he said. Besides, he's not a fighter. He joined the Navy to keep from taking over his father's feed store or falling into a dead-end mill job. The fighting was left to men like Uncle Buddy.

I lift my nose. "I know what a real gun is."

*　*　*

At Nandaddy's, I peel potatoes for boiling while Momma makes corn pudding—milk and eggs, flour and sugar mixed with the corn kernels and baked to a custard. I take pork chops out of the ice box, dip them in egg and roll them in flour. When the shortening melts in the cast iron skillet, I squeeze the pork chops in close together.

I find a box of brown sugar and am ready to sprinkle some over the chops the way Mamaw does for extra flavor.

"Burr might not like the chops that way. Just fry them with salt and pepper," Momma says.

Outside, Buddy is showing Burr the Packard he bought. Smiley is watching with Nandaddy. The Packard is at least a yard longer than Nandaddy's Model A, and I imagine he's complaining about the new automobile taking up too much garage space.

After Momma gets the corn pudding in the oven, she goes to check on Mamaw. These days it's a struggle for my grandmother to get any broth down at all, much less feel well enough to come downstairs and be sociable.

When I'm alone in the kitchen, I reconsider the brown sugar, thinking Burr wouldn't notice a little sweetening on his chops. I'm not sure how much Mamaw adds in, so I lift up the box, expecting it to sprinkle out like white sugar. Instead, a lump drops out, splattering grease onto my dress, six sunburned freckles on the pink smocking. Momma will yell at me, even though the dress is getting tight and shorter on me than it was last summer. She said I could get another season out of it, but I'm like Phoenix in the respect that we both prefer trousers.

I don't have time to worry about the smocking, though, and the sugar has already melted in the shortening. There's no turning back. For my taste, too much sweetener is better than not enough, and so I swirl the sugar around, hoping by some miracle to come out with a dish that bears a resemblance to Mamaw's. After a few minutes the sauce thickens to syrup and moves on to glue in the hardening stage. I try adding water, but it just boils off, leaving the sauce like caramel. I push the pan off the burner, hoping less heat will transform the sauce back to liquid.

Momma comes in to help me get the food on the table.

"What's this?"

"The pork chops."

"What did I tell you?" Momma's tone is accusing. She picks at the front of my dress. "And look at you."

"I couldn't help it."

"Well, tuck a napkin over yourself so we don't have to see it at the table."

The men come inside, and Burr holds a chair for Momma.

"Smells funny," Smiley says, climbing onto the seat beside Momma's.

"Did you wash up, boy?" Buddy examines the hands Smiley holds out. He nods. "Well enough."

I cringe when Burr sits at Mamaw's place.

Nandaddy is at the head of the table. "Would you honor us with the blessing today, Burr?"

"I'd be glad to."

We join hands, mine pressed in my grandfather's cool grip and the other nestled into Uncle Buddy's sweating palm.

"God is great and God is good, and we thank Him for this food. Amen."

"That's not a grace," Smiley says.

"Would you like to say one for us?" Burr says.

"Nope." Smiley scratches his head and Momma jerks his hand down. "But

I'da asked for a gun."

"What do you need a gun for?" Nandaddy spoons mashed potatoes onto his plate.

"Prowlers, Nandaddy." Smiley fans his eyelashes at his grandfather.

"Prowlers?"

"Yeah. Momma says we got prowlers. Need a gun to scare 'em off."

"I thought I heard someone at the door last night," Momma explains.

"Harlan said he saw a black man on Magazine Street two nights ago when he was out from the night shift." Nandaddy points his fork at Momma, his bulky hand attempting a delicate touch with the silver, but failing. "Didn't look like any of them that lives up on the hill."

Buddy stops his fork halfway to his mouth. "What was he doing?"

"It was after midnight. He must've been up to no good."

"Maybe he works at the mill. He could have been coming in for the shift after Harlan's." I'm thinking of Covey, but I won't utter his name.

Nandaddy butters a biscuit. "Harlan knows everybody on the payroll." He tears off a bite, his tongue catching a drip of butter. Talking around the bread, he adds, "Said he didn't know this fella."

Burr helps himself to a pork chop. The syrup stringing golden threads from the platter forces me to smile. He heaps potatoes next to the chops but declines the corn pudding. Momma passes around the biscuits.

"Doesn't sound like anyone from around here," Buddy says.

"Maybe he's kin to somebody in the African section," suggests Burr.

"If he gets seen by the wrong people, there'll be trouble," Nandaddy says.

"What kind of trouble?" Smiley asks.

I watch Burr cut into a pork chop and bring it to his mouth.

"I'll tell you," Buddy says, "more than once a man with brown skin pulled me from hellfire. They were some of the best soldiers I fought with overseas."

"I'd hate to see things get stirred up," Nandaddy looks seriously worried although I don't know what a prowler at our house has to do with him.

"Nobody knows if the person at our door was the stranger," I offer. "Someone may have been in trouble—a car broken down or a runaway." I've thought many times about vanishing, maybe to Penny Reardon's or Mrs. Davenport's. But if I'm going to run away, it ought to be far enough so that nobody will ever find me.

"Hey," Smiley says, "this is like candy." He's holding the pork chop in his fingers, gnawing on the bone.

Burr starts to chew then raises his eyebrows and picks up his water glass.

"How are the pork chops?" Momma asks.

He ducks his head. "They are—surprising."

Momma scowls at me.

"It's a fine dinner, just like Mamaw makes." Nandaddy gives me a wink.

"About this gun A.T. wants," Buddy says. "I've got one in mind."

"I'm not sure we should have a gun in the house, Buddy," Momma says.

"You either need a gun or someone to look out for you."

"Burr can look out for us." Smiley should shut his trap.

Nandaddy lays down his fork. "Well, Burr, what are your intentions?" He pushes against the table, straightens as if this is a question he's been waiting to ask.

"I ship out again soon," Burr says.

"Where are they sending you?" Buddy aims his fork at Burr.

"They don't tell us that, or how long we'll be aboard."

"Should be pretty calm out there now."

"Nevertheless—" Burr dabs his mouth with his napkin. "Being at sea puts a strain on a man—unless he has someone waiting for him when he gets home."

Nandaddy clears his throat. "Are you proposing something?"

"I've already proposed." Burr looks at Momma. "But she hasn't given me an answer."

"Why would a guy invite that kind of trouble?" Buddy winks to indicate he's joking.

"You have a beautiful daughter, Mr. Persinger." Burr shifts his eyes at Momma.

"Mug's a hard worker—strong as an ox."

"She's a fine woman," Burr says. "The finest I've ever known."

"That girl wants to marry you, she will. She says no and you might as well get back on that ship."

"I'm not shipping out unless I can slip a ring on her finger."

I bite into a piece of gristle.

"What do you children think?" Nandaddy looks from Smiley to me. I work the gristle between my front teeth.

"A.T., you want Burr to be your new pa?"

"I want him to move in tonight," Smiley says.

"Bobbie?"

I wish Nandaddy would call me Barbara or Marlene or another name I don't go by so I feel like someone else, someone not in the predicament of making a decision about whether Burr Burrows replaces my father. Daddy said when he started dating Momma, he took her to the movie *Morocco* starring Marlene Dietrich where she wore a man's tuxedo and sang in a nightclub. Androgynous was the word a movie magazine used to describe her. Daddy was so taken with the actress that he gave me the middle name Marlene. She once said, "I am at heart a gentleman." I suppose I am being called to answer Nandaddy like a gentleman.

I pinch the gristle and set it on my plate.

"The three of us are getting along just fine. Besides, if Buddy gives us that gun, I can look after us."

Buddy laughs. "With Bobbie around, I don't believe you all will have anything to worry about."

Everybody laughs. Everybody but me. I don't find his joke the least bit funny.

20
A Day for Killing

There's a saying that the bride will shed a tear for every raindrop that falls in the churchyard on her wedding day, so I'm not a bit surprised when the drizzle starts as Momma's repeating the vow to cherish, honor and obey. She's toasting her new husband with fruit punch in the basement of First Methodist Church when a downpour drenches the courtyard. As she dashes to Uncle Buddy's Packard, rain turns her blue suit the color of a bruise. Smiley and I ride with Buddy in the front seat, chauffeuring Momma and Burr in the back.

For the four days Momma and Burr are on their honeymoon in Washington, D.C., Smiley and I stay at my grandparents' house. I protested that we could stay in our own house and have Elsie look in on us, but Momma said we should try to be a help to Mamaw and tell her all about the wedding. Burr added that with the prowler on the loose, we shouldn't be staying alone. I think of asking Phoenix to move in with us, but she didn't come to the wedding so I figure she's crossed us out of her life.

I set up a fold-out cot for Smiley, and I take the single bed in the spare room. I have a hard time sleeping, thinking about Momma. Penny says marriage is about sex, but Momma has never mentioned sex except to say when Reverend Singer gets around to bringing it up, she'll be ready to tell me all about it. Until then, however, if it's not fit to be discussed at church, sexual activity will not be talked about in our house. My information comes from Penny and an encyclopedia she borrowed from her parents' bookcase. All it showed, though, was a diagram of a see-through woman with her inside parts labeled. The opposite picture was of a naked man who didn't look the least bit interested in what was inside her panties, which she wasn't wearing. If that's sex, I don't see what all the rumpus is about.

But just the same, after I hear Smiley's slow breathing, I creep a hand into my pajama bottoms to check around. It's too dark to see, even if I could gyrate myself around to look, so my fingertips become my eyes. Where my thighs meet, I can feel my pulse and the blood seems hotter than it does at my wrist or even at my temple. The vein rises and falls with a steady rhythm, but then a twitching begins, quickening as I press the flesh. The longer I keep my hand there, my fingers moving into the softness, the harder it is to stop. Sliding the pillow down, I stuff it between my knees and roll onto my stomach. I think of Covey's hand brushing mine and Uncle Buddy's cold metal pistol, his hand pressing apart my legs, my finger thrusting at the trigger—pushing, pushing, pushing. And suddenly the gun goes off. The detonation paralyzes me for half a minute, and then I drift down as if carried by a wide nylon parachute that floats me into the deepest sleep I can ever remember.

*　*　*

In the morning, fisted clouds punch blue sky over the hills from Lordsview Court. As usual, Nandaddy has gotten up at sunrise. I check on Mamaw, who's still sleeping, and then go out back to see if my grandfather is tending the animals. He has rigged a pyramid of poles under which a cauldron of water steams over a crackling fire. Covey adds wood to the fire and checks the steam rising straight into the quiet air. He doesn't acknowledge me. Of course not, I tell myself—he's working, saving up money for his education, no time for a moonstruck teenager.

Smiley comes out, rubbing his eyes. "What's going on?"

"It's a fine day for killing," Nandaddy yells. "'Bout time you all saw where your meat comes from."

A beam juts from the barn roof near the cauldron, and Buddy holds a rope that winds up through a winch attached to the beam. The other end is fastened to Bobo's hind leg. The rope is taut, but not tight enough to give Bobo a suspicion of what is about to happen. He sways side to side as if impatient but makes no attempt to get away.

Nandaddy, the twenty-two over his shoulder, marches to the sty like a soldier. Bobo stands at attention, watching him approach. The boar stretches out his neck, touches Nandaddy's knee with his snout, acknowledging, trusting. Across the yard, the cornfield sleeps, the trees stand waiting, and the chickens cease pecking in the yard, cock heads, twist nervous eyes in their sockets.

I press a hand flat at Smiley's back and hold it there. Covey comes over to us. I feel heat flush my cheeks as I remember thinking of him the night before.

"You ought to take the boy inside," he says. "It's cold out here. Anyway, he's not ready to see this."

Neither Momma nor Mamaw would have allowed Smiley to witness what's coming, but I know he won't be kept in the house now. He has experienced as much dying in the past few months as I have; he just hasn't taken it in. Maybe Bobo's slaughter is the best way to show him just how much dying is a part of living.

I wag my head. "We're staying put."

Nandaddy touches the rifle barrel to Bobo's lowered head. The bullet tears a hole in Bobo's skull and scatters dust in the dirt, sending him down onto his front legs just as his hind legs are rising into the air. Covey helps Buddy hoist the rope, hand over hand, and Buddy ties it off on the fencepost, hanging Bobo upside down by one leg.

When Buddy whisks the hunting knife out of the sheath on his belt, I see for an instant a German forest, a Nazi soldier lifted off his feet by the sleeve of a U.S. Army uniform, the flash of a blade across a shaved throat. He makes three giant steps to the hanging boar and cuts a vertical slit in the jugular. Maroon fluid spurts out, making a puddle at Buddy's feet. Bobo kicks with his free leg, running through air, his body jiggling with spasms. The metallic smell of blood cuts the cold air.

Buddy wipes the blade on a towel hanging from his waist and sheathes the knife again. He steps back and watches Bobo run from death, slowing down with each kick.

"Shouldn't take but two or three minutes," Covey says. He must have read that fact in his anatomy book.

Smiley buries his head in my jacket. I bend down and hold him, his face wedged against my neck.

"You're fine," I tell him gently. "You'll be fine."

Nandaddy starts humming "Up a Lazy River" as if it's a normal morning and he hasn't just taken the life of his prized hog. He pulls a thermometer out of the water and checks the temperature.

When Bobo ceases twitching, Buddy yells for Covey to loosen the rope from the fence post. Nandaddy buries a large hook in the boar's chin, and

Covey fastens the rope to the hook so that for a few seconds the boar hangs horizontal. Buddy unties the other end from Bobo's leg and holds it, bracing himself. Hooked by the chin, Bobo swings down, feet swaying over the cauldron.

"A.T.," Nandaddy calls, "you watch now. This here's the only time you'll see a hog get its ass washed before its face." He gives a belly laugh. Buddy lowers Bobo into the tub, water spilling out over the side.

"Bobbie, you get those candlesticks ready. And give one to your brother." He points at a box by the fence. Inside I find hollow steel balls cut in half with knobs atop them like biscuit cutters.

Covey helps me out. "They're for scraping the hair off."

Smiley shakes his head no.

"Let him be," Nandaddy says. "We'll save the second string for next year. Bobbie, you get over here and when I haul the pig out, be ready to scrape fast as you can, hear?"

Nandaddy pulls the rope as if he's ringing a church bell, and Bobo's head comes up. Covey starts in, dragging a candlestick across the forehead, over the ears, down the snout. I scrape the jowls and my side of the neck, and we keep abrading Bobo's skin as Buddy and Nandaddy inch him out of the tub. Buddy hikes him up and lays him over the edge, head on one side, tail on the other, and we work on his backside.

"You see the spot your grandfather shot the boar? That's the best place to stun him." Covey talks almost in a whisper as he works, studying the pig as if he's lecturing a class. "Lungs and heart are closer to the head than a deer's. A wild boar can run a quarter mile after taking a bullet to the heart, but you hit it here—" He touches the hog's muscular neck a couple inches below the ear. "You'll crack the spine and he'll drop in his tracks. You've got to finish him off, though." He tosses his head toward Nandaddy. "Your grandfather knows what he's doing."

I have no desire to shoot a wild boar, but Covey's baritone voice soothes the repugnance of what I've just witnessed.

In the February air, steam rises from the pig, skin pink as mine fresh from a hot bath. If I could choose a skin color, I'd pick Winona's—sweet toffee, toast. I'll never understand why white society hates such a beautiful hue.

The pig's plump flesh quivers and grows naked as we swipe metal across it.

"We woulda done this last week," Nandaddy says, "but there was a full moon. The hair don't come off good when the moon's full." He goes back to "the lazy, lazy river by the old mill stream," whistling this time.

I match Covey's rhythm as we scape the pig, and I pause to shake my arm when he does. Buddy hoists the pig again until it hangs free, and Nandaddy lights the blowtorch and goes over the skin, burning off the fine hairs. Buddy attaches a bar between the hind legs and lays the carcass back over the cauldron. Then he moves the hook from chin to bar and raises the boar upside down.

"Bobbie," says Nandaddy. "Get the washtub."

I retrieve the tub while Nandaddy works over the pig, cleaning out the ears, cutting off the tail, the feet, widening the slit in the neck. Covey takes the washtub from me, our eyes speaking different languages. Mine are magnets drawing him in. His reflect two worlds, neither to which he fully belongs.

Covey shifts his sights to my grandfather, who has stopped whistling. He's all business now, driving a knife into Bobo's chest and pulling it down hard all the way to the hole in his throat. Then he goes back and carves the belly upward, stopping between the legs. The entrails fall out into the tub, some dark purple, others a creamy color. The large intestines bulge with lumps of fecal matter, and the small intestines are webbed with small blue veins. When he cleans inside the carcass and hoses it out, I get a shiver of satisfaction at the gutting.

"Covey, I don't think my mother's up to pickling the feet—you can have 'em if you want," Buddy offers. "We'll use some of the intestines to make sausage, and you can take the rest."

Covey nods.

"Ellen, she likes the head cheese," Nandaddy says. "She picks the meat out of the cheeks and says it's the sweetest part of the pig." Mamaw hardly eats more than nibbles these days, and what she does manage to get down tortures her stomach. Nandaddy waves a hand at Covey. "You go ahead and take the head, too."

"If you don't want it," Covey says.

Smiley has been silent, but now he speaks up. "I want to go home." His cheeks are wet. I haven't realized he's been crying. Now he's looking at the pig, no longer Bobo who ruts in the mud behind his grandfather's house.

Nandaddy comes over to us, wiping his stained hands on his rubber apron. He whirls Smiley around and whisks him up into his arms. Smiley rears back and looks at him as if he's a stranger, searches his sagging chin, the top of his bald head, the nose just out of plumb, and burrows into him as if looking for something recognizable in his gentle grandfather.

"Your sister here's got a knack for slaughtering hogs," Nandaddy tells him. "Someday you can do it, too. Would you like that?"

Smiley moves his head from side to side. No, he would not like that.

What does it take to kill—a bullet, some rope, a knife? Panthers kill with fang and claw, soldiers with pistols, mills with explosions. Some kill in self-defense, some in the cause of freedom, some to eat. There are other ways to die, too—a disease that torments the body, cruelty, insult, a broken heart. But today a pig has died so two families can feed themselves. The taste of killing is in my mouth, and I find it good.

21
Moth to a Flame

On Monday morning when Buddy drives Smiley and me to school, it seems that the earth has rotated to a foreign realm. I have no map for where my life is headed. I'm no longer interested in Penny Reardon's stories about movie stars or even Kenny's teasing that I know is meant as flattery.

In class, I'm staring out the window when Mrs. Davenport calls on me to conjugate the verb "to lie."

"I'm sorry," I say. "What?"

"To lie," she repeats.

"I lied, I have lied," I recite.

Kenny chortles. Penny rolls her eyes. Mrs. Davenport forces a sigh.

"As in, lie down," she says.

I'm not stupid or I wouldn't be the best reader in the class.

"Today I lie," I start again. "Yesterday I lay. At other times I have laid."

"No, no," Mrs. Davenport says. "You have lain. You weren't listening, Bobbie."

"I guess not," I admit.

"See me after school," she says. Kenny snorts and I swear I'll lay into him at lunch, and that's no lie.

*   *   *

In the afternoon, the class is struggling through Shakespeare's *Much Ado About Nothing*. Mrs. Davenport says Shakespeare was being funny, but most of it goes over my head except the part about the notes Beatrice wrote to Benedick being paper bullets of the brain, which I consider a clever turn of phrase.

After school Mrs. Davenport asks me what's wrong, am I ill again?

I'd like to pour out my heart to her, but I say, "It's much ado about nothing." Mrs. Davenport smiles, but the truth of the matter is there isn't enough ado about a whole lot that's going on in my life. Mr. Shakespeare got it backwards.

* * *

That night, Burr is stretched out on the sofa, listening to a replay of Melody Ranch I have wanted to hear. Smiley is coloring in a book at the coffee table. Momma gives me a hug, but hugs won't convince me to accept Burr as a stepfather.

"How was Washington?" I ask. "Did you see President Truman?"

"No, we didn't get invited to the White House." Momma smiles at her joke. "But the monuments were all lit up, fancy people everywhere. I felt like a debutante."

"A what?" Smiley says.

Momma never used that word before and I figure Burr taught it to her. What else has she learned in four days?

"Set the table, honey." She hands me two candles. "And put these in the holders. Burr bought them just for dinner tonight." The yellow candles are each a foot long. "This will be our first supper as a family. It's cause for celebration."

My grandmother gave Momma the candleholders before the wedding. When her stomach ailment got worse, she started giving her possessions away—linen handkerchiefs to Nandaddy's sister, a china platter to the ladies' welcoming committee at church, and even a porcelain bowl to Covey for Aunt Regina. The silver candleholders belonged to her mother and are etched with a pretty scroll design. I hope to inherit them someday.

She starts setting out the food, and I get the wooden matches and light the candles. In midwinter it's dark by five o'clock, and Burr flips off the overhead light. The kitchen looks different by candlelight, like a fancy restaurant. Shadows dance on the walls like ghosts, and the wind moans outside. Smiley stares at a bead of wax dripping down a candle.

A moth wobbling on clumsy wings flaps its way to the light. It dips and rises, testing the heat but not getting too close. Smiley gets up on his knees and claps at it with cupped hands.

"Got him."

I peek into the cave of his palms and the moth twitches its antennae at me.

"How did he get in here?" Smiley presses an eye to his thumbs.

"He's been eating a hole in my wool sweater, I'll bet." I pout at the insect.

"He's fuzzy."

"Let me see." I squeeze my thumb and forefinger into Smiley's hands and pinch the moth's wings.

"What're you gonna do?"

"He's cold." I hold the moth over the candle. "I'll heat him up." Then I lower the insect toward the flame until its legs curl from the heat. The fire rises up blue around it, and its body fights to free its wings from my tight grip.

"Get rid of that filthy insect and wash your hands," Momma growls. "We're about to eat."

"Sister killed my bug," Smiley whines.

A burned moth smells like a scorched shirt. Is that what my father smelled like when he died?

"She helped kill Bobo, too." Smiley pokes my arm hard.

"Shut up, Smiley, or I'll kill you next." I'm ready for the flat of Momma's hand across my face, ready for a shaking, at least. What I'm not prepared for is the tenderness of her hands cradling my cheeks, turning my face up to hers.

"What in the world has come over you?"

I want to cry for joy at my mother recognizing that something has come over me. She's holding me with the candles flickering and her smelling of steak fried in Crisco, crispings scraped from the bottom of the pan for flavoring the gravy. I could bawl and wet her blouse with my tears, but she says, "Everything's going to be all right, I promise."

Why can't she see that nothing will ever be all right again?

I break from Momma and go to my room. Lying on the bed, I notice a crack I've never seen before in the flowered wallpaper near the ceiling. The pink roses must have distracted me from it before, but I study the line now, a thin ridge through three petals, meandering along a thorny stem. How deep is the fissure? Will the house snap in two with one hard stomp and send me tumbling into the foundation? I almost wish to be thrown into the underground—down, past the cellar, deep into mountain ledge and beyond, deeper than roots so that sound fades to a muffle then dull thud and finally a peaceful, deathly silence.

I don't know how long Burr has been standing in the doorway before I notice him. When I sit up, he thumbs over his shoulder at the table, then shields the side of his mouth as if he's telling me a secret.

"I hate those bugs, too." He lifts his brows, waiting for an answer. My stomach retorts with a rumble, and he swings his arm in front of him in an after-you-ma'am manner.

Burr is jovial at the table. "Your mother's a veritable chef. I want to savor the last of these home-cooked meals before I'm shipped off to finish my tour of duty."

"You going on the battleship?" Smiley has a look of adulation on his face I wish he'd wipe off.

Burr nods. "We'll be cruising around and testing those big guns."

Smiley wants to know when he's coming back.

"As soon as I can."

Momma says, "I'm going to New York this coming weekend to see Burr off."

"We'd like you to come with us, Bobbie," Burr says.

"Me?" Have I heard correctly?

"I don't want your mother to ride back alone on the train."

"I'll be fine," Momma says. "The train comes straight into town."

"Bobbie's never been to New York, have you?"

"I've never been much of anywhere." I'd rather not know it's Burr's idea that I go along. Instead, I make believe it's Momma who wants to spend time with me—two girls on a vacation together. We could amble through the park and window shop. I might even wear a dress.

"I'll go," Smiley says.

"Elsie wants you to stay with her," Momma says. "She'll be making fudge for the church bazaar, and she needs somebody to test it."

"Aw, hell," Smiley protests.

"A.T.—" Momma starts, but Burr stops her.

"It's fine," he says. And then to Smiley, "New York's a big city, boy. Not like hiking through the woods around here. Every concrete block looks like the next, and you might get lost."

"And we'd never find you again in all those people," Momma adds.

"Sister might get lost," he says.

The biggest city I've been to is Richmond when Daddy took us to the state fair. I'd never seen so many people at one time, and New York would make ten of Richmond. Wouldn't Momma's heart break if I disappeared in a crowd? The idea festers pleasantly as I watch yellow wax ooze down the silver candleholder and form a pus-like puddle on the tablecloth.

22
New York City

As the train rumbles toward New York, Burr rests his head on Momma's shoulder and dozes. I can smell the heavy spice of his hair tonic, and his lips make a popping sound with each exhalation. He finished off a bottle of whiskey before the train arrived, but Momma says he needed it to summon his courage for shipping out. I hope Momma knows what she's gotten herself into. I've seen her order a dress from the Sears catalogue that looked good on the model but once it came, it didn't fit the way she wanted. I'd have sent it back, but Momma took in a tuck, let out a seam, and held it all together with a belt. She makes the best of whatever we have, but I suspect she'll need to make major alterations to get Burr to fit.

Outside the window, lights blur by as we clatter down the tracks. Otherwise it's dark, and I'm getting sleepy myself. I lie back against the seat and for one split second before I drift off, I wish the head on Momma's shoulder belonged to Phoenix.

* * *

When I wake up, the sun is hovering low over the frozen cornfields of New Jersey, steaming with mist. It's late morning before the sun crowns Mud Mountain, but here it blinks through pine trees and then houses. A steward comes down the aisle with pastries, and Burr buys a cruller, two bear claws, and three cartons of orange juice. I finish my food while we rocket through a tunnel of tall office buildings.

The train rolls into Grand Central Station in the shadow of skyscrapers.

Daylight cuts through the concrete structures at angles, like knives slicing into the intersections. Momma packed one suitcase for both of us, and Burr carries it and his duffel onto Park Avenue, sets them down, lights a cigarette. Stubble has grown on his jaw during the night, which he'll have to shave off when we get to the hotel. His Navy uniform is crinkled from sleeping in it. Holding the cigarette between his lips, he grabs the bottom of the jacket and yanks it down. He takes off his white chief's hat and combs his hair with the fingers of one hand. Frowning at the smoke, he fastens the hat back on his head at a slight angle. In the uniform I can almost comprehend what Momma sees in him.

He crushes his cigarette on the sidewalk and picks up the bags. Momma takes my hand and I let her because I don't want to risk having her slip away. She threads her other arm through Burr's, and we saunter down the wide sidewalk three abreast as if we're in a parade.

Forty-Second Street is comprised of cement and stone piled as neat and straight as rectangular mountains thrusting miles into the sky.

"Don't look up," Burr says.

"Why not?" I ask, looking up.

"Yes, why not?" Momma echoes. "They're marvelous." Marvelous—another word I've never heard her use.

"People will think you're from the sticks."

I feel my face burn. Words like "sticks," "country," and "common" are terms for people who live in the back woods and who don't care about bettering themselves. I don't want to be thought of as one of those people. And so, much as I'm tempted, I will not look up again.

We wander down Madison Avenue, and Momma checks the shop windows for items that are beyond our reach—grosgrain hats and satin ribbons, sequined dresses and rhinestone earrings—or are they real diamonds? If we were with Phoenix, we'd go in and inquire about the price of a pair of snakeskin pumps. She would try them on and walk around the store, even if she wouldn't begin to have the money to pay for them. Phoenix would know how to talk to a salesman, and she wouldn't care if he thought she was country. She might even have a good laugh with him.

We pass a florist's shop where the sidewalk is strewn with rose petals that look like pink velvet in a shaft of sunlight.

"Look—a carpet of flowers."

"They're thrown out from yesterday," Burr says. "Don't make a big deal."

Nevertheless, I bend down and scoop two handfuls, tucking them into my pockets.

"Don't act like a street urchin." Burr swivels his head to see if anyone has noticed.

"Just picking up some souvenirs." It seems we embarrasses him no matter what we do. He's from the same place we're from—what makes him an authority on how to behave in the city?

He adjusts his hat lower and picks up his pace, pulling Momma behind him. I rub the petals with my fingers and when I lift my hand to my face, I bring the scent of roses.

*   *   *

"Let's get something to eat," Burr says.

We stop at a café. He pushes the bags against the wall beside his chair so he can keep a knee touching them, and the waitress brings three coffees and a whole pitcher of milk. Burr orders poached eggs on toast for himself and fried eggs with a side of scrapple for Momma and me.

The eggs come but they're overdone, a greasy crust around the edges, and the yolks are green, not like the deep orange of the fresh eggs we get at home. The scrapple is good, though, peppery on my tongue.

"Aren't you going to drink your coffee?" says Burr.

I've given up pretending to like coffee.

"No. You want it?"

He pours it into his cup. "You've got to be Rockefeller to let this stuff go to waste."

When we finish, he signals the waitress for the check. Outside, we walk east on Fortieth Street.

"Want to see Times Square?" Burr says.

"Yes." I am barely containing my excitement. "Let's see everything."

"What about the bags?" Momma asks.

"We'll take a taxi. Times Square is on the way to the hotel." He walks backwards a few steps and sticks out his arm into the street. A yellow taxicab stops, and Burr helps Momma and me in while the driver loads the bags into the trunk.

The taxi shoots down Forty-Second Street, "Straighten Up and Fly Right" thumping on the radio. The cabbie swerves through traffic, one hand on the steering wheel and snapping his fingers with the other. Outside, girls in bobby socks play hopscotch, teenagers roller-skate on sidewalks, and grown-ups hurry to who knows where. The taxi jerks and slows down in heavy traffic.

"Here it is," Burr says. "The Crossroads of the World. You should have seen the mobs of people when the war ended."

Busses and cars. Horns honking, engines gunning. Soldiers in uniform. Bond clothing store. Newsstands. People talking, laughing. The marquis for the Adelphi Theater announces Betty Condon starring in *On the Town* and at the Winter Garden Theater, June Havoc is on stage in *Mexican Hayride*.

"Look," Momma says. "Celeste Holm is here in New York City." She points to the marquis of the Shubert Theater where the actress is starring in *Bloomer Girl*.

Real movie stars. I might even see Celeste Holm strolling down the sidewalk or riding in a cab close by. Everybody seems important in New York. I wonder if people look at us and think we're somebody.

*   *   *

At the Franklin Hotel, Burr drops the luggage, unlocks the door to our room, and pushes it open. Then he whisks Momma up and across his arms as if she's as light as a kitten.

"Are you going to carry me every time we go over a threshold?" Momma is teasing him. I don't remember my father ever carrying her anywhere.

He laughs. "Just until I get used to having a wife."

I find the lavatory down the hall, fill the sink with hot water, rinse my face, my neck, my hands. I think of taking a bath, but New York is waiting, and two days will go by fast.

When I come back, Momma is lying with Burr on the double bed, intertwined with each other.

"It's ten o'clock in the morning," I grouse. "Are you two going to sleep away the weekend?"

Momma looks at Burr in an I-told-you-so way.

"I think she likes New York," he says, sheepish.

There isn't much to the hotel room—the bed, nightstands on either side, a desk with a wooden chair, two lamps. Heavy curtains border a window that looks out at a brick wall. A cot folded in a corner must be for me. I hadn't planned on sharing their room, but the way I see it, I don't have any choice.

* * *

Momma and Burr pry themselves out of bed and we wander into Greenwich Village. Burr buys a bag of popcorn and lets me feed the pigeons in Washington Square. We walk through Soho, Little Italy and Chinatown, neighborhoods flavored with smells of garlic, basil, ginger, and exotic scents that arouse in me a strange desire.

When we get hungry, Burr chooses a Chinese restaurant where see-through shrimp drift in tanks and flat fish eye me warily. Momma and I share a platter of fried rice because the portion is so large. We both eat with spoons in spite of Burr's apology to the Chinese waiter for our crudeness. At sidewalk markets, blue crabs piled in bushel baskets snap their claws next to bins of scaly chicken feet. I love the colors of Chinatown, red flags, green awnings, orange signs, streamers of green and yellow hanging from eaves. The Chinese sing their language in nasal tones, and it's hard to believe I'm in America.

We stand in line to take the elevator to the eightieth floor of the Empire State Building and climb the stairs to the top. From high up, the city looks like a postcard, yellow taxis crawling through the streets and Central Park a forest of skeleton trees. The chrome-topped Chrysler building points to the sky and boats almost too tiny to see leave comet-like wakes in the river. Massive steel ships wait at the docks, and to the south on a small island Lady Liberty stands alone, her torch raised.

I feel as if I can step off the balcony and float on the wind, my arms outstretched, lifting and soaring like the gulls that swoop over the harbor. I won't be Bobbie Grey anymore, but some winged creature flying above whatever cares harness people to the ground. A cold wind licks at the balcony, and Burr must sense I'm about to take the leap. He holds my coat sleeve as the sirens and the roar of the city fade to a purr.

Momma shivers. "I'm going inside and warm up."

We wander through the gift shop and Burr tells me to pick out a souvenir. I settle on a miniature Statue of Liberty with a pencil sharpener on the bottom which I'll give to Smiley so he won't be sore about being left behind.

We take the oily subway back to lower Manhattan and walk down West Broadway. Through the flood of shoppers, I spot a woman thin as bone staring from deep inside her skull. She's sitting on a rough board with small wheels like roller skates, and her legs end just above each knee. She's hunched in a blanket stained with some dark liquid and her head extends over a rusty cup, guarding its contents. I reach into my pocket.

"Don't," Burr says. "You give one of them money and they'll be crawling out of the woodwork with their hands out."

"But she looks like she's starving."

"Come on." Burr pushes us along, but I watch the woman over my shoulder until we round the corner and she's out of sight.

*   *   *

That evening we go back to the hotel and change into our best clothes. I wear the sweater Burr gave me, and Momma dons the blue suit she bought to marry him. Then we walk to the Café Rouge at the Hotel Pennsylvania with crystal chandeliers throwing light on the walls and flowers bursting out of giant urns. The waiter wears a tuxedo and bows when he presents the menus. Burr orders a bottle of champagne and steaks, medium rare for him, well done for Momma and me.

A band is playing, and Burr taps the table in time with the music.

"That's Charlie Spivak on the trumpet," he says, as if Charlie Spivak is someone we should know.

When the dinner comes, I pick up my knife and fork to dig in.

"Put that down," Burr says.

"But I'm hungry." I can't imagine what we're waiting for. Do New Yorkers say grace before a meal?

He nods at the waiter, who comes to the table and cuts Momma's meat into bite-sized pieces, then cubes mine the same way. Daddy used to cut up my meat when I was too young to use a knife. He'd saw the knife between the fork tines and leave dices of pork or beef on my plate, then he'd watch as I savored the first bite. I swore the way he cut it made the meat tender.

When the waiter leaves, I bite into the steak and it's delicious. I try not to fret about how much the bill will be for such a meal—steak, champagne, and who knows what else—but I've spent most of my life worrying about how much things cost.

"Can we afford all this?"

Burr lifts his champagne glass and sips from the wide lip, his elbow out. He sets it down before he answers. "A guy about to deploy deserves a decent meal."

"Not if it means sending us to the poorhouse." I look to Momma for consensus, but she's studying her plate, no doubt yet again regretting my presence.

"One topic people in Manhattan don't discuss is money," he says, an edge in his voice. "You just worry about tonight and let tomorrow take care of itself."

The meal, the train, the taxicab, the hotel—Burr must have spent a hundred dollars in just one day.

"What if you run out of money?" Momma asks, finally on my team. With the weather cooling down, Mr. Neddleton has started bringing coal for the stove again, and the grocery bills are higher now that the gardens have been turned under for winter.

"When I run out," Burr says, "we'll dip into yours."

Momma digs her fork into her baked potato. I know she's not about to open her pocketbook even for a swell time when we're scratching in the dirt as it is.

"Tell you what." Burr leans back and squeezes an arm around Momma. "I'll send you my paycheck every month, except for a little I'll keep for cigarettes and, you know, a drink now and then. You can be in charge of the money from now on. How does that sound?"

Momma clinks her glass to his. "That sounds like a deal."

I start to think about what we could buy with Burr's pay. A bigger place, maybe in Rosedale—even a car.

Charlie Spivak is blowing "Take the A Train" and when he starts in on "Moonlight in Vermont," I feel less like I'm from the sticks and more like I'm in a fairy tale and try to remember every detail to tell Penny Reardon when I get back to school.

*　*　*

That night I hear Momma groaning in her sleep. She sounds out of breath, as if a hoodlum is chasing her, so I do like Daddy did when I had a nightmare. He nudged me awake and said, "I'm here, Sister." Burr must be trying to wake her because he's tight against her back, rocking her, but I can tell by the light from the streetlamps that her eyes are squeezed shut.

"I'm here, Momma." I stroke her hair the way Daddy did mine.

"Aw, Bobbie," she says, out of breath.

"You were dreaming, Momma."

Burr rolls to the side and Momma turns over. "I told you this wouldn't work," she says.

"It's okay," Burr says. "You go run a bath and I'll join you."

Momma wraps herself in her robe and tiptoes down the hall. Burr raises up on an elbow.

"Your mother's just upset because I'm going to sea."

"I shouldn't have come." The realization that I interrupted their lovemaking mortifies me, and I want to melt into a puddle on the floor.

"Of course you should have come," Burr says. "You're part of the package."

"Momma didn't want me."

"Sure she did." Burr has gotten his boxers on and is wrapping a bathrobe around himself. "She's your mother."

I hope when Burr climbs into the tub with Momma, he'll think to remind her of that fact.

*　*　*

Sunday is our last day in New York before Momma and I see Burr off at the harbor Monday morning. He surprises us with tickets to an afternoon concert at Carnegie Hall. On stage, the grand piano shines like patent leather. Momma had piano lessons, but she never liked playing. She wanted ragtime and boogie-woogie, but her teacher assigned her to play hymns—"The Old Rugged Cross" and "Just a Closer Walk with Thee." She said she wouldn't make Smiley or me have to endure that agony.

I've never heard music like this. Chopin, Rachmaninoff, Mozart. Giant flower petals open behind my lids, pink and sticky—curly tulips, peonies. Vibrating fingers crawl up and down my body, and I quiver at the beauty of the sound.

When the music ends, people pick up coats and fold programs. No one seems changed by the notes that left frothy trails of delight down my spine. Did they not hear what I heard?

We come out to the smell of wet sidewalks and rubber raincoats. Rain is pouring down, splattering on the concrete in the same tempo as Mozart's music. Sheltered by the theater awning, we try to decide what to do. Momma suggests a taxicab, but all the yellow transports are occupied.

"There's a bar down the block," Burr declares.

He orders two whiskeys—a double for him—and a ginger ale for me. Momma and I go to the ladies' room to clean up. Her hair is sticking flat to her head, her mascara smudged, lipstick gone. She repaints her lips, rubs the black off her face, pinches her cheeks.

When we come back, Burr has finished his drink. Momma sips at hers and adds some of my ginger ale to her glass.

"It's my last night," Burr says. "Might as well have another. You two ready?"

"Not for me," Momma says. "But you go ahead."

So far by my reckoning, Burr has been a pretty decent husband. He helps out with the bills, and he's amenable to Momma's wishes. As a stepfather, he hasn't doted on either Smiley or me, and I appreciate his distance. That way I don't feel obligated to reciprocate.

After Burr signals the bartender for another drink, he says, "I think I'll stay up until the ship leaves just to keep you two in my sights."

"The chief would get all over us for bringing a sleepy sailor to the dock tomorrow. You'd better get a good night's rest to keep us out of trouble." Momma's cheeriness is not convincing. She doesn't act as happy as a new bride is supposed to. Even when she's with Phoenix, she holds back a piece of herself, as much as Phoenix tries to please her.

"To my family." Burr lifts up his glass. The rain is still coming down outside, and he orders beer chasers for his whiskeys. It's past suppertime, and Momma gets the bartender to bring us some hamburgers.

"You've got to eat something," Momma tells him. "You'll need your strength for tomorrow." He dilly-dallies with his hamburger and says the drink is filling him up.

At eight o'clock Momma says it's time to go.

"Don't be a ball and chain," he says.

I can tell Burr's comment is raising Momma's hackles.

"You've got an appointment in the morning." Her words have been raked over a whetstone, sharp and shiny.

"You don't like it here? Let's go. The band at El Morocco must just be warming up." He gets off the barstool, but his knees buckle. He grabs the bar and Momma helps him up.

"Let's go home," she says, meaning the hotel.

"I'm home wherever you are, beautiful." His lips are thick and the words slur.

Momma guides him outside. The rain has slowed to a drizzle, but she raises her arm to hail a cab, taking control. The situation needs to be set aright, and she will see that it is, drunken husband or not.

A taxi stops, and we push Burr in and scuttle in after him.

"What about El Morocco?" he says.

"We've got to get you into bed," Momma says.

"Driver," he mumbles, "the Elmo, 54th Street."

"No, driver." I take over. "To the Franklin Hotel, please."

"I'll be fine in a few minutes. You've got to see the Elmo. Cole Porter's playing." Then he starts snapping his fingers and singing. "You're the smile on the Mona Lisa. I'm a worthless check, a total wreck, a flop, But if, Baby, I'm the bottom, you're the top!"

"Which is it, lady," the cabbie says, "El Morocco or the Franklin?"

"The Franklin," Momma says. "Don't listen to my husband." She fumbles through his coat pockets for the room key.

"Listen," Burr says, hissing the word. "You're the top and I'm the bottom."

"I can't argue you with you there." The words are out of my mouth before I can stop them.

*   *   *

Momma and I drag Burr out of bed at daybreak and we walk to the harbor through a soggy mist, Burr between us. He smells of stale whiskey and staggers down the sidewalk as if it's afloat.

The mammoth ship looks like a metal she-dragon. The top, shaped like the tail of a huge airplane, seems distant through the haze. The American flag with its 48 stars and the U.S. Navy insignia flutters from its masts.

"Please be careful," Momma whispers to him.

"I'm in good hands." He taps her chin with his knuckle. "And so are you." He pats me on the shoulder.

Sailors are lugging their duffels across the gangway to the ship, their base for the next few months.

"You'd better get going," I advise. Cowboy Code number ten: The cowboy is a patriot. I'm not convinced the Code applies to Burr. He's neither a patriot nor a cowboy, and I'm glad to see him go. Even gladder to think of his paychecks coming to Pine Cliff with Momma's name on them.

*   *   *

We are waiting for the train when Momma checks in with me. "Did you have a good time?"

"Yes." I'm not lying. Even Burr's misbehavior didn't dim the bright glamor of the city. "Did you?"

She kisses my forehead. "Everything will be different from now on." She has said that before, but so far I don't see much difference.

"Different how?"

"Better, I mean."

Better than what—than having Phoenix around? Better than when Daddy was alive? The tide will never turn upward for me as long as I live in sooty old Pine Cliff. After seeing New York, I'm ready to leave it all behind.

When the train chugs in, I stick my hand in my pocket and touch Linda Stadler's crocheted change purse. When I draw it out, rose petals stick to my fingers for a brief instant and then flutter to the platform.

23

Mamaw

As the train hisses into the Pine Cliff station, Momma and I gather our bags and totter to the door of our rail car. Outside, a few passengers mill about like specters in the dust of morning. Momma swings the suitcase ahead of her and we step onto the platform.

The clock inside the station says six. We caught the crowded afternoon train and slept sitting up all night. Now I'm as drained as a gutter spout after a hard rain and just want to crawl into my own bed. Nandaddy is supposed to meet us at the station, but where is he? A man is lying on a wooden bench, his coat draped over him, hat covering his face. On the bench behind him, a couple whispers, their faces kissing close. A beefy woman in a wool coat clacks across the tile floor in fat-heeled shoes.

We walk out to the sidewalk and huddle against the station wall. Rope clangs against the flagpole. Morning has the tension of a cat before it springs. Daylight has not yet dispelled the cold wind that sucks at us, and I pull my coat collar around my neck. The smell of the mill is as rank as sewer gas. I half expected the business to shut down while we were gone, as if the whole town would cease to exist. But up Main Street, behind the courthouse and over the treetops, the mill's towers are belching their stink as they've done day and night since before I was born, through marriages and deaths, celebrations and sorrows, arrivals and partings.

In spite of the funk, I catch the faint aroma of fresh doughnuts from Blondell's Bakery a block down the street. The tan delivery truck waits out front, engine idling. Momma stirs the contents of her purse, brings out a cigarette and a matchbook with "Café Rouge" on the cover. She runs her thumb across the script and fingers the square edges. Then she drops the cigarette back into her purse. Nandaddy wouldn't like to see her smoking.

His Ford growls around the corner of Lexington Avenue, and I press the pebbles of sleep out of the corners of my eyes as we wait for him to stop. He glances at us and then looks back through the windshield. His elbow is resting on the window opening, and he rubs his forehead, his brimmed hat tilted back over his smooth pate.

"Hello, Dad," Momma says.

"Maggie. Bobbie." He's chewing on a cigar stub, twirling it with his tongue. It has gone out. He takes the butt from his lips and frowns at the dead end, then shoves it back in.

Something's wrong.

Momma pushes her suitcase into the back. Nandaddy picks at a tiny leather blister near the top of the steering wheel. He lifts his hat and scratches his head.

Then I know. My grandmother has been growing leaner every week, holding in the pain that wracks her gut, masking her agony with a thin smile.

"Where's Mamaw?" I ask, but I don't need an answer.

He yanks the cigar out of his mouth again, holds it with two gnarled fingers and rests his hand on the steering wheel.

"She's at Allegheny Hospital." He swipes at his nose with the back of his hand, bringing the cigar with it.

"Oh, no," Momma says. "How bad is she?"

He flicks the stub out the window. "Dern doctors won't tell me nothing."

"Take me there." Momma climbs in beside him. I get in the back with the suitcase and watch Nandaddy drive, one hand on the gearshift, one on the wheel.

*　*　*

The hospital smells of ether and disinfectant. We follow my grandfather down a tiled corridor, an empty stretcher alongside a wall. An old man with a growth of whiskers is slumped in a wheelchair. Nandaddy takes the left hallway, and I can hear Mamaw's groans before we reach her. She's lying covered with a sheet, her body shrunken and bony. She clenches both fists to her stomach.

"Mother, I'm here."

A demon has slipped through the pores of Mamaw's skin and left her bony and brittle. Her hand lifts to find her daughter's.

"Marguerite," she says. "Thank the Dear Lord."

Nandaddy stands near the door.

"Lawrence, get that nice nurse to bring me some medicine," Mamaw says. Nandaddy leaves with quiet steps.

"You're going to be fine." Momma tries to hide her distress. Her mother is dying.

Mamaw tries to lick her lips, but her thick tongue sticks to the dry membrane. She coughs, lets go Momma's hand, dabs at a corner of her mouth with her forefinger, turns her head and coughs again. The hand becomes a fist and joins the other at her stomach again.

A nurse comes in with a tray. "Need something to help, Mrs. Persinger?"

"Oh, sweet Jesus, yes."

The nurse gives her a shot, and her fists uncurl, but the palms still press her stomach.

"Look at me," Mamaw says weakly. "I haven't even said hello to my granddaughter."

I kiss her on the cheek, cool and soft as the spathe of a calla lily.

"How was your time in New York?" Mamaw struggles to talk. Even in her final hours, she's selfless. Her thoughtfulness humbles me.

"Fine," Momma says. "But I wouldn't have gone if I'd known how bad you felt. Burr wouldn't have let me."

"Don't you worry about me." She pats Momma's hand.

I watch the creases in her forehead relax and her lips curve into a slow smile.

"I need to sleep now. You tell A.T. Mamaw loves him." The soft wheezing of her breath tells that, for the moment, the demon has loosened its hold.

* * *

In the corridor Nandaddy is sitting on a bench examining the linoleum, his coat over one knee.

"Dad?" Momma says, but he doesn't react. He's watching the tan specks on a black background, like splattered paint.

"Dad, why don't we stay with you while Mother's in the hospital? Bobbie and I can keep the house up and make sure you and Buddy get some food into you."

"You'd just be underfoot," he says. "We've got too much work to be worrying about you all."

I'm glad he doesn't want us around. It seems like forever since I've been home. I even miss Smiley.

"Besides—" He gets up and slumps into his coat. "I'd best get used to doing for myself."

*   *   *

When Momma isn't at work, she's at her mother's bedside. I tend to Smiley's needs and after he's asleep, I drown myself in *The Great Gatsby*. Now that I've seen glitz and glamor, I can appreciate Nick Carraway's fascination with Gatsby's lush lifestyle. There are drawbacks to big parties and fancy cars, I'm sure, and I'm hoping the future won't be an either-or for me. I'd like to land smack dab between the doldrums of Pine Cliff and the pizzazz of West Egg.

When I'm about to wither from loneliness, I think about whom I could have a conversation with. It's too late to call Penny. Then the phone is in my hand and I'm telling the operator to connect me with Dr. Goode's residence in Rosedale. Even though she's working the evening shift, I hope I'll be lucky and catch Phoenix on a night off.

I hear the ring—once, twice, and a woman answers.

The sound of her voice causes a flood, and Daddy and Bobo and Covey's glove-pummeled face and Mamaw and the New York City lady with no legs all come gushing out. I must be babbling because I hear her say, "Sister?" and when I don't know how to answer, she says, "I'll be right over."

By the time Phoenix walks in, I've pulled myself together. She stops and holds out her arms as if she wants me to melt into them, which I'd like to do. I take step toward her and even though every nerve in my body needs to be held, I force myself to point to the bag she's holding.

"What've you got there?"

"Oh—ginger ale for you and Archer Timbers. Cures all ills." She sounds disappointed or uneasy, I'm not sure which. The circumstances have changed, and we both know it.

I pour us glasses of ginger ale and tell her about the Empire State Building and Carnegie Hall. She regales me about how she's operating the crane now, hefting spools of paper and lining them up atop each other like packed skyscrapers. I explain about Burr going off on the big ship, and she says, "Good riddance." I don't mention the wedding or Momma's blue suit getting all wet or the noises they made in the night. The situation is hard for Phoenix as it is.

*   *   *

Phoenix makes arrangements to switch shifts with Momma so she can sit with my grandmother during the day. Phoenix will stay with us at night. Momma tells her she's grateful and it will only be until Mamaw gets well. Which we all know will be never.

Phoenix helps herself to the empty hangers in Momma's closet and rearranges Momma's underclothes to make a drawer for her own. I could have taken care of myself—and Smiley, too. If the house were to catch fire, wouldn't I wake up and get us out? The prowler might come back, Momma says, but we haven't heard anyone outside since the incident. Nevertheless, I'm thankful to have Phoenix back.

Every night after Momma goes for a nap before her ten o'clock shift, I lie awake, listening to Phoenix in the kitchen, knife tapping the counter as it slices through bread, waxed paper rattling when she folds it around the sandwiches, one each for Momma, Smiley, and me. A ham or chicken sandwich, raw carrot sticks, a boiled egg and a pickle. She usually packs a treat, too—something she makes in those evening hours as a surprise for us. One week it's oatmeal cookies, another week chocolate fudge. I'm glad to have her care about us. If it weren't for Phoenix, I don't think anyone would give a thought about me.

It's strange, though, getting used to another person's habits. Phoenix plants seeds in paper cups of dirt and balances them on the windowsills. Getting ready for a spring garden, she says. She clips pictures from wildflower catalogues and arranges them on the table—planning a flowerbed. She likes cheese in her grits and Tabasco on her eggs.

One night I wake up when I hear a deep laugh. Outside the window is a blur of stars, and I'm not sure if I'm dreaming. My eyes adjust to the dark, and I pull the covers around me. A lamp is on in the living room, and long legs stretch out from the sofa.

I slide out from the covers to see what's going on. When I make my way to them, Phoenix stands up, Covey behind her. Now I know I'm dreaming.

"Momma gone to work?"

"Uh-huh," Phoenix says.

"Is that you, Covey?" I don't mean for it to sound like an accusation. Covey has never been in our house before—at least, not that I know of.

"Just came by for a talk," he says.

If he's come on some business, I can't think what it would be.

"It's late." Covey gets on his coat. "I'll be going." He has the same look in his eye that I saw when he boxed with Aubrey Hicks—desperate, as if he's not sure whether to fight or run.

"I'll see you," Phoenix says to him.

"You take care, Bobbie." He lays his hand on my shoulder before he shuts the door quietly after him.

*   *   *

At breakfast I corral Phoenix in the kitchen.

"What was Covey doing here last night?"

"We had some business to talk over," Phoenix says.

"You mean mill business?"

"How do you want your eggs this morning?"

Why is she avoiding my question? Is she sweet on Covey? I've had to bear so much—I couldn't bear that.

"Tell me what's going on."

Phoenix sighs. "Sister, there are some things you don't understand just yet. Let's just leave it that Covey and I had some matters to attend to. Believe me when I say that there's not a speck of romance between us." She sets a plate of toast and eggs on the table. The eggs are over easy, just the way I like them.

*   *   *

I've missed seeing Winona. She has a seriousness about her—earnest, Daddy would have said—that makes her more interesting than Penny Reardon. Winona doesn't care about movie stars or fashion designs. Prodigies care about important issues.

One afternoon I wander up the hill thinking I'll see her on her way from the settlement school. It's March and cold is stubborn to retreat, even though the worst of winter is over. The air carries the smell of pine and early spring mud. The mill doesn't reek so bad up on the hill, and the soot blows the other direction.

At the crisp white church, I stop. In the summertime when the windows are open, the singing of the congregation drifts down to our house. Winona said at noon they take a dinner break, start up again around three, and sing their way to evening supper.

I pass Gloria's Store where dark-skinned men gather to read newspapers and drink coffee and women buy groceries and fabric. The streets in Winona's neighborhood are packed dirt, softer under my shoes than the concrete sidewalks of downtown.

I make a point of getting home just before Phoenix comes in from work and Momma gets back from the hospital. On days I trek up to the African settlement, I make quick suppers—fried meat, boiled potatoes and slices of bread heated in the oven instead of fresh biscuits. Momma never knows the difference. Anyway, she's busy reading the latest letter from Burr, tapped out on his typewriter. She studies it until I call her for supper, and she comes to the table bubbling with news about what book Burr is reading, *Wuthering Heights* one week, *How Green Was My Valley* the next. Smiley is instructed to be a good boy, and I'm to help Momma around the house—as if I'm no help. I'm doing more than my fair share.

I hike almost to Winona's road one afternoon and then stop and look across the valley at the mountains. Filmy clouds float like silk scarves above the crests. I pretend the mountains are the skyscrapers of Manhattan, pretend for a minute I'm lost in a maze of buildings, on my own in that exhilarating place. I could hail a taxi and tell the driver to take me to Radio City Music Hall and try out to be a Rockette. Daddy said I have a dancer's legs. But here I am in this backwoods town where everything is either uphill or downhill, the black section or the white section, downtown or neighborhoods, and a long way from Radio City. If a Rockette had ever crossed the town line into Pine Cliff, she would create a buzz and get her photo in the *Messenger*. Aside from rumors of a prowler, our biggest excitement is burning ticks and running across an occasional poisonous snake.

Winona whizzes by me on her bicycle, startling me out of my contemplation.

"Hey," she says, and I echo. Her pigtails flap under a knit hat.

"Are you up here spying on us?" she asks.

"Just taking a walk. Anything wrong with that?"

"You were coming to see me, weren't you?"

"Maybe."

"Well, come on, then."

*   *   *

Aunt Regina makes us cups of hot cocoa and gives us each a gingerbread cookie. Covey closes a book he's been studying and says he'd better get ready for work so he won't be late. When I try to get back into his good graces and apologize for speaking harshly to him the other night, he interrupts.

"I'll be back usual time," he tells Regina but he never says a word to me, which wounds my heart.

Winona shows me the history project she's making, a relief map. She says it's the country of Ghana, where her ancestors are from. She has drawn an outline on a board and piled on paste, making mounds to represent mountains and a crooked groove which she says will be a huge lake she'll paint blue. Below the map will be a gulf, which is almost like the ocean. She has to label the towns, and she says I can come back and help her if I want. I believe Ghana is somewhere in Africa and I pretend to know where, reminding myself to look it up when I get to school.

I've forgotten all about the time until Regina tells me that I should get started if I want to be home before dark. Running down the hill, I stumble on rocks and try not to think of panthers lurking in the woods beside the road. It's dusky and lights are shining through the windows of our house. I know Momma will be there mad as a wet hornet.

I find her waiting with her coat over her arm.

"Phoenix is working my shift tonight, so you've got to stay with A.T." She doesn't scold or even ask where I've been.

"What's wrong?" I know Mamaw is worse because she doesn't answer me.

"Buddy's on his way to get me," she says, putting on the coat.

"You haven't had anything to eat."

"I'll get something at the hospital cafeteria."

After Momma leaves, I heat up leftovers for supper. I try to play a game of Old Maid with Smiley, but I can't help thinking about Mamaw. At eight o'clock, I get him to bed, but I decide to wait up for Momma. She might need someone to talk to.

At ten-thirty Momma still hasn't returned. I figure visiting hours are over, but I know in dire cases they let close relatives stay as long as they want. I try to stay awake, listening for Phoenix or Momma to jangle the door.

I must have fallen asleep hard because I never heard Phoenix come in. She has made a pot of coffee and some grits. She fixes an egg sandwich for Momma and wraps it in double paper to keep it hot, pours coffee into a thermos, and tells Smiley and me to get our clothes on because she's taking us to see our grandmother.

* * *

Momma looks as if she hasn't slept all night. She has circles under her eyes, and her hair has lost its luster. Phoenix gives her the sandwich, but she discards it on the windowsill. She seems grateful for the coffee, though, and drinks it from the thermos cap.

On the stand by Mamaw's hospital cot, someone has placed a picture of Nandaddy and her when they were young, when Mamaw's hair was dark and Nandaddy still had some, blond and wispy. There are two other pictures, one of Uncle Buddy in his uniform and another of Momma holding a baby—I'm not sure if it's Smiley or me. The shades in the room have been drawn and in the dim light Mamaw's complexion appears yellow. Her hair, always clean and fresh smelling, is a dingy halo about her hollow face. She looks as if her skin is holding her skeleton together. Mamaw was always pretty. She kept her hair in a neat bun and never wore makeup that I can remember. Now her eyes are clouded over and her lips sag open. She exerts what seems to take all her strength to close them. Every breath is a heavy weight she struggles to lift.

"Hello Mamaw." I keep my voice low so as not to startle her. Her eyes rotate toward me, but her head stays in place, as if the bones in her neck have fused into one piece. She squeezes my hand. Skinny as she is, Mamaw's knuckles are swollen. Not the fingers, narrow as bird legs between the joints. The knuckles are like knots in thick string. A ring slips around her finger, too loose to leave a mark. It's gold with a topaz stone cut into a heart shape. It's probably been years since she's taken the ring off, not since the knuckle has grown into a hard gnarl of twisted ridges. Decades of skinning meat, shucking corn and churning cream to butter have grown those knuckles large. After Nandaddy married her, when her hands were smooth and slender, she might have taken off the ring to reach inside a plucked chicken, grab hold of its gizzard and tear out the heart and lungs. I imagine she removed the ring and looped it over a nail by the kitchen sink. Did she remember the night my grandfather gave it to her, offering the box without ceremony, without speech or song or words of love? What must she have thought before she unfastened the satin cube? How must her pulse have skipped when she saw the golden ring and slipped it on her finger?

I hold her hand and rub the stone with my thumb, cut edges worn smooth. I believe I'm special to my grandmother, as if we have an unbreakable bond between us. Nothing seems so important to her as spending time with me, asking how school was, letting me help in the kitchen. Her love is different from anything I've felt from Momma or Daddy. It's like the love Reverend Singer talks about in church, always present and never demanding anything in return. It doesn't depend on my being well behaved or on loving her back. I know she was glad to have a grandson, but being her first grandchild, I trust that I'm her favorite.

Mamaw's lips work up and down and a rasping sound comes from her throat.

"I believe she's trying to tell you something," Momma says.

I lean close enough to smell her breath, like damp soil, and her fingers grip my hand and tighten. Her tongue threatens to fly from her, and her body jerks like a tethered falcon straining to take flight. Then a wail rises from her.

"Do you see him?" she says. "It's Jesus. Do you see his wavy hair? He's glowing."

She lets go my hand and reaches for the end of the bed.

"I can't feel my feet. Jesus is holding my feet. Take my hand, Jesus, and help me up. Lift me, please, Jesus. I can't stand this pain anymore."

"Phoenix, take the children downstairs," Momma says. Phoenix starts out with Smiley, but I don't move. Momma needs me and I have no intention of leaving.

The sheet is damp at Mamaw's stomach where the cancer has eaten through from her insides, and she smells like meat left too long in the icebox. She's rotting, and she isn't even dead yet.

"It will take her days to die like this," Momma whispers.

"Make them do something, give her something."

Momma brings her mother's fingers to her lips, but Mamaw's agony makes her strong and she reaches again for Jesus.

A nurse comes in, bringing the smell of alcohol, sharp as pins. She leans her weight over Mamaw's writhing body and pries a wooden paddle into her mouth.

"You don't need to do that." Momma is tense and hostile, protective of her mother.

"She'll swallow her tongue unless we hold it down." The nurse's hips are on the bed, and she's holding both Mamaw's hands in one of her own and directing the paddle with the other. "You'll have to leave now," she says.

"Let me speak with my mother for a few more minutes," Momma says.

"Look at her," the nurse snaps. "Does she look like she's in any condition to have a conversation with you?"

A second nurse comes in carrying a syringe pointed upward like a loaded pistol. She nudges Momma aside with her shoulder and punctures the crease of Mamaw's elbow with the needle. Within a minute or two Mamaw relaxes, and a placid look comes over her face, as if the beast that has been wreaking havoc with her has called a temporary truce.

"She'll be out for a while," the second nurse says. "You may as well go and get some rest."

"I'm going to stay a while longer," Momma says.

When the nurses leave, Momma says, "You go find A.T. and Phoenix, Sister. And make sure the door is closed when you go out."

"I'll stay," I insist.

"Go now." She sounds angry, and I turn to leave rather than upset her. Then she adds in a sad voice, "I'll be with you all in a few minutes."

I pull the door not quite shut and stand in the hallway so I can watch without Momma seeing me. She looks like a boulder teetering at the top of a hill, about to break loose. Then she starts rolling down, bending toward Mamaw, cradling her head with a palm as if she were a baby. She brushes a wisp of hair from her cheek and kisses her limp lips. Taking the extra pillow, she hugs it to her chest for a second. I should dash in and stop what she is about to do or call for the nurse, but Momma's face has such a sweet smile on it that I don't move. She leans in, lets gravity take the white puff of pillow to Mamaw's face, and presses her weight on it. I see her lips form the words, "Goodbye, Mother. I love you." Her own face is lit with love, and she is acting with love, and love flutters around her like weightless feathers, swirling in eddies, lifting and drifting and settling on Mamaw so she glistens like fresh snow in sunlight.

In the corridor's bright, clean light, the nurses go about their business while Momma stands by her own mother whom she has just sent off to be with Jesus. The alcohol smell slices into my stomach and I'm cold and shaking as if I have a fever.

Momma comes out of the hospital room looking as if part of her own spirit has left her. At the main desk, the nurse gets something from a drawer and dangles a golden chain into Momma's cupped hand.

"It would have choked her," she says. In Momma's fingers is the necklace Nandaddy gave Mamaw for Christmas. Then Momma closes her fist around the locket.

As we leave to find Smiley and Phoenix, I think about Mamaw's spirit. What is a spirit anyway? A thing that comes with the body when we're born and grows inside us. And when we stop growing, it keeps on, scrunching up inside and getting wiser as we grow older until it cracks out as a chick outgrows the shell and flies off—to be with Jesus or to cheer on spring flowers and be midwives to wild things.

When we reach the cafeteria, Smiley is sitting at a table eating cinnamon toast. Phoenix brings me a soda pop and a plate of French fries. I drizzle on vinegar from a shaker bottle. Momma sips at coffee and watches people carry trays of food to tables.

"When is Mamaw going to leave the hospital?" Smiley asks.

Momma twists her cup on the saucer.

"Angels have come for Mamaw," I tell him. Momma snipped the tether, and my grandmother has risen winged and free. "They've taken her to heaven, Smiley."

* * *

When we walk out to Phoenix's car, Smiley grows teary and Momma lifts him, although he's too big, and arches her back with the weight. She's strong— strong enough to take the frail life from a sick woman. She says I have my head in the clouds just like my father, but she sees what's on the ground, what needs to be done and how to get it done. I admire that about her. And I admire how she has chosen to do something about somebody else's suffering besides her own.

24
Paper Bullets

While Phoenix sorts through pinto beans for stones and scores a slab of suet to flavor them, Momma rereads Burr's latest letter. She wrote him about Mamaw dying, and he wrote back that if she contacts his commander saying she needs him, they might consider it a hardship, her with two children and no husband around. We don't have any hardship. Phoenix helps out with groceries and taking over the cooking, and Mr. Neddleton has slowed his coal deliveries to once a week because spring is around the corner. I can smell the earth working its way back to life. We're getting along very well without Burr's presence.

The beans need an hour to cook, so I take Smiley outside. The yard is muddy and either we'll get dirty and track mud into Momma's clean house or risk irritating her by playing in the street when she's told us a thousand times not to.

He tosses me the football Phoenix gave him. I hike it to him between my legs the way I've seen them do it at practices on the high school field. Then I go from center to tackle and chase him up the road. I catch him, of course, and grab him around the waist. He goes down with a thunk, and I hear silence for a minute—not even a wheeze from him. And then he squirms free and the football wobbles across the street. When he turns around, he's moving his mouth in a funny way. Then his wailing starts, blood spurting and coming and coming. I lift him and set him on the curb.

"Let me see." When I stick my finger into his mouth, I feel a gap in his tongue where he must have bitten it when he fell. I think of Bobo's slit neck and wonder if Smiley will bleed to death.

Phoenix and Momma fly out of the house. At that very moment I wish I were up on the hill at Winona's or at my desk in Mrs. Davenport's class memorizing the Mayflower Compact. I want to transport myself to Nandaddy's house or Buddy's secret shooting place, anywhere but here with Momma yelling at me for letting Smiley get hurt, not to mention playing in the road when I should have known better.

Phoenix has him up in her arms and he's bawling and bleeding all over her shirt, and Momma wads a cloth into his mouth.

"What were you thinking, Sister?" she yells. I can take her yelling—it's her disappointment that cuts through me like broken glass.

Elsie brings a towel and says she'll drive them to the hospital. Momma takes Smiley from Phoenix.

"Too bad Burr's not here," Phoenix says. "He's missing all the fun." Then they drive off to Allegheny Hospital with Smiley, leaving me standing in the road.

Inside, Phoenix must have been in the process of making up a skillet of cornbread to go with the beans. She has cornmeal in a bowl and eggs on the counter. An onion is peeled and ready for chopping. I love a bowl of beans in their own rich gravy, the crunch of onion and the grainy taste of cornbread to soak up the juice. I stand over the pot and breathe in the steam, worrying that they'll amputate Smiley's tongue or at least he'll lose his sense of taste. He's never minded much about eating anyway.

I turn off the burner under the kettle and put the eggs back in the icebox. Then I drift into Momma's room, looking for something to take my mind off Smiley, wanting to get close to Momma. I pull out the drawer where she keeps Burr's letters. She read us some of them, but she stopped when she got to certain parts. Her eyes would keep moving and she'd smile and blush and Smiley would say, "What's he saying?" And she'd say "Oh, nothing important" and get up and go lie down on the bed.

The envelopes are typed to Marguerite Burrows. Am I Bobbie Burrows now? Or still Bobbie Grey? I like the name Grey. It's neither black nor white, neither day nor night, the time in the early morning before the sun's rays bend over the earth. A quiet color. A cool color. The color of forgetting.

I lift up the pile of letters and settle on the edge of Momma's bed. On her side table are scissors, a button, a candy in its wrapper, a folded handkerchief. Which items are Momma's and which Burr's? Or does every item now belong to both of them? I open one of the envelopes and take out the letter typed on onionskin so thin I can see my hand through it. When I run my fingertip on

the back, I feel bumpy pinprick holes the period key has made. Then I read.

We set out this morning in the fog and I was in a fog or I'd never have crossed that gangplank and left you standing on the pier. It's late now, and you must be in bed. I'm jealous of the pillow that breathes the scent of your hair. I'm jealous of the bedsprings that feel your weight above them. I'm jealous of the sheet that rests on the rise of your breast.

The letter makes me creepy but I open another.

On the street, at the kitchen sink, while you sleep, I'm watching you.

My after-school milk films on my teeth and I have an urge to brush them. I read the second letter again. "I'm watching you." I watch Momma all the time—ironing, mending, dancing to Cole Porter's music, one hand at her stomach, the other up like the pledge of allegiance, eyebrows drawn up as if her belly hurts. Once she danced with me, wrapped my hand around her waist and held my left one out, twirling me around and laughing. I laughed, too, and then Smiley complained, wanting attention. Momma can never refuse Smiley, his silvery hair and blueberry colored eyes.

What is it that draws Momma to Burr? The letters—paper bullets—might offer a clue.

Now that I'm at sea, I haven't had a drink for two weeks. There's none to be had when we're at sea, and I'm mending my wicked ways.

Honey, last night I dreamed that we had a baby girl. What I wouldn't give to have a daughter, one of our own—a girl who looks just like her mother.

They replaced Daddy, and now they're looking to replace me. I hope Burr's ship sinks and he's stranded on some Pacific island. I hope he'll never get his hands on Momma again.

I fold the letters and settle them back into the drawer. Outside it's dusky, and a car drives by with its headlights on. It will be dark in less than an hour. If I hurry, there might be enough light to find my way up to Winona's house.

25
The Klan

Over the mountains the sky is layered in pink and blue. Sun hits the top of Oliver Mountain and then rests in the notch of two hills, falling slow—a lazy late winter sun. The cows in the lower meadow lie down in a clump. The river shines pewter, trees on Fore and Lick Mountains scarlet with cold, sap blood pumping with spring readiness. Far down the road, the town streetlights blink on and burn dimly.

Within a few minutes I cross the invisible line that divides the white neighborhood from the black. A broken plow frame rusts in the meadow of chopped cornstalks. A hen roost of unpainted pine, a crusty pile of horse manure in the road. On the porch of one house, a spindle-back chair, a broom, bristles worn to a slant. The houses here are square and stand shadowless and reverent in the dusk. Someone has neglected to bring in the laundry. Sheets hang straight as walls, a pair of dungarees, men's shirts pinned at the tails, arms hanging as if in upside down surrender. Even in winter if you leave clothes out after dusk, they'll stay damp and be prone to mildew. I resist the impulse to unclip them from their clothespins and leave them folded on the chair. Instead, I hurry by the bodiless forms.

Covey's dog yaps a greeting and someone tucks back a curtain and looks out. I'm hungry and hope Regina has something on the stove. Then it occurs to me that she might think I'm a burglar and I pray to all that's holy she doesn't have a gun.

There are no streetlights and no moon. Just a dim sliver of light comes from behind the curtain. I'm cold and want to go inside, want Regina's arms

around me, want to lay my head between her breasts and have her pat my back and say, "Poor child."

Just as I'm about to sink like a stone in frigid water, I'm inside and Regina is rocking me and smelling of rosemary. My body is heaving with sobs and so she rocks and rocks and sings, sweet and rumbly, "You be all right, child. Everything be all right."

*　*　*

Ironically, Regina feeds me the same dinner Phoenix had been making—cornbread and beans, except her cornbread is sweet and the beans are spicy with chunks of tender meat. Covey adds wood to the stove and places a seat beside it, and I'm warming from the beans, the fire, or Covey's presence. He seems unsettled tonight, not singing and joking the way he did on New Year's Eve. He paces, looks out the window, and paces some more. The dog is restless, too, yapping in a slow rhythm with a howling refrain.

"What's gotten into Franklin?" Winona asks.

Regina shakes her head. "I've had this feeling before."

She senses it, too—some sort of trouble in the air.

Covey fixes himself at the window, staring through the curtain fabric. "Phoenix warned me," he mumbles.

Regina sprinkles clothes for ironing, and Winona works at a skirt hem with a needle. I chew my thumb cuticle and listen to Franklin's warnings.

That's why Covey was at our place. But what was Phoenix warning him about?

It's not long before a car engine growls in the distance and guns up the hill. Covey makes fists at his sides.

"That's Elsie's car." I recognize its raspy hum. But Elsie wouldn't come up here.

Covey holds the door for Phoenix.

"Thought you'd be here," she says, looking at me.

"The boy okay?" Covey asks.

She hugs Regina and says, "Archer Timbers is fine, but he won't be eating hot dogs anytime soon."

"Maggie will spoil him on milkshakes, knowing her," Covey says.

"Nothing wrong with spoiling a child," Regina says.

Phoenix rubs her hands above the stove. "Sister, we should get down into town. I've got to get Elsie's car back to her. Regina, I think you all should come, too. You can stay at my house tonight."

"What's going on?" If Phoenix wants to take them all to Rosedale, what's about to happen is going to be trouble.

"They're after that prowler," Phoenix says. "Don't anybody know who he is, but every white man in town suspects it's a black man. How they can tell that in the dark is a mystery."

"It wasn't any black man," Covey says.

"Well, it doesn't make a difference, does it? They're bound and determined to teach somebody a lesson, and I hear tell your name won the lottery."

"Covey," Regina says, "you go on with Phoenix. They won't bother about Winona and me."

"I'm not leaving this house."

"Well, then." Phoenix pulls up another chair by the stove. "You got any supper left, Regina? We may be in for a long night."

Covey wouldn't steal, not as hard as he works. He's a lot of things—mill worker, boxer, farmhand—but not a thief.

He stands at the window again and Franklin resumes his barking.

"You know what today is?" He hasn't turned around, and I'm not sure whom he's asking.

"What day is it?" I say.

"It's the day his father—" Phoenix blinks at Winona and changes her tone. "The day his father died."

I remember Nandaddy saying Covey's father was a fine gentleman and didn't deserve what happened to him.

"It must be—what, eighteen years ago now?" Regina says.

I've heard the story—he fell off the Jackson River bridge. But the bridge has railings. Seems hard to have an accident like that, even if he'd been drinking. Some say he jumped, but with a wife and son to care for, Mr. Fortune had no reason.

"What do you reckon happened?" I ask.

Covey rubs his head. "He was dead before he ever hit the water."

"Nobody was charged." Phoenix holds a bowl of beans up to her chin and shovels it in.

"Courts don't protect a black man anyway." Covey speaks to the window, words that seep out through the glass and blow away with the wind.

Phoenix's spoon tinks against her plate, the fire crackles, and Franklin's slow howls come through the window.

"Bobbie," Regina says, "you and Winona may as well get some sleep, since it doesn't look like anyone's leaving tonight."

Winona has already gone to bed, and I climb in with her.

"You awake?" I ask.

"Uh-huh."

"What do you expect tonight?"

"I don't know." There's something in Winona's voice that makes me suspect she does know—if not from experience, then from a history of knowing.

The pieces of the puzzle are starting to come together.

"You have a father, Winona?"

"Papa? They ran him out of town when I was a baby."

"Who ran him out of town? And why?"

For a minute, she's quiet. Then she says, "Why don't you tell me, since you know so much."

Now it's my turn to be quiet.

In the darkness, Winona's face is so close I can feel her feathery breath on my nose. She smells starchy, clean. I touch my lips to hers and fall asleep like that, breathing Winona in.

*   *   *

I wake to thunder. Thunder forming words that make no sense. Thunder forming Covey's name. Outside the window, lightning sparks. Sparks again and stays light a second longer than lightning is supposed to. I get up and pull back the curtain, expecting rain.

Men. Flashlights. Cars pointed toward the house, headlights on.

The next words are thunderous.

"Covey Fortune. We said come on outside."

Ghost men, white ghost faces. Ribbons of light. Slender switches in their hands.

Before tonight, I have not been afraid of men. I've been afraid of other things—black widow spiders, rabid dogs, monster movies. Now I add to the list white men dressed in white.

Winona sits up in bed, her forehead pressed to her knees.

"They've come for him," she whispers.

I shuffle into the front room, sliding my feet on the wood floor in the darkness. Covey stands behind the closed door dressed in khakis and a cotton flannel shirt.

Phoenix is a shadow in the kitchen. "You're not going out there," she says.

"They'll set fire to the house," he answers.

"They'll give up after a while."

"Not 'til they've tasted blood."

She bolts up. "Let me go talk to them."

"It's not you they want." Covey holds up his palm toward her. "I can take a beating. Laying their outrage on me might spare another black man."

"Fortune, get out here now." The familiar voice brings the sweetness of butterscotch to my mouth, but it turns sour when Covey grips the doorknob.

Outside, he's silhouetted before the lights. Phoenix works her lips but nothing comes out. Regina bows her head toward the table and looks as if she's praying. Franklin coughs rapid-fire, straining at a rope. Someone has tied him to the tree.

The cold February night slinks into the house, but no one moves to close the door. No one moves at all. Even the five men outside stand stark still.

"Fortune," a tall one says, "you been trespassing on private property?"

Covey's back is to me, muscles tense.

"You know what private property is?

"I do," Covey says.

"I don't think you do, Fortune," the tall one says. "White women are private property and you been seen around town with a white woman."

Phoenix is poised to spring. Behind her, Regina stands ready to pin her to the seat. Is Phoenix the white woman they're talking about? I almost laugh. How can they count Phoenix?

Covey's fists hang at his sides. He jabs a look at Regina to hold her in place—this is his obligation—and steps off the porch.

Two men tussle him to the car. They pull his shirt off and bend him across the hood, one man holding his wrists. There is something odd about the men, and I realize they all have pillowcases over their heads, eye holes clipped out in uneven circles. Horn-rimmed glasses stick through the side of one pillowcase—Mr. Isobel?

A hefty fellow holds up a light and another the size of Aubrey Hicks raises the switch. It whistles through the air and slaps flesh once, twice, three times. The arm rises and falls, rises and falls and looks in the dim light almost like the choir director at church leading the offertory music. Whistle slap. Whistle slap. Whistle slap.

Phoenix bolts but Regina wrenches her into the chair.

If nothing stops them, the men will go on until morning and daylight will find them hypnotized by the rhythm of their flogging. Covey doesn't utter a sound.

I squint at the man holding the flashlight, short and stocky but robust. The build, the way he stands—a blast of recognition shoots through me bringing a sticky sweat to my skin. Some music is playing out of tune in my head, sour and so sharp it hurts my ears, like the scrape of chalk on Mrs. Davenport's blackboard. Lord, it's cold, but steam rises from Covey's skin, blood oozing from the snakelike wounds.

My heart flaps in my chest trying to get free, but my feet are gone. Somehow I'm standing, floating above the floorboards, floating down the steps without legs. Cowboy Code number six is the command to help people in distress, and without thinking about it, that's what I intend to do—to try and relieve what's causing Covey's distress, noxious as the mill's contamination.

The music is louder now and I realize it's Franklin yelping and pulling at the rope around his neck, his jaws snapping together, froth spraying from his tongue. I'm at the tree, pulling the rope, trying to untie it but there isn't enough slack. I hear Phoenix wailing at Regina to let her go, goddammit.

Where is God now? Not inside the white pillowcases cut for eye holes. Not in the switch that rises and falls on a black man's back. God is love, Reverend Singer preaches, and love is a man braced across the hood of the car, being punished for men's misguided sense of righteousness. Love is tender and malleable and when it is beaten, love turns to fear and fear to hatred, and hatred is the biggest distress.

Daddy said that growing up is a gradual process and I just need to be patient and wait. But he was wrong. Growing up happens in a moment, a single pulsing of the heart. One beat is the final thrum of childhood, taking innocence with it. The next beat marks the beginning of a different journey, one that guides me toward the headlamps of the car.

Familiar smells envelop me—gas station grease, cigar tobacco, leather, butterscotch, ether. I concentrate on the man holding the light. The eyes behind his white hood are tired and sad—my grandfather's eyes.

I start to say one word: "Nandad—." Before I finish, he grasps the arm that holds the switch.

"That's enough, Aubrey," he says. "We meant to scare him is all."

There is one more slap of the switch.

A group of men who have begun a thing is like the eruption of a volcano—it takes time to cool down. My grandfather must understand this because he repeats, "That's enough, I said." He wrenches the switch from Aubrey's hand and flings it across the yard into the night.

In a surge of strength Phoenix jerks loose and throws herself out the door at the gathering of men. She slashes at sleeves, claws at faces. The horn-rimmed glasses fly to the ground, doors slam and the car backs up, rolling Covey off the hood. He falls to all fours, vomiting in the pooled light from headlamps that turn like livid judgment and leave us all in the dark.

Regina comes outside and helps Covey up. Phoenix stands swiping the air and hurls "bastards" at the taillights and "bastards" again until Regina calls her to help. They half carry, half drag Covey in and take him to his bed.

"Put some water on to boil," Regina barks, but my feet are not attached to my legs. Whatever was holding me up gives way, and the crash of my body to the floor brings on a sweet and welcome blackness.

*　*　*

When daylight pours through the window, I find myself alone in Winona's bed. Phoenix comes and sits beside me, a cup of milky tea on her lap.

"Is Covey dead?" I ask.

"It would take more than five old white men to kill him."

"Why'd they do it?"

She frowns at the tea, sips to check the temperature, and hands the cup to me. "I wish I had an answer to that question." She slumps back to the kitchen, leaving the tea with me.

Winona has gone off to school, Phoenix says. She doesn't mention my going to school, and I don't bring it up. I can't face Penny Reardon after what occurred last night.

"Can I see Covey?" I whisper in case he's asleep.

"Go on, then." Phoenix swipes her hand toward his room.

When I go to Covey, he's lying on his side, face to the wall. Regina has wrapped a sheet tight around his torso, oozing red stains where the switch broke the skin.

"Covey?"

He doesn't respond.

"We ought to get the doctor."

He shakes with a short cough. "You go on down the hill where you belong."

I hold my breath to keep my heart from choking me.

"Phoenix." He lifts his head and winces. "Get her out of here."

"Let's go," Phoenix says. "Regina can take care of him."

Outside I untie Franklin and he lies down with head on his paws. He whimpers, and when I go to pat him, he ducks his head away.

26
The Apology

I decide not to tell Momma about that night, about the hooded men with flashlights, or about Covey's wounds seeping like the bandages on Mamaw's stomach. I go to school and multiply fractions and diagram compound sentences on the board when Mrs. Davenport instructs me to and wonder what Winona is doing and whether phantoms drift through her nightmares as they do mine. I don't tell Penny, either. How can I explain to her what I don't fathom myself—why white men will tear a black man from his house and beat him bloody. Why my grandfather hates Negroes. The men had not strung Covey up and slit his throat as I've heard they did to black men farther south. Nevertheless, I can sense the lashes cutting my ribs, slicing my lungs, razor licks at my heart. My skin is as white as the hand that held the whip, as white as the hand that held the light, the hand I know to clench cigars and fashion Christmas presents in his cellar. My hand is white, but my heart is turning as black as tar, black as despair. I feel glassed in. Canned. Sealed. Preserved. Stashed on a shelf in a tight, dark place.

*   *   *

I've just gone to bed when a car door thuds shut on the street. After a minute I hear a click in the lock and as if someone's trying to break in.

I slide out and creep to the living room. Momma's up, too, and I hear her bureau drawer slide open. As I'm trying to remember where she keeps the cleaver Nandaddy made, she comes out of her room with Buddy's pistol. I know the gun has its own language and once it speaks, there's no taking it back—and no apology.

The door shudders and then groans. Momma plants her feet on the linoleum and slips off the safety. A solid form is standing in the doorway, cold air passing in around him.

"I've got a gun," Momma says.

"Mug?"

Momma sighs but keeps the gun on him.

"Why are you here, Dad?"

"You gave me a key." He holds both hands out as if trying to stop an oncoming car.

"I mean at this hour."

"Put that gun down." He doesn't speak again until after Momma lowers the pistol and slips the safety back on.

"You scared the dogwater out of me," she says.

"I had a queer feeling. Thought I'd come and check on you, make sure you and the kids are okay." He rubs his finger under his nose and sniffs.

Momma switches on a lamp. "Sorry about the gun."

She lets him take it from her. "Where'd you get this thing?"

"From Buddy," I say, shuddering at my grandfather holding the weapon. "He got it in Germany." I don't go into details.

He stares at me and starts to say something. "I—uh—" A drip starts from a nostril. His tongue darts out and he sniffs again. "I didn't mean to get the whole house up."

I remember how he looked that night, the hood over the bald head, how he turned and saw me, registered surprise, then fright and an instinct to run. "This is the way it is," the eyes said. "I don't like it any more than you do, but it's the way it's got to be."

I remember thinking, no. No, no, no, no. He's got it wrong. How could my grandfather be so wrong?

He holds the pistol on its side, lifting it up and down. "It's got good heft. I'm not much for handguns, though. Take a twelve-gauge anyday."

"Buddy thought I needed some protection," Momma says.

"I'm glad to know you're not fearful about using it." He studies the gun.

"Why didn't you just call, Dad?"

"Don't like the dern telephone." He rubs a thumb along the pistol's barrel and adds, "Couldn't sleep anyway."

I shiver and realize no one has shut the door. I push it closed, pull a sweater off a hook, and drape it over my shoulders. A hush settles around us.

"Well," he says, laying the gun on the end table.

"Dad," Momma says, "you can stay here. I'll make up the couch for you."

"I guess I'll just get back to the house." He must be grieving—that's why he roams late at night. Maybe it's grief that drives him to do violence against a black man.

"How about some coffee?" I offer.

"Too much trouble." He half-turns toward the door. "You two go on back to sleep."

"I was about to get up and make a pot." I'm glad Momma lies to him. I hate to see even the vilest creature suffer, and my grandfather is suffering.

While I brew the coffee, Momma toasts bread in the oven. Nandaddy unbuttons his coat and hangs it over the kitchen chair, slides off his hat and places it on the seat, sits down at the table.

"Mug—" I wish he wouldn't call Momma by that name. It reminds me of a prizefighter after losing a match, face deformed with swelling, blue with bruises.

I set the coffee on the table. It shines like old motor oil.

"I know I have pretty peculiar ways." His fists circle the cup, not touching it, not just yet. There's something he has to say.

"What is it, Dad?"

He takes a swallow of the coffee but doesn't touch the toast.

"That boy's like my own."

"A.T.?" Momma says.

"He's not talking about Smiley," I say.

Cowboy Code number five: The Cowboy must not advocate or possess racially intolerant ideas.

Nandaddy rubs his thigh. Then our eyes clamp on each other as they did that night at the settlement. "I wouldn't for the world have him come to harm."

Nevertheless, my grandfather and the men he was with inflicted an injury that will never heal. They need to be held accountable.

"Why did you do it?" It's a demand rather than a question.

He waits, his lips working as Buddy's did that day in the forest when he talked about the Nazis. If he says he was forced against his will, that he'd never hate a man for his skin color, I might be able to forgive him.

"Why?" I ask again.

"Since the war ended," he says, "people've just gone mad."

"What are you talking about?" Momma says.

"I've got to live in this town and get along with folks. On occasion that means going along with—" He looks at the toast. "With unpleasant things."

At that moment, I know that everything I've ever been taught in unspoken ways about white people being superior to everybody else—none of that is true. Nandaddy and those other men beat Covey because they wished it were true. My grandfather, the toughest man I know besides Daddy, is a bully. Worse than a bully—he's a coward.

He runs a nubby finger around the plate and clears his throat. "I keep pretty busy and can't be running into town all the time. But if I could get the material, I'd go ahead and build you a house this summer over on Hemlock Avenue. I could help look after you and the children."

"And we could look after you." What I mean is, we can make sure whatever drove you to Covey's house is locked in a vault with the hood you wore that night.

Momma rubs her forehead. "I'll write Burr and see what he says."

Nandaddy throws down his coffee and pushes himself from the table.

"I'd write him myself, but you know I don't spell so good. But I'll do all I can for you all. If you'll let me." He sinks into his coat but leaves it hanging open.

Momma follows her father to the door.

"Make sure this is locked, you hear?"

"Thanks, Dad," she says.

He walks down the steps to the street. The car's engine starts before Momma closes the door.

"He's troubled about something," she says, watching through the window as he drives off.

"I'm not surprised."

Momma cocks her head to one side. "What do you mean?"

I shrug. "I mean, I know what he's going through."

She answers as a sympathetic stranger would. "Sure—I suppose you do."

27
The Discovery

Spring is creeping up on winter and I pry up the window sash to let in the wormy smell of earth. All living things buried deep from the cold push their way up—moles, bugs, pale shoots. Even rocks heave up from the melting ground. Pounding rains take us by surprise, and one day Elsie's laundry gets a good rinsing when she didn't get it off the line in time. Momma says it's time to pack winter coats in mothballs. Mothballs smell of spring.

One morning I start to make the coffee and discover the back door wide open. Momma's still in bed, so I walk out to the stoop where steps lead down to the yard, splotchy with mud puddles. The crocuses are up and tulip spikes have broken through the ground. The earth is coming back to life.

A twig cracks in the woods behind the house and Phoenix emerges with a fistful of wildflowers, dirt streaked across one cheek.

"Hey," she says, pointing back up the trail she made, "cowslip's up already." She pries off her mud-splattered shoes at the top step. In the kitchen, she rummages through the cupboard for a jelly jar.

"And look—this cress is growing by a spring." She fills a jar halfway with water and perches the jar on the counter. Pinching a stem, she says, "Dog violet. And this here's trailing arbutus." She holds a vine under my nose with small purple flowers smelling like cherry pies. I'm surprised by how fragile spring flowers are, and yet to bear March winds blowing off the mountaintops they must be tougher than they appear.

Phoenix wiggles the stems into the jar and fiddles with the flowers until they have some organization, then sets the jar on the table for early spring cheeriness.

"In a few weeks," she says, "you and I'll go out and till a vegetable garden. There's a perfect spot for it."

"I don't know anything about gardening."

She pours herself some coffee. "I'll show you. Not much to it."

She has found my weak spot. I'm crazy for someone to pay me any kindness, to teach me about flowers and plants and what makes them grow. I want to plant a garden and, to my surprise, I want to plant it with Phoenix.

*   *   *

On Saturday Phoenix takes Smiley to a matinee so Momma and I can do some spring cleaning at my grandfather's house. Buddy is treating his girlfriend Bertha Shaker to a picnic and Nandaddy has gone off to Clinton Forge for a tractor part, so we have the house to ourselves.

Two men without a woman can take a toll on the furnishings. Dirty dishes left in the sink, dirty handprints on the cupboards, dirty clothes thrown onto chairs. I scrub the bathroom while Momma mops the kitchen and sets the clothes to launder in Mamaw's wringer washer. We clean upstairs together. Buddy's room doesn't need much. He keeps his clothes tidy in a bureau and whisks the dust from under his bed—Army training. In Momma's old room the lacy spread and ruffled curtains are little cheer for the yellowed pictures on the wall—a watercolor of a vase of droopy sunflowers, a print of a snowcapped mountain, a small copy of the Lord's Supper in a thin frame, the glass cracked in one corner.

"Didn't you ever pin pictures of movie stars to the walls?" I ask Momma, thinking of old John Barrymore or Greta Garbo.

"No," she says. "Dad would have worn the handles off the razor strap if I had. Everything had to be just so." Then she smiles toward the bed. "But I kept a few under the mattress and pulled them out when I heard him snoring." I like thinking of Momma mooning over her stars the same way I moon over mine. I didn't have to keep the pictures a secret from my father, though. He teased me about it and asked me why I needed movie star magazines when I had him. He was more handsome than Spencer Tracy, that's for sure.

I wouldn't think of cleaning Nandaddy's personal space when he's there and risk aggravating him. We wait for his car to rumble down the driveway and the swirling dirt to settle back on the road. Momma is already looking into my grandparents' room. The light from the window shows the dust on

Mamaw's dresser, the faded bureau scarf. If Nandaddy had at least thrown a sheet over the bureau, it would have helped, but her things look as if they haven't been touched—as if they've become invisible to him.

Mamaw always had fresh linens on the beds. I loved that airy fragrance. But now the heavy odor of unwashed hair hovers around the yellowed pillowcase, and everything has the smell of cigar. Mamaw would never let him smoke in the bedroom, but now on the nightstand I find an ashtray filled with stinking butts like stools of excrement.

I open a window to let out the reek. Momma and I throw back the blankets and strip the bed, fold the covers and lay them on a chair with the pillow to take out and air on the clothesline. I dust Nandaddy's bureau, careful not to move his box of cufflinks, tie bars, and a pocket watch he never winds. In a picture of Mamaw and him on their wedding day, they are standing shoulder to shoulder, both looking straight ahead, Mamaw in a dark dress with a white collar, her hair pulled back, placid smile on her face. What did she see in my grandfather, a paunchy boy no taller than herself? Nearly bald even then, the large head was out of balance atop the starched shirt and crooked bow tie as if someone fiddled with the photo and glued Nandaddy's head on someone else's body. Heavy brows shadowing his round face, nose like a furrow's ridge—not like Momma's pug, which spreads cheekbone to cheekbone. Her hair is dark, like her mother's.

I wipe the glass with a cloth and straighten the picture. I want to handle Mamaw's possessions and hold them to my face. The fragrances might bring her back to life—lavender, rose, honeysuckle.

Momma finds clean sheets in the linen closet and lays them on the bed. I start on Mamaw's dresser. Pictures of Buddy and Momma as babies, a small jewelry box with a string of pearls, a cameo brooch, earrings of glass flowers. A crystal dish with a hatpin and some safety pins. A china lamp painted with pink roses, a bud vase, a perfume atomizer with a rubber squeeze balloon, empty.

I stroke each separate piece with a cloth, dust the bureau and shake the scarf, then replace the items as they had been. Maybe Momma would let me have the jewelry box and the pictures, something of Mamaw's, something dear.

"Clean out the drawers," Momma says, "and we'll get some boxes from the basement. We'll give what we can't use to the church."

I start on the bottom drawer—sweaters, heavy woolen scarves, a pair of slacks Momma gave her one Christmas and which still has the tags on them. My grandmother never wore trousers that I remember. In the second drawer, cotton tops and two boxes. The smaller one holds doilies separated with tissue paper. Crocheted disks of slender ivory thread in delicate curlicues starched stiff. A card on top reads, "To Lawrence and Ellen—Best wishes, Mavis and Bucky."

"Look at these, Momma."

She takes a doily and runs her fingers over it. "Probably a wedding gift she was saving for an occasion that never came."

I think of our drab furniture and how something lacy under a lamp or an ashtray would brighten it up.

"Could we take them?"

"We wouldn't want to ruin them." The box goes on the pile for the church charity. I resent Momma's practical nature. If you treasure a thing, you keep it close so you can see it daily to remind you of its importance. If you treat it with love and care, it won't get ruined. She is sending away the doilies just like she sent away Mamaw—and like she emptied my father from her heart.

I push the lower drawers closed and tug the top one open. Cotton panties, folded flat and laid in a neat row. Two limp bras and flesh-colored stockings—thick cotton rolled into perfect balls. A slip of starched linen, a tiny pansy centered at the top. Square handkerchiefs, a pair of short white gloves. I pull the drawer out farther, bracing it with my hip, and swipe my hand along the back. There has to be something for me.

Momma lifts the lid of the chest that sits at the foot of the bed. "You'd think Mamaw would have a decent blanket in here," she says, pulling out a worn quilt, squares peeling up at the seams. A threadbare coverlet, a spread with rips in it. As she lays them folded on the bed, the scent of cedar wafts out with a sweet, woodsy odor. She lifts out a flannel blanket that looks like it has some use and places it next to the others. As she's about to put the bedclothes back, she stops.

"Why aren't these with the linens?" She reaches in for a pile of sheets, brings them out, puzzles over them, fingers the edges. A pillowcase, creased into a triangle, falls to the floor. I think about scooping it up to keep Momma from finding out. But no. I decide to watch for her reaction. She must see as well as I do the rough holes cut out, two of them, eye-width apart.

She is left holding the sheet, staring at it as if the sheet must be folded and stacked in the linen closet where it belongs. Then she sees the mud stains, the rough stitches of the sleeves. She registers curiosity. I lift the hood from the floor with my fingertips, careful not to touch it with my palms while she turns the sheet about, trying to make sense of it, the material falling into the shape of a man, a stocky man. Then she holds the sheet by the shoulders, looks from the garment to the cap I clasp limply in my hands, and back at the robe.

"Dear Lord," she whispers. We've never spoken about the Klan. Nothing about its outings has been published in the *Messenger*. But I've known of its existence, of the fact that most of Pine Cliff's upstanding residents have been members at one time, even Mr. Townsend, the *Messenger* publisher. I know— from murmurings, from the way men I've encountered at my grandfather's house stop talking when I walk into the room, from the way they eye black men on downtown business—I know the Klan is a larger part of life than anyone is willing to let on. I've seen them in action.

Momma balls up the sheet and jerks the hood out of my hand. Without saying anything, she starts down the stairs. I figure she's either going to dispose of the evidence or hang it on the line and broadcast it to the neighbors.

In the cellar, the furnace is simmering with hot coals. Momma wraps the skirt of her dress around her hand to pad the hot handle and cranks open the heavy door. She stuffs the maw with the white fabric, picks up the metal rod leaning against the furnace, and pokes the sheet down into the coals. Flames rise up hungry around it.

When the edges of the fabric scorch, Momma closes the door. She replaces the rod and then fastens her eyes on me. "We will never speak about this," she says and then whisks by me and goes back upstairs.

*　*　*

In the kitchen I'm wiping water spots from the blades of the dinner knives and laying them in their compartment in the sideboard when the knock comes on the door. Whoever is knocking must not have seen my grandfather drive off.

Regina is in a Sunday coat buttoned up to the neck, a shawl over the shoulders in a touch of fashion. Both hands press her purse, big and black and solid.

"Hello, Regina." Momma opens the door wider. "Please come in."

Regina doesn't move. She has changed. Steel is in her eyes—she hasn't come to visit.

"I need to see Mr. Persinger." Regina is firm, Momma's equal in their staunch presence. It has been two weeks since I've seen Winona. Does she hate me for what happened to Covey?

"Dad's gone to Clinton Forge," Momma says.

Regina raises her chin. "Then give him a message for me. Tell him he's got to get someone else to help him with his—" She hesitates. "His gentleman's farm."

Mrs. Davenport taught our class about verbal irony. The word "gentleman" carries the full weight of that irony.

"Is Covey going somewhere?" I ask.

Aunt Regina ignores me and squares off against Momma, a barrier of color separating them. They haven't done each other wrong, but Momma matches Regina's indignation as if they have. They are two proud women standing in defense of their families.

"It's time we moved north," Regina says. "Covey's going to school in Washington in the fall, and Winona can get professional music lessons."

What Momma says next sends me into a whirlwind of confusion.

"It's going to break her heart."

Momma can't mean my heart—she doesn't know how I feel about Covey. And I don't believe Winona's heart will break about leaving this stinky old town. Whose heart, then?

Regina answers without a blink. "He'll write her as he's always done."

Always? Who is this mysterious woman with a fragile heart? And when does Regina plan the move? When can I come to say goodbye to Winona and Covey? Could I take the train up north to visit? But before I ask, Regina turns around and starts down the steps.

28
The King of England

Mail from the Pacific is slow in coming. Smiley's tongue is all healed when Momma gets the letter of concern from Burr. He writes again to say if Momma were sick and couldn't take care of us, he might be able to get that hardship leave, but I hope Momma isn't so lonely for him that she'll pretend sickness. Phoenix is adequate company. She even makes the chores fun, scraping a rhythm with the washboard and singing a sprightly song. We've dug a garden together and seeded rows of radish, lettuce, peppers and tomatoes. When the first sprout comes up, she yells, "We've given birth, by George!" Then she plucks a red globe, mud crusted, wipes it with a thumb and hands it to me. I pop the radish into my mouth and relish the sharp, peppery flavor of a thing I planted with my own hands.

Phoenix is sharing Momma's bed, like sisters, like Winona and me, even though most girlfriends outgrow sleeping arms around each other once their redheaded cousins start making regular visits, but no one at school—not even Penny—mentions our living arrangement.

In class Mrs. Davenport rehashes recent history. "It's important to be aware of what the Nazis did to the Jews, gypsies, and the insane so it will never happen again," she says. When Kenny calls Jamie Mitchell a Nazi one afternoon, Mrs. Davenport says it's worse than using the "n" word, which I never would. The Germans skinned people and if they had tattoos they used the skin for lampshades. And they starved the Jews and performed experiments on them, like soaking them in ice water to see how long it would take for hypothermia to kill them. Penny Reardon says she heard about a woman they mated with a dog, but she doesn't think the woman ever had the baby. Mrs. Davenport says what we did to the American Indians, taking their land and slaughtering the women and children, and to the Africans we brought over on slave ships was bad enough, but we've made up for our mistakes with reservations and emancipation. The Germans have a ways to go before they give their victims retribution.

I raise my hand.

"Yes, Barbara?"

"What about the Klan? I mean here in Pine Cliff."

"The Klan? You mean the KKK?"

What I mean is how decent men like my grandfather can turn into devils. What I mean is beating innocent black men for no good reason.

"Yes," I answer. "The KKK."

She gives me a blank look that I can't read. Then she says, "We have to move on to the role of the Japanese in the bombing of Pearl Harbor."

*   *   *

Smiley usually comes down with colds in the winter, but even though it's May, he's sneezing and complaining of a sore throat.

"I'm going to stay with him and keep camphor rubbed on his chest," Momma says.

It's just one day off work, but when she goes back, the shift foreman warns her she's used up all her leave and she shouldn't think about taking any more time off, no matter how sick her children are. Momma does not take well to threats. I get a kick out of her replaying for us how she told him he can have his damned job because A.T. and I come before those rolls of paper piling up in the pit. Phoenix says she wishes she'd been there for the show.

I fear we'll be in the same old predicament—no money coming in and scrimping and going into debt so that I can hardly hold my head up at school. But Momma says Burr's paychecks will make up the difference and we aren't in bad shape. If she's counting on Burr, I'm willing to bet she's fooling herself.

In fact, Momma is frisky, teasing with Phoenix and even holding hands when we walk downtown. Phoenix is deluding herself about her chances of winning Momma away from Burr. I guess when you love someone, you take whatever bone they throw you.

Quiet settles on Pine Cliff after the supper hour, except when the seven o'clock train comes in and locals gather around the platform to see who's returning from a trip or who's coming to town for business at the mill. One evening just before seven, Phoenix insists we walk downtown. Newspaper reporters and photographers are clustered by the station's tracks, cameras and notepads in hand, pencils wedged over an ear.

"What's going on?" Smiley leans around bodies to try to get a view.

"You'd think it was the King of France," Momma says.

"Close," Phoenix says. "He used to be the King of England."

"Um-hm." Momma plants a fist on her hip. "And I'm the Queen of Hearts."

"Don't you all read the news?" Phoenix walks backwards to keep the conversation going.

"Since the war ended, I just look at 'Tilly the Toiler' and the ads," Momma says. "Did I miss something?"

"Old Townsend buried it inside the *Messenger*, but seems like word got out anyway. The Duke and Duchess of Windsor are due in on their way to the Homestead."

The Homestead is a grandiose hotel perched on two thousand acres outside the village of Hot Springs. Buddy drove us up to see it one Sunday afternoon. The resort channels two steaming springs into a spa where the rich and famous soak in the mineral waters. Thomas Jefferson went to the Homestead to treat his rheumatism, and other presidents stayed there, too. I promise myself that someday—one way or another—I'll wallow in that kind of richness.

Phoenix elbows her way through the bodies to get closer to the tracks, holding Momma by one hand and Smiley by the other. I'm close on Momma's heels. Who is the Duke of Windsor, anyway? Mr. Townsend has a photograph on the wall at the *Messenger* office of Harry Truman getting off at the Pine Cliff station, but I don't believe royalty has ever graced the platform.

"Is the Homestead ritzy enough for them?" Momma asks.

"They're slumming," Phoenix says. "They've been traveling all over the globe for the past couple years. Don't have anything better to do with all their spare time."

Smiley catches the eye of a mahogany-skinned girl about his age. She looks at her Sunday shoes, regards him from under the brim of her Sunday hat, and swishes her skirt around her legs. Smiley watches her, not at all self-conscious about the fact that he's staring.

"Look what I can do," she says, flirting. "I can go like this." She makes a face by pressing her bottom lip to her top teeth. Smiley makes the face back at her and she looks away, shy. When Smiley is older, there's a chance he'll catch her eye again. By then maybe he can court her without throwing the town into an uproar, without the Klan calling out his name in front of our house to dole out punishment for falling in love with the wrong girl.

When she starts taking baby steps toward Smiley, her mother calls to her.

"Niquette, come on. Train's pulling in."

Bulbs flash, hats wave, hands reach toward the moving railcars. Phoenix lifts Smiley piggyback so he can see over the crowd. The train screeches to a stop, and men in dark jackets push the crowd back. I step up on a bench to see over heads. The car spills out people in business suits, a few men in uniform, a woman struggling with a suitcase, and they all merge into the horde.

In the doorway of the railcar, a woman pauses and the platform grows quiet, or at least it seems that way to me. She's wearing a plain, tailored suit with a string of pearls at the neck, no hat, smooth hair coiled behind her head. She's tall and stands straight, making her look even taller. Statuesque, Mrs. Davenport would say. Someone calls out, "Duchess" and another, "Your Highness." Her lips curl down at us and she rotates a gloved hand in the air.

Niquette stands behind her mother and looks around her waist. The woman—is it the duchess?—has the air of pride I saw on Momma and Regina that Saturday they had the showdown at Nandaddy's house, the sense that they deserve better than the circumstances in which they've found themselves. They lift their heads above the town's stink, above the effort to make ends meet.

I look down at the scuff marks on my shoes and feel clumsy. My thumb comes to my mouth, and I bite at the cuticle. I don't think I can ever learn to endure my circumstance with dignity and swear someday I'll go to New York or Washington and make something of myself.

"Look," Phoenix says. "There's the Duke."

A middle-aged man appears behind the Duchess. He has Burr-like handsomeness but with more polish. He motions toward the platform and someone gives a hand to help the Duchess down from the train. Then they're lost in a sea of bodies. Reporters follow them to a waiting car, and they're gone.

The crowd thins out and Phoenix slides Smiley off her back.

"What'd you think of the royals?" she asks.

"She's beautiful," Momma answers.

"You call that beautiful? Plain, if you ask me." Phoenix takes Momma by the wrist. "Come here—I'll show you beautiful."

We hoof up the sidewalk to Leggett's Department Store, and Phoenix stops by the window. The sunlight is fading but Momma's reflection holds her posture straight, waves of hair flowing down her face and resting on her shoulders. Dark lashes line her dark eyes and her cheeks are flushed with pink.

"Now, that's beautiful," Phoenix says.

It occurs to me at that moment that Phoenix loves my mother, loves her more, I suspect, than Burr does. Loves her even as much as Daddy loved her. Momma knows it, too, which must be why she lets Phoenix nestle into her bed, nestle into our lives.

"Phoenix," Momma says, "you're as crazy as a June bug."

*   *   *

In the following weeks, school lets out and our household falls into a kind of contentment. Our garden starts producing, and nothing tastes more like summer to me than cucumbers peeled and cut into spears or sliced with onions and floated in vinegar. The wet pop of the seeds between my teeth is a delight. Phoenix enlists Smiley to pinch suckers from the tomato plants while I shell peas. We eat tomato and mayonnaise sandwiches and crunch hot radishes sprinkled with salt. When the summer squash comes in, Phoenix fries it, stuffs it, grates it, makes loaves of sweet bread and still has a hard time keeping up with the new blossoms. She makes a creamy sauce with peas and carrots in it, and we have it over toast for supper.

After the washing is done and the furniture dusted, Momma has time to play four-way catch. In the afternoons she writes letters to Burr. His are wistful, saying how badly he wants to come home. He sends messages to Smiley about how he should try putting a bar of chocolate in the ice box and letting it get cold before he eats it or how he should get Momma to practice making sweet-potato pie so she'll have the recipe perfected when he comes back. He writes about the movies he watches at night, like *The Magnificent Ambersons* and *Hail the Conquering Hero*. Life aboard ship seems pretty nice and I hope he'll stay there.

29
Aunt Ruby

Momma says she'd like to plan something out of the ordinary for Phoenix's birthday on Saturday.

"Maybe we can get Buddy to drive us over to Humpback Bridge," I suggest. Humpback is Virginia's oldest covered bridge, and some people claim it's haunted.

"Sorry—I'm busy," Phoenix says.

Momma looks disappointed. So am I.

"You've spent almost every Saturday with us."

"Got an appointment."

"Got yourself a boyfriend?" Momma teases.

I can't imagine Phoenix falling for a guy.

"Naw, just something to do is all." She stands with one fist on her hip and scratches her ear.

"What've you got to do, Phoenix?" I figure she'll confide in me.

"Did I ever tell you about Aunt Ruby?"

"Your aunt?"

"My mother's sister. She's having heart trouble and they've got her over in the convalescent home."

"I'm sorry to hear that. Why haven't we been to visit her?" Momma asks.

"She kept to herself in her big house in Fairlawn."

"We could take flowers to the convalescent home," I suggest. "I'll cut some roses for her from the yard."

"She's pretty weak, the doctors say. A parade of visitors might do her in." Phoenix looks at Smiley.

"Maybe you're right," Momma says.

"Tell you what," Phoenix says. "Can you pack us a picnic?"

"Sure." Momma looks toward the mill and curls her lip. "But we'll have to get out of town if we don't want that smell spoiling our lunch."

"You leave that to me. Just pack the basket. And throw in your swimsuits, too. I'll be back by noon."

"Can I go with you?" I'm curious about Phoenix's people—she's never given us much information.

She studies me a minute. "Sure—that would be nice, Sister."

* * *

Tall white pillars hold up the portico of the Valley Convalescent Home. It could have been someone's fancy house in the antebellum era.

"Does your Aunt Ruby have any children?" I ask and then remember Phoenix said she isn't married.

"Well...," Phoenix starts. Then she changes directions. "She loves kiddies and she loved her gardens—gardening's a curse among our kinfolk." I figure Aunt Ruby is in the right place. An island of flowers is abloom in the garden, and by the portico—roses, hydrangeas and lupine bordered by clouds of impatiens. Mimosa trees offer feathery blossoms, and the scent of magnolias perfumes the air.

I ring the doorbell, and a nurse in uniform opens. Phoenix asks to see Ruby Olney. She leads us down a hall to a room where a frail looking woman sits in an upholstered chair by a window.

"Why, Phoenix!" Aunt Ruby says, struggling to straighten herself. "It's about time you came to see me." Auburn tresses tied in a careless knot atop her head makes her look like an angelic version of Phoenix. Crow's feet mark the corners of her eyes, but otherwise her skin is smooth. It's hard to believe she's dying.

"This is Bobbie Grey." Phoenix bobs her head toward me. "A friend of mine."

Aunt Ruby offers a freckled hand and presses its cool palm to mine.

"Have them make you something to eat—it must be lunch time."

"We just have a minute, Aunt Ruby," Phoenix says, not wanting to wear her out.

"You two get comfortable, then." She points to a wooden chair. The dresser and a nightstand crowd the small space. Phoenix parks herself on the bed. I'm drawn to the silver-framed photographs lined up across the dresser. One shows an old-fashioned couple on a settee, two girls standing behind. Young women, fancy dresses, formal poses.

"That's my mother and Aunt Ruby with my grandparents," Phoenix says. "Ruby looked after them 'til they passed away." She points to a picture of a frowning baby in a stroller. "This is me."

Another baby donned in a bonnet stands on a stool. A tan-skinned baby, toothless smile. The same baby I saw in the photo on the Goode's mantel.

"Look at that one, will you?" Phoenix motions to a photo of herself, perched on a chair, hands folded in her lap, eyebrows lowered in disapproval. And one more framed shot of the dark child, this time in knickers, a tie at his throat. Youthfully handsome and somehow familiar.

"Who is that?" I ask.

"Quite a gallery, isn't it?" Aunt Ruby says. "Father liked to document the offspring, bless his soul." She coughs.

My questions are being ignored, but I'm starting to get the picture.

"How's my brother-in-law?"

"Dad's busy but doing well, Ruby." Phoenix twists a button on her shirt.

"He never had another woman in his life after your mother died."

"He knows I wouldn't have stood for it." Phoenix is trying to be funny, but she poked a wound and a pain shoots from my heart to my backbone. Maybe I shouldn't have stood for it, either.

Aunt Ruby takes in a jagged breath as if there's something she's been waiting to ask.

"Tell me, then—how is he?" We've just discussed Dr. Goode—who is she talking about now?

"He's just fine," Phoenix says.

"Is Regina taking care of him?"

"More like he takes care of Regina. You keep forgetting that Covey's a man now."

Covey—his father thrown from a bridge. Aunt Ruby giving him up to protect him. It all falls into place.

"I know his age to the minute," Aunt Ruby says. "He was nineteen October tenth. How could I forget such a thing?"

"You don't need to worry about him," Phoenix says.

"I do, though."

Of course—those pictures on the bureau are Covey as a child.

"You know Covey well?" I ask.

Aunt Ruby looks at her fingers intertwined as if in prayer and her mouth melts into a sad smile. "I knew his father."

"I thought his mother was dead."

"No—not dead," she says. "His mother is very much alive."

Heat rises to my face when I realize my ignorance, and I take a giant leap in my understanding. Covey's hair, wavy and reddish instead of the black curls of Winona's. His skin, a twilight color, not the earthy tone of Regina's. Penny Reardon and I have whispered about white women going off with black men when boyfriends were off at war. I've seen fair-skinned children playing in swept yards with dark-skinned half-sisters and half-brothers, and Phoenix loves my mother without reservation. The boundaries to love are artificial ones.

Liver spots dot Aunt Ruby's cheeks. She must have been a beautiful woman when she was younger, and here I am wishing to be old—at least old enough so I'll know what's to become of me. There are so many lines that I've been told not to cross. I came close to one and even pushed my toe over it when I spent the night at Winona's house. But Aunt Ruby marched directly over one of those lines. She might have had any man she desired, but she desired a black man. She must have loved him—maybe loves him yet. My heart aches for this sad woman who holds a secret she has kept for twenty years. And now I've been given her secret to guard—another weight to carry over the threshold into the abode of women.

A sharp tap on the door brings a nurse in.

"Time for your medicine, Miss Olney."

"I guess we should be moving on," Phoenix says.

When Phoenix goes to kiss her cheek, Aunt Ruby touches Phoenix's arm.

"Tell him something for me," she says.

"What's that, Ruby?"

"Tell him he won't have anything to worry about when I'm gone."

"I'll tell him."

"And see that it's so."

"I'll see to it."

Aunt Ruby rests her head back and we squeeze by the nurse, who waits with a tray of pills.

I stop and turn to Aunt Ruby. "I'm very glad I met you."

30
Happy Birthday, Phoenix

Just after noon Phoenix drops me off and says she'll be back for us in half an hour. Momma has fried chicken, and I ice a cake she made the night before.

On schedule, Phoenix appears wearing a wide grin.

"We goin' somewhere?" Smiley asks.

"For a ride," she says.

"What are you up to, Phoenix?" Momma and I both know Phoenix is full of surprises.

"You all ready? Chariot's waiting outside." She grabs the picnic basket and hurries us out the door.

By the curb is the most beautiful car I've ever seen, a convertible with top down, whitewalls like party shoes, and a silver necklace of chrome around the hood.

"What in the—" I start.

"It's a Phaeton—1935, I think. My dad keeps it stored in the winter. He's just letting me borrow it because it's my birthday." She gets behind the wheel and Smiley and I scoot into the back. Momma rides gunshot.

"Where we going?" Smiley bops up and down on the seat.

"We're seeking the healing waters," Phoenix says. "Everybody ready?"

Lifting a hand, I let the wind push against it and ruffle my hair. Then I pet the stitched leather seat. This is how I want to live, in the lap of luxury.

We're heading out of town toward North Mountain. Smiley stands up, holding onto Momma's seat.

"Sit down," she orders, but he continues to stand.

"You're not taking us up to visit the Duke and Duchess, are you?" It wouldn't surprise me for Phoenix to walk up to the Duke's hotel suite and yell, "Put the kettle on—y'all got company."

"Nope—why would I spend my birthday with a bunch of stuffed shirts?"

There's not much traffic on Route 220—just a few houses scattered along the road and no businesses. I'm not worried about Phoenix navigating this boat of a car around the steep curves. She's taking the driving seriously, both hands on the wheel, checking the mirrors. A wall of rock rises up on the right, trees hanging on for dear life, a sheer drop-off on the left.

"Let me honk the horn." Smiley strains toward the steering wheel.

"I said sit down," Momma barks.

"Honk the horn!" he says.

Phoenix pushes on the horn, which sounds like a flock of migrating geese. "How's that, Archer Timbers?"

"Do it again," he says, and she does. Then she lights in singing Old MacDonald. I join in on the sheep baa-baaing and we get through snakes, porcupines and skunks, making up sounds before we run out of animals.

Phoenix glances over at Momma.

"What say we look for a bigger place this summer? Maybe one that'll give Sister more privacy. She's getting to that age."

Whatever "that age" is, I'm definitely getting to it. One minute I'm down on the floor playing cars with Smiley and the next I'm mooning over Gene Autry and Audie Murphy. I'm grouchy a lot of the time, and I hardly know who I am anymore. It's nice to know someone recognizes the changes coming over me.

"A bigger apartment would be nice," Momma says. "Wouldn't that surprise Burr?

"I'm not thinking about Burr." Phoenix is thinking about setting up house with us, being Momma's companion. I know they're more than friends.

"What I'd like is to give Burr the surprise of his life," Phoenix says.

"What kind of surprise?"

Phoenix shrugs. "I mean, what if he came back to the house and you had moved out?"

Momma shakes her head. "You're talking crazy."

We ride without speaking. Finally, Phoenix pulls onto a wide stretch of shoulder and turns off the engine.

"Ladies and gentleman." Her disappointment has subsided. "I present to you—Falling Springs."

Creeper vines snake around the trees. A mossy cliff rises from the slope where water, spraying mist and making rainbows, cascades fifty feet down into a basin surrounded by boulders big as automobiles.

"I haven't been here since I was a little girl," Momma says.

"You've got to see it up close." Phoenix climbs out, lets Smiley out of the back, and starts down the path.

Momma doesn't budge. She's not going to leave the fine car to haul herself into snake and varmint territory.

"Come on, Momma—I'll help you down the slope."

"Well, darn if I'm going to stay here by myself," she says.

I lead, holding onto low bushes to keep my balance. Up ahead Phoenix is working her way over the rocks with Smiley close behind her, going straight for the falls. Momma yells at them to be careful but her voice is lost in the roar of the falling water. She's having trouble going downhill in her sandals, but once she sets her mind to something, my mother does not give in.

The footing is slippery near the falls and I walk in a crouch, holding onto rocks to steady myself. I look up in time to see Phoenix and Smiley disappear behind the liquid wall. When I look back to check on Momma, she has frozen, searching the cliff, the water.

In a minute, I hear Smiley's voice. "Come on, Momma!" He's peeping out from the falls.

Carefully Momma and I make our way toward him and squeeze ourselves into a cave big enough for a small party, the falls hanging like a sopping wet blanket walling us in. Moss soaks up much of the noise, and by shouting we can hear each other.

"Feel it." Phoenix pokes her hand through the cataract. I reach mine out, expecting it to be freezing, but it's like bath water.

"Comes directly from the warm spring," Phoenix says. "Smell the sulfur in it?"

I catch a faint scent of matchheads.

She grabs Smiley's overall straps and lets him inch toward the falls. Before he can touch it, the spray soaks through his clothes and he squeals. Even Momma tests the falls, holding Phoenix's hand for balance.

We huddle together until Phoenix points to her mouth and rubs her stomach. She's hungry—and so am I.

While they hunt for a picnic spot near a swimming hole, I climb up to the car and get the lunch basket and the thermos. Phoenix finds a flat rock by a pool, and we feast on Momma's cuisine. I think about the royals at Hot Springs and wonder what they're having for dinner. If they're not licking their fingers after tasting chicken fried in fat or using a biscuit to swab up that last bit of pickle from the potato salad, I pity them. The fresh crunch of a homegrown cucumber, twisted off the vine this morning and washed down with sweet tea—I can't imagine any meal as fine.

After we eat, Momma brings out the cake and lights two candles. "Two for twenty-two," she says.

Momma was seventeen when I was born. My father was her first love. It was seven years later when Smiley announced his impending arrival, which surprised all us. Phoenix has some catching up to do.

Smiley helps Phoenix blow out the candle and after we each have a piece of cake, he and I wade at the edge of the swimming hole, picking up stones and tossing them into the pool. The bottom slopes off steeply.

"I'll show you how to skip a rock, Smiley." Daddy taught me to skip them over the river. "You need small, flat ones." I find a perfect stone and sling it sidearm so that it skips five or six times before dropping. When I find another rock, I give it to him to try. His splashes once and sinks.

"Aw, hell," he says. He tries again without success. "Hell, hell."

"Smiley, sometimes I feel like that, too." I consider that it's better to give up the game before he gets overly frustrated.

"Make a rock pile on the shore, but don't go in the water," I warn. "I'm not jumping in after you if you slip—I just ate."

Sun filters through the pin oaks and dots the rocks a buttery yellow. Phoenix lies back and weaves her fingers over her stomach. Momma unbuckles her sandals and dips her feet in the water. I have a way of pretending I'm preoccupied while I'm listening to what the adults are saying, having grown adept at doing two tasks at once, playing and listening, which provides me with a valuable education.

"Want to have a swim?" Phoenix asks.

Momma says, "I never go in past my waist."

"You ask me, you're already in up to your neck," Phoenix says.

"What's that supposed to mean?"

"Nothing." Phoenix changes the subject. "How's Buddy doing?"

"I don't see much of him," Momma says. "He spends most of his time with his girlfriend in Buena Vista."

Phoenix taps her stomach. "He's a pretty sharp pool player."

"How do you know that?"

"He whupped me that weekend you went to New York."

"You played pool with Buddy?"

"Yep. At the Gypsy Tavern."

"What were you doing there?"

"I told you—playing pool. We went back to his place and played rummy 'til three a.m."

"You and Buddy?"

"Did you know he gets mad if he doesn't win?"

Phoenix is still running after Buddy, for all the good it will do. She's determined to be a member of our family, even if she has to take second best.

"That winning impulse runs in the family," Momma says.

"You think Burr is a prize?" Phoenix shoots back.

"He's a husband and father for my children."

"Are you sure that's what you want?"

Smiley tries to catch minnows in his hands. When they evade him, he plunks stones into the pool until he gets bored. Then he pokes me with a stick.

"Let's go explore."

"Naw, I like it here."

"You ain't seen anywhere else."

"Hush," I say.

I make as if I'm looking for a certain kind of rock and pick up one with indigo veins running through it, turn it around on my palm and let it slap back into the water.

"Burr's a good man," Momma says.

Phoenix rubs her forehead. "I thought you'd see the light. Guess I figured wrong."

"I guess you did."

"Well, anyway, the papers say they're doing a lot of peacekeeping in the Pacific. Sounds like he'll be gone a long time, Mags." Phoenix tickles Momma's arm with a blade of grass.

"Didn't I tell you?" Momma scratches her arm. "I wrote a letter about us having a hardship without him, and they're sending him home."

"You what?" Phoenix sits up.

"He should be showing up in a few weeks. The paperwork takes some time, but he'll be flying out of the next port."

Phoenix perches her elbows on her knees, ready to spring. "Were you keeping it a secret?"

Why would Momma keep the secret from *me*? She's playing Parcheesi with my life. I'm at least entitled to know how the dice are rolled.

"He's my husband," Momma says. "I don't have to lay out my entire life for you."

I resent Momma for her meanness to Phoenix. There's no call for it. Why does she spend time with Phoenix if she means to hurt her?

"You owe me some explanation," Phoenix says. "You owe me that, at least."

Momma breathes a half exasperated, half wistful breath. "He'll be in Washington and wants us to move up to a place he's found in Arlington, just outside the city."

Phoenix winces. Momma must know how that information stings her. But Washington—that's where Winona moved. Maybe we'll live near one another. I can learn to play the piano and we can perform duets.

"What about me?" Phoenix says.

"We'll always be close," Momma answers.

"Not with that prickly cactus pulling us apart."

"Phoenix—"

"Damn it, Mags—don't you ever think of me?"

Momma rakes at a mosquito bite on her leg. Phoenix clutches her wrist to stop the scratching.

"At least look at me when I'm talking to you."

"I've got things to sort out," Momma says.

"You've got to sort things out with *me*."

Momma raises her head and focuses at a spot beyond Phoenix. "The children love you, Phoenix."

"And what about you?"

Cowboy Code number three: Always tell the truth. But what is the truth?

Momma answers by draping her arm around Phoenix's neck and pulling their foreheads together. Phoenix wipes her cheek then rubs her palm on her pants. She rests her forearms on her knees and looks at the rocks between her legs, crumbles the spear of grass into a fist and throws it.

"Let's get out of here," she says and jumps to her feet.

"Where's A.T.?" Momma is scowling at me.

"He was here a minute ago." Why is it my job to look after him?

"There he is." Phoenix points to the falls and starts running over the rocks,

slipping, cutting her knee, scrabbling apelike on hands and feet.

"Stay where you are, A.T.," she calls.

He's going back toward the cave, climbing on a boulder with a sheer face that dives straight into the deep water. The rock is slippery, and I watch his foot shoot out from him, see him grab for a hold on the air and tumble in a slow cartwheel into the water.

The thought of losing him, no matter how much he goads me, is intolerable. I've had my share of loss. I disregard the fact that I've never been in water over my head. Momma's of no use and precious time is wasting. My brother is drowning, and I have to save him. In the seconds before I throw myself into the pool, I contemplate a life without Smiley. Momma clinging to me in her grief, giving me all her time. But then I imagine her balling me out for Smiley wandering off, never forgiving me for losing him, even sending me away so I won't remind her of this tragic event.

I'm surprised at how the water sucks the breath from me, but I dogpaddle like mad toward Smiley's splash until I get to the spot where he went under. Then I let myself sink down, searching through the green liquid. When I spot his flailing limbs, I grab him and push him upward. His body rises to the surface, his kicking legs leaving a trail of froth. Phoenix snatches him and he disappears.

In the silence afterward, I hear the liquid throbbing of my heart, feel the blood pass through my arteries, feel the surges in my temples, fingertips, toes. Swaying reeds anchored in black mud wave below me and I drift above them in wingless flight. Silver bubbles sail sideways and dark webs weave about me. Funny, though, it's growing dark so early in the day. Funny that the light is fading when I should be rising toward it.

* * *

When I come to, I'm lying on stone, smooth and cool. Phoenix's lips are pressed to my own, Phoenix's wet hair dripping onto my face, Phoenix's breath filling my lungs, giving me life.

I hear Smiley wailing, "Sister's dead! Bobbie's dead!" and Momma shushing him. Then Phoenix has Smiley, carrying him up to the hill, and Momma's arms are around me, rocking me.

"What a fool thing, jumping in like that." But her voice is soothing, not scolding, and I read her panic in the hoarseness. I don't cry, not even when she whispers, "We almost lost you." She cradles me like a loving mother is supposed to. Even so, I resent her for neglecting me and for her cruelty toward Phoenix.

"Why do you hate me?"

She stops rocking. "Oh, Sister," she moans.

"Why?"

"You're just in shock, honey."

"No, I'm not." I pull away so I can look at her. "How can you forget about Daddy?" I've taken a second leap, and I'm swimming for my life. I have nothing left to lose. "Why are you so selfish?" The last word sounds like splashing water.

Momma searches my face. She has something to say to me—another confidence—perhaps the weightiest of all.

"Your father—" She starts then stops to sigh.

"What about my father?"

She fastens onto me as if she's looking for the words. Finally she finds them.

"He married me because I was carrying you." She huffs a breath, almost a sob. "He said it was the civil thing to do." Her thumb runs across my dry cheek. "But he loved you. Oh, my, how he loved you." She kisses my forehead.

Blurry mysteries come into focus. The car stopped at the curb. Daddy's head on a woman's lap, her red fingernails stroking his chin. Daddy stepping out, awkward, and sticking his head back through the window. Daddy struggling up the stairs and the red fingernails waving out the window as the car drives off. Daddy going past Momma sitting on the porch glider, neither of them saying a word.

I lay my head back on the calm stone and watch two starlings chase a crow across the sky, dipping at its back, pecking at its wings. When I fill my lungs with life-giving air, a terrible black thing flutters out with my breath, flaps around my head and flies away.

*　*　*

On the drive home, Momma anchors Smiley and I sit up front with Phoenix. She looks straight through the windshield—no singing, no joking. I study her profile—her straight nose, her stubby eyelashes, her small ears—burning her image into my memory.

*   *   *

That night Phoenix is curled up on the sofa with a book while Momma gets Smiley to bed. I stay up to read some Rudyard Kipling stories, keeping Phoenix company. Momma says the excitement wore her out and she's going to turn in.

I doze off and when the creak of floorboards wakes me, it's dark. Someone has turned off the lamp, but in the starlight coming through the window, I see Phoenix in Momma's room, standing by the bed. Momma reaches up, squeezes her hand and brings it inside the covers. Phoenix slides under the blanket. I can hear them whispering through the door, something about Aunt Ruby.

"She had a real love. Every woman should have a real love once in her life." Phoenix's voice.

"Not if you have to hide it," Momma says.

"Even if you have to let it go." Phoenix's suede tones are the last thing I remember before I drift back to sleep.

31
The Locket

On Saturday afternoon Burr's sister Grace arrives for a visit. She and Momma do their best talking as they're playing gin rummy.

"Your deal," Grace says.

"What am I up to?" Momma asks.

"You had two-fifty, but you just lost twenty with those tens in your hand. You should've gone out three rounds ago. You're not concentrating."

"I guess I've got a lot on my mind."

What's on her mind is Burr coming home. What's on my mind is missing Phoenix. She hasn't been over since her birthday. I know Phoenix will show up sooner or later because she left clothes in Momma's closet, her favorite cup, a special tea she likes to drink. I wish she'd come back soon, and not just to claim her belongings.

"How are the children doing?" Grace asks.

"Fine," Momma says. "We're all fine."

"You spoiling them?"

"Not much chance of that." Momma bites her cheek. "We pinch every penny."

"Our mother spoiled Burr rotten. He had some spell over her. In fact, there's not a woman in Virginia he can't charm."

Grace likes to brag on Burr. She measures her husbands—past and present—against him and once she gets started, her tongue is like a runaway train.

"You remember June Bushey? She was one of Burr's girlfriends, but she wasn't too smart. Burr wised up after she showed him a good time. And when he broke Alice Corbin's heart, she ran off with Sam Isabel's boy. I swear Burr had a different girl every night of the week."

"Well," Momma says, "he's mine now. I consider it a compliment that he had so many girlfriends and picked me to marry."

Grace looks around our shabby apartment. "Burr deserves to indulge himself after putting in his time, pinching pennies or not."

"Dad said something about building a house for us." Momma lays her card hand face down on the table. "He found some land for sale near his place, but I don't see how we can find the money."

Building a house is a commitment to staying in Pine Cliff. I'm hoping once Burr gets back we'll move to New York. I'm suffocating in this Podunk town, but nobody consults me. If Momma asked, "Okay with you if we do such and so, Bobbie?" or "How do you propose we handle this or that?" or "Are you happy, Bobbie?" I would have to tell her the truth.

"It's so far out. I don't think Burr would like it if he couldn't get downtown," Momma says.

Grace taps a finger on the table. "Farther up Allegheny Avenue, Walter Jenkins is finishing his carriage house to rent out. New fixings and everything. I think you can make it real cute. You want me to talk to him?"

"Oh, Grace, would you?"

"I'll do it—" She sweeps up the cards and starts shuffling. "For Burr."

*　*　*

The rent on the apartment is $24 a month, but with what Burr sends us, Momma says she thinks she can pay the bills. She wants to think about it, though, before we start wrapping the dishes in newspaper.

"A new house would be wiser." Momma sits on the couch smoking a cigarette and eyeing the faded walls. "Something of our own." She settles the cigarette in an ashtray. "Sister, come here a minute."

I sit down beside her. She's holding what looks like butcher paper folded flat.

"Your birthday's next week—did you forget?" she says.

I haven't forgotten that I'm turning fifteen but I assume everyone else has, and I decide not to get excited about it.

"Mamaw would want you to have this." Momma passes the bundle onto my lap.

"What is it?"

"Something of the past to take into the future."

I stare at the gift.

"Go ahead and open it."

I take my time until the paper lies flat. Mamaw's necklace lies curled, delicate gold on the tough paper meant to cover butchered meat. I try to speak, to express how the common paper makes the locket even more lovely, as if my delicate grandmother has found her way back to my rough and practical grandfather.

Momma unfastens the clasp. "Lift your hair." I raise my hair from my neck, and she clips the necklace on me.

"You think Nandaddy will mind?" I wouldn't wear the necklace if it bothered him to see it on me.

"I'm sure he's already forgotten about it."

I slip my fingernail into the crack in the heart and pry it open. Mamaw didn't have time to put a picture in it. I'd like a small photo of Daddy if Momma can find one. Has it been almost a year since he's been gone? What is he now, skull and bone? Flesh rotted to the earth? Heart, lungs, the fur of his forearms, the force of his grip—all decomposed to dirt? Is he in the spring flowers? The summer vegetables? The autumn colors? The breezes that signal the coming of winter? Is he in the silence of the cold, the glint of frost? Or is he here, inside me—always?

I click the locket closed. For now, I'll leave it empty.

That night I lie awake, feeling an undercurrent of excitement, like a ship's motor at port churning the water, not going anywhere but roiling with possibility. Momma wanders around the rooms, then turns out the lights. I can barely see her outline standing between my bed and Smiley's, listening for the sound of our sleeping.

32
Strange Ideas

When summer comes, the community wanders out of their houses and onto the sidewalks. High school boys smoke cigarettes on the corner of Main and Lexington and watch girls whose arms and legs are bare in the heat. When a pretty one passes, they flick a knowing look at each other and snicker or stare dumbly, then stick a hand in a pants pocket and give a private yank. I may not know much, but I'm aware that an older boy walking hand in hand with a smart-looking girl signals more than a stroll. Yearning will give way to touching and touching to more serious things. One of these days my turn will come. Not that I'm interested in any boy in Pine Cliff.

Momma takes us downtown to shop for the leather aviator cap Smiley has been wanting. In front of the Gypsy Tavern, Lowry Trott is holding the waist of a woman I haven't seen before. A stringy mane drips down her shoulders and plasters to her shirt, ashen strands tangling with black. She looks like a scraggy skeleton. Her skirt ends just below the knee, and varicose veins color her legs with blue webs. Ten years older than Lowry, I'll bet. Lowry's whiskers are a field in need of bush whacking, and his shirt and pants are stained with motor oil.

Momma grabs Smiley's hand when we pass. Lowry wobbles, catches his balance, and looks at us but doesn't speak. Momma stares straight ahead. I'm glad that Burr's not uncouth. He likes a drink now and then, but I don't think he'd flaunt himself around town like that.

To get myself ready for Burr's arrival, I take to reading his letters, which come on paper as brittle as chapped lips. When I read the one dated May 17, 1948, I realize that I should have left some letters in their airmail envelopes.

My Darling Maggie,

I have three, no, four things which are with me most of the time. Two of them you haven't seen, but you will. The one I often misplace is my wallet that has your picture in it. And my identification bracelet that has your name on the back. And my tattoo that has your name inside a blue heart. Oh, did I forget to tell you about the tattoo? I had been having a few cocktails at the Cathay Bar and was in a jovial mood when I got the idea. But I won't tell you—I'll show you when I see you, which will be soon, my love.

This morning, after thinking the matter over, I believe I will live after all. I had to clutch this typewriter with both hands to keep it from getting down on the deck and running around like a mad dog. That's why I won't drink any more cocktails for a long time, and that's a promise.

Maggie, I'm an awful beast and don't rate such a wonderful girl as you. I hope you're thinking about us having a baby. I'd be afraid something would happen to you, but I'm willing to try. You do love me, don't you?

All my love, Burr

I turn the letter over and examine it. One small stain smudges the lower left-hand corner, a drop sloshed from a drink. I fold the letter and slide it back into the envelope—a bullet in the chamber. It's not the first time he's mentioned a baby. He must have his heart set on it. Phoenix will not be happy if she finds out what he has in mind. Not that she has much say in the matter.

* * *

Momma decides we'll save money by keeping the old place, which makes me glad because I can still hear Daddy's laugh echoing off the linoleum. I'll have to settle for sharing sleeping quarters with Smiley a while longer, small consequence for being able to stay in our home—Daddy's home.

When Momma tells Mr. Neddleton she's getting rid of her old bed, he says he'll take it. She orders a new model from Ruggle's with a box spring and mattress. It has a high headboard made of tan leatherette, puffed out and bolted with matching leatherette buttons, the kind of bed I imagine Myrna Loy slept in. It will take Momma six months to pay for it, squeezing five dollars each month from the allotment, but she says it will be worth it. We take down the old curtains and wash them, and I unpin them from the line while they're still damp and press them dry. Grace shows up with a throw she crocheted for the couch and an accent pillow she made by cutting up one of her skirts that had grown too tight in the hip. The living room is starting to take on a refined look, even with the old furniture.

* * *

I'm glad when Buddy shows up. We haven't seen him for ages, and I insist he stay for dinner.

"You sure you have enough for one more?" He has an impish smile.

"Always plenty for you," I say.

"I mean besides me."

As if on cue, Phoenix walks in without waiting for an invitation. She has cut her hair so it hangs straight to her chin, parted in the middle. She must be trying for high fashion, but in my opinion she comes across looking like an overgrown tomboy, which I suppose she is. She's shed a couple pounds, and the waist of her pants droops below the cinched belt.

Momma looks her up and down. "You're a wreck, Phoenix. What's happened to you?"

Phoenix shrugs. "Busy is all." She surveys the house. "Looks like you've spruced the place up."

Momma bought a copy of an artist's painting with a real wood frame—a print of a sandy marsh, cattails in the foreground, sun pressing through gauze clouds, a stone farmhouse on the horizon. The scene stretches out, as if I can reach into it and not touch a wall, a tree, a mountain. I'm sick of looking at mountains.

"Nice," says Phoenix. She runs her fingers over the upholstery of a chair, the corner of a table, the bottom of a lampshade.

"Want to see what we've done to the bedroom?" Momma means her room—hers and Burr's. Or is it Phoenix's and hers?

Phoenix shakes her head and looks at her shoes.

Momma tugs her by the hand. "Come on."

I watch Phoenix stand by the bed without touching anything. "Pretty high quality," she says.

"Try it out." Momma corrects herself. "I mean, sit on it."

Phoenix appears to think about it and says, "No thanks." At the bureau she studies the picture of Momma and Burr taken in New York on their honeymoon. Momma in her wedding suit, a black hat with a short veil, Burr in the dark Navy uniform.

"You look happy in this shot," Phoenix says.

"I was." Momma corrects herself a second time. "I mean, I am."

"Are you?"

Momma bites her bottom lip. The moment is fraught with tension, as Mrs. Davenport says about McCullers's book *The Heart Is a Lonely Hunter*. A lonely hunter indeed is the heart—my heart, at least, and probably Phoenix's, too. I can't think what to do with my hands, so I clasp them behind me. Here are the two women I love most in the world, now that Mamaw's gone. Two women who love each other, if I'm not mistaken. And yet they're engaged in a battle of wills, both wanting what their pride keeps them from ever having. Lonely hunters.

"Hey," Buddy yells from the kitchen. "I thought you asked me to dinner."

During the meal, he carries the conversation. Buddy's not one to discuss his romantic inclinations, so he keeps the topics to chickens, his automobile, and baseball—the first black pitcher in the majors homered for the Brooklyn Dodgers his first time at the plate, looks like the Yankees might be in the World Series, and some team had a no-hitter against the Washington Senators.

Smiley slides down from the table, and Momma examines her meatloaf, but Phoenix soaks up every word.

"Who pitched the no-hitter?" she wants to know.

"McCahan for the Athletics," Buddy clarifies.

"Hot dog!" She's enthusiastic at least about one subject.

After supper Phoenix does the dishes and I dry. Buddy keeps us company in the kitchen.

"You women can get some strange ideas. In fact, I'm giving Bertha a little breathing space for a few days."

"Her time of the month?" Phoenix is not one to mince words.

"I wouldn't know about that, but I'd like to have a clue about what's going on with her."

"Say," I break in, "have you ever made the table rise?"

"Me?" Buddy says. "I've made tables sit up and beg."

Phoenix chuckles. I like hearing her laugh again. "What say we have a session?" she says.

I've been thinking about consulting the table. I have some concerns that need addressing.

After Momma tucks Smiley in, she says a table session would be entertaining. I set it up, and when she gets the north legs into the air, she asks, "Who's going to start?"

"I will." Buddy clears his throat. "Table, will I find the nerve to pop the question to Bertha Shaker?"

The table taps the floor once—yes.

Phoenix's face is stony. I don't think she cares. Buddy isn't the one she wants.

"Buddy, I didn't know you were thinking about marrying Bertha," says Momma.

"It just seems like the next step."

"How does she feel about you?" I ask.

"Why don't we consult the table?" Momma poses the question, and the table taps yes.

"I'll be darned," Phoenix says. "Hey, Bud, I'm real happy for you."

Buddy purses his lips and nods toward her. So that's that. Phoenix has lost her chance to join the Persinger clan. Having her marry Buddy would have been a nice convenience, but in all honesty I can't see it happening. The air between them is cool.

"I'll ask a question," Phoenix says, looking at Momma. "Will Burr be back by the first of August?" The table taps once. That's two weeks away. I keep up my concentration for the table's sake, but I'm none too happy. I like everything the way it is.

I summon the gumption to jump in. "Will he keep his promise about not having another drink?" Two taps, hitting the floor hard each time—no.

"Have you been reading his letters?" Momma frowns at me.

"You read them to us." I avoid her question.

"Not all of them. Sometimes he writes things that are just for a husband and wife."

"And the censor," Phoenix adds.

"Can we get on with it?" Buddy says.

"Okay," Momma says. "Table, tap the floor once if Burr and I will have a daughter someday and twice if it'll be a son."

The table hesitates and taps once, twice, three times.

Buddy frowns. "I think you confused it."

"I'm the one who's confused," Phoenix says. "When did this baby business come up?"

Momma lifts one shoulder in a movie star pose. "I'm not too old."

"That's not the point. You have a baby and you'll never get out of that marriage."

"What makes you think I want out?"

The table shakes under my fingertips. Or it might be my fingers shaking.

"This table's not working right tonight." When I take my hands off, it seems to exhale a sigh of relief as it lowers.

"Look what you've done," Momma says.

"I've had my fill of this nonsense." I push back my seat. "I'm going to bed."

33
Homecoming

Every afternoon I dread the mail's arrival. A slim envelope bordered in red stripes with "airmail" stamped across it reduces Burr to two dimensions, black typewriter ink on white paper. Even so, I have a fear that one day Momma will slit open an envelope and the ink will take form, rise and swell, and he'll pop out, fresh and plump and real.

When he writes that he's on his way back to Pine Cliff, Momma waxes the floor, scours the kitchen walls, beats the rugs on the line. Clean sheets on the bed every week, just in case. She rearranges the cupboards and gets into the corners with a toothpick. Every night she sets her hair in finger waves and every morning makes up her face. He might come while she's at the store, and she keeps her lipstick in her pocket, ready to uncap it at the vaguest hint of a blue uniform.

Then on the last day of July, the call comes. Smiley picks up the phone and holds the receiver to his ear. He doesn't even say hello, just stands there looking dumb.

"Archer Timbers," I hear him say. He's taken to calling himself that after Phoenix started it. "Uh-huh," he says. "When will you be here?"

Momma takes the phone from him. "Where are you, Darling?" He's in Norfolk. Be home tomorrow. Can we meet him at the station?

* * *

We go downtown early, walk up and back Main Street, keeping the railroad tracks in sight. When the train pulls in, Momma counts the cars, holding her breath. The engine hisses, slows and clangs to a halt. Momma squeezes my hand. She smells of lilac and talc.

And then there he is, princely in his Navy suit. He stops at the top of the steps, duffel in hand. Squinting in the daylight, he settles the chief's hat lower on his forehead. Momma swings her arm in the air. He sees her, stumbles coming down the steps, catches himself with the handrail. No cameras flash, no guards hold back the crowd. It's just Burr, thinner and wirier, if that's possible. He swings Momma off the platform. Arms around her, hands on her face, tangled in her hair. Taking off his hat, he kisses her. Then he bends over and shakes Smiley's hand. He doesn't know what to do with me. I didn't want to come. I asked if I could go over to Penny Reardon's, but Momma said we had to make a family showing.

Smiley wants to carry Burr's bag but can't manage it. I don't offer. Burr holds the bag in one hand and loops his other through Momma's arm as we walk toward the house.

"How was your trip?" she asks.

"I'm beat," he says. "But I've got thirty days before I get the next orders. I'll be stationed on the East Coast. So, we've got to celebrate. You still have that bottle?"

"No," Momma says. "No bottle. I threw it out."

"We'll stop and pick one up." He makes puppy eyes at her. "Just this once. You don't know what I've been through. I couldn't describe it in the letters— guns going off all the time. It wears on you."

"But the war's over," Momma says.

"They're practice salvos," he says.

I guess Momma figures he deserves one night of drinking because we stop at the liquor store on the way.

*　*　*

Burr takes it all in—the pictures on the walls, the books on the shelf. On Smiley's bureau, toy cars lined up, rubber horses with cowboys astride them. In Momma's room, he sinks onto the bed, leaning his head on the leatherette headboard. Smiley sits beside him, staring at his face as if he's a celebrity.

When he says, "It's good to be home," I realize the old place is starting to feel less like home to me.

*   *   *

That night I have trouble falling asleep. I can sense by the sounds in the other room most of what's going on. The rest I fill in with my imagination. Burr kisses her and rubs his hands over her breasts. She's shy with him. It's a hot night, and the fan on their dresser must push the air about as much as shuffled cards.

Burr is home, and if Phoenix dares to enter Momma's mind, she'll nudge her out.

*   *   *

"Good morning, Sunshine," Burr says. "You want coffee?"

"I'll get it myself," I say.

"Suit yourself." He pours a cup and takes it to Momma. I watch him set it on the bedside table and rub her legs through the sheet.

"What time does A.T. get up?" he asks when he comes back.

"He should be up by now," I tell him.

"Then why the devil isn't he? We'll see about that."

He rummages through the cupboard. Then he switches on the radio and spins the dial, fragments of voices and music sputtering out. He settles on a march, a tinny drum thumping the rhythm. "Here," he says, handing me two pot lids. He clangs a wooden spoon on a pot and hikes into the living room, lifting his knees high. Looking back at me he says, "Well, come on. Time for reveille." I am dumbfounded. Does he expect me to make a fool of myself?

I hear Smiley mumble, "What's goin' on?"

Burr says, "Fall in, Chappy."

In a minute Smiley emerges, marching with Burr and banging away on the pot Burr hands him. Burr has a whistle in his lips, his hand over an eyebrow in a salute. It's the most ridiculous thing I've ever seen, and I laugh even though I try not to. The two of them march out the back door and down the steps, around the house, and come back in the front.

"Parade rest," says Burr. Smiley follows Burr's salute, his pajama bottoms wet with dew.

"Everybody on the street must think I've married a lunatic," Momma says. She's wrapped in a new bathrobe of pink satin. Burr must have bought it for her. She fixes oatmeal with sugar syrup while I make toast.

"Can we do this tomorrow, too?" Smiley asks.

Momma brightens. "Tomorrow and every morning."

I've started drinking coffee again and squeeze the handle of my cup, holding it tight as if it will slip away.

*   *   *

During his first week back, Burr stays close to home. His navy whistle is used to call the sailors to order on the ship, and he teaches Smiley and me a whistle that means we should come home right way if we're outside. He spiels stories about ports he visited, recites poems after dinner, walks us downtown, plays catch in the yard.

"Phoenix throws it under her leg, like this," Smiley says. It's about time someone brought her up. "And then she catches it with her other hand. Can you do that?"

"That's no way to toss a baseball," Burr says. "Somebody should show her the right way to throw it."

"She was just fooling around," I say.

"Sure she was," Burr's voice is edgy. I'd forgotten their run-in on New Year's Eve. It's just a matter of time before they have another confrontation. Phoenix isn't likely to give up her territory easily.

*   *   *

Every evening people stop by to say hello—Elsie, Pansy, Esther, Grace, almost everyone we know—except Phoenix. One night Buddy comes over with a narrow paper sack. I have a feeling what's inside. Momma takes Smiley into our room while Buddy and Burr mix drink after drink and pour them down. Buddy catches him up on baseball scores and boxing matches, and Burr spins some stories about bare breasted women in the South Pacific. I halfway listen, rolling a die from a Parcheesi game to see how many times I can make it come up six. When they start in on Phoenix, I perk up. Burr says he's just as glad she hasn't been over because she upsets Momma.

"I think the culprit might be you," Buddy says.

"Me?"

"Phoenix is not too friendly toward you."

"I don't think she goes for men in general."

I resent Buddy's laughter—I thought he liked Phoenix. If I tell Burr about Phoenix sharing Momma's bed while he was gone, he might get mad enough to leave, but that would make Momma unhappy. She's invested too much in Burr.

"How's that Packard of yours?" Burr asks.

"Great car," says Buddy. "You should take it for a spin sometime."

"Well, that's just what I was thinking. How about you let me use the Packard to take Maggie and the kids out to Dunlap Creek tomorrow? It's supposed to be a hot one."

"Well," Buddy says, "I guess so, sure. Long as you treat her with kid gloves."

"I'll drive her like a baby." Burr stands up. "Here, let me get you another drink."

"Sure, but easy on the whiskey this time. I'll have to drive home tonight."

"There's plenty of leg room on the couch," says Burr.

They banter back and forth about whether Buddy will stay or go, but it's not my business to wait it out with them.

34
Packard

Sometime before daylight, the door opens and Momma says, "You're loaded." A bump against the wall leading to the bedroom, and Momma mutters, "Let me help." One shoe clunks to the floor and then the other, and a zipper whistles. The springs creak, and Burr garbles something before falling to heavy breathing.

I know Momma's staring into the dark, thinking what to do. She is forgiving when someone makes a mistake, but if he repeats the offense, her tolerance wears thin. She has to find a way to make him mend his ways—or else. But I'm not sure what the "or else" is.

*   *   *

Buddy brings the Packard to the house the next morning, as he promised. Momma makes coffee, leaving Burr to sleep it off. I cut up celery kitchen match size and Momma devils eggs. I pack tomato, mustard, and lettuce sandwiches into a box.

"I'm sorry, honey," Burr says when he gets up. "Don't be sore at me."

She takes her time wrapping peanut butter fudge squares in waxed paper and doesn't look up when she says, "The car's out front."

"I'll just scrape these bristles off and be ready to go."

*   *   *

Burr puts the basket of food and a jar of iced tea in the trunk.

"You sure you can drive?" Momma sounds doubtful.

"I started driving my father's truck when I was eight." He tries to sound jovial, but his hand shakes when he combs his fingers through his hair.

I'm wary about Burr at the wheel when he's groggy. Smiley tries to pull me out because he wants to sit behind Burr, but I hold my ground.

"I'm already here."

"Go on." He shoves me.

"I'm not moving." My stubborn streak kicks in.

"Move, Sister," Smiley orders.

"Listen," Burr says. "You take starboard on the way over, Sport, and Bobbie'll give you the port side on the way back." I would object to the Navy lingo except that it pacifies Smiley into a compromise that I find suitable, and we're off.

Burr stops at Lowry's gas station, buys an inner tube Lowry has patched, and has him inflate it. When Burr wedges the tube into the trunk with the lunch, Lowry spits sideways.

We make a second stop at a store just outside town.

"What're we doing here?" Smiley asks.

"Just going to run in for a minute," Burr says. "Sit tight." He comes back with a large paper sack. Momma glares at him. "Got some pops for the picnic," he says.

"But I brought tea," she says.

"Let's make this nice, okay? Besides, I need a little hair of the dog."

I'm afraid the outing is spoiled before it even gets started. I lick at my thumb and bring my lips down to the knuckle. The sharp mustard under my thumbnail stabs and I bite down until the pain turns to pleasure.

*   *   *

In our geography unit, I learned that Dunlap Creek is part of the James River watershed. A tributary of the Jackson, it takes three-quarters of an hour to drive to the swimming hole Burr has in mind, so he says. I roll down the window and invite the hot wind to blow in my face. Deep in the woods, between the trees I can pick out a stump or a fallen log where the sunlight flecks like confetti. If I focus, I might catch sight of a deer or a mountain lion camouflaged by the leaves and branches. Animals spread out, signal to one another with howls or huffs, and gather now and then for warmth and the comfort of their own kind. The young stay with their mothers. Fathers go off on their own. Seems to me a fine way to live.

*   *   *

Dunlap Creek is no exotic vacation resort. It's nothing more than a muddy river at a curve in the Blue Ridge Mountains with furry trees mummified by Virginia creeper. A rickety pier leans out over the creek. The water is calm and cool but not arctic, and I can wade in without getting chilled. Burr helps Smiley into the inner tube, his butt in the center, legs dangling in the water, and pushes him out to where the river is up to Burr's thighs.

"Watch out for nibbling fish," he says, sliding under. He tweaks Smiley from below, and Smiley lets out a yelp. Burr tries to grab my toes, but I crawl up onto a rock. Smiley gets a ride and then Burr tells him it's his mother's turn. Smiley digs in the pebbles on the bank, and Momma lies back on the tube. Burr splashes water on her shoulders and dribbles it down her bathing suit. When I trudge past her to get to shore, I smell the wet heat from his body mixed with the hot rubber of the tube. Momma rests her head on the tube and lets the sun soak into her. Burr swims around, eyeing her like a crocodile.

Smiley and I pile stones into towers, but I'm getting impatient.

"I'm hungry," I call. Momma and Burr exchange low laughs, and I can tell he's doing something to her under the water. "It's way past lunchtime," I complain. Burr starts pushing her for the shore, the stream slapping the rubber with a licking sound. When the tube rubs bottom, Momma wrestles to get up. Burr helps her and then presses himself to her and massages his hands into her back. It's enough to spoil my lunch.

At the picnic table, Burr hands a bottle of pop to Smiley and one to me. He flips the cap off a green bottle for himself, raises the bottom and takes a long gulp. When he lowers it, the bottle squeals against his mouth. Smiley tries to imitate, sticking his tongue into the bottle so that it looks like a pink slug wedged in the neck.

"Want a pop, honey?" Burr asks.

"No," Momma says. "I'll just have tea."

The beer bottle is half empty before Momma can unwrap Burr's sandwich, and a glaze is sliding over his irises. We're nearly finished our meal when Burr starts on his third, and in the bag I find two others, wet with perspiration, and an empty which he must have drunk back at the store.

"Better lay off," Momma says. "You've got to drive."

"Beer doesn't affect me. I'm fine."

He comes up behind her and swaddles an arm around her chest, hand holding the bottle. She twists loose and says, "We have to pack up."

He digs a hole in the pebbles just underwater and sets the bottles in to cool. At the picnic table, he finishes off another beer then lies back on the bench, his shirt under his head, and falls asleep.

When Momma is done packing, she says, "It's late. We have to be getting back." Burr jerks awake and almost falls off the bench but catches himself with one leg. He sits, knees apart, rubbing his chest. Three sheets to the wind.

Momma puts the lunch basket in the car while Burr goes to a tree and urinates. Staggering back, he trips on a tree root, stumbles to the car, and props himself on the door to steady himself.

"You gonna be sick?" Smiley asks. A gut-wrenching vomit would do him good, in my opinion.

"No," Burr mumbles. "Climb in."

Smiley grabs the port side, but by that time I don't care. Burr is careful, looking before he accelerates onto the road, and shifts into second without revving the engine. By the time he shifts to third, Momma has her feet braced on the floorboard and a grip on the door handle. Smiley is quiet, looking out the window and humming to himself. I watch Burr, willing him not to nod off.

The road twists around curves, trees crowding the shoulder. I'm grateful there are few cars on the road. Down a hill, the Packard picks up speed.

"Slow down," Momma says.

"Just relax." Burr takes his eyes off the road to give her a crooked smile, and the car drifts to the left.

A car horn blares. Momma sucks in her breath. Her arm is over the seat, holding onto Smiley's knee. Burr yanks the steering wheel to the right to avoid the oncoming car, overcompensates, and the fender catches the trunk of an evergreen. I hear a thud and my shoulder jams into the armrest. When the car comes to a stop, I check Smiley. He has a red mark on his forehead but is not seriously hurt. Blood trickles down my calf from a cut on my knee. I lean over and lick it. My shoulder hurts, but I don't think I've broken any bones. Burr sits staring out the windshield, both hands tight on the wheel.

"That moron came out of nowhere." Burr shoves an apologetic look at Momma. "I swear he came out of nowhere."

Momma gets out of the car and I climb out after her. The fender has a dent, and the hubcap is bent, grass and bark sticking out from under it. The tire hisses and goes flat.

Burr comes around the car and grimaces at the damage.

"Buddy's going to murder me," he says.

"You're lucky you're not dead already," I growl. "Lucky we're not all dead."

He runs his hand over the dented fender. "You think he carries a spare?"

"I dearly hope so," Momma says.

Burr works his way to the trunk, leaning on the hood, the roof. He clanks around, dropping metal pieces on the road, bouncing the spare to check for air pressure. I wander through the woods to the stream running along the road and dribble water over my knee. Momma appears with Smiley. She nestles him onto her lap, dips her hand in and presses her palm to his head.

"What'll we tell Buddy?" I ask.

"He'll understand." She wags her head. "It's been a while since Burr's driven a car."

"Especially in his condition."

"Be quiet, Sister," Momma says.

I don't have to listen to her. She's pitiful.

"He could've killed us. Is that what you want?"

Momma presses her forehead to Smiley's neck.

The woods are tranquil. It would be nice to stay by the creek in the forest, but Momma has a husband and he is changing the tire, and when he's finished we will all get back into the car and head to town. All this I know, but I can't help wishing it were otherwise.

*   *   *

The following week, Burr does not go to the Gypsy Tavern and does not touch a drop of alcohol. The accident must have startled him sober. Buddy took it well, but we have to exercise frugality to pay for the repairs to the Packard. Burr keeps busy with tasks. He fixes the fan that has been rattling in its cage, even though his hands are shaking. He cuts the grass and trims the tall weeds by the house. He tightens a wobbly chair leg and greases a squeaky hinge. The month is winding down. Momma praises him for not drinking, but a few days before his orders come, he gets restless, pacing the porch, walking to the corner and back. I sense a storm coming.

"I'm going for a stroll," he says.

Smiley's child-size rocking chair had been mine. He's almost too big for it now, but he likes to throw his head back so that the rocker rears up. When he rocks forward, the chair slips backwards, and in this manner he works his way around the house. Now he's kangarooing his way into Momma's room.

"Honey, I have to get the children into bed," Momma tells Burr. I resent her putting me in the children category. Besides, I'm able to get Smiley to bed so she can go trawling behind Burr to keep an eye on him.

"You don't need to come. I'm just going a little stir-crazy."

"You won't drink, will you?"

"I might have one. That's all, though."

Out the darkened window, I catch him jogging down the steps and watch until the sidewalk swallows him up.

Momma irons some clothes in the kitchen and after I go to bed I see her curled up on the couch, listening to the radio turned down low. Sometime later, I hear the door and get up to see if Momma needs help with Burr. He stumbles, steadies himself on the casing and flops onto the bed, stinking drunk.

"This is the last time," Momma says.

We untie his shoes, setting them one at a time on the floor. "You should go back to bed." I hear concern in her voice—and gratitude.

"After I help get him settled." I swivel his feet up.

When we roll him over to get at his belt, he bolts upright, knocking me backward. His look has terror in it as if he's seeing the enemy attacking or a brawl in the Cathay Bar—but I've given him no cause to draw his fist back, to let fly with all his weight. When he hits my jaw, my head flies back, thumps the wall, and my hip catches the edge of the bureau. In one shooting instant of pain, I know what Private Stevens felt, burned and hanging from a German tree, I know the slice of the switch into Covey's back, and I know the ripping of flesh and cracking of bone when the metal tower blew up my father. Daddy never laid a hand on me, not even when I dropped Momma's perfume bottle. Glass had tinkled on the floor, and the aroma of wild rose permeated the air like a sudden garden. He had bought that perfume for Momma, and the scent stayed for weeks. I can smell it now, sweet and flowery.

I sit wedged in the corner where the dresser meets the wall and think of Nandaddy's cleaver, its heft, the rough grip in my hand, the slap of flat steel, the bite of sharp edge. What God hath joined together, let no man rend asunder, Reverend Singer said, but I'd like to rend Burr with that cleaver and sunder him from Momma and from me.

Momma's teeth are clenched, and her growl is feral. "No-you-don't." She has Smiley's rocker raised over her shoulder like a heavy pack, like the pillowcase of Daddy's things. I'm amazed at her strength to heave the wooden rocker up. It pauses above her, teeters, and comes down onto Burr's head.

I hear the crack and don't care whether it's the wood or his skull. He falls backwards and the rocker crashes to the floor beside the bed. Blood runs from his forehead down his face and onto the spread, and he lies there without moving. Momma checks to see if he's breathing. He groans, his hand paws the air, and then he falls still. I think of cleaning the blood from the spread before it leaves a stain and wobble getting my feet under me.

"I'll get a washrag," I say, but Momma misunderstands.

"Leave him be."

She carries a pillow and an extra blanket to the couch and switches on the lamp.

She turns my cheek to the light with her fingers. "You'll have a bruise."

I'm glad. Burr will be reminded every time he looks at me.

"What are we going to do, Momma?"

She fixes the pillow at one end of the couch. "I have to figure that out."

Whatever Momma decides, it will involve Smiley and me. I wish we would pack up and move to New York that very minute and leave Burr bleeding on the bedspread.

Momma lays the blanket over the couch, and then she does something she's never done before—she holds my face in her palms and kisses me square on the lips. I can smell the salt of her perspiration, or the tears she's holding in.

"We'll talk about it tomorrow." She lies down and draws the blanket over her.

I go to my room without saying good night. It's almost morning anyway.

*   *   *

Burr says he doesn't remember what gave him the case of dry heaves and the knot on his head the size of a lemon. When Momma tells him what happened, he says she should have killed him for hurting me. And he will never, ever drink again. A hundred times he mutters "I'm sorry," none of which erases

what he did nor gives me assurance he won't repeat the crime. He leaves at the end of the week and will be stationed in Washington. To save money, he has taken an apartment with a lieutenant and will come home weekends on the train. If I had my way, he'd stay in Washington. But Momma declares it an agreeable arrangement.

35

Queer

I have a dream one night that someone came and touched my elbow, a gentle contact but making its presence known. I was reading and didn't look up, just kept on to the next chapter, but I sensed her over my shoulder. Her breath feathered my cheek. She smelled like a summer garden, and then she kissed me on the earlobe and her breathing sounded like wind.

When I wake up, I think about who she could have been—not Momma. Not Winona. Not even Phoenix. An angel maybe. I've never felt love like that. She had no skin at all but a radiance like the fluorescent lights in the school hallway. I have to believe in the day when we can walk down the sidewalks of Pine Cliff and not notice skin color but, instead, see the light shining from within.

I must be under the influence of the August heat that gets trapped in the house like steam from the mill's dryers. Momma used to talk about how hot it was inside when she worked with Phoenix, both of them sweating so much that Phoenix's shirt stuck to her breasts. Coming out at quitting time was like stepping into spring. I never minded summer heat before, but now it wraps around me like cellophane and closes off the air.

Phoenix calls one day to make sure we're surviving, as she puts it. Momma is friendly to her and says we should all meet for lunch soon. She tells Momma she's going to steer clear of us when Burr is around. No use in stirring up the soot, but Momma says not to worry, soot has already been stirred.

I'm afraid to get my hopes up about Phoenix coming back into our lives, even when in the cool of morning Momma and I make a picnic lunch and meet Phoenix by the river. She perches by a tree and munches a cold meatloaf sandwich, letting Momma lead the conversation about getting Smiley ready for school, people at the mill she wants to catch up on, trying to sound sunny.

She never mentions Burr, and Phoenix never brings him up. What Phoenix does say is, "What happened to your chin, Sister?" When Momma clutches the basket handle, I say, "Must've tripped." Phoenix looks for confirmation from Momma, but she folds waxed paper and scrapes her nail over the crease.

"You sure?" Phoenix sounds suspicious.

"Uh-huh." It's a feeble lie and I know Phoenix knows it. Maybe that's why she starts coming over again, to keep check on us.

We build a barbecue pit in the yard out of rocks Smiley and I drag from the woods. On some evenings we roast sausages and wrap them in soft bread spread with mustard. When we have corn on the cob from Nandaddy's field, Phoenix eats like a typewriter, dinging the bell every time she returns the carriage. She brings popsicles or caramels, and a couple times she showed up toting cupcakes with frosting. But every Friday she disappears, and we don't see her until Monday. On Friday Burr comes home.

On Saturday Burr winds black tape around a worn lamp cord, weaves a patch on a torn screen. He tries to be on best behavior, and for those two days of the week he does all right. He catches the last train out of Pine Cliff on Sunday evening and goes straight to work from Union Station early Monday morning after a few hours curled up on a rail car seat when he can find an empty one. We're keeping two households now, guarding every nickel and making do. Momma captains the home team. She loses ground every time Burr takes a drink, but she will not quit. My mother never starts a game expecting to lose, no matter what the odds.

Every Monday Burr writes from the Navy Bureau where he has a job as record keeper. They are hopeful letters listing everything he has spent—three dollars to have his suit pants let out (our cooking is too scrumptious), a dollar and a quarter for a trolley pass, ten cents for shoe polish, sixty-five cents for a Salisbury steak dinner, seventeen-fifty for rent. Momma cashes his checks and gives him an allowance to live on during the week, and he mostly adheres to his budget. A few times he has asked for more—he's out of writing paper, shaving cream, needs a new watchband—and Momma doles it out to him. Daddy used to handle the bills, but she's done a fine job of taking over. It does seem to me like an odd arrangement, though, Burr being like an older brother rather than a stepfather. Momma may be too strict with him because one Friday the following letter arrives in the mail:

My Dear Maggie,

I'm down in the dumps. It's the same old story—money. I can live off Lieutenant O'Malley until payday but do not want to ask him for more than I have to. I made a promise to myself not to take any more from you—and even if it hurts, I'll have to stay here this weekend.

All my love, Burr

I'm not disappointed, but Momma sets her mouth when she reads the message, and I know she's preparing herself for battle. On board ship, the vastness of the ocean keeps him out of trouble but on land he's free to roam alleys if he chooses, and with Momma's name tattooed on his skin. Guttersnipes, riffraff, and stray cats all know her name and know that she is beloved of a scoundrel.

Momma flirts with the telephone. I hope she'll call him and confirm her worst suspicions. Instead, she opens the table drawer and finds a sheet of paper. She's more comfortable with pen and paper than a faceless voice. Fine stationery is a luxury we can't afford, and all she has are coarse leaves flecked with tiny fibers. The pen leaves rat tracks, and the ink bottle is empty, the fountain pen useless. So she finds a pencil. Pencil is good enough for him anyway.

"What did you say to him?" I ask.

She folds the paper twice and starts to address the envelope, circling the pencil tip above the paper, getting the rhythm of the cursive. She has nice penmanship.

After she finishes the address, she says, "How would you feel about moving away from Pine Cliff?"

There is pleasure to be sopped out of such an important question, even if my answer doesn't matter, even if Momma has already made a decision.

"Depends."

She licks the envelope and smooths the flap closed without pressing her usual pink lipstick kiss across the seal.

"You wouldn't miss your friends?"

Penny Reardon and Kenny? I haven't heard from them all summer. And Winona is already gone. But what about Phoenix—would she move with us? My stomach cramps up when I think of never seeing her again.

"You just fixed up the house and now you want to leave it?"

"If it comes to that."

*   *   *

We don't go to the station Friday night to meet Burr, and he doesn't show up at the house, although I wake up several times in the night listening for the door. Momma calls Phoenix on Saturday, and she takes us to a matinee and window shopping and then plays cards with Momma late into the night.

On Sunday Momma looks at the telephone a dozen times and turns away. It's Burr's move.

*   *   *

School is to start after Labor Day, just two weeks away. Smiley needs clothes but for me, Momma lowers the hems of my skirts, moves buttons over and says I can tie one of her scarves around my waist and it will be like a new outfit. She buys Smiley a pair of trousers and a pullover, compensation for which we'll have to lay off going to the movies for a week. Phoenix wants to lend us some money, but Momma won't have it. She knows how to stretch a dime.

Burr hasn't sent one word. You'd think he'd call, at least. By Thursday Momma has stopped walking to the telephone and glaring at the receiver. And wouldn't you know it? On Thursday afternoon his letter arrives.

The paper is slick, like a page from a magazine, with ink so thick it bleeds through the page. When Momma unfolds the note, the sheet slices her ring finger, leaving a neat slit. She stares at the part in the skin for a second, and then it fills with blood and overflows. She wipes it on the top of the letter, a red smear across her name. Then she reads.

He's sorry about the past weekend, will make it up to her. He wants to get back in her good graces. He'll be home on Friday night—sober. He sends her his undying love and his best to A.T. and me.

*   *   *

"From now on," Burr says that weekend, "I'm going to be totally honest with you." He pours evaporated milk from the can into his coffee. Momma doesn't put the milk into the little china pitcher for him anymore.

"What have you lied to me about up until now?" she asks.

Everything, I should say, but I hold my tongue. I don't intend to ruin this Saturday by talking ugly. Phoenix is coming to take me shopping in Clinton

225

Forge for a birthday present for her father. She's thinking about having some cufflinks etched with his initials.

"Well...." Burr blows into his cup. "There is one thing—I know you'll laugh about it now."

"What?" Momma says.

"You remember that night last winter you heard someone rattling the door?"

"That was you," I snarl. I knew it wasn't Covey. Burr came back drunk and tried to get in, but Momma had locked the door and he didn't have his key.

Anger flames in me. "Why'd you let Covey take the blame for it?"

"They didn't beat him for that." Burr sucks in some coffee and swallows.

"You know about the beating?"

"He was lying to people about being half white." He sets down his cup and lights a cigarette.

I point a finger at him. "Covey wouldn't say that. It wasn't anything he'd brag about."

"I'm just telling you what I heard." The cigarette smoke drifts over my head.

"You hear that from Nandaddy?"

Momma intervenes. "Sister, Phoenix'll be here in a minute." She wipes the table, raking crumbs off the edge into her hand. "Are you ready to go?"

Burr sniffs. "I don't want her coming over here when I'm gone."

Momma drops the dishrag into the sink, pulls the cupboard door open with the toe of her shoe, and tosses in the crumbs. "Is that why you stayed away last weekend?" She tightens the tie on her apron.

The pot's about to boil over and I'd like to watch and see who ends up cleaning the mess, but I'm still in my pajamas and have to get dressed before Phoenix comes. All the same, I listen from the other room.

"Look." Burr clears his throat. "Seems like everybody in town's talking about you two."

"Who's everybody?" Momma says.

"Lowry Trott swears she's queer."

"She doesn't go for Lowry, that's for sure."

"Aw, honey, I just don't want people getting the wrong idea."

"Why do we care what Lowry Trott or anyone thinks for that matter?"

I'm watching out the window for Phoenix but take a quick look into the kitchen. Burr has hold of Momma's elbows and is mumbling into her hair, something about Grace saying Phoenix is aiming to take her away from him. Momma pushes him away.

"Phoenix is my friend." I hear a note of annoyance in her voice. "And Grace is a gossip."

"Have you given thought to the children?" he says. "Sooner or later they're going to hear about it, true or not."

Between minor disasters like the fire in the projection booth at the Visulite Theater and the Jackson overflowing onto River Street last spring, a small town gnaws on itself for amusement. Momma stopped taking us to church because of wagging tongues. Phoenix doesn't go either. Burr may have a point—Momma and Phoenix are like an old married couple. She knows Phoenix likes her pork chops fried crispy, likes a spoonful of sugar in her peas, a sprig of crushed mint in her iced tea, stirs her coffee with the fork handle. She reads *Life* magazine back to front, licks her pencil lead before she writes, always sits in the fourth row at the cinema. She likes a hot dinner and a tepid bath. Has Momma learned such details about Burr?

"It's just talk," Momma says.

Burr pinches her cheek. "Let's hope so."

When Phoenix honks the horn, I prance down the stairs to the car. She has the door open, waiting for me.

36
Womanhood

"Your dad make it home?" Phoenix asks.

"He's not my dad." I wiggle on the seat. My stomach is upset.

"For the moment, he's all you've got."

I roll down the window. The hot wind does nothing to settle my insides. I think maybe I need to have a bowel movement, and when I tell Phoenix, she doesn't ask me why I didn't go before I left the house or complain at all.

"I have to fill up anyway," she says. "Think you can wait fifteen minutes for the station up the road?"

"I think so."

Phoenix doesn't say much while she drives, just looks over at me now and then. I have a lot on my mind—new teachers, the possibility of moving, Burr and Momma playing tag with each other. I hope I'm not getting sick.

We pull into the gas station, and I go into the ladies' room. I line the seat with lengths of toilet paper as Momma taught me to do in public bathrooms so I won't catch a disease, and then I sit down. There's blood on my underpants that I didn't see the last time I looked. I keep forgetting to count the days so I can prepare for my redheaded cousin's visit, and I have nothing with me to deal with her. I'm trying to figure out what to do when Phoenix knocks.

"All clear in there?"

When I don't answer, she opens the door I neglected to lock, and here I am in plain view, nowhere to hide and stuck in a compromising position. Phoenix takes one look at the crotch of the panties around my ankles and then reads the expression on my face.

"Uh-oh," she says. "How old are you now?"

"Fifteen. But it's been happening for a few months."

"I was thirteen. You're lucky you had some time before you had to deal with this mess." She wads up some toilet paper and sticks it in my panties. "That'll have to do until we can get to a drug store."

"Thanks," I say with some relief.

"This is your mother's job, but since she's preoccupied at the present time, I'll have to serve as a substitute. Trust me?"

Even if I had a choice, I would have trusted Phoenix. I feel flooded like some spring cellar and but for Phoenix I would drown. Phoenix—my rescuer. My solid ground.

Outside the car window, a power line threads itself through the blue fabric sky beside the highway, and I focus on its silver slenderness and the invisible needlepoint that curls around and sticks itself into my belly. In that sharp pain, I find satisfaction.

*　*　*

When Phoenix tells Momma that my visitor has arrived, she takes me into her room. We sit side by side on the bed, on the nubby petals of the new spread, white with embroidered flowers. Momma looks straight at the wall and I watch the tops of my knees, the pale fuzz growing thinly. She has tutored me in using the belt and pads, but now when she sighs and clears her throat, I know she wants to talk about being a woman.

"There are things you need to know," she says.

"You don't have to explain—I already know."

"You know about the birds and the bees?"

I nod yes at my knees. Penny Reardon has educated me.

"And dogs and horses and men and women."

She plants her knuckles on the bed beside her. "Well, then." She breathes a sad, ragged breath. "Well." Then she gets up and goes out, leaving me sitting in the embroidered garden where she and Burr act out what we never speak of.

37
Prince Charming

Phoenix calls on Monday morning, but Momma tells her we'll be having dinner with Nandaddy and will see her later in the week. Tuesday we're going to Buena Vista with Buddy to get his watch repaired, stay to see the latest Errol Flynn movie, and eat supper at Bertha's. Wednesday Momma gives her the excuse that she's feeling feverish and will send us to bed early and then turn in herself.

Thursday Phoenix shows up at the door.

"What's going on?" She's standing on the back stoop. She uses the back door these days.

"Nothing's going on," Momma says.

"Is he coming this weekend?"

"You mean Burr? Of course he is."

"You free to do something tonight, then?" Phoenix is fingering a wild daisy plucked from the yard. She could throw some chicken on the barbecue, play some catch, a few hands of rummy. But Momma has her guard up. She looks up and down the back yards of the neighbors' houses.

"You must have better things to do," she says.

Phoenix flinches as if she's been stung. "Yeah, I guess I've got things to do." She throws down the flower and disappears around the house without looking back.

* * *

I start tenth grade with reservations. My body has become a stranger, erupting fluids without warning and sending me into sulks the reason for which I cannot fathom. My gym instructor is a man and, worse, he insists that our physical education consist of tumbling activities—somersaults and building pyramids with the biggest boys on the bottom and the tiniest girl at the top. I'm on the middle layer, and Cheryl Housner climbs up on me and digs her sharp knee into my kidney. When Mr. Wolf is pleased with our pyramidal form, the big boys collapse, and we topple into a human ruin. I dread having to ask Mr. Wolf to excuse me from tumbling when my time of the month comes.

Smiley says he likes second grade, and after a week he stops waiting for me after school and wanders home on his own, stopping to check for tadpoles in every puddle so that we arrive at the same time. I don't bother tattling on him, for all the good it would do.

Burr writes that he's looking for a two-bedroom apartment in Washington, but housing is tight. He has found a one-bedroom for $36 a month, but we need two, and there's no telling when the bigger place will come up. I hope for three bedrooms. I'm too old to be sharing with Smiley. And anyway, I'm starting to change my mind about leaving. Tenth grade is not as bad as I anticipated, I like our little house when Burr's not home, and Phoenix is in Pine Cliff. I can't bear to think of leaving her.

Once a week Burr checks on housing for military families, but a dozen names are on the list ahead of us. Meantime, we cut every corner and live like squirrels. Burr tries to get by on less than four dollars a day, which includes a weeknight movie and comic books he buys for Smiley. The fare to Pine Cliff and back is $22.50 a month, laundry costs four dollars, and cigarettes amount to five dollars. Out of his monthly paycheck, his expenses leave him with $23.70. Of course, he doesn't account for the weekend bottle, but even that he rations, stopping at two drinks on Saturday night when we sit on the porch and watch the lightning bugs rise, slow and groggy, picking up speed until they streak like gunfire across the night. When the mosquitoes start feasting, we go inside and listen to the radio.

After one Sunday dinner, Smiley and I are playing catch in the side yard, and Momma is fixing a covered dish of banana pudding to send back with Burr. I see Phoenix come to the back door and knock. I don't think she notices Smiley and me.

Burr pushes screen door but doesn't step out.

"Oh," he says. "What can we do for you?"

"You can't do anything," Phoenix says. "Is Mags here?"

"Yeah. Hang on." He lets the screen door slam.

When Momma comes, she talks through the screen.

"I thought the bastard would be gone by now," Phoenix says.

"You know he catches the Sunday night train." Momma sounds irritated. "And he's not a bastard."

"Right—he's Prince Damn Charming. I forgot."

"Then you're acting like the ugly stepsister." Momma steps out onto the stoop rather than have Phoenix come in.

"Listen," Phoenix says, "keep your glass slippers on. I just came over to see if you all wanted to go to Blacksburg next weekend for the Virginia Tech game. It's alumni weekend, and there's going to be a parade, floats and everything. We can spend the night, on my dime."

"Phoenix, you know Burr is here every weekend."

"Seems to me he's skipped a few."

"One, but that was just a misunderstanding."

"I'd love to go to Blacksburg," I say, coming around the corner of the house. The weekdays drag by, and when Burr comes home, we've got nowhere to go and no money to spend.

"Seems to me he owes you a weekend. Come on, Mags. You, too, Sister."

"I suppose it would be fun." Momma is considering Phoenix's invitation. I hope she'll tell Burr not to bother catching the train next weekend.

Before she can commit, though, Burr wanders through the kitchen and out back. He snakes his arm around Momma's neck, his hand dangling over her left breast. "Want to let me in on your girl talk?"

"Phoenix, we'd better not," Momma says.

"Better not what?" Burr says.

"Just think about it, will you?" Phoenix squeezes Momma's hand.

"She's got plenty to think about already." Burr ushers Momma inside.

"I'm sorry, Phoenix," Momma says over her shoulder, leaving Phoenix standing on the stoop.

38
Lies

Momma throws her weight into being Mrs. Burrows. She cuts back on cigarettes so she can buy steaks for Saturday night's dinner, a big one for Burr and two smaller ones for three of us to share. Burr unwraps the butcher paper and hums.

"What say I cook these on the barbecue? Give them some outdoor flavor."

I don't tell him Phoenix built the pit and that Phoenix has used it to cook many meals for us. I do, however, watch him make a neat stack of logs and throw on a match, watch him stare as the match burns out and the logs sit cold. He sends Smiley into the house for newspaper, wads it up and pushes it under the logs. Flames this time, blowing up white ashes like hot snowflakes, but the logs still don't catch. I worry that he won't get it started. Momma will want him to have success with this domestic gesture.

"Why don't I give it a try," I offer.

"Oh, you think you can do better? Have a go at it, then." He backs up with his hands on his hips. I pull the logs out, ball up more newspaper, find some twigs and make a teepee over the paper, then strike a match. When the paper and twigs flame up, I stack the logs on top, leaving spaces between them for the fire to breathe, and in a few minutes the logs catch.

"Where'd you learn how to do that? Are you a boy scout or something?"

My nasty streak boils up. "That's how Phoenix does it. See, you've got to start small and work up."

"Well," he says, "my way would have made coals faster."

"Your way we'd be eating raw steaks."

His lips twitch. "Why don't you see if your mother needs some help. I think I can handle it from here."

When the steaks are done, Burr brings them in and sets them on the table. Momma has spread a fresh cloth and lighted candles in Mamaw's silver holders. The sun is going down, and the candlelight casts shadows. Burr turns on the radio and "Don't Get Around Much Anymore" warbles out.

"Hey, I like this song," he says. "I haven't heard music all week."

"Don't you listen to the radio?" Momma asks.

"It's on the fritz. I've been meaning to take it in to be looked at. Just a blown tube, I think. Guess I've been playing it too much."

Momma pours wine from a tall, thin bottle into two tumblers. It's cheap wine, and I watched her empty half of it into a Mason jar before dinner, fill the bottle with water and add a drop of red food coloring. No point in fueling Burr's craving.

"A toast." Burr lifts his glass and Smiley reaches with his juice glass, slopping some onto the cloth. Momma holds up her wine, but I'm reluctant to join until I know what we're toasting.

"To us," Burr says.

"To us," Momma echoes.

They clink their glasses together, but I put mine down. Burr taps his to mine and says, "Say, you want to see where we're going to live?" He gets up, finds a piece of paper and pencil on the telephone table and brings it back, sketching a map, a maze of single-story row houses on the bus line within a mile of the Navy Annex.

"The housing project is in Virginia, but see how close we'll be to the District of Columbia?" he says, excitement seasoning his voice. "We can go into town on weekends and see old Lincoln sitting up on his big seat, staring at the Washington monument." He pecks the pencil lead on the paper. "And if Buddy ever gets ready, he might sell us his Packard."

"We going to get a car?" Smiley bounces on his seat.

"Why not? We can take a summer vacation and stay in a motel with a swimming pool. You two can even jump on the bed."

"I'm too old for that," I say.

"Then you'll be in charge of getting cold pops and ice from the machines in the office."

He means well, I'll give him that, but I'll be surprised if the plans take form.

"When we going to get us a car?" Smiley is persistent.

"Well, I'm working on it. It's just on paper for now, but if you eat your dinner and start growing, it'll happen before you know it."

"How are things at work, honey?" Momma always asks that question when he comes home on weekends. It's a small thing, but hearing her ask it makes life sound almost normal.

"It's been pretty hectic," he says. "I've been meaning to tell you about it. They may ask some of us to work overtime." He's talking to his plate, which makes me suspicious.

"How much overtime?" Momma raises her eyebrows.

"Weekends, maybe," he says. "A new section moved into the office last week, about fifty recruits. All I hear all day is clacking typewriters."

"All Navy men?" Momma stops her wine tumbler before it reaches her lips.

"Mostly. And about a dozen WAVES."

"Women, you mean?" I'm thinking about all those girlfriends he had before he married Momma.

"They're all homely as sin," he says.

"When will this overtime start?" Momma asks.

"I'm going to try my best to get out of it."

"See that you do," she says.

*   *   *

On Friday night Momma, Smiley, and I wait at the station for Burr, but the train arrives without spitting him onto the platform. Momma sits up that night listening for the ring of the telephone. He calls on Saturday afternoon saying he missed the train and was so upset that he borrowed some money from O'Malley to drown himself.

"I wish he *had* drowned," I say.

"Don't talk like that, Sister."

"Why didn't he call last night, then?"

"He stayed at a friend's place. He didn't think he could make it to the apartment, the state he was in."

When is Momma going to wake up? Phoenix would never play those tricks on her.

"It's hard for him getting back late on Sunday nights," she says. "He's going to start taking the Sunday morning train."

More time to ourselves, I'm happy to note. More time with Phoenix.

"Funny, though," Momma says. "I thought I heard the faintest sound in the background when I was talking to him, something like the hum of a fan, a cat purring. He must have had the radio on."

"Has he had it fixed?"

Momma adjusts the hang of a curtain. She studies the stitching in the seam and scratches at a spot with a fingernail. The two o'clock train whistles a shrill blast.

"He'd just better be on that train Friday night," she says. Or what? She'll hang him by one leg and slit him open? She'll grind him into sausage?

"What'll you do if he's not on the train?"

"Never mind," she says.

*　　*　　*

Burr's face is puffy when he comes in the following Friday, as if he hasn't had much sleep. He pours a drink and downs it, pours another.

I watch him fill the glass. "I thought you were going to cut out drinking."

"I've got good reason. They're shipping me out."

"They can't do that," Momma says.

"Any sailor who's been ashore for four months is being sent back to sea." He slides a cigarette out of a pack but doesn't light it.

"What about the apartment in Washington? What about the car and the vacations? You made promises to us." I've already told the school principal we're moving, and he said he'll write a letter to my new school about my academic performance to date. I didn't try out for a part in the Christmas pageant just in case I'm forced to withdraw. I'll look foolish if we haven't gone by then.

"How soon?" Momma says.

"They don't say." He sets down his drink so abruptly that liquid sloshes out. Then he grabs Momma's shoulder, a desperate look in his eyes. "Do you want me to stay?"

"How can you ask me that?" Momma doesn't give him a direct answer. Burr wanted to be a family man and Momma's going to make sure he gets it— wife, children, a house with curtains on the windows and all the furnishings. Whether that's what she wants or not, that's the decision she has made.

"Get Elsie, Buddy, your dad, my mother, anyone you can think of to write letters." He's pacing across the living room, four steps, turn, four steps, turn.

"They don't have to be fancy. Address them to the Bureau of Naval Personnel. All they have to say is that it's a hardship on you, my being away." He points at her with his cigarette. "Ask Dr. Cummings for a statement, too. You've paid him plenty, so he should be willing to do it. He could say you're not strong enough to care for the children and the house by yourself."

It's all lies. We can take care of ourselves fine. Except for the little bit of cash we get from him, we're on our own anyway.

Momma presses her lips together, a sign that she's thinking.

Burr pulls her rough stationery from the telephone table. "You can write them yourself. It'll be quicker that way, and they can sign them." He points to me. "Bobbie, get your school notebook. She shouldn't write them all on the same kind of sheet."

"Momma—" I stop myself. If she writes those letters and he sticks around, we'll be in the same predicament as before—getting hung-over professions of love and promises to be a better man in the future. It's a moment when we Grey women have a decision before us, like a rabbit thinking about whether to stare down the predator or run for her life. I wish the choice were mine to make but Momma has stared him down, and she has given in.

"Go ahead and get the paper, Sister."

I try to hold onto any thread of hope I can grasp. Maybe he'll reform. Maybe he'll keep his promises. But it's probably wishful thinking.

She smooths out a sheet and he gives her a pen. Burr dictates, and Momma writes four letters, changing her penmanship—perky backhand, square print, pinched vertical, looping forehand—with various phrases but all saying the same thing.

"They have to be notarized," Burr says, drink in hand. He slowed down while Momma was writing. "We'll have to take them to the bank first thing Monday morning."

"Don't you have to be back on Monday?" I ask.

"I'm taking half a day off. It'll be worth it if I can bail out of this outfit."

"And do what?" I ask. "Will you move back to Pine Cliff or are we moving to Washington? Smiley and I are wrapped up in this plan, too."

He shuffles through the sheets of paper. "We'll talk about that later."

*   *   *

Momma calls the people Burr suggested and asks them to meet her at People's Bank when it opens on Monday morning. Buddy says he can pick up Elsie, and

Grace will bring Mom Burrows. No one mentions Phoenix, and it's ridiculous to think she'd be party to keeping Burr in Pine Cliff.

On Saturday Burr is well behaved, thankful to Momma for helping him out of a jam, I suppose.

"Did you call Doctor Cummings?" he asks Momma.

"No," she says. "He's awfully busy. You've got to make an appointment a week ahead to get in to see him."

"What does it take for him to sign his name to a letter?"

When Momma doesn't answer, Burr tosses a dime up and grabs it midair.

"It was a longshot, I guess." He tosses the dime up again. I try to imagine him living in Pine Cliff, taking over his father's feed store or working at the mill, but I can't picture it. He would never be able to do what Daddy did, the sweaty work of checking digesters in hundred-degree heat, putting his life on the line. Burr has been at war, if you count taking stock of toilet paper rolls, but he isn't cut out for mill work.

"Say, isn't Phoenix's father a doctor?" he asks.

"Yes, but I've never been a patient of his." Momma avoids looking at him.

"Phoenix could talk to him. Maybe she'd get him to write a letter."

"I won't ask her to do that."

"Why not? You're chummy with her." His tone has a sarcastic edge, and then he softens. "I mean, she'd do just about anything for you, wouldn't she?"

Momma hesitates. Phoenix would turn the earth on its axis if she thought it would please Momma, but would she be an accomplice to Burr getting out of a deployment?

"Bobbie, you can run interference," he says. "You've got Phoenix wrapped around your finger."

Even if that were true, I don't see any benefit for Phoenix in a Lesley Burrows discharge from the Navy.

* * *

Burr has the letters notarized and takes them to the post office before he gets on the train. He says they'll buy him time while the head of personnel reviews his case.

Meantime, in late October the garden gives up the last of its offerings. Phoenix harvests the vegetables, carries them in and unloads them on the kitchen counter—winter squash, fat carrots, piles of kale and collards, mounds of potatoes crusted with earth. At the threat of frost, she picks all the green tomatoes, and we dip them in egg and cornmeal and fry them up. Phoenix cooks the collards in bacon grease, then sprinkles the crumpled bacon over them. We are all plumping up, except for Momma, who picks at everything. How she can resist Phoenix's cooking, I do not know.

I start to dread weekends. It isn't just that the cooking falls to me—but Phoenix disappears, and Momma holds vigil over Burr. Will he drink too much? Will he wander down to the Gypsy Tavern? She's on edge and he's moody. Each time Momma presses him about what's wrong, he says he's worried about money, having a wife and two kids is a greater weight on him than he thought it would be, he's just down in the dumps. He brings a full bottle of whiskey Friday night and leaves it empty on Sunday when we pack him onto the train with a bag of leftovers on his lap and a hangover pounding in his head.

*　*　*

When an envelope arrives for me with a Washington, D.C., postmark, I stare at it for a minute thinking it must be from Burr. But why would he write to me?

I tear the flap and find a card—Happy Thanksgiving on the front. Inside, it's signed by Winona with a note. Her penmanship is small and neat, the ink black. She's getting proficient at the violin and thinking of taking up piano, she writes. Then she mentions Covey, and my heartrate speeds up. He has promised to buy her a spinet if he can find a fair deal on a used one. He came into some money from a rich relative—Aunt Ruby, I'm sure—and is enrolled in a science course at Howard University, wants to be a veterinarian someday. That makes me smile. Covey an animal vet. He'll be kind and patient with them.

I wish she'd say more about Covey, but she goes on about how you can win baby alligators at the fair for knocking over three pins with a softball. You can stick your finger in its mouth and it doesn't hurt. You keep them in a box with sawdust and a bowl of water. They eat bananas, peel and all. She says she saw it herself when she went to the Fourth of July celebration on the Mall. Regina wouldn't let her try for one, though. When they get too big and start climbing out of the box, you have to flush them down the toilet and they end up in the river. That's why you shouldn't swim in the Potomac. Some of the alligators are ten feet long. She's never seen one herself, but if I ever come to Washington, she'll take me to Haines Point to look for them.

I read the letter over and over and make a pledge to get to Washington somehow. Winona and I could go see the Constitution and monuments. Maybe Covey would come, too. All that's required is that I think of Burr as my father, but it's a dear price to pay.

We expect him home the day before Thanksgiving. He promises to catch the train after work and be here before we go to sleep. The four of us will have a quiet Thanksgiving dinner. Buddy will be spending the holiday with Bertha's family. Phoenix plans to have supper with her father—not that she's been asked to dine with us. Nandaddy is going to his brother's house in Roanoke and invited us to come, but Momma declined. She wants to have the first Thanksgiving with her new husband, a big meal, turkey, mashed potatoes, rutabaga, fresh biscuits, pumpkin and butterscotch pies.

Wednesday after school, the butterscotch pies are cooling on the counter, their meringue peaks toasted, their caramel aroma tempting. Momma is washing mixing bowls and pots in the sink. She doesn't turn and say hello when I come in.

"What's the matter?" I figure her mood has something to do with Burr.

"Read the letter for yourself." Her voice has defeat in it, a tone I'm not familiar with. I pluck the letter from the table. As usual, it's typed with the periods punching holes in the paper.

Dear Maggie,

I know it's Thanksgiving, honey, but it seems silly to get on a train two days after I just got back. It hurts me as much as it does you, but it'll save a few extra bucks if I just stay here this week. Besides, I don't want to leave O'Malley all alone. His family lives in Iowa, and he wants to save his leave for Christmas. We'll have a hot turkey sandwich downtown Thursday, and then I'll give you a call before I settle in with a book.

I'm putting in for a week's leave at Christmas, and we'll have some fun then. It won't be long, sugar.

Love, Burr

I fold the letter and slip it back into the envelope. Mrs. Davenport says letters are sometimes called missives, like missiles, weapons used in wartime, and I think how appropriate that is.

"Maybe you shouldn't have tried so hard to get him that shore duty, Momma," I say. "You might just live to regret it."

39
Football

"Smells delicious in here." Phoenix comes by on Wednesday after work. Momma has made the stuffing but the turkey won't go into the oven until the morning.

"Hello, Phoenix." Momma is sitting at the kitchen table.

"Thought I'd sneak over and see you all before your ornery husband's train comes in," Phoenix says. "What time is he due?" Her hands in A.T.'s armpits, she swings him around in a circle, his legs flying out.

"Anything happening at Virginia Tech over Thanksgiving?" Momma taps her cigarette on the ashtray.

Phoenix stops twirling, staggers one way and Smiley reels the other. She plants her feet and cocks her head.

"What?"

"We're ready to take you up on that offer of a football weekend."

"What about your little family get-together?" She plops down on a chair.

Momma puffs and blows smoke toward the ceiling.

Phoenix doesn't wait for an answer. "VMI's got a game at noon." She whacks Smiley playfully on the behind.

"Would that be okay with you two?" Momma looks at Smiley and me. Her throat sounds tight, as if she's about to cry. Taking a trip to get her mind off Burr is one thing, but she's giving Phoenix false hope.

"What about Thanksgiving dinner?" I say.

"Takes less than an hour to drive to Lexington," Phoenix says, nearly breathless. "We can be back by late afternoon."

"Yee-haw," Smiley yells.

And so it's settled.

*   *   *

Phoenix has borrowed her father's car and I sit in the back, trying to keep Smiley from jumping around. He's all over the seat, acting out plays—passes, fakes, blocks. Phoenix looks over at Momma.

"What's on your mind?"

Momma has a powerful will but is she willing to go through it all again—Burr's distraction, hauling him into line? She gives a slow head shake and stares at the dashboard.

Phoenix studies the road. "Mags—when was your last period?"

"I'm not sure. Just before I bought the new bed, I think."

"That was three months ago, Momma," I say.

"I'm just not sure of anything anymore." She sucks in her cheek and chews on it. We have money problems enough as it is, and who knows whether Burr is going to stay in the picture? This isn't the time to be expecting.

"Listen," Phoenix says, "when we get back to town, you've got to promise me you'll go see the doctor."

Momma rubs her temple.

"How about letting my dad take a look at you this afternoon? You can stay for supper."

"We'll see—"

"A baby," Phoenix says. "Now doesn't that shed a different light."

"Phoenix," Momma says, "if something should happen with Burr and me—"

Phoenix hazards a glimpse at Momma. "What kind of something?"

"I mean, if we should decide to call it quits—"

How far is Phoenix willing to go for Momma? She's already endured more than she deserves.

"You know I'm here. I'll always be here."

With looking after her family, Momma has never had time to look after herself. If she has to ask herself what she wants, will she be able to answer? Burr represents all she is conditioned to believe is proper and acceptable. He's not so bad when he's at his best—funny and solid, father and fixer. But at his worst, Momma and the rest of us have our hands full.

*   *   *

When VMI wins the game by a field goal, Phoenix buys Smiley a pennant to stick on his wall. I can almost taste the stuffing and butterscotch pie we'll have for supper. Momma says she's too worn out to be sociable with Phoenix's father and we'll just fix dinner for ourselves. I suspect she's trying to avoid the examination. Momma has the attitude of what she doesn't know won't hurt her.

Phoenix says she'll come in for a minute and parks the car. Halfway up the steps, Momma stops to catch her breath.

"You all right?" I ask.

"Honestly, what's wrong with me? I should be able to jog up these stairs without breathing heavy."

"Not in your condition," says Phoenix. "Take it easy, girl."

The door is ajar, and it opens when Momma pushes without turning the knob.

"Didn't I lock this?" she says.

"Maybe you-know-who came down after all," Phoenix spits.

"Honey?" Momma calls.

A half-empty liquor bottle rests on the table, a puddle spilled beside it.

"I'll just mosey along," Phoenix says. She looks at Smiley. "Where's your pennant, Archer Timbers?"

"Forgot it in the car," he says, and Phoenix goes with him outside to retrieve it.

"Burr?" Momma calls again.

"We didn't leave a note," I offer. "He's probably gone for a walk."

"Everything is closed on Thanksgiving—even the Gypsy Tavern."

"At least he can't get into much trouble. Anyway, isn't this his coat?" I lift the Navy pea coat and find a brown one underneath. "Whose is this?"

The door to Momma's room is closed, and a queasy feeling grabs hold of me. My hand comes to Mamaw's locket and I rub the etching with my thumb.

Momma pushes open the bedroom door as carefully as if a fanged creature is lying in wait on the other side ready to spring. The covers are messed up, a pillow propped against the tufted headboard, Burr's head on the pillow, his mouth gaping in sleep. He's bare chested, hairs curling like bug antennae around his nipples. In the crook of his arm, a dark head, black strands splayed over his shoulder.

Cowboy Code number eight: A cowboy must keep himself clean in thought, speech, action, and personal habits. Burr has violated every law of the Code, but this one is the ringer.

Momma hesitates two seconds and then bends to the bottom drawer of her dresser. Burr licks his lips at the scraping of the drawer. Momma has the pistol aimed at him when he manages to pry open his lids.

"Hello, darling," Momma says sweetly—another lesson in verbal irony.

He blanches. Not pale as if he hasn't been in the sun for a while, but ashen, as if he's about to be sick. The woman squeezes the sheet to her neck. Her pink lips are swollen, eyes frozen wide.

I try to think of something to say, something that will slash them, pierce them. Then I think, wouldn't it be nice to have Phoenix replace him, Phoenix who loves my mother, who loves me. Wouldn't it be nice to set up house with Phoenix someplace where no one will talk, where no one cares about two women and two children—three children. No boozing, no womanizing, just easy living. But I know even if she feels the same way I do, Momma will not rest until she retrieves her husband, and at this moment it doesn't matter to her which way he comes back—walking, crawling, or riding in a box.

Momma looks as if it's taking all her energy to hold the gun. She's holding the grip with both hands, finger of her right hand on the trigger. Burr pushes the woman away with his elbow.

"She followed me here, Sweetheart. There's not a train out 'til tomorrow. I gave her money for a hotel, but she forced her way in." He shifts a look to the woman and then back at the gun. "See, I came down to surprise you."

Momma cackles. "Well, I'm not surprised."

"Mags." The calmness of Phoenix's voice shocks me. I'm anticipating a firestorm, not Phoenix's familiar timbre. "Much as I'd like to see his blood spurt, you don't want it on your hands. Not with a baby coming." She presses Smiley behind her.

"A baby?" Burr gasps.

If he expects an answer, I'm not sure Momma is able to force the air from her lungs to give him one.

"I wouldn't blame you if you shot me," Burr says. "Go head. Pull the trigger."

"The hell you will," Phoenix says to Momma. "The lowdown dog's got a family he's responsible for."

In slow motion Momma's hand moves to the safety and she clicks it off.

"We came to tell you," the raven-haired woman says, her voice husky.

"He's leaving you." She looks at Burr. "We love each other, don't we, Lesley?"

Burr is riveted on Momma.

"Lady," says Phoenix, "if you know what's good for you, you'll get your britches on and vamoose."

"You'd better go, Linda," Burr says.

"You coming with me?" She leans up on an elbow.

"No. I'm staying here."

The woman jerks herself out of bed. Her breasts are smaller than Momma's and below her flat abdomen, a swatch of curly black. I imagine a bullet going through her stomach, red splattering out like the paint from Uncle Buddy's cans in the clearing. She grabs a white shirt from the bed and fumbles into it, tail falling to her thighs, sleeves over her hands. Burr's shirt.

When she passes Momma, she knocks the gun, and I jump at the crack that follows. A fifty-cent-piece hole in the headboard appears just starboard of Burr's right eye. I think, spread your feet, Momma, get a stable base. Cradle the pistol in one hand and squeeze nice and slow on the trigger. At that range, I could hit him dead in the center of his forehead. But Phoenix is right—killing Burr isn't the answer.

I grab for the gun and it goes off again, hitting the lamp on the nightstand and sending shards of glass splattering. Burr sits up and raises both hands. He looks pinned like a moth specimen to the headboard. His lips move as if he's praying, trying to negotiate some last-minute peace with his maker.

Phoenix grabs Momma but she jerks loose, and the next shot draws crimson. Burr's lips round, and he grunts. One hand holds his shoulder, and blood flows between his fingers.

The gun clanks to the floor.

Phoenix grabs a piece of cloth from the rug—a pair of panties, I think. Then she's at Burr's side, pulling his hand away and pressing the panties to the wound.

"It's not bad," she says. "Just grazed the skin. You're all right."

He's crying, mucous running from nose to lip, looking at Momma.

"I'm a bum, a miserable bum."

"Got to agree with you there," Phoenix answers.

I snatch up the gun and snap the safety back on. Then I take the clip out just to be sure Momma doesn't try to finish him off.

Elsie appears asking what happened.

Burr squeezes the panties on the wound. "I was just showing off that old pistol, and it backfired on me. No harm done."

"In bed?" Elsie sounds as if she knows more than she's letting on.

"I'm fine," he insists.

She draws her mouth to the side. "I have a sneaking suspicion that wasn't your sister just stormed out of here, was it?"

Burr shakes his head.

"What's going on?" I've forgotten about Smiley.

"You come on over to my house with me, boy," Elsie says. "I believe there's a drumstick with your name on it."

I've forgotten it's Thanksgiving. I suppose I have a lot to be thankful for. If Momma had killed Burr, she'd have gone to jail, and then what would we do? I know one thing, though—from now on Burr is going to play by Momma's rules. And if he doesn't play fair, I think he learned the penalty for cheating.

40
Cowboy Code

"Sweet Gertie Garbor," Burr sings.

"Went to the harbor," Smiley answers.

"Married a barber." Burr again.

"A yo-de-yo-de-yo." Smiley finishes, off key. One of the silly songs Burr taught us.

"First thing we're gonna do when we settle in Washington," Burr says, "is go to the zoo. Are you ready for the monkey house?"

"Yes, sir," Smiley says.

"How about you, Bobbie?"

In the four months since Momma got her revenge with the pistol, I have made a kind of peace with myself. My father is gone, my grandmother is gone, and I'm ready to forgive. When we move to Washington, I'll be near Winona and Covey, and I'll be a city girl. Whatever comes next, I know I won't be bored.

"Yeah," I say, "I'm ready."

"Got your coats?"

"Yes, sir," Smiley says.

"Got your hats?"

"Uh-huh."

"Got the clothespins for your noses?"

I can't help but laugh.

"Aw," Smiley says, "monkeys can't smell that bad."

"You wait and see." Burr turns to Momma. "This is it. Starting from scratch." He kisses her hair. "I'm going to make you happy."

"I know you will," she says. "I just need a little time with Phoenix."

"Yeah," he agrees. Burr has changed in many ways, not the least of which is his attitude about Momma's best friend.

"I'm coming, too."

Momma pushes the bangs off my brow. "Of course you are."

*   *   *

Phoenix is hovered over a mug at Marilyn's Café, the *Messenger* pinned under an elbow. Her hair is pulled back on one side and fastened with a barrette. She rotates a cigarette with her thumb and forefinger. When she sees us, she twists a smile. One thing I count on is Phoenix's pleasure at seeing us. She hugs my neck, then crushes out the cigarette in the ashtray and presses both palms on Momma's swollen stomach.

"How you three doin'?" We haven't seen her in at least two months. She said she was going to give Momma time to figure things out.

Momma falls into the seat next to her. "When did you take up that bad habit?" She scowls at the cigarette butt.

"I just fool with it. I like to watch the smoke." Phoenix folds the paper and pushes it aside. "Looks like we're still playing cat and mouse with Japan."

"All wars end sooner or later," Momma says.

"So history says." Phoenix's face is pinched and the spark is gone from her eyes. "Some demons are hard to shake loose, though."

I don't think she's hinting at international conflict.

"We're just about to leave," I tell her.

"Your place ready for you?"

"We'll see when we get there," Momma says. "Commander Fredericks pushed our application through. It's a small apartment, but it'll do for now."

Phoenix pulls at her earlobe. "I'm proud of you, going to see him like that."

Momma went back to Washington with Burr, marched up to his commanding officer's desk and told him about the woman—Linda. He said he'd be glad to ship Burr out, but Momma said she thought he was sorry and she would take it from here.

"What choice did I have?" Momma says.

"I thought you had a pretty good alternative." Phoenix must know the term sardonic, which I learned from a British author. "I remain a caged and rather sardonic lion in a particularly contemptible and ill-run zoo," he wrote. In the past year, I've learned that being an adult is equivalent to living in one

of those zoos, and I share Phoenix's contempt for it.

Momma smooths her dress down over her belly. "Commander Fredericks has already put in the discharge orders. We'll find out pretty soon if it goes through."

"You think he's done with that woman for good?" Phoenix asks.

"She was a WAVE. They sent her back to the Pacific. She won't see U.S. soil for at least a year and then she'll be stationed on the West Coast."

"By that time my little sister will be crawling all over the house," I say.

"You got your heart set on a girl?" Phoenix, I think, wishes that in some other dimension, in some magical way, this maybe-girl-child would be hers.

"I think Burr does." I've already got a brother. A sister will be fun to dress up all girlie.

Phoenix sighs and looks at the ceiling. "I'll miss the heck out of you all."

My throat feels like it has a peach pit in it, and I swallow hard to keep from choking. "You'll come to see us, won't you, Phoenix?"

"Sure." She crosses her arms on the table. "But it's going to be different from here on out."

Momma touches her fingers to Phoenix's face. "You're the best friend I ever had," she says.

Phoenix lifts a fist to her mouth and coughs. She studies her empty cup, leans her head to the right, and wipes a cheek on her shoulder.

"Come see us off," I say.

Phoenix nods. "I can use a walk."

*   *   *

Outside February is showing signs of spring. In the flowerbed by the courthouse, green tulip leaves are poking through the ground. I sense the expectation of their beauty in spite of the nagging uncertainty that they'll blossom this year. A frost will nip them or some villain will cut off the buds before their time and their glory will never come. Maybe it's better to cut their young lives short to make sure old, withered petals will never be strewn on the ground. But it's too late for that kind of thinking. Spring will come, the tulips will bloom and die, and then in the spring they'll come back. Hard times are payment for moments of splendor. It's the way of things. The way they'll always be.

Phoenix slips an arm through Momma's as she has done a hundred times before, as if nothing has changed.

"You'll write me, won't you?"

"Of course I'll write you." Momma bumps her head to Phoenix's. "You don't mind a few drips of mother's milk on the paper, do you?"

"I'll take a letter from you in any shape, long as you haven't used it as a diaper."

Momma chuckles.

"Say," says Phoenix, "I've got something for both of you." Phoenix is carrying a bag, the top rolled down for a handle. She pushes it at Momma.

"What is it?"

"That old gun. Sister gave it to me to keep for you."

Momma takes a step back. "I don't want that thing."

"I've got no use for it—" She presses the bag into Momma's hand. "But you might."

Momma hesitates, and then she accepts the bag, holding it out to the side like spoiled garbage.

Phoenix pinches something in her shirt pocket. "This is for you, Sister." She hands me a picture. It looks like some skinny boy, but then I see the gummy grin and the pigtail slung over the shoulder, the way she used to wear her hair.

"I thought you should have something to remember me by." Then she kisses me on the forehead.

Mamaw once said you're supposed to carry your love in your locket, and Phoenix is as close as I've ever come. I'll put her picture there.

Down Allegheny Avenue Burr sits in the Packard with the engine running, Smiley bouncing on the seat.

"We'll be back for Buddy's wedding next month," Momma says. "Are you coming?"

"He sent me an invitation." Phoenix swipes at her nose with her wrist. "But I've got some big plans about then. Don't think I'll make it."

"What about May? I'd like you with me when the baby comes."

"You don't need me, Mags. Besides, you've got your husband. At least he'd better be there. If he's not, you give me a call, you hear?"

"Phoenix!" Smiley is leaning out the car window. When she gets to the car, he tumbles out the door and grabs her around the waist.

"Archer Timbers, you rascal," she says, but her voice has no energy.

"Dad's got our stuff packed," he says. I haven't called Burr by that name. I probably never will, but I don't begrudge my brother.

Phoenix bends to look into the car. Burr lays an arm over the back of the seat. A glimmer of a smile passes between them. Phoenix, still hugging Smiley, signals with one hand—a wave of surrender.

The wind in February can be raw, and I reach my hand into my jacket to warm my knuckles. In the pocket, I wrap my fingers around something hard— a small cylinder. I added two laws of my own to Gene Autry's Cowboy Code. Number eleven: A cowboy must know when to call a truce. And number twelve: He must make peace with the enemy.

When the Packard starts away from the curb, I watch Phoenix through the rear window, hands stuck down in her pockets, growing smaller as we drive out of town. She taught me how love is unconditional devotion regardless of race or gender. It's generosity and joyfulness. It's forgiveness.

When we turn up Magazine Street, I twist around to watch the smoke from the mill's chimneys curling like strips of torn paper and rising into the sky.

Reading Questions

1. Can you pinpoint on a map where the fictional town of Pine Cliff might be located?
2. What would be the reason a paper mill might be located in a mountainous area?
3. What were the advantages of living in Pine Cliff? The disadvantages?
4. What were some of the taboos of Pine Cliff society?
5. Why would The Homestead be established in such a remote landscape?
6. Why would a Japanese family operate an Italian restaurant in town?
7. How did the character of Phoenix differ from Bobbie's family?
8. Did Maggie commit a crime in smothering Bobbie's grandmother?
9. Should Bobbie have accepted Nandaddy's apology for Covey's beating?
10. Would you consider Burr a villain or a victim?

Acknowledgments

Cowboy Code in many ways is a true story. I couldn't have written this book without stories my mother told me and the dozens of letters my parents wrote back and forth when my father served in the Pacific. My half-brothers Don and Ron Vanness are to thank for teaching me about guns and how to use them. Ron is the keeper of Uncle Bud's German pistol, which misfired once and shot a bullet through his wall. Anecdotes from my brothers and my Virginia aunts Hilda Morris and Gladys Fugaro added detail and color. Gratitude goes to Westvaco, which allowed me to tour its paper mill in Covington, Virginia. I owe appreciation to the brilliant writer and mentor Sena Jeter Naslund, who put me in touch with my Virginia roots and started me on this book's two-decade journey. The author Julie Chibbaro helped the novel find its focus at a Highlights retreat in Pennsylvania. Ann Kensek did an exemplary job of proofreading a final draft. The editor Reagan Rothe believed in this manuscript, for which I owe appreciation. Mostly, I'm thankful for my mother Margaret Bush Vanness Bryant and the overwhelming obstacles she surmounted to raise her family with dignity and love.

About the Author

Louella Bryant is author of While in Darkness There is Light, winner of Southwest Writers Award, and the collection Full Bloom, which won the Premier Award for Fiction. Her young adult novels Black Bonnet and Father By Blood also have won awards. Louella has acquired prizes for short stories and poems appearing in magazines and anthologies. Formerly with Spalding University's MFA in Writing Program, Louella now works as independent editor. Visit her website at http://louellabryant.com.

Other Books by Louella Bryant

The Black Bonnet

Father By Blood

While In Darkness There Is Light

Full Bloom Stories

Children's book

Two Tracks in the Snow

NOTE FROM THE AUTHOR

Word-of-mouth is crucial for any author to succeed. If you enjoyed the book, please leave a review online—anywhere you are able. Even if it's just a sentence or two. It would make all the difference and would be very much appreciated.

Thanks!
Louella

Thank you so much for reading one of our **Women's Fiction** novels.

If you enjoyed the experience, please check out our recommended title for your next great read!

The Apple of My Eye by Mary Ellen Bramwell

"A mature love story with an intense plot. This book has something important to say." –William O. Shakespeare, Professor of English, Brigham Young University

View other Black Rose Writing titles at www.blackrosewriting.com/books and use promo code **PRINT** to receive a **20% discount** when purchasing.

www.ingramcontent.com/pod-product-compliance
Lightning Source LLC
Chambersburg PA
CBHW011131100726

47898CB00009B/2935

9 781684 333004